Diana was the Painted Butterfly—
beautiful, treacherous, destructive and . . . irresistible.

Holt was as rugged and implacable as the mountains
that rose proud, tall — and threatening — above the desert floor.

Each was a mystery for the other to solve— a stunning
secret to be revealed and cherished — or buried forever. . . .

Under the Wild Night Sky

"We'll go back to camp."

"We still haven't caught the other horse," Diana protested.

"We don't stand much of a chance of finding it in the dark, not now. Besides, one fall is enough. The next time you might break your neck," Holt told her roughly.

A yearning shivered through her.

"Would you care, Holt?" she asked in an aching whisper as he gazed down at her. His head moved downward.

An inch from her lips, he growled, "What do you think?"

There was reluctance in his kiss, as if he resented the fact that he found her physically desirable. It mattered little, as his kiss provided fuel for the smoldering embers of their passion. White-hot flames melted them together. There was a searing, sweeping urgency to their embrace, an insatiable lust that transcended physical bounds.

It was a wild coming-together. Afterwards, Diana lay in his arms, awash from the primitive delights that had swept her high on a tidal wave of pure passion.

Books by Janet Dailey

The Rogue
Touch the Wind

Published by POCKET BOOKS

Janet Dailey

The Rogue

PUBLISHED BY POCKET BOOKS NEW YORK

Another *Original* publication of POCKET BOOKS

**POCKET BOOKS, a Simon & Schuster division of
GULF & WESTERN CORPORATION
1230 Avenue of the Americas, New York, N.Y. 10020**

ISBN: 0-671-82843-6

First Pocket Books printing February, 1980

10 9 8 7 6 5 4 3 2 1

Trademarks registered in the United States and other countries.

Printed in the U.S.A

The chronicles of the Old West are filled with legends about a pacing white stallion. Many noteworthy personages have mentioned sighting the wild mustang in their diaries and papers. Among the first was Washington Irving. The range of this magnificent stallion was said to extend from Texas to Oklahoma into New Mexico and Colorado. His exploits were legion. He was known by many names: the Pacing White Stallion, the White Steed of the Prairies, and the White Mustang. The Indians called him the Ghost Horse of the Plains.

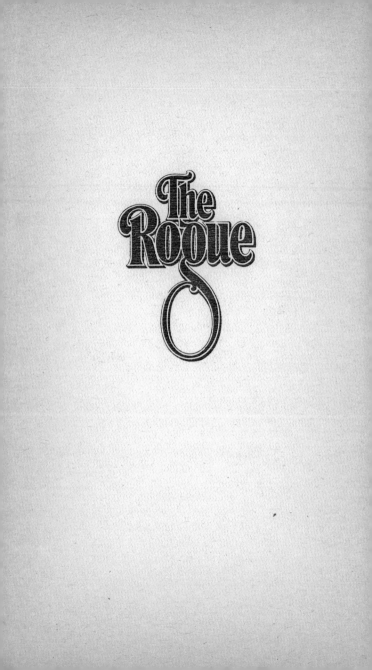

The Rogue

Chapter I

The eastern range of desert mountains cast long morning shadows onto the valley floor. Its slopes were blackened with thick stands of pinion and juniper trees. Coming from the south, the breeze carried the scent of water from the irrigation pipes spraying the fields where Nevada sage and ricegrass gave way to a green carpet.

Stacks of hay, like golden mounds of bread, stood beside the outbuildings of the horse and cattle ranch. Stables, corrals, and equipment sheds dotted the yard, dominated by the unpretentious ranch house sitting on a rise, the slightly higher elevation giving it an over-looking view of the entire operation. Precious water wasn't wasted for lawns, and hardy desert growth claimed the land around the buildings.

A trio of sleek Arabian yearlings was cavorting in one of the corrals. Two people watched from the rail. One was young and one was old. With arms draped over the top board, the grizzled man was supple and weathered like a good rope. There was a permanent squint to his eyes from long years of looking into the sun and wind. Experience was etched in his sun-beaten face along with a certain sourness that came from dreams lost.

The closest Rueben Spencer had ever come to making it big was shooting a hard eight in an Ely casino and winning a month's pay. The closest he had come to a home was one unit of the ranch's fourplex—room and board and wages, courtesy of his boss. And the closest Rube had come to a family of his own was the teen-aged girl perched on the rail beside him, the boss's daughter. He had made no tracks in his lifetime that the Nevada wind couldn't wipe out in a minute.

For Diana Somers, it was all ahead of her. The world was waiting at her feet, as it had since the day she was born. Having held the status of a teen-age for almost one full year, Diana was beginning to realize the privileges that came with being the boss's daughter and only child, privileges she had taken for granted before.

The knowledge gave her a sense of authority and power. It showed in the way she carried herself—the faintly regal tilt of her head and the willful set of her chin. Only to one man did she bow her head, and that was her father. He was the driving force in her life. It was only in his company that vulnerability glimmered in eyes as vividly blue as a clear Nevada sky.

Her mother was a blurred memory, a shadowy presence in her past who had died when Diana was four from complications brought on by pneumonia. A picture in a photograph album confirmed her mother's previous existence, but Diana felt no sense of loss for someone she barely remembered.

The Somers ranch consisted of a thousand deeded acres plus thousands more leased federal acres for grazing. Diana was the princess in this small empire, her father the king. It never occurred to her that there should be a queen. She needed only her father, and her father needed only her. The world was complete.

The rattling thump of a pickup truck as it bounced over the rutted lane leading from the highway to the ranch yard drew her attention. Glancing over her shoulder, Diana frowned at the unfamiliar vehicle. The crease in her forehead deepened at the Arizona license plates.

She turned to Rube Spencer. "What do you suppose that stranger wants?"

Rube looked and spat out a sideways stream of tobacco juice from the chaw in his mouth. "Goddamned if I know." He shrugged. "Could be that new man the Major hired."

"What new man? The Major never said anything to me about hiring someone."

Everyone called her father the Major, including Diana.

John Somers had resigned his commission in the army a few months after Diana was born. He had given up a promising military career to return to the family ranch when his older brother was killed in a car crash. He had brought with him military discipline and command, and the title of Major had stuck.

"Just the same, he did."

"Where was I?"

Rube paused to recall. "It must have been when we was hayin' and you was out drivin' the tractor. Yep, that must have been the day. I was dosing the gray mare." Rube despised farm work and shirked it every time there was any to be done. The Major had finally stopped fighting with him and assigned him strictly to the horses. "I come out of the stable and saw the Major talkin' to this fella, showin' him around."

He continued to ramble on about the day, but once Diana had gleaned the information that Rube had questioned the Major and had been told he had hired a new man, she stopped listening. Few people listened to all that Rube had to say. The Major had once declared that Rube could talk a man deaf.

The battered pickup stopped in front of the main house. The slamming of a screen door brought an abrupt end to Rube's recounting as he suddenly remembered work to be done, his sixth sense warning him of the Major's appearance.

Diana paid no attention to Rube's sudden interest in his job. Swinging around, she hopped down from the

corral fence, intent on meeting the man the Major
hadn't told her he had hired. The idea didn't set well.
Over the years, he had always confided in her, teaching her every facet of the ranch business until Diana
knew its workings almost as well as the Major did.
This closeness between them was something she trea-
sured, and discovering this gap in their communica-
tions made her uneasy.

Slim, and tomboy-clad, Diana crossed the ranch
yard with long, eating strides, copied from the
Major's. In a nervous but essentially feminine gesture,
she reached up to smooth one side of her raven-black
hair, cropped close to her head in a boy's cut.

The Major descended the porch steps and walked
toward the pickup. With shoulders squared and posture erect, he weighed not an ounce more than when he
had resigned. His ranch-cut trousers in a dark tan,
durable material, had a military crease. The print shirt
he wore had a stiffly starched collar, and his boots
were polished to a high sheen. His dark hair was short,
not coming anywhere close to touching his shirt collar,
sideburns liberally sprinkled with gray. The Major was
a vigorous, vital man, born to command.

A handsome, distinguished man, his position in the
community alone would have made him a target for
unattached females. That, coupled with his looks,
made him doubly desired. Once Diana had been jealous of the fawning attention women at church or in
town displayed for her father, but his indifference
eventually assured her that he had no interest in
marrying a second time. All his life he had lived in a
male-oriented world, from his childhood on this ranch
to the military and back to the ranch. Bachelorhood
suited him. Any feminine companionship he sought
was done discreetly. Diana didn't feel threatened by
these odd evenings out and viewed with contempt any
woman who tried to establish a more permanent
relationship with her father. She silently laughed at
those who told the Major she needed a mother. She

needed only him, and she was determined that he would need only her.

His voice was crisp but friendly as he greeted the man stepping out of the pickup to meet him. The two were shaking hands when Diana arrived at the Major's side. Her carriage was as straight as his, her bearing equally authoritative. He gave her a warm, indulgent look but made no display of affection, such as placing a hand on her shoulder. Not that Diana expected any such gesture.

"Your welcoming committee is complete, Holt, now that my best girl is here." The Major addressed the man they faced. "This is my daughter, Diana. Our new hand, Holt Mallory."

Her gaze openly inspected him, as if her approval was needed before this Holt Mallory actually started work. Tall—at the six-foot mark—and whipcord-lean, he courteously removed the straw Stetson from his head. The rumpled thickness of his brown hair had been bleached by the sun to the variegated shade of tobacco. His tanned features were carved in implacable lines. His eyes were a hard, metallic gray, like shards of splintered steel. They looked old, old beyond his years. Yet he couldn't have been more than twenty-six.

"How do you do, Miss Somers?" His voice was low-pitched, with a cool, drawling sound.

"Fine, thank you." Prickles of dislike crawled over her flesh, a feeling that intensified when Diana glanced at the Major.

"Is that your son?" The Major was looking beyond the new man, and Diana's gaze followed.

"Guy, come here and say hello to the Major." For all the quietness of Holt Mallory's voice, it was definitely an order.

A nine-year-old boy stood beside the truck. Thin and pale, he looked lost and frightened. An attempt had been made to plaster down the cowlicks in his sandy blond hair, but it hadn't been very successful.

Hesitantly and reluctantly, he came forward to limply shake the Major's hand.

"How do you do, sir?" he mumbled.

The Major straightened and smiled. "He's a fine-looking boy, Holt."

Diana looked again at the young boy, trying to see what her father had found so "fine looking" about him, but she didn't find it. He seemed a nondescript little boy, small and sensitive and frightened of his own shadow. Diana felt a surge of contempt for the boy's lack of strength, but it was tempered by an inexplicable desire to protect.

"I'll show you where you'll be staying, Holt," the Major announced, then turned to Diana. "You bring Guy along. It will give the two of you a chance to get acquainted."

Diana had no desire to become better acquainted with the young boy. But, if it was what her father wanted . . . she concealed a sigh and reached for the boy's hand. He hid it behind his back and Diana shrugged her disinterest.

"Come along, Guy," she said and fell in step behind her father and the new man.

When the small boy trailed them, Diana slowed her pace to walk with him. She never had much to do with children, except those her own age in school. She glanced at the downcast eyes of the boy and tried to think of something to make conversation.

"Are you from Arizona?"

There was a moment of silence after her question. Diana thought she wasn't going to get an answer. Then the pair of rounded blue eyes looked up at her.

"No. My dad lived in Arizona, but my mom and me lived in Denver."

"Where is your mother?"

His bottom lip quivered. "She's dead."

"Mine, too." Diana offered the information in polite empathy. "She died when I was four." She stared at the man ahead of them, walking beside the Major.

"How come you lived in Denver and your father lived in Arizona? Were your parents divorced?"

There was an affirmative nod of the boy's head. Diana didn't blame the boy's mother. She didn't like the man, either, but she was surprised when the boy indicated a similar opinion.

"When my mother died last month, *he* showed up and said he was my father and that I was to live with him now." There was a wealth of resentment in the boy's tone.

"Do you mean you had never seen him before?" Diana frowned.

"My grandma and grandpa said he is my father, so I guess he is," he admitted. "My mom told me that my dad went off and left her after I was born, because he didn't want either of us."

Remembering those hard, gray eyes, Diana could believe that. "If that's the way he felt, why is he bothering with you now?" She spoke her thoughts aloud.

Little Guy Mallory seemed to flinch at the question. "He claims he always wanted me," he answered skeptically, "but that my mother wouldn't let him see me. But she would have. I know she would have."

The defensive outburst on his mother's behalf drew an assessing look from Diana. The boy might be sensitive, but he wasn't completely meek.

"I'm sure your mother would have if he really wanted to see you," she agreed. Poor kid, Diana thought, and spared a moment of pity that the boy had a father who didn't want him. No wonder he looked so bewildered and frightened.

They were passing the stud pens where the Major's prize Arabian stallions were kept. Breeding and showing purebred Arabians was one facet of the ranch's operation. In addition to the thirty broodmares and their offspring, there were yearlings and two-year-olds, some being kept as show prospects and others being readied for sale. Plus, the ranch had a remuda of working horses. The two Arabian studs were penned some distance from the other horses. The magnificent bay Shetan raced to the rail to whicker to his master. There was nothing unusual in that, but Diana noticed the wide-eyed stare the boy gave the horse. "Can you ride?" she asked.

"I've never seen a horse in person before, only on television and from the truck when we were driving here," was his reply.

"You'll see plenty from now on," she said. "You can even learn how to ride while you're here. It's easy."

"Is it?" His breathless voice made it seem as if she had just offered him the whole world.

"Sure." Diana shrugged. "I'll teach you." And she immediately regretted the impulse that had made her volunteer. She didn't want to spend her summer playing nursemaid to a green kid.

"Wow!" Guy Mallory was already erupting with joy, animation entering the previously strained features. "That's terrific!"

His exuberant voice caught the attention of the two men pausing on the doorstep of the largest unit in the fourplex, the one that had stood vacant for more than a month. A smile softened the rough contours of Holt Mallory's features as he looked curiously at his son, who was practically skipping with delight.

"What's all the excitement about, Guy?"

"She promised to teach me how to ride a horse!"

A frown flickered across Holt Mallory's face. "You never told me that you wanted to learn," he said with forced lightness. Obviously, Guy had confided more in the few short moments with Diana than during the hours with his father.

"I do!" Guy declared. "And she's going to teach me!"

"That's very generous of Miss Somers, but there's no need to trouble her. If you want to learn, Guy, I'll teach you—that is, if the Major doesn't object to us borrowing a horse."

"I have no objections, Holt, but since Diana has offered to teach him, I think it would be a good idea to let her," the Major insisted. "The ranch is going to be pretty busy for the next couple of months. Diana will have more free time than you will. And she will be good company for the boy, help him settle into his new surroundings."

Holt Mallory didn't look pleased with the logic of the Major's argument. "That's true," he admitted and leveled a steel look at Diana. "As long as you don't mind, it's all right with me."

"I don't mind," she lied.

"Great!" Guy exclaimed. "I'd rather have her teach me, anyway." The boy missed the sudden flexing of muscles along his father's jaw, but Diana noticed it. So did the Major. "When can we start?" questioned Guy. "Today?"

The Major smiled. "Not today. Your father is going to need your help unpacking and settling into your new home. Here's the key, Holt." He handed it to him. "Diana and I will leave the two of you to explore the place on your own. If you need anything, or have any questions, I'll be at the house most of the day."

"Thanks, Major."

Diana wondered if Holt Mallory was thanking him for the job or for smoothing over the awkward moment. It didn't really matter which it was. She turned with her father and walked to the main house.

They were nearly to the porch before she remarked, "You never mentioned that you had hired a new man."

"Didn't I?" he replied absently, his thoughts elsewhere. "It must have slipped my mind."

"He doesn't want the boy."

The Major stopped to stare, now giving her his undivided attention. "What put that idea in your head?"

"Guy told me."

"The two of you did quite a bit of talking on that short walk."

"Enough to know that man is virtually a stranger to him. Guy never saw him until his mother died. He deserted both of them when Guy was just a baby."

"It isn't quite as cut and dried as that, Diana. Guy's parents were barely sixteen when they married. It was one of those 'have to' things. They were simply too young, and like a lot of teen-aged couples, they couldn't make it work. After they separated, his wife left Arizona with the baby. Holt never heard from her again until her parents notified him of her death. It wasn't a case of not wanting to see his son. Holt didn't know where he was."

It sounded plausible, but Diana preferred Guy's version. "I don't like him," she stated.

The Major frowned. "It isn't like you to make snap judgments."

"I don't like him," she repeated.

"You'll change your mind. He's excellent with horses and has a working knowledge of cattle. More than that, he has management potential."

"Management? Why is that so special?"

"I'm not getting any younger. In a few years, I'm going to need somebody to run the ranch, take some of the load off my aging shoulders. Holt is going to need a few more years of seasoning. If my instincts haven't failed me, he's going to be a good leader someday."

Diana made no comment. She knew that if she had been a boy, the Major would have been thinking about turning the ranch operation over to her in a few years instead of to a stranger. The knowledge hurt. The summer ahead didn't look as pleasant as it had before Holt Mallory arrived.

Entering the house a step behind her father, she followed him through the living room to the connected dining room. The furnishings in the house were austerely male, arranged in precise order. Everything was comfortable, yet very utilitarian. The table was set for morning coffee, a daily routine in the Somers' house.

As the Major pulled out a chair at the head of the table, the housekeeper came from the kitchen carrying a pot of freshly brewed coffee and a plate of homemade doughnuts. Sophie Miller was a gaunt, unprepossessing woman. Although she was only in her late forties, her brown hair was salted with gray and severely styled in a crown of braids atop her head. Widowed for many years and childless, she had lived on the ranch for the last six years as the Major's housekeeper. She was a drab person, doing her work without ever drawing attention to herself.

Diana sat in the chair to the right of her father. Ever since she could remember, she had always joined him in this morning break, actually drinking coffee from the time she was eight. Father and daughter shared almost everything together. This was not one of the times that Diana sat back and enjoyed it. She was still disturbed that the Major had failed to inform her that he had hired a new man. She was also bothered by the way he had so casually dismissed her dislike of this Holt Mallory.

Coffee was steaming from the Major's cup as Sophie filled the cup in front of Diana. The Major had unfolded his napkin and laid it across his creased trousers. He glanced at the plate of doughnuts and smiled at Diana.

"Chocolate, your favorite, Diana," he commented and received a disinterested nod from her. "Sophie made them especially for you."

The quietly prompting statement shook Diana out of her silent contemplation. "Thanks, Sophie." She tossed the words indifferently over her shoulder, and the housekeeper smiled briefly in return, having learned not to expect more from Diana.

To Diana, Sophie was merely one of a series of housekeepers who had gone in and out of her life. Sophie had simply lasted longer than the others. Most of them hadn't liked the isolation of the ranch since it prevented them from seeing family and friends. Sophie had no family and, apparently, few friends, so the job suited her.

Diana had no interest in the housekeepers. Her life centered around the Major. The housekeepers were faceless souls who worked for him. She had never formed an attachment to any of them. There was only her father. What interested him interested her. At the present, he had shown an uncommon interest in the new ranch hand. And Diana did not like it.

Over the next few weeks, her first impression of Holt Mallory didn't change. He was polite to her. He treated her with the respect due a boss's daughter, yet never with the indulgent affection the other ranch hands expressed. To the others, she might be the darling, the pet of the ranch, but not to him.

As for Guy, he had virtually become her shadow, whether Diana liked it or not. Most of the time she didn't, although there were moments when his almost worshipful attitude soothed her ego.

This was not one of those moments. As she walked swiftly to the stud pens with Guy trailing at her heels, she fervently wished he would get lost—permanently.

"Can't I ride with you, please?" He repeated the request she had turned down seconds ago. "I'm getting good. You said so."

"No! I'm going to exercise the stallions." Something she did regularly in the arena, a safe distance from the broodmares and potential trouble. "I've told you and told you that you can't ride your mare with me when I'm on one of the studs."

"Why not?"

Diana flashed him an irritated look. "Hasn't your father told you anything about the birds and the bees?"

Guy blushed furiously and fell silent, but he never left her side. At the pen, he peered through the rails as Diana climbed over the top, a bridle draped over her shoulder. The bay stallion danced to her, knowing the routine and eager to stretch his legs.

"If you want to make yourself useful, Guy"—there was a faintly acid ring to her voice as she slipped the bit into the stallion's mouth—"go get the saddle out of the tack room for me while I work Shetan on the lounge line."

"Okay." He darted off, eager to do her bidding.

When he returned, it was without the saddle and not alone. Diana glanced around to see Holt Mallory walking behind his white-faced son. She flicked him a dismissing look and turned to Guy.

"I thought I told you to bring the saddle."

"I—"

"What do you think you are doing, Miss Somers?"

There was something in the quiet way he put the question that set her teeth on edge. She stopped the circling bay cantering around her on the lounge line and faced him. She was every inch the boss's daughter looking at a mere hired hand.

"I don't see that it's any of your business."

"Guy tells me you are planning to ride that stallion."

"I am."

"Does the Major know?"

"Of course, he knows," Diana retorted indignantly.

"He must be out of his mind to let a slip of a girl like you—"

He never had a chance to complete the sentence, as Diana broke in angrily: "I am a better rider than practically everyone on this ranch, maybe in the county."

"That isn't saying much." He opened the corral gate and stepped through, latching it behind him. "Hand me an end of the lounge line."

"Why?" She eyed him warily.

"Call it a test," he answered. Diana sensed a challenge and couldn't refuse. She handed the end to him and he stepped back. Less than three feet separated them. "Hold on," Holt instructed. "Don't let me pull it out of your hands."

Wrapping the long leather lead around his hand, he gave a steady pull. Diana dug her heels into the ground and resisted, successfully. A sudden, hard yank sent her stumbling forward into his chest. His hands closed around her shoulders to steady her, his superior strength jolting her like a cattle prod. Diana jerked away.

"That was a dirty trick," she accused. "It doesn't prove anything."

"Doesn't it?" His mouth quirked in a taunting, humorless smile. "If that stallion took a notion, he could jerk the reins right out of your hands, the same as I did."

"Shetan is a well-trained horse," Diana defended. "And I never ride him around the mares, only in the arena, and only after I've worked him a bit on the ground. I am perfectly capable of controlling him."

"Even the best-trained horse can rebel, if only for a few seconds. With someone like you on his back, that's all the time it would take."

"I've been riding these stallions for years." Which was stretching the truth quite a bit.

"I don't care what you've been doing. While I'm around, you aren't going to," he informed her.

"You're nothing but hired help," Diana declared with haughty scorn. "You can't tell me what to do."

"I just did."

"Holt has a good point." At the sound of a third voice joining the heated conversation, Diana spun on her heel to see the Major standing at the corral gate. "I think it would be best if you don't exercise the stallions anymore, Diana. I've had misgivings about it from the beginning. There are times when you have to man-handle even the best-trained horse. And you couldn't do it."

Every nerve in her body screamed in protest, but not a sound passed from her lips. She shoved the line into Holt's hands and walked rigidly out of the corral. Her eyes were dry, but there was an enormous lump in her throat. She thought she would choke on it.

Diana walked blindly, not caring where she was going, heading into the open spaces beyond the corrals. It was several minutes before she heard someone hurrying along behind her. Diana glanced back and saw Guy.

"If you still want to ride," he began hesitantly as she finally acknowledged his presence.

All the pent-up anger suddenly exploded. "You dumb little kid! This is all your fault!" she accused. "Why did you have to open up your mouth and tell your stupid father what I was doing?"

His small face whitened. "I didn't mean to, honest."

"I didn't mean to," Diana repeated in sarcastic mimicry. "I thought you didn't like your father, so what were you doing talking to him about me?"

"I don't like him," Guy insisted, "but he asked me what I was doing with your saddle and—"

"—you told him," she finished. "You said you wanted to be my friend, but you are no friend of mine. Go away and leave me alone. I don't want you around! You're nothing but a pest!"

"I'm sorry. I didn't mean to." Tears filled his eyes as he stared at the ground, his chin quivering. He began sniffling, seemingly unable to move.

Diana was still glaring at him with contempt when the tears began spilling over his pale lashes, streaming down his cheeks. His small hand couldn't stem the flow. She was suddenly uncomfortable. She couldn't remember the last time she had seen anyone cry. Diana didn't know how to handle it.

"Stop being a cry-baby," she muttered, but that only seemed to increase the volume of tears, despite Guy's valiant attempt to obey. "Come on. Stop it." Impatience and unease brought a frown. Diana turned partially away, not wanting to watch him cry. "Forget what I said. It wasn't your fault. It was your father making trouble, trying to worm his way into the

Major's favor by pretending he was concerned that I might get hurt. He doesn't give a damn about you or me."

"Then you're not mad at me?" Guy asked for more assurance.

"I'm just mad in general." She gave him a sidelong look and grudgingly extended a peace offering. "I'm going to the irrigation pond to cool off. Do you want to come along?"

He hesitated. "I don't have my trunks on."

"So?" Diana lifted her shoulders in an uncaring shrug. "Neither do I. Do you want to come along or not?"

He accepted eagerly, scrubbing the last traces of tears from his face. Now and then he sniffled at his runny nose as he walked beside her to the pond.

The summer went from bad to worse as far as Diana was concerned. More and more of her activities were curtailed. In previous summers every minute of the day was filled with things to do. Now she was fighting boredom.

Kicking a rock out of her path, Diana shoved her hands into the rear pockets of her Levi's™ and glanced impatiently around the ranch yard. Surely there was something to do. She breathed out a disgusted sigh. There was always Guy.

Diana changed her direction and walked to the fourplex. The door to the last unit was open. Not bothering to knock on the screen door, she walked in and paused at the sight of Holt Mallory standing at the kitchen sink shirtless, halted in the act of wiping his face dry with a towel.

"It's polite to knock before entering someone's home." He finished wiping his face and hands.

"I'm looking for Guy. Where is he?" Resentment glittered darkly in her blue eyes.

"Somewhere outside."

As he turned to hang up the towel, Diana's eyes widened curiously. A network of scars lined the tanned flesh of his back. "How did you get those marks on your back?" she demanded.

There was an instant's hesitation before Holt reached for his shirt. "I don't remember."

"Somebody beat you. You wouldn't forget a thing like that," Diana accused.

He looked at her for a long, hard moment. "You can forget anything if you try." His attention became absorbed in buttoning his shirt. "You said you were looking for Guy; he's outside."

Diana eyed him with curious speculation, but knew he would tell her no more. Finally she turned and left, going in search of Guy. But she didn't let the matter drop. She revived it at lunch with the Major.

"Did you know Holt Mallory had scars all over his back? It looks like somebody used a whip on him." She offered it into the conversation with seemingly idle interest.

The Major's look was swift and piercing. "Really?" His response was deliberately bland. "Pass the salt."

"How did he get them?" Diana set the salt and pepper near his plate.

"Did you ask Holt?"

"Yes."

"What did he tell you?"

"He said he couldn't remember. Of course, it's a lie." She dismissed the answer with an infinitesimal shrug of her shoulders. "How did he get them, Major? Was he in prison before he came here?"

"I don't believe they whip people in prison anymore, Diana," he replied in an indulgently dry tone.

"Maybe not anymore, but . . . how did he get them?"

"I really can't tell you, Diana." He said it as if he didn't know, yet Diana suspected that he did. He simply wasn't going to tell her. He had always told her everything. There had never been any secrets between them. It hurt, but it didn't stop her from fantasizing about how Holt had acquired the scars, even if she didn't bring the subject up again.

With summer's end came the fall round-up. It was one of Diana's favorite times. Riding for long hours, miles from the ranch yard, sleeping beside a campfire under a canopy of stars, it was adventurous and exciting out in the wilds. There was always so much to see, mule deer grazing, an occasional glimpse of a desert bighorn, or a fleeing band of wild horses skylined on the crest of a hill.

By the golden light of dawn, Diana retightened the cinch of her saddle, a bedroll tied neatly behind the cantle. Everywhere there was movement, others quietly and efficiently preparing for the start of the annual event. All the faces were familiar. Year round, the ranch usually employed an average of eighteen men on a regular basis, but extras were hired during round-ups or haying time. They were generally locals. It was rare for the Major to hire strangers for part-time help.

Over the seat of her saddle, Diana saw Holt Mallory approaching with an air of being in command of the operation. What had begun as instant dislike on his arrival at the ranch had magnified over the last few months. It smoldered in the look Diana gave him. There was a hesitation in his firm stride when his cool gray eyes saw her. They flicked from her to the saddled horses and bedroll before glancing thoughtfully away.

When Diana saw him stop to speak to the Major, her lips thinned into an unpleasant line. Her pulse started hammering in ominous premonition as she saw them both glance at her. She didn't like the way the Major was looking at her, nor the short nod he gave to Holt after a relatively lengthy exchange. When the Major started walking toward her, Diana pretended not to notice, looping the reins over the horse's neck and preparing to mount.

"Diana." His crisp voice called for her attention.

Damn! she cursed beneath her breath, but pivoted to face him. She adopted an expression of bland unconcern while an inner sense warned her in advance what his next words would be.

"You'll be staying home this year, Diana." Her father came straight to the point.

"I've been going on the fall round-ups since I was eight years old. Besides, you need all the help you can get. And you know I can ride and rope with the best of them."

"The work is too hard for a young girl like you."

"I've never complained," Diana reminded him. "I don't mind the dust and the heat and the sore muscles."

"I know you don't complain." Major Somers had always spoken to her as an adult. His attitude had always been very honest and frank. This time was no different. "You are growing up and filling out, Diana. It isn't proper anymore for you to be sleeping out for several nights in the company of men."

Diana replied with equal candor. "You aren't suggesting one of the boys might try to molest me, are you? They are all my friends." *Except Holt Mallory.* "It's ridiculous. Besides, you'll be along."

"Not this time. I'm getting too old to be sleeping on hard ground," he informed her. "But that isn't the point. I don't want you to grow up to be a rough-talking, hard-riding Calamity Jane. I want you to be a lady and not quite so much a tomboy. Do you understand?"

"Yes, Major." She surrendered to his wishes.

"Good." He looked satisfied with the outcome. "I'll be driving out every day in the Jeep™," the Major continued. "It will be relatively quiet around here for you. Why don't you arrange to have Sophie take you on a shopping expedition for some new clothes—something a bit more feminine than those Levi's?"

"All right," Diana agreed.

If it was a lady her father wanted, she was willing to comply. From that morning, Diana began the transformation. She went shopping and bought new clothes designed to accent her femininity without going over-board with a lot of ruffles and bows. She began to take an interest in what she believed were womanly things, learning to cook and sew. However, she didn't go to extremes. She continued to ride frequently and do less arduous chores around the ranch.

As a rule, only single men made use of the accom-modations afforded by the ranch. The small handful of married ranch hands lived off the ranch, generally on small holdings of their own. It was rare, if ever, that Diana came in contact with their wives.

However, that winter, their closest neighbor, Alan Thornton, who owned the ranch ten miles away, was married. It was only natural that Diana became ac-quainted with his young schoolteacher wife, Peggy. It was her first real association with an adult female. It was Peggy who persuaded Diana to let the black silk cap of her hair grow to a more complimentary length and made suggestions as to the type and amount of makeup she should use.

Diana listened to Peggy's dreams, trying to com-prehend the older woman's romantic imaginings. The Thornton ranch was considerably smaller, thus con-siderably poorer than the Major's massive holdings. When Peggy spoke of her plans to remodel the small ranch house, Diana would try to be enthusiastic, but she knew there would never be the money to spare to do a third of the things Peggy envisioned. It was impossible for her to understand the woman's bubbling contentment.

It was equally difficult for Diana to understand her female classmates in school. Their preoccupation with pop stars and pimply faced boys and titillating gossip seemed silly. As always, Diana excelled in her schoolwork and was a favorite of the teachers. The combination of shining black hair, brilliant blue eyes, and a slim and increasingly shapely figure made her even more popular with the boys. Diana was more comfortable with them, having been raised in an almost

solely male environment, but they seemed very
juvenile much of the time.

Her attitude toward Holt Mallory didn't change. She
continued to regard him as her enemy. And she waged
open warfare whenever she could, trying to undermine
his steadily growing influence on the Major. An-
tagonistic, Diana took every opportunity to issue orders to him, assuming on her position as the boss's
daughter. She sought to constantly remind Holt that he
was only hired help, paid to do the Major's bidding—
and hers. Whenever he was around the stable, Diana
never saddled her own horse, but demanded that he do
it. She used any means she could to get at him, secretly
hoping she would push him to the point of quitting.

Guy was still her puppydog, trailing after her
whenever he could. It didn't seem to matter how Diana
treated him. He was grateful for any scrap of attention
from her. And Diana gave him just enough to be
certain the wedge between Guy and Holt remained
firmly in place. If he liked her, he couldn't like the man
who was his father.

Chapter II

At the beginning of the summer that would bring her seventeenth birthday, Diana had her first intimation of what it was like to have a crush on someone. A new man had been hired, skilled in horse showmanship, to train the Major's prize Arabians. His name was Curly Lathrop.

Tall and muscular with curling dark hair and flashing brown eyes, he had an easy charm and a ready smile. To Diana he was a Greek god come to life. A boss's daughter was never ignored, but she set out to make Curly Lathrop regard her as much more than that. She flirted with him, and he flirted back, but always with an indulgent air, as if he thought of her as a mere child. It frustrated her that he wouldn't see her as the woman she felt she was.

Her birthday came on a hot day late in July. It was little different from others she had celebrated. Sophie had dutifully baked her favorite cake and decorated it for the evening meal. Guy had painstakingly made her a hand-tooled leather key case with her initials on it.

Peggy had stopped by in the afternoon to give her a present of a silk scarf and to relay the news that she was expecting their first child. And Diana listened to the plans Peggy had for the spare bedroom. The money it had taken two years to save to remodel and modernize the kitchen was now being set aside for baby things, doctor bills, and the hospital costs that would come. Diana voiced the expected congratulations, but wondered to herself why Alan and Peggy hadn't waited a few more years before starting a family. She didn't see how they could afford one yet.

At dinner that evening, the Major presented her with the usual lavish assortment of birthday gifts. Diana wore her newest party dress for the occasion and exclaimed over the presents with the right degree of happiness. With just the two of them at the table, ignoring Sophie, who merely occupied a chair, Diana wasn't in a party mood.

Afterward, she wandered onto the front porch and leaned against the railing to gaze at the stars overhead, taking care not to let a wood splinter catch on the white eyelet lace of her dress. Diana fingered the buttons down the front and wished Curly was standing with her.

Her gaze swung wistfully to his quarters. No light shone in the unit he occupied, but his truck was parked outside. Then Diana spied a light in the tack room at the stables. The sudden sparking of an idea caught at her breath.

Before discretion or pride could blow it out, she hurried into the house. Her father was in the study doing paperwork, and Sophia had already secluded herself in the privacy of her small room at the rear of the house. Diana walked into the kitchen and cut a slice of birthday cake.

Wrapping it in a napkin, she took it down to the stable. Diana pretended surprise when she entered the tack room and saw Curly cleaning the equipment.

"Oh, it's you. I saw the light and thought Holt was here," she added in explanation.

"Really?" He eyed her with mocking skepticism.

"Yes, really." Her gaze flashed him a look of provocative challenge.

"What do you have there in your hand?" Curly glanced at the napkin.

"A slice of my brithday cake. As I said, I saw the light and thought it was Holt. I was bringing him this piece of cake to give to Guy." Diana walked farther into the small room shrugging her shoulders. "But since he isn't here and you are, you can have it, instead."

His smile said that he still didn't believe her story but he would go along with it. "I wouldn't want to deprive Guy of his treat."

"You won't be." She offered him the napkin-wrapped cake. "I'll take Guy his tomorrow. Sophie baked a big cake. It will go stale before the Major and I can eat it all."

"I do have a taste for sweet things," admitted Curly with a glint in his eyes that made her pulse beat faster. A faint tremor of excitement went through her as his fingers touched her hand when he took the cake from her. "So it's your birthday today, is it?"

"Uh-huh." She watched him unwrap the napkin and take a bite.

"How old are you?" he asked between mouthfuls.

Diana wished she could lie, but he probably already knew how old she was. "Seventeen."

After several minutes, he finished it. "That's good cake." He brushed the crumbs from his hands. "I wish I'd known it was your birthday today."

"Why?" she murmured a shade breathlessly.

"I would have bought you a present."

"I wouldn't have expected you to do that." But wouldn't it have been wonderful if he had? Diana dreamed silently.

"What did your boyfriend give you?"

"I don't have a boyfriend."

"Come on. As beautiful as you are, all the guys at school must be crazy about you."

Her heart skipped a beat when he said she was beautiful, especially when the same sentiment was echoed by his look. "They all seem so immature." Diana tried to sound very adult when she answered. At his low chuckle, she turned away, hurt that he should find her amusing.

"That's a pretty dress," he commented. "I suppose the Major threw a big party for you up at the house."

"No. We just had a quiet dinner." Her indifferent tone indicated she hadn't expected anything else.

"Birthdays should be celebrated with more than just dinner, a cake, and some gifts," Curly said in a reproving manner.

"Oh?" She gave him an over-the-shoulder look. "And how do you celebrate your birthdays?"

"With a few drinks and some dancing, and, hopefully, the right company." He held her gaze. "It isn't much of a birthday without those three items."

"Mine hasn't been much of a birthday, then," Diana sighed, because it hadn't.

"Since I didn't buy you a present, I'll see if I can't supply the necessary ingredients for a celebration." Curly winked and walked to the near corner where several footlockers were stacked. Briefly touching a finger to his mouth in a gesture of secrecy, he reached behind them and brought out a bottle of whiskey. "I keep it here for strictly medicinal purposes—to keep me warm on cold nights," he explained, knowing the Major was death about drinking on the job. "Tonight we'll put it to its proper use." He took two small paper cups from a stack inside a wood cupboard and poured liquor into one. He hesitated before pouring the second, glancing to Diana. "Do you drink hard stuff? I wouldn't want to be accused of corrupting a minor."

"I've drunk liquor before." Once in her whole life, but she wasn't about to admit it to him. Maybe if he thought she was a little more worldly than she actually was, he might treat her like a woman instead of a child.

He added liquor to the second cup and handed it to her, lifting his in a toast. "To a young and very beautiful lady. Happy birthday, Diana."

When he downed his drink, she did the same. Fire burned her throat, stealing the breath from her lungs.

Diana tried not to cough and succeeded in keeping her reaction to a choking gasp.

"It does make you warm, doesn't it?" she laughed, her voice husky.

"It does," Curly agreed and refilled her cup. "And it helps you relax, too."

After a couple of sips, Diana discovered he was right about that, too. It still burned going down, but not nearly as much as the first time. And it made her feel pleasantly relaxed, giving everything around her a rosy glow. They talked about trivial things. He refilled her cup again. She was beginning to feel delightfully lightheaded when Curly snapped his fingers.

"I promised you dancing, didn't I? Come on." He reached for her hand and led her out of the tack room.

In the wide stable corridor that ran lengthwise to divide the stalls, Curly turned on the radio her father had installed there to soothe the horses. A dreamy instrumental ballad played from the speakers. Only the light from the tack room provided illumination.

He turned, flashing her that bewitching and seductive smile. "Will you dance with me?" he asked, as if they were at a nightclub instead of in a stable.

"Yes." Diana seemed to float into his arms.

He was strong. She could feel his powerful muscles as he held her close. They swayed with the slow tempo of the music. Diana had never danced this way before; she could feel the pressure of his thighs against her hips and the hand spread near the small of her back.

"How do you like this birthday celebration?" His handsome face seemed only inches away. "Drinking, dancing—"

"—and the right company," Diana said, supplying the last ingredient.

"And the right company," Curly agreed. His gaze roamed over her upturned face. "It's a pity I wasn't here last year for your birthday. Sweet sixteen. I don't suppose you have reached your seventeenth birthday without being kissed?"

"I've been kissed a few times," she said, making it sound like an understatement. She studied the dark, springing curls of his hair, wanting to touch them and run her fingers through them.

"Today?" he asked.

"No."

"No birthday is complete without a birthday kiss," Curly said.

She had been kissed before, but when his mouth moved onto hers, his kiss didn't resemble the awkward exchanges that had come previously. He claimed her lips with practiced ease. The relaxing effect of the liquor she had consumed permitted Diana to let instinct direct her response.

"Not bad for an amateur," he commented when it ended.

"My teachers haven't exactly been professionals." She tried to sound as calm as he had, but his kiss had been as wonderful as her romantic imaginings had dreamt it would be.

"Let me give you some free lessons."

"Okay."

Any pretense of dancing was abandoned. Her arms circled his neck, fingers sliding into the thickly springing curls at the back of his head. She smelled the whiskey on his breath and knew hers carried the same odor. The driving pressure of his mouth forced her head back.

Diana wasn't certain whether it was the liquor or the long, drugging kiss that was making her feel so faint. She decided it was a combination of both when he began nibbling at her neck and starting a whole new flurry of sensations. She moaned in reaction and clung even more tightly to him. He came back to her mouth and kissed her again with devastating expertise.

"Come on." He moved away, taking her by the hand and dragging her behind him as he walked to the far end of the stable corridor. Her head was swimming, not quite aware of what was happening or why. Loose straw was piled against the wall. "We'll be more comfortable here." He knelt down and pulled her with him.

"My dress," Diana managed to say in a brief protest.

"Don't worry about it, baby." They were lying in the straw, his mouth again just above hers.

Something told Diana this was wrong. "But—"

"You said I was the right company," Curly reminded her, a hand caressing the length of her arm.

"Yes," she admitted in a whisper, and her gaze slid to his mouth, so close to her own. "Please, kiss me again, Curly."

And he obliged the request thoroughly, over and over again, each kiss more passionate than the last. His tongue parted her lips and probed at her teeth. She resisted, drawing away from its penetration, a confused fear splintering through her.

"Come on, baby," he partially taunted her. "Hasn't anyone ever showed you how to French-kiss?"

"N . . . no."

"It's easy." He kissed the corner of her lips, a teasing sensation. "I'll show you." She didn't seem to have any will except to learn whatever he wanted to teach her. "Just open your mouth."

Diana did so, slowly, and his lips settled moistly over it, his tongue sliding between her teeth to explore the inner hollows of her mouth. For a second, she merely submitted. Then, gradually, there was a desire to respond. Tentatively, she let her tongue move against his, finally returning the erotic intimacy of the kiss.

"Oh, God, baby." He was breathing heavily as his lips moved lightly over her cheek to the curve of her neck. "You're something else."

He moved to her ear, licking at it with his tongue. Diana shuddered at the delicious shivers that danced over her skin. His hand slid over her hip, drawing her more closely to his side, then gliding up to the swell of her breast. Diana tried to push his cupping hand away, but she didn't seem to have any strength. His caresses were becoming too intimate. Her mind gave orders to stop them, but her muscles couldn't coordinate to offer more than a token resistance.

Curly was back kissing her lips again and his hand had stopped rubbing her breast and had moved to the scooped neckline. Everything seemed all right again until Diana realized he was unbuttoning the front of her dress. She twisted away from his kiss.

"Don't!" she gasped in angry protest and reached to draw the material together when he pushed it aside, but her efforts were completely ineffectual.

"Don't fight me, baby."

His breath was hot and moist on her cheek, his mouth seeking her evading lips. Her head was swimming dizzily. The kissing was all right. She liked it, but this petting was further than Diana wanted to go. Her fingers circled his hairy wrist, but she couldn't stop the hand that slid inside her brassiere and lifted her breast free of the lacy cup. He wasn't content until the other was free, uncaring that the bra was binding her painfully.

"You got great tits, baby," he muttered thickly. "Just look at them staring up at me, so young and firm."

Before Diana could guess his intention, his head was lowering to kiss their bunched roundness, licking and biting at the nipples. Desperately, she tried to push him away. Fear was beginning to pierce the alcohol mist that was fogging her mind. But a part of her felt a certain sensual stimulation for the erotic attention.

"Curly, I don't want you to do this." A thread of anger ran through her panicked whisper.

"Sure, baby, sure." But he paid no attention to her protest.

Diana felt his hand touch her knee and glide under the hem of her skirt. All unconscious pleasure she was deriving from his touch vanished at this new and dangerous intimacy. She tried to twist away, hammering at his head and shoulders with her fists, kicking as he lifted up her skirt.

"Stop it! Let me go!"

"You damned little tease," he growled and rolled on top of her to hold her down with his weight.

She opened her mouth to scream, but he covered it with his, muffling the sound. He grabbed a handful of hair, pulling at the roots to hold her head still. Animal sounds of fear came from her throat, only to be smothered by his brutal kiss. Her skirt was up around her waist and he was forcing his legs between hers, unphased by her glancing blows. A raging anger was quickly taking the place of her fear, an anger that he should dare to violate her. His fingers were clawing at her panties, the pressure of his swollen manhood hard against her bare thigh.

One moment he was on her, and the next he was rolled off. For a dazed second, Diana thought it was something she had done as Curly pushed himself to his feet.

"Get out of here, Holt!" he snarled. "This is none of your damned business—unless you want to be next after me."

Diana's eyes focused on the second figure looming in front of Curly. Of all the people to come to her rescue, Holt Mallory was the last she would have chosen.

"Forget it, Curly," was his deadly quiet answer.

"Like hell!"

In the dim light, Diana saw Curly aim a right swing at Holt's face, but it glanced off an upraised left arm. At the same instant that Holt blocked the first punch, he jammed a right fist into Curly's loin. Curly doubled up, falling to his knees, mouth open, his glazed eyes wide with pain. Diana waited with savage anticipation for the next blow, but none came. Holt had stepped back, his arms lowered.

She scrambled to her feet, determined that Curly would not get off so easily after he had nearly raped her. A pitchfork was stuck in the side of the pile of hay. She grabbed it and ran toward the kneeling figure, sobbing with her desire for vengeance.

"Bastard!" she cried hoarsely. "I'll—"

So intent on Curly, Diana didn't see Holt move into her path until his fingers were closing over the wooden handle of the pitchfork to wrench it from her grasp. She fought to regain possession of her only weapon, but Holt tossed it into the hay pile like a spear. She would have retrieved it, but a steel arm circled her to crush her to his chest.

"Let me go!" Diana twisted uselessly in his hold. "He tried to rape me! He deserves to die!"

"Shut up." Holt covered her mouth with his hand, his cold gray eyes boring into her when she tried to bite him. Behind her, Diana could hear Curly staggering to his feet. Holt's sharp gaze fixed on him. "You're fired, Lathrop. Pack your things and be gone within the hour."

"You can't fire me because of her." Curly's breathing was still labored from pain. "My God, she's been asking for it. She's been following me around since I got here, watching me, teasing me, walking around with her blouse half-buttoned and wearing those tight pants. You've seen her. She's been like a bitch dog in heat."

Diana was sickened by what he said. It was too uncomfortably true. But it didn't change the fact that he had been going to take her against her will. The anger brought on by humiliation served to fuel the rage she felt toward Curly.

"Officially you are being fired for drinking on the job." Holt made no other acknowledgment about the accusations Curly had made. "The evidence is that whiskey bottle sitting in the tack room. You're through, Curly. Now clear out!"

His hand continued to smother Diana's cries of protest. She struggled against his constricting arm, the buttons of his shirt scraping against her breasts. Holt didn't let her go until the stable door had closed behind

Curly. She pivoted away, hastily buttoning the front of her dress.

"How could you let him get off scot-free like that?" Her eyes were a murderous blue as she turned on Holt. "What kind of a man are you to let him walk away after what he tried to do to me? The Major would have beat him to a pulp."

"For what?" he challenged. "For taking you up on one of your many invitations? Everybody has seen the way you've been strutting around him. Curly was right. You were asking for it. If it wasn't for the Major, I wouldn't have interfered."

The shame of his words burned through her. "He isn't going to get away with it." Her voice was tight as she turned to leave. "The Major will see that he's punished."

Hard fingers on her arm spun Diana around. "You aren't going to say a word to the Major about what's happened," Holt ordered.

"I am," she defied him. "He'll call the police and have Curly put in jail. And I'll tell him the cowardly way you handled everything. Before I'm through, you won't be working here, either!"

"You spoiled little bitch." His expression was carved with contempt. "We just lost the best horseman in the state, and all you can think about is blood. You want the Major to publicly defend your honor, knowing you chased after Curly like a cheap little tramp. You don't care if the Major looks like a comic figure in front of all his friends, just as long as you get your pound of flesh. He's too fine a man to deserve a daughter like you."

The attack demanded some kind of retaliation. There weren't any words to argue what he said, so Diana swung her open palm at his face, striking his cheek. His eyes took on the color of molten silver. He clamped a hand around her wrist and dragged her to the short bench in front of a stall. Holt bent her over his knee, her skirt falling around her head.

"No!" Diana screamed in shocked protest, suddenly realizing his intention.

It was already too late as her panties were pulled partially down and the first hard slap was administered to her tender flesh. A strangled cry of pain wrenched from her throat. All the struggling in the world couldn't free her. She sunk her teeth into her lips after that, permitting only grunting moans to escape. Diana didn't want anyone hearing her cries and finding her in such a humiliating position. Holt made no attempt to check the force of his blows.

The spanking seemed to last for an eternity before he stood her up. Red-faced, her eyes brimming with tears she wouldn't shed, Diana flashed him a proud and wounded look, her knees quivering, but keeping her upright.

"Are you satisfied?" she challenged in a wavering voice.

The hard lines of his face were impassive. "Somebody should have done that a long time ago."

"For your information"—Diana made a miserable attempt to sound sarcastic—"I did come here tonight to see Curly. I did want him to notice me. I wanted him to kiss me, but I didn't . . . He offered me some whiskey and I drank it because I didn't want him to think I was a child. After that, when he . . . I couldn't seem to . . ." She was having difficulty using the right words. "I never wanted him to do what he was going to when . . ."

What was the difference? Diana turned away in frustration. Holt probably wouldn't believe her, anyway, and she didn't care whether he did or not. Why did he have to be the one to come in and find her with Curly? Why couldn't it have been someone else? God, how she wanted to cry—but not in front of him.

He rose to stand beside her. When Diana wouldn't look at him, his fingers closed around her chin and forced her head around.

"Supposing what you say is true, the next time

something like this happens, and with your kind there will always be a next time," he inserted, cold and insensitive, "there are two things you can do. You can take your lovely manicured fingernails and scratch his eyes out or ram your knee into his crotch as hard as you can—*if* you really don't want him to make love to you."

"Thanks for the advice," Diana responded acidly. If her legs weren't so shaky, she would have tried out the last on him.

His eyes narrowed. "And not a word of this to the Major or anyone else," Holt ordered. "Not even so much as a hint. The Major knows I already warned Curly once about drinking. He isn't likely to be suspicious unless you make him so. You got that?"

"Yes, I've got it."

"I am not going to let you hurt or shame the Major," he warned.

"Your sense of loyalty is overwhelming." The very last thing Diana wanted to do at this moment was talk to anyone about what had happened tonight. She just hoped she could forget it, but she had the feeling that the sight of Holt Mallory would always remind her. She pulled her chin out of his hand and turned away.

"Where are you going?"

"To the house," she snapped.

"Not like that," Holt answered just as sharply. "Hold still." And he began brushing the hay from her dress and picking it from her hair. When he was through, he offered her his handkerchief. "Blow your nose."

"It doesn't need blowing." Diana refused it and blinked the last tear from her eyes.

As she walked to the door, Holt's voice followed her. "Remember what I said."

"I'm not likely to forget." Her terse answer was the truth. Her bottom was so sore that Diana knew she would have to sleep on her stomach tonight.

Diana didn't say a word to anyone about that night. She pretended surprise when the Major mentioned, regretfully, that Curly had been fired. Those who noticed the way she moped around the ranch for the next couple of weeks blamed it on the fact that Curly had left, without realizing there was any connection. Now Diana hated Holt.

Diana graduated from high school with honors, addressing her valedictory speech to the proud face of the Major, seated on the aisle near the front. She enrolled at the university in Reno at the Major's suggestion.

At first Diana had tried to argue against going on to college. She had no desire to further her education. As far as she was concerned, it was complete.

"But what's the point of going on to college? I know everything that I need to," Diana had insisted on a late summer afternoon. "There isn't anything a professor can teach me about ranching that I can't learn from you. I know how to keep the books and make all the entries."

"I am not going to let you waste your intelligence. Besides, there is more to college than classes and professors." The Major had smiled indulgently. "There are sororities to join, activities to participate in, and parties to attend. You need to taste more things in life before you can be so positive that you know what you want."

But Diana had been skeptical. "I won't change my mind."

"Maybe not," he had conceded, "but at least you will have experienced something more than the life you've known."

A knock at the door had interrupted their discussion. When the Major had opened the screen door to Holt, resentment had welled up inside Diana. He had read her expression and glanced at the Major.

"I'm sorry. I didn't mean to intrude." His apology had been smooth, with the proper degree of respect. Diana could have told him that his presence had been an intrusion in her life since the day he'd arrived. But each time she had tried to shut him out, the Major had welcomed him in. It had become a losing battle.

"You aren't intruding," the Major stated. "Diana and I were just discussing her college plans." Diana could have corrected that, too. They were "his" plans, not hers. "What is it?"

"There are a couple of buyers here interested in your Arabians. They specifically want to look at the yearlings," Holt had explained. "Rube is bringing the Jeep around to drive them out to the pasture. I thought you'd want to ride along; the buyers seem to have an eye for the good stock."

"You can handle it without me." It had been a flat pronouncement of trust in Holt's ability.

Diana had stared at her father, shaken by his statement and its implication. The Major had delegated responsibility to others before, but never when his prized Arabians were involved. Holt had become firmly entrenched, and she could no longer ignore the fact. The discovery had deafened her ears to the rest of their conversation. The shutting of the screen door had brought her sharply back.

"Your four years at college will go by so fast that they'll be over before you know it." The Major had picked up the threads of their previous discussion with hardly a break in rhythm.

In agitation, she had turned away. The Major had come up behind her and rested a hand on her shoulder. She had found scant comfort in this rare display of affection. The Major had always been a very controlled man emotionally, rarely expressing his inner feelings, part of the rigid discipline he acquired in the military, plus a natural male reticence.

"I have always planned for you to attend college, Diana," he had told her quietly. "Every father dreams of his child obtaining a college degree. I'm no different."

Diana could find no argument with that. All her life she had done what he wanted. It was too late to break the habit now. She had not wanted to endure his disappointment in her if she refused. Besides, after his conversation with Holt, there had seemed to be little reason to stay at the ranch.

Still, she had offered one small protest. "But Reno is so far away, on the other side of the state."

"Not so far that you can't come home on long weekends and holidays," he had consoled.

So Diana had given in. Consoling herself that she was pleasing him, she threw herself into college life. Her class schedule did not permit many weekends home that first year, restricting her visits to vacation times that were all too short and too far apart. To make the time pass more swiftly, Diana involved herself in more activities and campus parties. She made many surface friends, but her crowded hours never contained the extra minutes to allow deeper relationships, male or female.

The summer came and went almost overnight. It seemed she had barely arrived at the ranch and she was leaving for the fall term.

There were two momentous occurrences in her second year of college. In October, she was called to the dean's office, where she was informed her father had suffered a mild heart attack and was in the hospital. Diana caught the first plane home to Ely.

As she stared at him in the hospital bed, she noticed he looked pale but otherwise unmarked. The Major had always seemed so invincible. It was a shock to discover that he was not. A vigorous light still burned brightly in his eyes, not flickering, but not eternal, either.

"Don't look so worried, Diana," he admonished the concerned expression on her face. "I have plenty of years left in me. I just have to slow down, that's all . . . take it a little easier than I have been."

"I'll make sure that you do."

"What does that mean?" the Major demanded.

"I'm staying home until you're better."

"It was one thing for you to leave college to fly home to see for yourself that I'm all right, but it's

completely unnecessary for you to sit around holding
my hand," he informed her sternly. "I have Holt and
Sophie to take care of me."

Diana wanted to point out that as his only child, it
was her right to look after him and not the privilege of
some hired help, but the Major didn't give her a chance
to speak.

"I'm turning over the operation of the ranch to Holt.
He's more than capable of handling it now. I'm lucky
to have him." There was no mistaking the admiration
and respect in his voice.

"I want to stay home with you."

"Young lady, you can make me happiest by going
back to college and getting your degree. After that, I
hope you find an intelligent and ambitious man to
marry, maybe have a few children later on. The
chances of accomplishing any of those things by
isolating yourself out on the ranch is next to impossible."

"Yes, Major." But Diana wondered if he would be
sending her away if she were his son instead of his
daughter.

Diana stayed at a motel in Ely until her father was
released from the hospital. She claimed it was because
she didn't want to make the hour-long drive each way
from the ranch. The truth, however, was she didn't
want to stay at the ranch knowing Holt Mallory was in
charge.

That February, Diana attended a special lecture of
her political science class. The guest speaker was a
professional lobbyist for Nevada mining interests. His
name was Rand Cummings. Tall, extremely good
looking, with dark curling hair and blue eyes, he was
charming, eloquent, and intelligent. Diana felt an in-
stantaneous attraction to the man, but her experience
with Curly had made her wary.

At the end of the afternoon lecture, Diana and a few
of the others who had no class afterward remained,
ostensibly to ask more questions. Only a blind man
would have failed to notice Diana, and Rand Cum-

mings was not blind. They "happened" to walk to the parking lot together. He asked her out and Diana accepted.

It wasn't exactly a whirlwind courtship, since Diana was determined not to let her emotions carry her away. Rand met most of the criteria she had set. He was mature, in his late twenties, well established in his chosen profession, and ambitious. He was enough like Curly to arouse her physically, yet he didn't press her to have intimate relations. During the most heated embraces, Diana sensed his responses were controlled, even when she trembled on the edge of losing hers. His discipline increased her respect for him.

The weekend before her summer break, Rand had driven up from Carson City to spend the time with her. Sunday night was their last evening together. When Rand brought her home, parking the car near her dorm, Diana turned readily into his arms. She abandoned herself to his possessive kisses, in a way testing his control. Before desire could overpower him, Rand was unwinding her arms from around his neck, but he didn't set her away from him. Instead, he shifted her sideways on his lap and satisfied himself with a leisurely exploration of her neck and throat.

"I'm never quite sure about you, Diana," he murmured.

There was experience in the sensual way he nibbled near her ear. It sent pleasurable shivers over her skin. Her fingers sought the curling waves of his dark hair to slide through their thickness.

"Aren't you?" she whispered.

But Rand didn't seem to find it essential to be sure of her. "You are a beautiful woman. You'll make an excellent wife for a lobbyist. As a matter of fact, you'd be an asset."

Diana drew back slightly, eyeing his handsome features through the upward sweep of her lashes. "That sounds very much like a proposal," she teased.

"It is a proposal. I want you to marry me, Diana," he stated.

For an instant, she made no response. She tried to see him as the Major would, wondering if he would find in him the same positive attributes that she had found.

"Can you arrange to fly home with me next weekend?" she asked. "I'd like you to meet the Major."

"I fully intended to, anyway," Rand said and smiled, "so I can formally request his daughter's hand in marriage."

"Not right away," Diana said quickly. And she hurried to explain: "I'd like him to meet you first and let him have a chance to get to know you, however briefly, before you ask him. Sometimes fathers can become overly critical if they find out immediately."

"Whatever you say," he agreed. "When we have his consent," Rand went on confidently, "we'll go pick out your engagement ring together."

Between kisses and nuzzling caresses, they discussed the future. Not even to herself did Diana admit that she had avoided agreeing to marry him until after she had obtained the Major's opinion. She cared for Rand, and his touch was not distasteful to her. He seemed to be all the things she had ever wished for in a husband. But she wanted to make sure the Major approved of her choice.

When she called home the next evening to let her father know she had invited Rand to return with her for the weekend, he didn't ask any questions. The last week of college seemed endless to Diana, but the flight to Ely was quickened with anticipation.

The Major seemed to have made a full recovery from his heart attack, although Diana noticed on her return that he tired more easily now, and there was considerably more gray in his dark hair. She let him surmise that Rand was someone special without knowing how special and gave him time to form his own impression.

On the last night before Rand was due to fly back,

Diana met her father alone in his study before dinner. They talked for a few minutes in generalities before she asked, "What do you think of Rand?"

"He seems very intelligent and charming. Is it serious between you? I presume it is, since you brought him home."

"He's asked me to marry him."

"And you want my approval," the Major concluded.

"Yes."

"What about your degree?"

"Rand and I have talked about it," Diana admitted. "I'm going to continue, but I'll carry fewer hours than I do now. It will mean we'll have to wait a few years before starting a family, but it will give us time together, too."

"Then I don't see that I have any objection to put forward. I like him, and as long as you want to marry him, there isn't anymore to be said, is there?" He smiled.

"No," she agreed. "Rand is waiting on the porch to speak to you. He wants to ask your permission to marry me."

"Don't keep him waiting. Send him in," the Major ordered with mock severity.

An August date was set for the wedding to enable the newlyweds to have time for a honeymoon before Diana returned to college for the fall term. It left little time to plan the wedding. Her whole summer seemed to be consumed with all the necessary arrangements. It was to be a big wedding, with the reception at the ranch afterward.

Even at the most hectic moments, Diana was relieved that she had something to do. There had been changes at the ranch since the Major's illness, small changes, but disturbing just the same. Holt and Guy now took their noon meals at the main house. There was a twofold purpose to it. The Major insisted it was senseless for Sophie to try to cook a meal for two.

There was always too much. Plus the noon hour permitted Holt time to confer with the Major and get his advice on any problems that had arisen.

Holt had suggested, on Diana's return, that the practice be discontinued to give the Major time with his daughter, but it had been rejected as unnecessary. Diana made no comment, but tried to arrange to be elsewhere for the noon meal. She still disliked Holt as intensely as she had before, but she no longer tried to oppose his presence at the ranch and chose to ignore it as best she could.

The weekend before the wedding, Rand flew to Ely to be with her. Diana was at the airport to meet him when his plane arrived on Friday. No words were wasted in greeting as Rand immediately swept her into his arms and claimed her lips in a long, possessive kiss. When he finally dragged his mouth away, his hands remained locked behind her back.

"Have you missed me?" Rand demanded. "It seems like a month since I've seen you, instead of two weeks."

With all the last-minute wedding preparations and gown fittings, the time had flown as far as Diana was concerned. But his statement pleased her.

"When have I had time to miss you?" Diana teased. "You've called me every single day."

He kissed her with hard, punishing force, his dark eyes blazing over her face when he lifted his head. "I had to call you every day or go out of my mind wondering what you were doing and who you were with."

That hint of jealousy was exciting. "Don't you trust me, Rand?"

He seemed to force a lightness into his voice. "How am I supposed to know what you are doing when you are so far away from me? You could be seeing some of your old boyfriends, not to mention all those rugged-looking cowboys on your father's ranch."

Diana tilted her head back and laughed. "You haven't taken a close look at the men who work for us." Still smiling, she assured him, "Outside of the Major, there is only one man in my life—and that's you."

His hold loosened around her as he lifted a hand to lightly stroke her cheek and the outline of her jaw. "You are so beautiful, Diana. I don't know if I'll ever trust you out of my sight."

The burning intensity of his gaze made her uncomfortable. His jealousy was unnecessary. When she gave her allegiance to a man, it was total. Rand was to be her husband. She had been raised with too strict a sense of moral values to not take her marriage vows seriously. Vaguely unsettled by his attitude, Diana shifted his attention from her.

"What have you been doing these last two weeks?" she issued in mock demand. "Did you find a couple of showgirls in Reno to keep you company during the lonely nights? I'm here at the ranch with the Major to keep an eye on me, but there's no one to watch you. You might be sowing a few last wild oats."

"But there is a difference, my love." Rand kissed the tip of her nose. "How I am spending my last, precious days of bachelorhood is none of your business."

"Chauvinist," Diana accused with a laugh.

"Now you know the truth about me," he chuckled and curved an arm around her shoulders to walk to the terminal exit. "Seriously, though, I found out yesterday that a larger apartment is available in the complex where I'm living. I mentioned to the manager that we might be interested in it. My place is rather small. I don't want us to be rushed into buying or building a home in Carson City."

Diana nodded in agreement. "I wish there was time for me to see the apartment next week."

"Don't worry," Rand assured her. "The manager promised to hold it for us until we come back from our honeymoon. He owes me a few favors."

When they had collected his luggage from the baggage claim area, Diana directed him to the ranch station wagon. She handed him the keys to stow his suitcases in the rear.

"Peggy Thornton, our neighbor, gave a wedding shower for me last week," Diana informed him. "Wait till you see all the presents! I'll show them to you as soon as we get to the house."

"I'm afraid it will have to wait until later, honey," he said, closing the rear door of the wagon and walking to the driver's side. "I have some business calls I have to make first."

"But I thought you came to spend the weekend with me," she protested.

"I did. That's why I'm getting these calls out of the way today." Rand opened the door so Diana could slide under the wheel to the middle of the seat.

"Can't you forget business this one weekend?" she demanded with faint irritation as he sat in the driver's seat.

"Not if I want this trip to be a tax deduction, which I do." He smiled and started the car. "All I have to do is talk to a couple of men at the copper mines and take them to lunch. I want you to come with me so you can get some early practice in what it's like to be the wife of a lobbyist."

"Are you sure you want me to come with you? I don't know all that much about mining," Diana admitted.

"Darling, you don't have to." He slid her a twinkling glance. "All you have to do is look beautiful, smile, and be nice to the men, flirt with them a little. You see, it isn't going to be hard being married to me." Rand grinned. "You should be able to do it with one hand tied behind your back."

"It's a snap." Diana was willing to do what Rand wanted, just as she had been willing to do whatever her father had wanted in the past. "The Major is expecting us for lunch," she remembered.

"There will be a phone at the mine," Rand stated. "You can call to tell him we won't get to the ranch until sometime this afternoon."

Diana's initiation into Rand's world was a pleasant one. She wasn't the least bit ill-at-ease with their men-talk, having been surrounded by it all her life. Occasionally, the discussions about mines and their operation became too technical for her to follow, but they rarely lasted for long. One of the mine operators would notice her silence, smile, and shift the conversation to include her. And Diana remembered Rand's advice. She was friendly, smiled a lot, and flirted a little.

When Rand finally pointed the station wagon toward the ranch, Diana glanced at her watch. "Your estimate was off. It's almost four o'clock. The Major was expecting us a little after two. Maybe I should have called."

"He knows you're with me. I doubt if he's worried." Rand dismissed her concern.

Diana was sitting close to him, her head resting on the seat back. She turned her head slightly to study his profile and smooth good looks. Rand had been fairly quiet since they'd left the mine.

"How did I do?" she questioned softly.

"You were a smashing success." He slid her a brief, arrogantly smiling look.

The compliment warmed her and Diana smiled. "Wasn't I supposed to be?"

"Yes, but don't overdo it," Rand cautioned.

"Did I?" Uncertainty glimmered in her eyes.

A straight stretch of highway was in front of them. Rand put his arm around her and snuggled her closer to him, kissing her hair.

"No," he answered. "I guess I'd better get used to looking at men and seeing the way they covet my wife."

"One more week and I will be your wife," Diana murmured and let her head nestle against his shoulder.

Diana was as nervous as any bride on the dawning of her wedding day. There was no need. The ceremony was flawless. The ranch yard was crowded with guests. Not even the summer heat could dampen the high spirits and festive atmosphere that claimed everyone. Rand was well known, and a lot of his important clients had attended the wedding and the reception. He and Diana were surrounded by several of them now, accepting the champagne toasts being offered in their behalf.

The Major was with them. Diana could tell by the look on his face that he was pleased she had married so well. It made her feel proud when she glanced at Rand, her husband.

As glasses were lifted in another toast, one of the men exclaimed, "Do you know I haven't kissed the bride yet?"

"Neither have I," a second chimed in.

More claimed to have neglected the same privilege. Diana knew better, but she said nothing. None of the men was offensive, nor did any attempt more than a friendly kiss. She obligingly submitted to each of them. As the last moved away, she tipped her head back for the next. The smile froze on her lips as she saw Holt Mallory standing in front of her.

"You are just in time, Holt," the Major declared. "Diana is letting everyone who forgot to kiss the bride at the church make up for it now."

The hard mouth twitched in a mocking smile. Holt made no response to the Major, but offered an exceedingly polite, "Good luck, Mrs. Cummings." Briefly his head bent, his mouth insultingly cool against her lips. Then he was turning to Rand. "Congratulations." He shook hands with her new husband.

Her lips were chilled by the feather touch of his, a touch so light, yet sufficient to prick the bubble of happiness she had felt. She hated him for spoiling her day, for making his presence known when he was aware how much she despised him. It didn't matter that the Major would have noticed if Holt hadn't come forward. She just knew she would never regain the special feeling that had been hers before he appeared.

Resentment shimmered in her eyes as she watched

Holt moving away. It was several seconds before Diana realized someone else was standing before her. A tall and gangly Guy bent his head and kissed her cheek.

"I hope you'll be happy, Diana," he mumbled and shifted uncomfortably, a faint blush staining his suntanned face.

"Thank you, Guy. I will." She tried to sound sincere; but there was a bitterness in her tone left over from her encounter with Guy's father.

"Yeah, well . . ." He grimaced uncertainly and turned to Rand. There was nothing friendly in the look Guy gave him. "Congratulations."

Awkwardly, Guy shook hands with Diana's husband and moved quickly away, losing himself in the crowd as Holt had done. Diana stared after him for a second. Then Rand's arm circled her waist and he murmured near her ear.

"Do you think I could kiss the bride?"

She forced a smile and lifted her head to him. "Of course."

Chapter III

Diana stared out the porthole of the aircraft. In the distance below, she could see the smoky haze of the smelting plant north of Ely. Soon they would be landing and she would be home, this time for good.

Her hands were clasped in her lap, her thumb absently rubbing the finger where her wedding ring had been. The divorce decree was in her purse, dissolving the marriage that had lasted almost four years. The "NO SMOKING" light came on, indicating the plane's final approach, and Diana leaned back in her seat, closing her eyes and wondering for the thousandth time where she had failed.

It had been so good in the beginning, filled with all the passion of new lovers discovering each other. It had burned too hot too quickly. Trouble began brewing under the supposedly blissful surface in less than a year. At first Diana had accepted the bitter arguments as something every new couple experienced, and had ignored the vicious accusations as something that would go away when they learned to trust each other.

When she realized they were warning signals, it was already too late. She fought to the bitter end to save the marriage, refusing Rand's demands for a divorce and enduring more than a year of separate bedrooms. Finally Rand had taken the situation out of her hands and the whole affair had become messy and ugly.

The wheels bumped once on the runway, then rolled smoothly forward. Diana opened her eyes and sat up straighter in the seat. Once the combination of black hair and blue eyes had made her strikingly attractive. Maturity had added beauty. She looked out the window as the plane taxied to the small terminal building.

When it rolled to a stop on the cement apron, she joined the few other departing passengers standing in the aisle. It was April and the morning sun was pleasantly warm as she walked down the steps of the ramp.

Entering the building, Diana glanced around, but recognized no one in the miniature terminal. Was the Major so upset that he hadn't sent someone to meet her? Her chin lifted a bit, a defense mechanism against the pain of the thought. It was more than two years since she had been home, two years of wanting to go but postponing the trip until things got better between her and Rand.

"Diana."

She stared at the young man who seemed to know her. Tall and leanly muscled, he had hair the color of desert sand and light blue eyes. He stepped forward, dressed in crisp new Levi's and a clean white shirt.

"Welcome home," he offered in a low voice husky with emotion.

Diana stared at the sensitivity of his mouth and his slightly tousled hair, cowlicks tamed by the weight and length of it. Disbelief trembled through her.

"Guy?" She identified him hesitantly and laughed naturally for the first time in months when she realized she was right. "Guy! I can't believe it's really you. You've changed so."

"You haven't." His grip was fierce as he held both of her hands, his look as adoring as it had always been.

His comment sobered her. "I have changed, Guy," Diana corrected him quietly.

"How are you?" His concerned gaze searched her face, noting the strain and tension through the paper-thin mask of composure.

"I'm fine," Diana lied. She felt broken, her world scattered like pieces of a puzzle. She didn't think the picture would look the same when she put it all together again. "I never expected the Major would send you to meet me," she said, changing the subject.

"Who else? Wasn't I always your slave?" Guy teased, but there was something very serious in his eyes.

She realized he was still holding her hands, and she gently withdrew them from his grasp. "I guess you were." She smiled and pretended, too, that it was a joke. "Where are you parked?"

"Right outside. We can pick up your luggage when we leave."

"It should be there now." She looked around but didn't see any of the passengers who had been on the plane with her. Besides the ticket agent and the security guard, the only other people in the one-room terminal building seemed to be waiting to board the flight out.

"I guess so," Guy agreed as he also became aware that they were the last to leave. Outside, only her two suitcases were sitting under the sheltered canopy. "Is this all?"

"Yes. The rest of my things will be arriving by freight in a day or two."

As he carried her luggage to the car, Diana studied him. Except for his coloring, there was little about him that resembled the pale, thin boy who had arrived at the ranch ten years ago. *Ten years ago*, she thought. That would make Guy nineteen. She hadn't seen him the last time she was home. She'd come only for the weekend, and he had been off somewhere on the ranch checking fences.

The last time Diana had seen him, Guy had just turned sixteen. He had been thin and gangly then. He had muscled out and become a good-looking young man, not handsome in the classic way Rand had seemed. There was something very fresh and clean about Guy, and Diana felt strangely tainted in contrast.

"What's the matter?" Guy frowned and Diana realized he had noticed her staring.

"I was thinking about what a stinking mess I've made of my life." There was a soft, bitter sigh in her voice as she climbed into the cab of the pickup.

Guy closed her door and paused beside it. "Everybody makes mistakes, Diana."

It was more than a mistake. She had failed utterly and miserably, but she appreciated his attempt to console her. "Some are just bigger than others." A tense smile curved her lips. "Right?"

"That's the idea." Guy returned the smile and walked around the front of the truck to climb into the driver's seat. Leaving the airport, he turned south on the highway. "Do you want to stop in town for coffee or something to eat?"

Diana shook her head. "No. I just want to go to the ranch."

"I'm glad you've come home."

"So am I." She should never have left, but there was nothing to be gained by dwelling on that. "How are things?"

"Fine."

Diana glanced at him. The strong profile reminded her of his father. "How are you and Holt getting along?" she asked, remembering the estrangement between them, aided many times by her.

"We're getting along better." There was a self-mocking twist of his mouth. "I guess you could say we've learned to tolerate each other. Holt is a hard man to get to know. I've never been able to figure out what goes on inside him or why he bothered with me. Guilt, I suppose."

Diana had difficulty imagining Holt Mallory feeling guilty about anything. She suddenly didn't want to discuss him.

"How's the Major?"

"Improving." Guy slowed the truck to turn at the signal light.

"Improving? What do you mean?" She frowned.

"Didn't you know?" he questioned with a surprised look. "The Major had another bad spell a couple of months ago."

A cold chill ran down her spine. She stared sightlessly ahead at the road. "No, I didn't know. He hasn't even hinted that he wasn't feeling well, not in his letters or when I talked to him on the phone. Why didn't someone let me know? It was Holt's place. Why didn't he?"

"Maybe he thought you knew." Guy wasn't attempting to defend his father, merely offering a possibility.

"Two months ago. That's when I finally told the Major Rand and I were having problems," Diana remembered aloud.

"That had nothing to do with it." Guy seemed to follow her train of thought. "The Major had been overdoing it. We had a long cold spell at calving time, and we were all working pretty hard to keep our losses down."

Diana let herself be convinced that Guy was right. "How did he take it when he learned about Rand and me?"

"He was pretty philosophical about it. Naturally he was upset for you, but . . ." Guy hesitated. "Why did you marry him, Diana?"

"I don't know." She shrugged and looked out the window. "I guess I thought I loved him. Rand was handsome and intelligent and successful. He wanted to marry me, and the Major liked him. I don't know why I married him," she repeated. "Maybe I just wanted someone to love me."

After that, they rode in silence for a long stretch of miles. The highway wound over a mountain pass through a desert forest of stunted pines, down to a valley of sage and grass. When they talked again, it was about unimportant things; they were both carefully avoiding the painful subjects.

At the end of the hour-long drive, Guy turned into the ranch yard and stopped in front of the main house.

Diana stared at her childhood home. She had half-expected to see the Major walk onto the porch to meet her when he heard the truck drive in, but the porch was empty.

"Diana?"

Guy was holding the cab door open, waiting for her to step out. She did, running a nervous hand over her tailored skirt.

"Go ahead," he prompted when she hesitated beside him. "I'll bring your suitcases."

He was only a few paces behind her when Diana entered the house. Everything looked exactly the same as when she had lived there. Not even the furniture had been rearranged. There was a lump in her throat as she looked around. The housekeeper appeared from the hallway that led to the kitchen.

"Hello, Sophie." The woman didn't look a day older to Diana.

"Hello, Miss. The Major's in his room, resting."

"How is he?"

"Fine, but the doctor insists he spend a couple of hours every morning and every afternoon lying down," the woman explained. "You go on to his room." Sophie glanced at Guy, standing just inside the door, suitcases in hand. "I'll show Guy where to put your luggage."

Now that the moment had come, Diana realized she was apprehensive about facing the Major. She felt like the prodigal daughter returning, uncertain how she would be greeted. Her gaze slid to Guy, who in his quiet way had been so supportive this last hour.

"Go ahead." He smiled. "I'll see you at lunch."

"Thanks for meeting me at the airport," Diana offered, then hurried to her father's room before she lost her courage.

The door was closed and she rapped once, waiting until she heard a crisp, male voice give her permission to enter. The Major was lying atop the quilt cover of his bed, fully clothed.

"Diana." He smiled. "I thought I heard the truck

outside and wondered if it was you." He made no attempt to rise from the bed at her approach.

"Hell, Major." Impulsively, Diana leaned down to kiss his cheek. "How are you?"

"Fine." He patted her hand resting on his arm. But Diana could see that illness had taken its toll on this once vigorous man. He had lost weight, although still physically fit, and his color was not as good. His once-dark hair was now almost completely iron-gray. The muscles in her throat constricted. "I'm sorry I wasn't at the airport to meet you," he offered, pulling a wry face. "I've been told I have to get my rest. It isn't easy to take orders when you are used to giving them." His eyes were just as sharp as ever and they studied her closely. "But what I want to know is, how are you feeling?"

"Fine," Diana lied, not for the first time, and turned to walk away from the bed, hugging her arms about her. Her eyes were bright with unshed tears as she stared at the ceiling. "I've let you down, haven't I?"

"Diana"—he was reproving—"don't speak such nonsense."

"It isn't nonsense. I have a college degree with no interest in using it. My marriage is finished. I didn't even bring you home a grandson." Diana listed her failures as if needing to confess her guilt.

"A college degree is never wasted, and a lot of marriages fail. As for a grandchild, I am grateful you and Rand didn't have any children, considering the way things worked out. It is difficult for one parent to raise a child. I know," the Major reminded her. "I won't have you feeling sorry for yourself. You tried. A man can't ask more from his daughter than that. In time, you'll have another chance and things will work out better for you."

"I don't want another chance." Diana had blinked the tears away at his admonition. "I've come home to stay, Major. It's where I belong. This time you can't send me away." Looking at him lying there on the bed, a shadow of his former self, Diana felt that he actually needed her.

"I have never sent you away."

She didn't argue the point. "Anyway, I'm back." She lifted her shoulders in a careless gesture. "You are stuck with a twenty-four-year-old daughter on your hands . . . whether you like it or not."

"It doesn't look as if there is much I can do about it, does it?" the Major queried with an indulgent look.

"I'm going to take care of you from now on, sir." The bright smile she gave him was not matched by the intense blue of her eyes, poignant in their plea for him not to object.

"Have I told you lately that you are the best daughter a man could ever have?" His voice was gentle with affection.

"Not lately," Diana admitted. "But you can tell me later after you have rested some more. I have some unpacking to do. Then I thought I might wander around a bit, re-explore my old haunts."

"I'll see you at lunch."

As she closed his bedroom door, her smile faded. She walked slowly to her old room, where her suitcases sat. There was a sense of security in the familiar walls, comfort and protection. Nothing could threaten her here. In this house, on this ranch, she was safe from all harm. It had been a mistake ever to leave it.

The messy, embittered divorce Diana had just gone through seemed long ago. She was home and everything was all right again. Diana unpacked swiftly and changed into the only pair of jeans she still owned, suddenly eager to explore the ranch and pick up the threads of her past life. Her old boots were in the closet and she tugged them on.

Outside, Diana strolled to the stud pens. Contentment radiated from her face as she rubbed the graying muzzle of the bay stallion that came to greet her. Far in the distance she could see dark shapes grazing on the rich grasses at the foot of the mountains. They would be the young horses, Diana knew, the yearlings and two-year-olds.

Her attention returned to the aging Arabian stallion whose ancestors were desert-bred, as he was. His advanced years did not detract from his classic beauty. The delicately proportioned head, with its large and luminous dark eyes, and the flawless conformation of his body were the marks of a purebred.

Petting the sleek neck one last time, Diana moved away, wandering toward the stables, shining white with a new coat of paint. The door stood open and she walked inside. Her eyes couldn't immediately adjust from the brilliant sunlight.

A horse snorted in the relative darkness, hooves shifting to rustle the hay covering the floor of his stall. The familiar smells of hay and horses, leather and saddle soap, brought a smile to her lips.

Footsteps approached the stable door, accompanied by the sound of stirrups flapping from a carried saddle. Diana turned to greet the ranch hand entering the door, anticipating that it might be Rube Spencer or one of the other men who had worked a long time for the Major.

It was Holt Mallory. His gaze touched, identified, and ignored her as he moved past her to the tack room. In that brief second, Diana was struck again by the feeling that his gray eyes were a hundred years old, that there was nothing he hadn't seen or experienced. It was the same thought she had had the first time she met him. And, like the first time, a rush of intense dislike prickled her skin.

Irritated by the way he hadn't acknowledged her presence with a greeting, Diana followed him, pausing in the doorway of the tack room. She watched him swing the saddle from his shoulder and drape it over the wooden saddle rest. Wide shoulders tapered to a slim waist and hips. His tall frame carried not an ounce of unneeded flesh. She had the feeling a knife blade couldn't penetrate those steel muscles.

"I see you haven't changed, Mrs. Cummings." His back remained to her, his cold, drawling voice taunting in its indifference. "You are still running around in tight pants with your blouse half-unbuttoned. Who are you after this time?"

Her hand rushed defensively to her blouse front, fingers refastening the button that had slipped loose. Heat stained her cheeks while a fiery resentment blazed in her eyes.

"No one," Diana retorted, "and the name is Somers. I have legally reverted to my maiden name. I can see you haven't changed, either, Holt. You are the same cold, arrogant bastard you always were."

He turned to face her. The years had molded his features into abrasively masculine lines. Gold glinted in the brown of his hair, visible beneath the curved brim of his Stetson hat. Diana studied him, his seemingly indolent stance masking a coiled alertness. He was as fascinating and as deadly as a swaying cobra before it strikes.

"Why have you come back?"

Diana found his question infuriating. "What a ridiculous thing to ask! This is my home!"

"How long do you intend to stay?" Holt did not let her barely controlled anger deflect him.

"This is my home," she repeated. "I am not leaving."

"Haven't you done enough damage?"

"Damage?"

"I warned you before about hurting the Major," he informed her coldly. "He may be ill, but he isn't blind. If you plan to continue your numerous affairs, you won't be able to hide them from him. When that happens, you'll answer to me."

"My affairs!" Her stricken look was telling. "What do you know about—"

"Did you honestly think the sordid little tales about your marriage wouldn't get back to this side of the state?" The muscles in his jaw hardened with contempt. "Wasn't it your infidelity that your ex-husband used as his grounds for divorce?"

"How . . . Who . . ." Her mind was whirling. She

had never dreamed that the ugly gossip had traveled this far.

"This is copper country," he reminded her. "The stories probably made the entire circuit of mining companies, considering your ex-husband's involvement with them. The gossips had a field day when the rumors about the Major's daughter reached here."

"Oh, God," Diana moaned and turned aside. "They were lies. I never had an affair with anyone. Rand thought . . . He . . ." She looked back to Holt, holding her breath. "The Major—did he hear them, too?"

Holt's eyes had narrowed on her, sharply gray and assessing. "I imagine. I never asked."

It was an effort to hold her head up. "I'm surprised you didn't tell him."

"I try to make things easier for the Major, not harder."

"Oh? Is that why you didn't bother to inform me when the Major suffered this last attack?" Diana challenged.

"I wasn't aware you didn't know about it," Holt replied evenly. "But if I had, I still wouldn't have told you."

"He's my father. I had a right to know."

"So you could drag the dirty proceedings of your divorce to his front door? That would have really made him feel better," he said with dry contempt.

"What kind of daughter would I be if I didn't want to be at his side when he needed me?" she demanded.

"I know what kind of daughter you are—spoiled and self-centered."

Diana swung at his face, her palm stinging sharply with the hard contact against his cheek, but there was satisfaction in the pain. She had only a second to enjoy the sensation before something exploded against her cheek, the force of it snapping her head to the side and drawing tears to her eyes. Stunned, she covered the smarting area of her face and looked back to the man who had slapped her.

"Now I know what kind of a man you are. You

enjoy hitting, don't you?" she said coldly. "Does it make you feel strong and powerful?"

"What did you expect me to do? I stopped turning the other cheek a long time ago." Holt was quick, hard, and dangerous. Any gentleness he possessed was buried deep and guarded.

Holt didn't say anything as he brushed past her, tall and formidable, cutting her dead. Never had anyone made Diana feel so small and worthless. She turned, but his long strides had already carried him out of the tack room and ultimately out of the stable.

"Damn you!" she cursed him in a sobbing breath.

Chapter IV

Diana was helping Sophie set the table for the noon meal when Holt and Guy entered the main house. Holt nodded briefly in the general direction of the two women before walking to where the Major was seated. Diana simmered, knowing the acknowledgment hadn't been intended for her. Two could play the same game.

"Do you want some help?" Guy asked.

At Sophie's startled glance, Diana realized the offer wouldn't have been made if she hadn't been there. "We're almost finished. Thanks, anyway, Guy." She set the last glass on the table. "All that's left is to dish up the food and bring it out."

She followed Sophie into the kitchen and returned with a steaming bowl of gravy. The screen door slammed as Rube Spencer shuffled into the long living room and dining room. He caught sight of the Major and removed his dusty, sweat-stained hat, holding it in front of him in both hands. Wiry, dark gray hair sprang in all directions, as if it had been weeks since it had seen a comb.

It was to Holt whom Rube spoke. "I looked under every rock, but there ain't no goddamned sign of that chestnut mare. I told you she wasn't there, but you wouldn't listen to me. I had to spend the whole goddamned mornin' searchin' for a horse I knew wasn't there. As if I didn't have nothin' better to do."

"What mare is that?" Diana questioned.

"Nashira," Guy said when Holt failed to answer. "You remember her. She had a star on her forehead and four white feet. Her colts always turned out to be little replicas of her."

"I remember." She nodded. "She was foaled the spring after you moved here."

"She proved out barren this year and wouldn't breed with either of our other stallions. Holt turned her out with the yearlings," Guy explained.

"Did you find where she might have gotten out?" Holt questioned Rube.

"I found a place where the top wire was down. There was some tracks on the other side," he admitted. "I figured they was hers and followed 'em for a while 'fore they got messed up in a bunch of tracks of some wild ones."

An eyebrow flicked upward in a thoughtful frown. "Did she join up with a herd?" asked Holt.

"I ain't no goddamned Indian," Rube protested. "All I know is the ground was pretty rocky, and I couldn't tell one hoof print from another. As near as I could tell, there was only about four horses, maybe less. It ain't likely to be a wild stallion and his harem. It's more apt to be some yearlings forced out of a herd, if you ask me. Don't know of any herds that range this close to the ranch. Those wild studs usually like more distance between them and humans, unless it's a dry year and we've had some good rains so far. Not like a few years ago when—"

"We remember how dry it was, Rube," the Major interrupted.

"Yes, sir, I know you do." Rube nodded respectfully. "I s'pose now you'll be sendin' me back out there to find that mare. If she's got the roamin' itch, ain't no tellin' how far she might have wandered. Why, she could be—"

"No, I don't think it will be necessary," Holt stated. "She'll probably come back in a day or two—for water, if nothing else."

"She might not," Rube argued. "I told you, we've had us some rains. She wouldn't be needin' to come back here for water. She could find it up there, especially if she joined up with some wild ones."

"This is her home range. The mare isn't likely to stray far from it. She has never shown any inclination to wander before," Holt pointed out.

"That don't mean nothin'." Rube started to spit out a stream of tobacco juice in disgust and remembered in time he was in the Major's house. "There ain't nothin' that can get wilder than a tame horse after it's tasted its first bit of freedom. Every wild horse came from your so-called tame stock. There weren't no such thing as a wild horse until them Spaniards brought over their ridin' horses. A few got loose and—"

"Lunch is ready." Sophie's announcement came just in time to spare them from a history lesson on the introduction of the horse to North America.

"Well, if you don't think I need to go a-lookin' for that mare, I'll get back to my work. I won't be keepin' you from your food," Rube said and sniffed the air appreciatively. "Sure smells good. I don't remember the last time I et food that didn't come from a can."

Diana took the broad hint and suggested, "Why don't you join us, Rube? There is plenty for all of us."

"I wouldn't want to be imposin' on you." But he was already moving toward the table. "As long as you're sure you have enough, it'd be a real treat for me."

"Of course we do," Diana assured him and hid a smile at the Major's exasperated, yet twinkling, look. "You just sit down anywhere, Rube, and I'll bring in another place setting."

When everyone was seated, Diana was at the opposite end of the rectangular table from her father, with Guy on her right and Rube Spencer on her left. After the Major had said grace, everyone was too busy passing the dishes of food to talk.

The concentration remained on the food until Guy recalled, "You used to catch wild horses when you were young, didn't you, Rube?"

"Sure did," he answered between mouthfuls. "But that was way before your time. Hel——" A glance at the Major and he quickly changed it to: "Heck, I was just a kid myself back then, younger than you. Those were the times, racin' pell-mell through the sage after a band of bangtails, knowin' if your horse put a foot wrong, you'd both break your neck." His eyes were shining as he talked, remembering the danger and the excitement. Then he sighed and came back to the present. "Course, that was before they made that law to protect 'em."

"But if it wasn't for the law, there wouldn't be any mustangs left," Guy pointed out.

"Yeah, well, there's a sight too many of 'em now," Rube insisted. "A wild horse ain't got no more natural enemies now, 'cept man. Oh, there's a rare mountain lion around here and there. An' once in a while, a coyote will bring down a cripple or an old horse. But the rest of the mustangs—" He shrugged to indicate there were no predators to threaten them.

"There isn't a more beautiful sight than a wild horse running free." Diana ignored his practical argument. "I was riding up an arroya once and rounded a bend. There was a mustang. I'll never forget the way he lifted his head and snorted at me in alarm before he bolted for the hills."

"Shore, it's a beautiful sight," Rube agreed. "So is comin' on a doe and her fawn, but if it wasn't for hunters keepin' down the number of deer, they'd be the plague of every farmer and rancher in the country. I ain't sayin' I want to get rid of all the mustangs. I'm like the Major here"—he gestured toward his boss with his fork—"and most of the ranchers. I don't mind sharin' the range with wild horses. But the rancher knows what it's like when there's a bad year. A horse, just like any other animal, has got to have so much land to forage on. If an area gets overcrowded and a dry spell comes along, it ain't a pretty sight to see then. Bags of bones strippin' bark from the sagebrush.'' Rube shuddered. ''I've seen it. And I'd rather see a horse shot than die like that.''

''It culls the herds,'' Holt inserted. ''The weak die out and the strong survive.''

''Maybe so,'' Rube conceded.

''In a bad year, couldn't the government feed them?'' Diana suggested.

''Soon they wouldn't be wild horses if they started doin' that. They would get like the bears, waitin' by the roadside beggin' for a handout. An' those proud, wild creatures you keep picturin' wouldn't exist. No.'' Rube shook his head. ''If they're goin' to be wild, let 'em be wild. But it you want 'em tame, then I say round 'em up.''

''I wouldn't like to see that.'' Diana shook her head.

''Neither would I,'' agreed Guy. ''Remember that time when Alan's waterholes dried up,'' he said, referring to the owner of the neighboring ranch, ''and the Bureau rounded up the herd of wild horses ranging on his place? The Major took us over to see them because I'd never seen a wild horse. They didn't look like much, standing in that corral, their heads hanging.''

''Yes, and you begged me to open the gate and let them loose,'' the Major recalled. ''It took a long time before I could convince you, and you, too, Diana, that catching those horses had been a humane act.''

''I remember.'' Guy nodded with a boyish grin.

''A wild horse ain't much to look at when he's caught,'' Rube stated. ''If them goddamned Easterners that are always screamin' at Washington to save the wild horses, if they ever saw one, they'd laugh their sides out. Half the little school kids think they're savin' Fury. Them mustangs are the shortest, scrawniest, ugliest bunch of nags you'll ever see. Most city folks think a wild horse is goin' to look like the Major's A-rabs. What we should do is get us a bunch of them Easterners out here, plant 'em in a saddle, and ride 'em three or four hours out into them desert mountains where they can see a herd for themselves. But they ain't interested in seein' a wild horse. They just want to know that they're out here. Hell, they're out here, all right," he muttered, oblivious to the reproving look from the Major. "Too goddamned many of 'em, I say. Why, of all the wild horses left in this country, half of 'em are here in Nevada. More'n fifty thousand, some say."

"Not all the wild horses that I've seen were poor specimens." Diana handed the platter of meat to Rube and he took a second helping. "Some had good conformation and a well-muscled build."

"That comes from ranch stock that's strayed. Introduces new blood to a herd that's been inbreeding for years."

"Plus I believe the army turned some remount stallions loose when they disbanded the cavalry," the Major inserted as further explanation of Rube's statement. "That was some years ago, of course."

"No matter what they look like, it is still a thrill to see them." Diana looked up from her plate after she spoke, accidentally glancing in Holt's direction. She saw the cynical glint in his eye. "You haven't taken much part in this conversation, Holt. What is your position on the wild-horse issue?" she asked with sardonic politeness.

"As it stands now"—his cool gaze swept the people sitting around the table—"you and Guy have come down strongly on the side of the mustang. Rube is for the ranchers. The Major has diplomatically decided to stay in the middle of the road. The score is two for the horses, one for the rancher, and one abstention." Holt ignored the housekeeper and her opinion, but Sophie seemed to take it for granted that he would. "I cast my vote with Rube. I'm against the law that protects the mustangs." He gave Diana a mocking look. "I expect you and Guy will now accuse me of being in favor of shooting Bambi.''

"Are you?" Diana questioned, bristling under his taunting regard.

"Yes," he answered simply.

"I thought as much," she retorted.

"Do you two ever agree on anything?" The Major smiled.

"Never." Diana stabbed her fork at the last bite of meat on her plate.

"Shall I bring the dessert in now, Major?" Sophie asked.

"Yes, please." He nodded.

"I'll help you." Diana pushed her chair away from the table and rose, needing to escape, however temporarily, from Holt's presence.

On her third day home, Diana decided it was time she paid a visit to Peggy Thornton. Holt's information that the sordid lies surrounding her divorce had reached her home community initially made Diana want to isolate herself at the ranch, but she realized that was impossible. It would only give credence to the stories.

So far, the Major hadn't asked any questions about the reasons for the divorce. As long as Diana wasn't certain whether he had heard the rumors, she wasn't going to bring up the subject, not if there was a chance he didn't know. The avoidance of the topic made her tense, prompting the decision to spend a few hours away from the ranch.

After lunch, she took one of the ranch pickups and drove the few miles to Peggy's. Diana hadn't visited the Thornton ranch since the summer she and Rand were married. It hadn't prospered in the interim.

Broken fence posts were propped up and staked into position, rather than being replaced by new ones. The white paint on the house was chipped and peeling, giving the small home a moth-eaten appearance. Toys were scattered across the front porch and into the yard. The car parked under a tree was the same one Alan had owned when he and Peggy were married.

With a sense of depression, Diana stepped out of the truck and walked to the front porch. A cacophony greeted her at the screen door: a radio blaring, children's voices, the banging of pots and pans, and a baby crying. Diana knocked loudly, uncertain whether it would be heard over the racket inside.

A figure appeared behind the wire mesh. "Yes?" The question was followed instantly by a delighted cry of recognition. "Diana! Come in!" The screen door was pushed open.

"Hello, Peggy." But the smile she gave her friend didn't reach her eyes.

The woman looked thin and tired, no doubt caused by the squawling baby she was bouncing on her hip. There was no luster to her auburn hair, although her brown eyes were as bright and twinkling as ever.

"I heard you were back," Peggy said and paused to scold the three-year-old girl sitting on the kitchen floor amidst an assortment of pots and pans. "I told you to stay out of the cupboards, Sara. Go outside and play with your toys." A lower lip jutted out in brief mutiny before the carrot-haired child obeyed. "Kids!" Peggy laughed and shook her head in mock despair. "You spend all that money for toys, and they'd rather play with your aluminum pans."

"I've come at a bad time, haven't I?" Diana murmured apologetically. The baby on Peggy's hip was still crying and trying to jam a small fist into his open mouth. "I should have called."

"Believe it or not, this is a good time." Peggy laughed and walked to the old stove, where a bottle was warming in a pan of water on a burner. "It's chaos around here anytime. Right now, you are in luck because one is sleeping." She tested the temperature of the milk on the inside of her wrist, somehow managing to avoid dropping the wiggling baby, and slid the nipple into its searching mouth. "And little Brian here soon will be," she crooned to the hungrily sucking infant. "Sara should be taking her nap. That is the real trick—getting all three of them to sleep at the same time."

"You have three children?" Diana had lost track over the years.

"Sara is three. Amy will be two in July. And Brian is four months, the apple of his daddy's eye. And all of them are in diapers," Peggy sighed. "I have to count Sara because she still wears them when she goes to bed. But Alan finally has his little boy. He's been working so hard lately that he hasn't had much of a chance to enjoy him. Brian always seems to be sleeping whenever Alan is home. He loves the girls, too, but a son is something special for a man."

"Yes, I know," Diana murmured.

"Goodness! Here I've been so busy jabbering away that I haven't even offered you a chair or something to drink. Sit down." Her hands were occupied feeding and holding the baby, so she nodded with her head toward the chairs at the kitchen table. "There's still some coffee in the pot that I can warm up, or would you rather have something cold?"

"Neither, Peggy, thanks." She sat down in one of the chairs and Peggy moved to another.

"I'm so glad you came over. When I heard you were back, I wanted to stop by and welcome you home, but I don't have anyone to take care of the kids. With your father being ill, I didn't want to bring my noisy trio over there. Alan has been working so late in the evenings that by the time I've fixed him supper and washed the dishes, it's time for bed."

"I understand."

"Tell me, how is the happy divorcée getting along?" When Diana whitened at the terminology, Peggy's bright expression was immediately replaced with a look of concern. "I'm sorry. That was a bad choice, wasn't it? I know the divorce must have hurt you. I didn't mean to put my foot in it."

"You've heard, haven't you?" Diana asked in a calm, level voice.

Peggy didn't pretend not to know what Diana was talking about. "That gossip about your extramarital activities." She wrinkled her nose in dismissal. "It sounded like a bunch of nonsense to me, unless you had changed drastically, which I don't think you have."

"None of the stories was true. Rand did accuse me of having affairs . . ."

"Why? I mean, surely . . ." Peggy hesitated, trying to word her question tactfully.

"It was one of those crazy, mixed-up things. Rand knew a lot of important people—executives of various mining firms, as well as state officials. After we were married, he was always reminding me to be nice to them. If they asked me to play tennis or golf or dance, I was supposed to accept. I was to always smile and be friendly, treat them specially. It was important to him and his work," Diana explained, glad to have someone she could speak freely with. "So I did it to please him. Then Rand began believing I was being more than just 'nice' to them. He became so jealous that I stopped accepting the invitations altogether. It didn't help. Rand accused me of sneaking off to meet them behind his back. Those arguments just led to more, until finally neither of us could take anymore. Too many things were said in anger that couldn't be forgotten or forgiven."

"It must have been rough," Peggy sympathized, "but in the long run, I'm sure everything will work out for the best." She tipped her head to the side. "Do you still love him?"

"I don't know what I feel." Confused, she ran a hand through the black silk of her hair. "I tried to be so sure I'd made the right choice before we were married. And to have it all turn out like this . . ." Her voice trailed off in defeat.

"To tell you the truth, I wasn't surprised when I heard you were getting a divorce. I had a feeling you were headed for trouble when you married him, but I was hoping I was wrong."

Diana frowned. "What made you think it was a mistake?"

"There were two things, I think." She paused to set the empty bottle on the table and lifted the baby to her shoulder to burp him. "You and Rand had such a totally different outlook on things. You were raised in the shadow of your father, and I don't think there is a higher-principled man around than the Major. I don't mean that he's a saint or that he expects you to be one, but he has certain values that you have acquired simply by being exposed to them all your life. Rand lived in an essentially political world where the end justified the means. I wouldn't be surprised if the accusations he made against you weren't what he would have done if the roles had been reversed. Do you see what I mean?"

"Yes, I think I do," Diana sighed. "I only wish you had mentioned the way you felt before."

"I don't think it would have done any good." Peggy rubbed the baby's back and glanced ruefully at her younger friend. "You seemed to be more impressed with the fact that your father approved of your choice than with any one else's opinion of Rand. You've always been more concerned about his reaction to what you do . . . or don't do. It's natural, I suppose, that he became the central figure in your life. Your mother died when you were so young. But sometimes I think you consider his opinion too important. I hope I haven't offended you by saying so."

"You haven't, and you're probably right, too." Her marriage to Rand had virtually been over a year ago, but she had refused to admit it because she hadn't wanted to face the Major with her failure. Perhaps if she hadn't been so stubborn, a divorce a year ago might have been a less embittered and abusive one.

Peggy was looking beyond Diana. "Here comes Alan." She frowned. "I wonder what's wrong." She glanced down to the baby, his head resting against her shoulder in sleep. "Wouldn't you know it? Brian is asleep again. Alan is going to think he's never awake."

There were footsteps on the porch. "Hi, honey." Peggy smiled the greeting when the screen door opened.

"Hi." His smile was a tired one as he walked in with his red-haired daughter skipping alongside him. "Hello, Diana." He nodded to her. "Welcome home. I saw the pickup outside and wondered who had stopped over from the Major's."

"Hello, Alan. How are you?" She returned his greeting.

"Fine." He glanced at Peggy. "Is there any beer in the refrigerator?"

"There should be," Peggy answered, then rose to get him one when he sat down at the table. "I'm glad to see you, but I thought you said you would be working all afternoon."

Alan tipped the straw cowboy hat to the back of his head and sighed, "The alternator wore out on the tractor."

Diana could see the lines of stress etched in his face that came from large responsibilities and small income.

"Oh, no," Peggy moaned in commiseration and handed him a can of beer.

"Oh, yes," he grimaced and pulled off the pop-top. He gulped down a swallow of beer and frowned at the can. "This isn't very cold."

"Nothing is. I think there's either something wrong with the thermostat or the cooling unit in the refrigerator," Peggy answered.

"That's all we need," he grumbled. Little Sara crawled onto his lap and tried to steal a sip of beer. "Aren't you supposed to be taking a nap, Sara? Why isn't she in bed?" The second question he directed at Peggy.

"I was going to put her there right after I gave Brian his bottle," she explained, but in an apologetic tone that irritated Diana. "Come on, Sara. You and Brian are going to bed now."

The little girl started to whine and was dragged by the hand out of the kitchen. Diana waited until Peggy returned to make her excuses to leave. Alan's thoughtless attitude toward his wife had brought a constraint to the conversation.

"You can stay a little longer," Peggy said, attempting to coax her to remain.

"No, really, I can't. I was just going to slip over for a few minutes while the Major was resting," Diana insisted. "I'll be back."

"Maybe it will be quieter next time."

They both walked onto the porch with Diana and waved as she drove out of the yard. All the way home Diana tried to understand how Peggy could be so bright and cheerful. She had neither a nice home nor nice clothes, and not much hope for either in the future. She did have three children who were working her to the point of exhaustion. To top it all off, Alan didn't seem to appreciate her.

But Diana did. Those moments of private conversation had eased a great many of her guilt feelings about the failure of her marriage.

Chapter V

It was becoming Diana's habit to help Sophie with the meals, especially at lunchtime. It gave her an excuse not to become involved in pre-dinner or after-dinner discussions where Holt was included.

She was setting the table when Guy walked in. "Hi. Holt won't be here for lunch, so there's no need in setting a place for him," he informed her.

"He won't be here?" Diana repeated. "Where is he?"

"Nashira, the mare, hasn't come back yet. He and Rube rode out to see if they could find her. He said if he wasn't back by eleven-thirty not to fix him any lunch."

"Well, lunch is already fixed."

"That's all right. I'm hungry enough to eat his share." Guy ignored her ill-tempered answer. He was accustomed to her attitude toward Holt.

Guy hadn't just been making idle conversation when he had declared he was hungry. He didn't lean back in his chair until he had emptied his place three times.

"What have you been doing to acquire such an appetite?" The Major regarded him with amusement.

"Working," was the smiling answer. Guy darted a twinkling glance at Diana before he explained to the older man. "I should be done with everything Holt gave me to do by mid-afternoon. Since he isn't around to give me more work, I thought I might ask Diana if she'd like to go riding with me this afternoon.''

''It seems I've heard that before,'' the Major remarked. ''When the two of you were younger, you were always asking if Diana would go riding with you.''

''*Hounding* me into going riding with him,'' she corrected with a teasing smile.

''That's because Holt wouldn't let me go riding alone until I was twelve,'' Guy defended himself good-naturedly. ''If the Major is willing to turn a blind eye to the fact I'm taking half the afternoon off, will you go riding with me, Diana?''

''I don't want to get you into trouble with Holt.'' Such a consideration would never have occurred to her in the past.

''I don't see why it should,'' her father reasoned. ''If Guy can do a day's work in less than a day, I don't see how Holt could have a complaint.''

''That settles it,'' Diana declared. ''With the Major on your side, Holt wouldn't dare say a word to you. What time shall we go?''

''Around three.''

''I'll have the horses saddled and waiting at the stable,'' she promised.

Diana had gone riding almost every morning since her return, but she was looking forward to the outing with Guy. He did so much to bolster her sagging self-esteem with his friendliness and little attentions.

A few minutes past three, he appeared at the stable looking tanned and fresh. Diana caught the scent of a spicy after-shave cologne as she handed him the reins to his mount. She realized he had showered and shaved before meeting her. It was a pleasing discovery to know he had taken extra time with his appearance.

''You don't look as if you've been working hard,'' Diana observed.

''Thanks to a shower and a clean set of clothes,'' he said, admitting what she had already guessed. He agilely swung his tall frame into the saddle. ''It's the first time we've ridden together in four years. I thought the occasion demanded a little extra effort.''

"You look nice." And she meant it. "Where shall we ride?"

"Wherever you like. Lead the way."

It did seem like old times as Diana urged her horse forward and Guy followed. Avoiding the green of the hay fields, they cantered through desert sage until the ranch yard was far behind them. The only sounds they heard were those they created, the squeaking of saddle leather and the thud of the horses' hooves pounding on the sandy soil. When Diana slowed her horse to a walk, Guy brought his alongside.

Without the breeze the cantering had generated, the sun felt sticky to her perspiring skin. "It's hotter than I realized."

"Summer is coming."

"What are you going to do, Guy?" She changed the subject, suddenly curious about him.

"When?" he grinned, finding her question too ambiguous to answer.

"You've been out of high school a year now. Do you have any plans? Are you thinking about college? Or the service?"

"Holt wanted me to go to college, but . . ." He shrugged. "I don't know. I'm tired of school and studying. Naturally, the Major suggested that I might try one of the armed services."

"Is there anything you'd like to do?"

"What I'm doing. No, seriously," he insisted when Diana smiled, "I like working here. I enjoy working with horses. Holt says I'm good with them."

"You always have been, once you finally got over being afraid of them."

"I wasn't afraid of them," he protested. Then he conceded, "Well, maybe a little in the beginning. Anyway, working with horses is what I want to do. It's always been at the back of my mind that someday Holt might save enough money to buy a place of his own."

"Do you think he will?" Diana had often pictured

him leaving the ranch, but she had never thought of Holt owning a ranch of his own.

"I don't know. He's only thirty-five; he's young enough to do it. But I don't think he'll leave the Major, especially now that he's been sick."

Why? Diana wondered, her mouth suddenly tasting sour. Was Holt staying out of a sense of loyalty? Or did he hope when the Major died there would be something in the will for his years of faithful service?

"What about you?" Guy countered. "What are you going to do?"

"Stay here. Take care of the Major. Beyond that, I'm not planning." Her answer was abrupt, shutting him out with its curtness.

"He hurt you, didn't he?" he said quietly.

With her thoughts centered on Holt, it took her a second to realize Guy was referring to her ex-husband. "Only people you care about can hurt you. Rand and I stopped caring about each other a long time ago. If anything, I am a shade disillusioned by the supposedly blissful state of marriage. Let's change the subject, shall we?"

Guy complied with her request, steering the conversation to more general topics. Diana noticed how much more self-assured he had become, like his father, only Guy was gentle where Holt was hard. Guy was serious and sensitive, yet good fun, definitely not the pest he had once been.

As they talked and laughed, mostly over old times, their horses ambled along with little guidance. They were headed back for the ranch before either Guy or Diana noticed their direction had changed. The earthen dam of the irrigation pond rose on their right, the green of water willows peering over the top of the dam's wall.

Diana reined her horse in. "Guy, let's go swimming," she suggested.

He hesitated, something flickering in his expression. Then he agreed. "Okay."

Riding their horses around to the opposite side of the

pond, they dismounted, leaving the horses in a grassy area near the water's edge to graze. Gravel bit into the bare soles of Diana's feet as she tugged off her boots and socks and rose to peel off her clothes.

She didn't think twice about stripping to the skin. All her life she had swum nude, alone or with Guy. She folded her clothes into a neat pile and laid them beside her boots, aware that off to the side, Guy was doing the same. It never occurred to her to look. She had no curiosity or interest. A man's anatomy was not new to her, certainly not Guy's.

Tiptoeing over the rough ground, Diana wasn't in the least self-conscious about her naked body. Warmed by the sun, the water was pleasantly cool as she waded in. When it was past her knees, she dived forward, not hearing the splash that followed hers.

Treading water near the center of the pond, she turned and called out, "The water is beautiful, Guy. Come on in." The last word was punctuated by a strangled cry as she was pulled under by a pair of hands around her ankles.

Freed, Diana kicked upward toward the light, surfacing with a sputtering gasp to find a laughing Guy only a few feet away. Her hand sent a spray of water at his face before she turned and swam away. But she was no longer the superior swimmer of the pair. He caught up with her easily, a hand reaching over to dunk her head.

After a quarter of an hour of horseplay, Diana pleaded for a truce, unable to best him as she once had. Their swim became a more leisurely exercise, alternately swimming and floating, enjoying the water that cooled the heat of the sun from their skin.

Wading from the pond, Diana picked her way over the gravel to a patch of fine sand. She paused to squeeze the water from her dripping hair. A contented smile was on her lips as Guy walked gingerly over the rough ground to join her.

"Do you want to dry off with my shirt?" he offered.

"No." She sank to the sand, sitting with her legs

stretched in front of her and arms propped behind her, her face uplifted to the sun. "The sun will dry me off in no time."

"That's true." He sat down beside her, Indian-style, leaning forward to rest his arms on his thighs.

"That was fun," Diana sighed. "We used to go skinny-dipping here all the time, remember? In the summers when it was hot, I used to think I'd melt before we got here."

"I remember." Guy nodded and raked a hand through his hair to force it into some kind of order.

"Remember that time Holt caught us?" she recalled with a laugh. "He didn't even know you could swim."

"Yeah, and he whaled the daylights out of me back at the house." He picked up a flat rock and skipped it across the surface of the pond.

The laughter faded from her expression as she gave him a sidelong look. His wet blond hair was darkened by the water to a rustic gold shade. Lean muscles bunched in his shoulders and arms. He wasn't a boy anymore.

But his statement had brought back memories of the boy he had been and of that time Holt had descended on them in a cold fury. At sixteen, Diana hadn't been frightened then. It had happened before she had felt the flat of Holt's hand on her backside the night of her seventeenth birthday. He had ordered Guy out of the water, but Diana had stayed, swimming alone after Guy had dressed and ridden off with his father.

Diana hadn't learned what happened until the next time she and Guy had gone swimming, and he had worn his undershorts into the pond. When she learned that Holt had forbidden him to swim in the nude, she had teased Guy unmercifully. How many times had she dived under the water and tried to strip his shorts from him? She couldn't recall, but it was countless times. On a rare number of them, she had succeeded and twice had sent his shorts to the bottom, weighted down by a rock. Diana wondered how Guy had explained the missing underclothes.

At the time, it had just been a funny prank. Only now did it occur to her that it had been cruel. She realized that she never had been very kind to him, regarding him as a pest and a nuisance, taunting him and teasing him about everything from the cowlicks in his hair to his difficulty in reaching the stirrups of his saddle when he was younger. She was sickened by the way she had behaved.

"What must you think of me?" Diana murmured aloud, her blue eyes clouded with shameful regret.

Guy turned his head to look at her. His gaze touched her wet hair, which caught the sunlight to gleam blue-black, and roamed over the fine details of her face. There was something suddenly very intense in his expression.

"I think you are the most beautiful woman in the world, Diana," he answered in a low, deeply emotional voice. "I've always thought so."

A breath of a sob lodged in her throat. That he could think that after the way she had treated him years ago tore at her heart. She stared at him, searching for some word to say.

"Guy." Diana issued his name in a choking whisper for forgiveness.

With a groan, Guy turned to her, rising to his knees to clasp the soft flesh of her upper arms and draw her forward. The years hadn't changed the way he had worshipped her as a boy, she realized. It had simply added another element.

His head moved down, his mouth tentative against her lips. Diana knew she could push him away, but she had pushed him away so many times in the past. She couldn't bring herself to reject him again. When she failed to object to his kiss, it deepened possessively. Diana responded, hearing the pounding of his heart.

She could feel him trembling with virginal passion. His hands were hesitant in their caresses, avoiding the intimate area of her breasts that might bring an end to the embrace, but the adoring fervor of his kiss made up for his lack of experience.

Guy began raining eager, feather kisses over her face, whispering her name over and over again. Diana was overwhelmed by his gentleness and vulnerability. His touching plea for her to return his affection was so like the silent requests of the past. Always before, she had ignored them. This time she couldn't.

"Yes, Guy, yes," Diana whispered against a smooth cheek.

Her hands slid to his neck, fingers intertwining behind it to pull him down with her to the sandy soil. A moan of raw desire came from Guy's throat, cut short by the driving kiss he ground onto her lips. The need to make up to Guy for the way she had treated him blocked all other considerations from her mind. Opening her legs to let his slide between, Diana guided and directed his movements, initiating him into the art of making love.

The experience was short-lived, ending when he shuddered with completion. His crushing weight remained on top of her for several more seconds before Guy rolled weakly off to lie beside her, an expression of satisfied exhaustion on his youthful face.

Neither spoke immediately: Guy, lost to the wonder of what had happened; and Diana, questioning the wisdom of her kindness. But the quiet happiness shining in his eyes when he turned to gaze at her seemed to be the only answer she needed for the time being.

He reached out to hold her hand, as if needing to touch her to be sure it was all real and not a dream. Shifting to prop an elbow beneath him, he gazed at her hand, carrying it almost reverently to his lips.

"Are you sorry?" Guy questioned, his look suddenly vulnerable as he lifted his gaze to her face.

No matter what doubts she might be experiencing, how could she say anything but, "No, I'm not sorry"? Diana touched his cheek with her fingertips in a caress meant to soothe and reassure. She felt so much older than Guy, almost maternal.

"I'm glad." His voice trembled with emotion. "It

was more wonderful than I dreamed it would be." Diana pressed her fingers to his lips in an effort to silence him, not wanting Guy to talk about something they both might regret, but he wasn't so easily deterred. He merely kissed her fingers and held her hand away. "I always wanted you to be the first. The guys were always trying to get me to go with them when they . . ." A faint blush tinted his face as he left that sentence unfinished. "But I kept waiting, hoping. Somehow I just knew you would come back."

"Oh, Guy," she murmured, helpless to stop the outpouring from his soul.

"I love you, Diana," he declared. "I've always loved you. I can't remember a time when I didn't."

"Don't say that," Diana protested.

"Why not? It's true. I love you. I know you're older than me," Guy admitted, as if he believed that was the reason for her protest. "But now we're both grown up, and five years doesn't mean anything."

"Please." She wanted to cry from frustration.

He frowned. "I know you care about me, or else—"

"I do care about you," Diana assured him, trying to explain. "It's just . . ." What could she say that wouldn't hurt him?

His forehead cleared as he guessed: "You're thinking about your divorce, aren't you?"

She seized on his suggestion. "It's too soon, Guy. I'm not ready to become seriously involved with anyone yet."

"I understand, and I can wait until you're ready to love me as much as I love you. All I want to do is take care of you. I'll never hurt you, Diana, I swear," he vowed.

"I know you wouldn't, Guy." When he moved to kiss her, Diana eluded him, gliding to her feet. "It's late. We'd better be getting back," she offered as an excuse for her rejection. "The Major will think we've gotten lost."

Walking to her pile of clothes, she picked up her jeans, aware that Guy had risen to his feet. He came up behind her, his hands settling on the curve of her shoulders.

"I wish we had gotten lost. I don't want this afternoon to end."

Diana wanted to turn into his arms, be held close and be comforted, to ease the crazy, empty ache she felt inside, but that would be taking unfair advantage of a love she didn't return and doubted that she ever would. She lowered her head, her fingers digging into the denim material.

"But you're right," Guy sighed and let his hands fall away. "We have to go back."

"Yes," she agreed tightly and began to dress.

There was little said during the short ride back to the ranch yard, both keeping silent for their own reasons. The presence of others at the stable kept everything casual as they unsaddled their horses. Diana escaped to the ranch house without having to listen to more ardent declarations from Guy.

After sharing a quiet dinner with the Major, Diana sat alone in the long living room-dining room combination. Her father had gone to his room, intending to read for a while, then have an early night. She felt restless and fidgety, half-expecting Guy to come to the house that evening, and she tried to think of what she could say to him.

Footsteps sounded on the gravel path leading to the front porch. Diana hurried to the screen door, seeking to keep Guy outside, where his voice or their conversation couldn't be accidentally overheard by the Major.

Through the wire mesh, Diana saw the tall figure emerging from the night's darkness, the lean physique reminiscent of Guy's. Only it wasn't Guy. It was Holt, and she stiffened as he walked up the porch steps.

"The Major has gone to bed," she informed him before he could speak. "You'll have to wait until morning to talk to him."

The light shining from inside the house didn't reach his face, but there was a deadly threat in his voice when he spoke. "I'm not here to see the Major. I came to see you."

A little pulse hammered in her throat. "We'll talk out here." Diana opened the screen door and stepped onto the porch. "I don't want the Major to be disturbed."

"Fine," Holt agreed.

Diana walked past him to the far end of the porch and leaned against the railing, aware that he followed, his gaze never leaving her. A gold moon was rising in the east, spotlighting the jagged peaks of the mountains. Night was beginning to lower the temperature, and the faint breeze was cool against her skin.

"What do you want?" Behind the bored impatience of her voice, Diana was wary.

"Stay away from my son."

The coldly flat order sent a wave of crimson heat over her skin, but the betraying flood of embarrassment was hidden by the night's shadows. She managed a falsely incredulous laugh.

"What a ridiculous thing to ask," she declared, ignoring the fact that it hadn't been a request. "Guy and I have known each other for years."

"I had a feeling when you came back that it wouldn't be long before you would be up to your old tricks, but it never occurred to me that your object would be my son."

"I don't know what you are talking about." Diana had started out on a course where there was no turning back. She had to try to brazen it out, taking the chance that Guy had not hinted how he felt about her and possibly that she returned the feeling.

But that hope was brutally dashed by Holt's response. "I am referring to your seduction number this afternoon." At her wide-eyed look of alarm, his hard mouth curved into a thin smile. "Yes, I happened to pass by the irrigation pond on my way back to the ranch. I saw you and Guy. I hope you aren't going to try to convince me that you nearly drowned and he was pumping the life back into you."

Diana was first hot with shame, then cold with rage. "What's the matter? Are you jealous because I considered your son more of a man than you?"

"Hardly." He was contemptuous of her suggestion. "When I want sex, I find a woman, not a selfish bitch with hot pants."

"Then what's your problem?" she taunted him, trying not to reel from his hurting insults. "Or are you just upset because I stole your son's virginity? Are you playing the outraged parent?"

"I'm not concerned with his lost virginity. It would have happened sooner or later. I'm here to make sure the whoring brat that took it stays away from him in the future."

Her brittle control snapped. Her arcing hand slapped his face with all the force at her command. That last time she had done that, Holt had retaliated in kind, and Diana was now prepared to elude his striking hand.

But the target of his lightning-quick hands wasn't her face. She ducked futilely as he seized her shoulders and yanked her hard against his chest. The air left her lungs in a stunned breath. A constricting band of steel circled her waist while rough fingers twined around a handful of hair to jerk her head back.

Before Diana could utter a sound, her lips were being ground against her teeth by the driving force of his. The hard, punishing pressure was demeaning, ravaging her mouth the way a man would take his pleasure from a whore. There was a buzzing in her ears, humiliation racing through her veins. Only the rough hand at the back of her head kept her neck from snapping under the force of his kiss.

Her hands strained against his chest, but the effort to gain breathing space arched her hips more fully against him, molding her lower body to the hard, male contour of his. He was sapping her strength, her heart hammering like a mad thing while his beat steadily beneath her hands.

As swiftly as her lips had been seized, they were

released. His hands moved to her waist, holding her firmly, as if he expected her to bolt. She lifted her head to glare at him. Mirrored in his silver eyes was her own angrily resentful expression and nothing more. Diana pressed the back of her hand to her throbbing mouth, wanting to scrub away all memory of his derogatory kiss.

"What's the matter?" His lip curled in a derisive smile. "Didn't you like that? Didn't you want me to kiss you?"

"No!" she hissed, disgust for him flashing in the violent blue of her eyes.

"Liar!" Any trace of amusement, contemptuous or otherwise, vanished from his face. His hand closed around her wrist, capable of snapping it at the slightest provocation. Holt jerked it so her hand was in front of her face. "If you hadn't wanted it, you could have used your claws."

Diana went hot with the memory of his instructions about warding off unwanted advances. She tried to twist free of his talon-hard grip and accidentally brushed her hip against him. The searing contact with the hard male shape of him ended her struggle.

Pressing close, Diana taunted him. "And you wanted me, didn't you?"

Holt pushed her away, rejecting her suggestion as he physically rejected her person. "I'm warning you to stay away from Guy. I won't have him mixed up with the likes of you."

"That isn't for you to decide," she retorted, determined to defy him to her last breath.

"He's not in your league. I am not going to let you amuse yourself with my son. Stay away from him."

He pivoted on his heel and walked from the porch, disappearing into the night. Hatred welled in her throat, a bitter and vile thing. It choked Diana into silence, leaving the last word to him.

Chapter VI

Shouting voices from outside filtered into her bedroom. Diana moaned and glanced at the clock on her dresser. It was barely six A.M. She rolled onto her side, trying to shut out the sounds of activity.

"Doesn't anybody know it's Sunday morning?" she grumbled.

It had been midnight by the time she and the Major had gotten home. Some friends of her father had given a party the night before to celebrate their twenty-fifth anniversary. Diana hadn't wanted to go, had no desire to see whatever old friends who might attend, but the Major had been insistent. He had decided she was isolating herself and needed to get out. When he threatened to attend the party without her, Diana had given in, concerned that he would overdo it if she wasn't there to keep an eye on him.

In the end, it had turned out to be a good thing. It provided her with an ironclad excuse to turn Guy down when he asked her to go into town with him. Not that she was obeying Holt's order of three nights ago to stay away from him, because she wasn't. She simply didn't want to become emotionally involved with Guy, nor did she want to hurt him. It meant walking a fine line. So far she had succeeded, but Diana was aware her success was mostly due to the subtle intervention by Holt and the enormous workload he had put on Guy to keep him busy from dawn until dusk, leaving Guy little free time to pursue Diana.

A sense of urgency seemed to be in the voices coming through her window, echoed by the slamming of the screen door. Finally, curiosity overcame Diana's irritation. Throwing back the covers, she brushed the tousled black hair from her face and walked to the window.

All the activity seemed to be centered somewhere near the stables, beyond her view. Diana glimpsed the Major striding in that direction, the hurried air about him being that of a man reacting to an alarm.

Something was wrong. With a frown, Diana slipped into her cotton robe and slid her bare feet into a pair of sturdy slippers. She was buttoning the last button on her robe as she half-ran and half-walked out of the house.

There was movement everywhere about the stables, yet the commotion seemed to be revolving around the stud pens. Diana hurried in that direction, her nerves stretching thin as the apprehension mounted. Was one of the stallions sick? Had someone been hurt?

Between the solid planks of the corral, Diana saw the Major standing inside with Holt and two others. The gate stood open and she hurried through it.

"What's wrong? What happened?" The questions were barely out when Diana saw the answer. The bay stallion lay on the ground, inert in death. "My God! Shêtan!" She took an instinctive step toward the body.

The one step closer permitted her to see the chunks that had been gouged out of the once sleek hide of his chest and neck. The ground around the mound of horseflesh was stained with blood, the juglar vein torn. Her stomach churned in a sickening rush of nausea that sent her reeling away from the sight. Diana stumbled to the Major's side and felt a comforting arm circle her shoulders. She buried her face into his chest, trying to shut out the mental image of the battered stallion.

One of the hands called out, "The vet's on his way,

Holt!'' And Diana's dazed mind wondered why. The stallion was already dead.

"It's incredible,'' the Major said, his chest heaving in a sigh. "How badly hurt is Fath?''

The name pierced her consciousness. Fath was the chestnut stallion the Major had purchased several years ago as an eventual replacement for the aging bay stud.

"It's hard to say,'' Holt answered. "He's lost a lot of blood.''

"How on earth did it happen?'' the Major mused aloud.

Diana lifted her head from his shoulder, realizing that somehow the two stallions had gotten together. She had heard stories of stallion fights, but she had never witnessed the result of their destructive prowess.

"I swear I latched the gates last night.'' There was a sickly pallor to Guy's face as he defensively answered the Major's question.

"I wasn't suggesting you didn't,'' her father responded.

"Both gates were securely latched this morning,'' Holt inserted.

Diana glanced around the corral, avoiding the spot where the dead stallion lay. The earth was churned up in evidence of pawing hooves, the scene of the fight. One section of the fence had a splintered top rail, the thick board hanging to one side.

" 'Pears to me,'' Rube joined them, "that the chestnut kept circlin' his pen until he found a weak rail. There's hoof marks on the boards where he'd reared up and tried out some rails. When he found the right one, he pounded at it 'til he knocked it loose, then came over here an' did the same thing to get inside the bay's pen. 'Pears to me that's the only way it could 'ave happened.''

"The flaw in that, Rube,'' Holt said dryly, "is why did Fath jump back out of the pen after he had killed Shêtan, and why didn't he return to his own corral? Considering that crippling wound to his right foreleg, I find it hard to believe he could have jumped out of the corral after the fight.''

"It is puzzlin','' Rube shook his head and spat out a stream of tobacco juice.

"Didn't anyone hear the fight?'' Diana questioned. "Couldn't they have stopped it?''

"It happened last night,'' Holt said, as if that explained it. "Evidently sometime before midnight, since that seems to be about the time everyone began coming back to the ranch.''

The Major frowned. "I thought I understood that Guy was staying at the ranch last night to keep an eye on things while the rest of you went into town.''

Holt didn't answer, but cast a piercing look at Guy, who shifted. "I got drunk, sir,'' Guy mumbled. "I think I passed out around nine or ten. I'm sorry, sir.''

"I am disappointed in you, Guy.''

Diana knew the effectiveness of those few words of reprimand from the Major and how heavily they weighed. She felt a measure of responsibility, too, for what had happened. She guessed that Guy's drinking had been in some way connected with her and the fact she had refused his invitation last night.

"It's done and it can't be undone,'' Holt stated. "Where did you put the mare?''

Guy looked at him blankly. "What mare?''

"Cassie, the four-year-old mare that was here to be bred to Shêtan for her first foal,'' he answered impatiently.

"She wasn't here when I found them. I forgot she was supposed to be. I didn't even look for her,'' admitted Guy, a stricken expression taking over his features.

With a muffled curse, Holt turned and walked to the section of the corral with the broken rail. Diana's gaze followed, searching the desert pasture that extended beyond the stud pens. All she saw were the rusty-red coats of grazing Hereford cattle. The Major's prize-winning bay mare wasn't in sight.

"Look at this,'' Holt called over his shoulder.

Diana, together with her father, Guy, and Rube, walked to the fence where Holt stood. In his hand, he held some short white strands. "I found them caught on the wood," he said.

"Horse hairs," Rube identified. "Probably left there when the stallion jumped the fence."

"Yes, but white hairs?" Holt questioned. "One stallion was a bay, so was the mare, and the other stallion was a chestnut. So where did the white hairs come from?"

"The chestnut has white markings," the Major pointed out.

"Or maybe one of them white-faces came up and rubbed their head against the rail," Rube suggested.

"Yes," Holt agreed, but in a tone that wasn't satisfied with either explanation. "Guy, go take a look at the tracks on the other side of the fence," he ordered. "See if you can pick up the mare's. She was wearing shoes."

Guy vaulted over the fence, anxious to make amends for last night. Holt didn't wait to see how successful his son was. Instead, he walked over to where the dead stallion lay and crouched down beside the mangled form with a composure that irritated Diana. She had to look away as he calmly began inspecting the death-stiffened body.

Several minutes later, Holt straightened and came back to the group, his expression grim as he met the Major's look. "More white hairs," he announced.

"Where?" the Major asked.

"There were a few clinging to the bay's forelegs and around his muzzle."

"What are you gettin' at?" Rube frowned. "You ain't sayin'—"

At that moment, Guy came running back to the corral. "I found the mare's tracks!" he called, puffing slightly when he reached the fence, a faintly triumphant light in his eyes. "She's headed straight for the mountains, but there's another set of tracks along with hers. I got the impression she was being driven."

"Aw, come on, Holt. You ain't thinkin' what I think you're thinkin', are ya?" Rube declared.

"You don't believe she was stolen, do you?" Diana glanced at Holt.

He ignored her question to ask Guy, "The second set of tracks—was the horse wearing shoes?"

"No, and it had a peculiar stride."

"To answer your question"—Holt turned to Diana—"I think the mare was stolen, but not by anybody on horseback."

"You're sayin' some wild stallion came down an' took that mare." Rube shook his head. "You're even thinkin' that wild stallion is the one that fought with ours. In the first place, no goddamned pint-sized wild stallion could do the damage you're claimin' this one did. And in the second place, there ain't no goddamned white stallion in these parts. You and me rode all over lookin' for that mare a couple of days ago. We didn't see no white horse, an' a white horse would stand out like an eyesore."

"The stallion could be an offspring of some ranch stock gone wild, which would give him some size. And he wouldn't necessarily have to be white. He could be a pinto with a lot of white to him," Holt reasoned.

"But if it is a wild horse, why would it come here?" Diana frowned. "The wild stallions have never bothered with our mares before."

"That doesn't eliminate the possibility," the Major responded to her question. "This stallion might be too young or too old to win any wild mares from other herd stallions. The evidence seems to point to Holt's conclusion."

"It might also explain the disappearance of the other mare," Holt added.

"We'll have to contact the Bureau," the Major stated.

"Why involve the BLM?" Holt asked in smiling challenge. "We don't know for a fact that a wild horse has anything to do with our missing mares. There is no reason for the government to search for our strays."

The Major had always been one to go by the book. Diana was surprised when he didn't immediately reject Holt's suggestion as not following the proper channels. But she was even more surprised when she saw the glint in her father's eye, a veiled but twinkling approval, as if he admired Holt for bending the rules as long as he didn't break them.

"It would be a waste of taxpayers' money, wouldn't it, when the mares are our responsibility?" he agreed.

The grooves around Holt's mouth deepened in a smile of satisfaction. "How do you feel, Major? Are you up to looking after things for a couple of days? Floyd Hunt's a good man. I can put him in charge while Guy, Rube, and I ride out to find the mares."

"Floyd is a good man. I think between the two of us, we can keep the ranch from falling apart until you get back. I just wish I was up to riding with you."

Diana's pulse accelerated. Behind all this talk of searching for strays lay the true fact that they were going on a wild-horse hunt to reclaim their mares. The idea excited her imagination. It would be challenging, much more adventurous than anything she had ever done.

"I'm going along," she announced.

Holt's head jerked in her direction, his eyes narrowing into gray slits. "It isn't going to be a joy ride."

"I know. It will mean a lot of hard riding over rough country. I can keep up and I won't complain. Ask the Major." Diana didn't care whether he wanted her along or not. She wanted to go. "Besides, I'm a good camp cook."

"That is reason enough to have her along right there." Guy championed her cause.

But there was a personal side to Guy's reason for wanting her to come. He saw it as an opportunity to spend more time with her, an opportunity that hadn't been part of Diana's desire to go. And Guy's wish to have her accompany them would be the very reason Holt would do everything possible to see that she didn't. He would succeed unless she obtained more influential support.

"Major"—Diana turned to her father—"I want to go."

It was the most animation the Major had seen in her face since she had returned; her face was alive and glowing, the way it had been before her disastrous marriage. The hesitancy that had been in his expression softened into consent.

Holt saw it the same instant that Diana did. "We'll be sleeping out, Major," he reminded him. "Three men and one woman—"

"I'm an adult, over twenty-one, and divorced. I am not bound anymore by proprieties." That reasoning had been valid several years ago, but Diana was determined it wouldn't hold up again.

The Major agreed with her. "Under the circumstances, I don't see why she can't go along."

It was up to Holt to either come up with another reason or accept the Major's decision. His features hardened in resigned acceptance.

"If you say so, Major." His light-colored eyes were anything but friendly when he glanced at her. "We'll be leaving within an hour, as soon as we've saddled and packed some supplies."

"I'll be ready when you are," Diana assured him with faint smugness. His down-sweeping glance took note of the cotton robe she wore, reminding her that she was still in her nightclothes. "Excuse me." Diana moved swiftly toward the house.

An hour later they were riding out of the yard with Rube leading the packhorse. Out of necessity, their pace was slow as they followed the horse tracks. The sun was at its zenith when they reached the foothills. They stopped often to rest their horses from the stress of the climb and the midday heat. The noon meal consisted of sandwiches Sophie had fixed and packed for them.

In the afternoon, the trail was lost in a rough section of rocky ground. Holt ordered Guy and Rube to spread out in different directions to find it again, while commanding Diana to stay with him.

When they were alone, Diana taunted him. "Aren't you being a bit overprotective, Holt?"

"Am I?" He looked at her coolly. "Guy thinks he's in love with you. Can you say the same about him?"

She carefully avoided his gaze. "That isn't any of your business."

"I think you just answered my question."

"Did I?" Diana challenged. "What was it?"

"You don't give a damn about him. You are using him just like you did when he was a boy, throwing him a crumb of your attention whenever it amused you to do so. You hurt and confused him then, but I'm not going to let you destroy him now."

Diana didn't argue about her past behavior. "I care about Guy," she said.

The silver glitter of his eyes mocked her assertion. "You aren't going to further your conquest over Guy on this expedition, so get that idea out of your head."

"I came to look for a stray mare. Don't you think it's time you stopped talking and started looking for her trail?" she asked haughtily.

Their eyes locked in a clash of wills, a duel that neither won as a shout from Rube brought it to an abrupt end. Rube had picked up the trail where the two horses had crossed a dry wash. They rallied to his call and started off again.

By late afternoon, Diana was beginning to feel the effect of the long hours in the saddle. Her calf muscles were cramping and her inner thighs were sore from constant rubbing against the leather. She was the last to dismount when they stopped for a ten-minute rest. Guy's hand was on her elbow to help her down.

"Thanks." She smiled tiredly and arched her spine to ease the stiffness in her back. "I'm not in condition for this ride, not like I thought I was."

"Want a rubdown?" he joked.

"Don't tempt me," she said with a wry grimace, but her gaze slid warily to Holt.

Guy followed her look, his expression turning grim. "I suppose he's said something to you."

"About what?" Diana asked with false ignorance and reached for her canteen.

"About us."

How could she tell Guy there was no "us"? "Did he say he had?" she countered.

"No. I told him to stay out of it, that what was between you and me was none of his business."

"I'll bet he didn't like that." Diana lifted the canteen to her mouth, aware that she had used the same statement earlier.

When she had taken a swallow of tepid water, she recapped the canteen and looped its strap around her saddlehorn. The horse shifted its position, blocking them from Holt's view. Guy seized the moment to span her waist with his hands, turning her to him, the frustration of checked desire blazing in his eyes.

"Diana," he moaned her name. "It seems like so long since I've touched you."

"Guy, don't." She stared at his shirt, opened at the throat.

"I wanted to see you so badly last night," he murmured.

"I explained about that," Diana reminded him.

"I know you had to go to that party with your father, but I'd been wanting to see you, and talk to you, and hold you. And Holt kept finding all this work for me to do so I wouldn't have time. Finally, I had a whole evening to spend with you, and you went to that party. It seemed like the last straw."

"It couldn't be helped."

"I know, but last night I kept thinking about you. I've been thinking about you all the time, only last night it was worse, because I was alone and you were out having a good time with your friends. I had a beer, then another, and another. Pretty soon I started wondering if you—"

"Guy, stop it." She began feeling suffocated by the jealous ring to his voice.

"I know," he sighed. "You don't want to get serious yet. But I can't help the way I feel. I've loved you for so long, Diana. It's a relief not to have to hide it anymore. I'd shout it from the highest mountain if you'd just say the word. When I'm with you, I'm the happiest man in the world."

"Don't say things like that."

"I know. I know." His hands moved on her waist in a caressing manner. "We're together now and that's all that's important. Diana"—there was a new urgency in his voice—"when we camp for the night, would you lay your bedroll next to mine? I know we can't do anything, not with Holt and Rube there, but just to know you're lying beside me would mean so much. I—"

In a strangled voice, she denied his sweetly touching appeal. "No, I can't do that." Diana twisted away from his hands, a wild knot of despair claiming her.

"Why?" He was bewildered by her agitated response.

"It isn't wise," she snapped.

There was a pulsebeat of silence. "What's the matter?" Guy's voice was taut, bitter at the rejection. "I'm not good enough for you, is that it? You are the Major's daughter and I'm just some young punk who works for your father."

Diana pivoted, staring at him. "Those aren't your words," she accused. "They came from Holt, didn't they? That's what he told you, and you believed him. That's why you got drunk last night, isn't it?"

"No, I didn't believe him," Guy denied, not quite meeting her sharply blue gaze.

"But he made you doubt. He made you wonder—"

"Forget I said that," he broke in. "I didn't mean it."

Too late Diana realized she should have kept silent. But when her intuition had told her Holt had issued those disparaging comments about her, her reaction had been automatic. In consequence, she had again permitted Guy to believe she cared more deeply than she did. *Damn!* she cursed inwardly. The mere thought of Holt was like a red flag waved before her eyes. She invariably charged without thinking.

"It's all right, Guy. Consider it forgotten," she offered with a stiff smile.

"Diana, I—" he began.

"The blanket has slipped under your saddle, Guy." Holt was there to break up the conversation. "You'd better adjust it before you end up riding a horse with a sore back."

Guy hesitated a fraction of a second. "I'll take care of it," he agreed before moving off to do so.

As he left, Diana met the metallic sheen of Holt's gaze. He would see to it that she spent little time alone with Guy. The determination was there in the ruthless line of his mouth. Her chin tipped upward in defiance, but Holt seemed unimpressed as he walked to his own horse.

Ten minutes later, Diana was hauling her protesting body into the saddle, the others mounting as well to resume the trail. Two miles farther, they crested a knoll and a high mountain valley spread before them. Holt stopped his horse at the top of the rise and reached behind him to the saddle bags and the binocular case inside.

With the aid of the binoculars, he began a slow, searching sweep of the valley. Diana strained her eyes and saw nothing. Holt's arc was half-completed when he stopped, adjusting the focus on the object that had caught his attention.

"D'ya see something?" asked Rube.

Holt lowered the glasses, his gaze remaining fixed on a distant point. He handed them to Rube, instructing, "Look straight down from that notch in the mountain."

"Is it the stallion?" Diana asked, her vision not equal to the distance to see for herself.

It was several seconds before Rube answered and

her heart pounded in anticipation. "It sure enough is," he said at last. "A goddamned white stallion. Wouldn't have believed it if I hadn't seen it for myself. An' you're right, Holt. He looks big for a mustang. Fifteen hands if he's an inch. Canny, too. He's lookin' straight at me."

"We're downwind of him. He's probably caught our scent," Holt said.

"Do you see the mares?" Guy asked. "Are they with him?"

Rube let the glasses waver from the stallion. "Could be they're grazin' in that hollow. Can't tell. Oh, oh, he's movin'. Must not have liked our smell. Look at that! Look at that!" He excitedly shoved the glasses at Holt. He hardly waited for him to focus on the location before he was demanding, "Do ya' see him?"

Diana saw the sudden frown furrowing Holt's forehead. "What is it?"

"He's a goddamned sidewheeler!"

"He's pacing," Holt inserted in explanation, a hint of astonishment in his voice.

"You saw him, too. Hot damn!" Rube slapped his thigh in satisfaction. "I thought m'eyes was goin' funny on me. Whoo-ee!" Diana had never seen the grizzled cowboy so animated before. "Ain't this somethin'! Wait 'til the others find out! Their mouths are gonna be droppin' open."

"He's gone." Holt lowered the glasses and replaced them in their leather case. "He only had three mares. Two were ours. He drove them up that canyon on the far side." Gathering his reins, he glanced sideways at Guy. "I guess that explains why there were times when we were trailing him that his stride seemed so peculiar."

"The stallion was actually pacing?" Guy frowned at Holt.

"Yes."

"But how? Why?" Guy expressed the stunned thoughts that were running through Diana's mind. "Where did he come from?"

"That's easy," Rube declared. "Ain't you never heard the stories about the Pacing White Stallion?"

"No." Guy gave the old cowboy a disparaging look. "This morning, before we started out, you swore there weren't any white stallions in the area. Now you're claiming to have heard stories about him," he scoffed.

"Not about this one." Rube was quick to deny. "No, I'm talkin' about the most famous wild stallion that ever lived. It was back in the 1800s. He was white as snow, 'cept for his ears, which were ebony-black. Stories said his mane was two feet long an' his tail was so long it touched the ground. His only gait out of a walk was a pace, an' he could out-distance the fastest race horse an' keep it up for days. This here stallion must be a throwback to him."

"It sounds like a tall tale to me."

"T'ain't no story." Rube bristled. "Leastwise, I didn't make it up. Lotsa famous people saw him. Why, even that fella that wrote the book about the whale tells about the White Stallion in the book. Just 'cause you never heard about him don't mean he didn't exist."

"Okay, Rube, I believe you," Guy conceded.

Chapter VII

After they had cantered across the mountain valley, they had been forced to slow their pace to resume tracking the stallion and mares. They didn't get close enough again to see the small band before dusk came and they had to stop to camp for the night.

As they dismounted, Guy said, "I'll get some firewood."

"Rube can do that." Holt walked to the pack horse. "You get the horses unsaddled and rubbed down." Aloof gray eyes glanced Diana's way. "Can you cook?"

"I said I could," she reminded him.

"I know what you said," he returned dryly.

"I guess you'll just have to take a chance and find out."

He lifted the pack off the horse and set it on the ground. "The food is in here. Get started."

Concealing her irritation, Diana began unpacking the food and utensils she would need. Rube gathered enough wood to start a fire. Once it was going, he went back out to get more for the cool evening ahead. Using canned beef, Diana fixed a pot of stew and hung it over the fire. She was mixing bannock biscuits when Guy and Holt carried the saddles into the camp circle, the horses staked out for the night.

"Did that stallion really pace?" Guy asked, still skeptical.

"Yes." Holt began shaking out the ground sheets.

"I wish I had seen him," Diana remarked.

"You will, hopefully tomorrow," Holt answered, his expression remote. "How long before the food is ready?"

"A few minutes."

"Smells good," Guy offered in encouragement.

Considering her primitive working conditions, Diana thought the food was delicious. Agreement with her opinion was evidenced by the stew pot, which had been empty when she had cleaned it, although the only one who voiced it was Guy.

"I'm stuffed," he declared, leaning back and patting his full stomach. "That was great, Diana. Didn't I tell you it was a good idea to bring her along to cook?" He tossed the challenge to Holt. "You wanted her to stay behind and make Rube and me eat your cooking. You aren't a bad cook, but you sure can't make biscuits like hers."

When Holt's silence became heavy, Diana spoke up: "Thanks, Guy. It's nice to be appreciated."

"You know what they say." There was a certain intensity to his smiling look. "The way to a man's heart is through his stomach. You've found a place in mine," Guy said, the tremor of his voice adding extra meaning to his words.

Holt leaned forward, a muscle flexing in his clenched jaw as he blocked Guy's line of sight to Diana. "Is there more coffee?" he asked her, holding out his metal cup.

"One more cup for sure." Using a handkerchief to protect her hand from the heat, Diana reached for the gray-speckled pot sitting near the edge of the fire and filled his cup.

"Might as well empty the rest of it into my cup," Rube stated.

He sat on the other side of the fire from Diana. She

rose stiffly and walked around to pour all but the dregs into his cup. Guy observed how gingerly she moved.

"Still sore?" He smiled sympathetically.

"That's putting it mildly. But I'm not complaining." The last statement was directed to Holt.

"Come sit beside me and I'll massage your shoulders," Guy offered.

"That invitation is much too tempting to turn down." She ignored the impaling thrust of Holt's gaze to sit cross-legged in front of Guy, offering her back and shoulders to his ministrations.

His hands closed firmly on her shoulders and began to gently knead the constricted muscles. A mixture of pain and enjoyment drew a sigh from her lips. Lowering her head, she closed her eyes, a black curtain of hair falling forward. His fingers were working magic on her aching flesh. It struck her again how thoughtful and considerate he was.

"Mmmm, you are going to make some girl an excellent husband." And she immediately regretted the remark and the construction Guy would make of it. "Too bad it's my legs that are so sore instead of my back."

"I'll work my way down," he murmured.

Beside them, Holt moved to add a dead limb to the fire. "We're going to need more wood, Guy," he said sharply.

"Why tell him?" Rube demanded. "He don't know where I found that dead tree. He'd be wanderin' around half the night lookin' for it. It's just as easy for me to go get it as it is to tell him where to look. 'Pears to me, you oughta be smart enough to figure that out for yourself, Holt. Be goddamned if I know why you didn't. You just sit right there, Guy." Rube uncurled his wizened frame and rose to his feet. "I'll fetch the wood."

The situation filled Diana with a sense of unease. "Which way are you going, Rube?"

"Over thisaway." He waved a hand to his right. "Why?"

"As much as I hate to move"—she shifted onto her knees, out of Guy's reach—"it's time I made a nature call. I didn't want to run into you out there in the dark."

"Well, if you run into anything out there, it ain't a-gonna be me," he declared.

Rising to her feet, Diana said offhandedly, "I won't be long," before moving off into the night the opposite direction that Rube had taken. If Guy suspected she had a more urgent reason for leaving, it wasn't revealed in his expression as he watched her go.

Desert nights were always cool. At this elevation, the temperature dropped even lower. Diana didn't tarry long in the chilling air, but hurried back for the circle of warmth around the campfire. As she neared the light, Guy's voice carried clearly to her.

"Why don't you just shut up, Holt? I'm old enough to know what I'm doing. Besides, you don't know Diana the way I do."

The context of Holt's low reply was lost to her, but she didn't miss hearing the dry contempt in his tone. Diana stiffened, knowing his opinion of her and guessing he was trying to convince Guy of the same.

Whatever he said brought Guy to his feet. "That's a lie."

Holt rose to meet his son's challenging stance. "You want to believe it's a lie. Grow up and open your eyes."

For all his relaxed air, Diana sensed his coiled alertness. The firelight outlined his rugged profile, playing over his cheekbones to hollow his cheeks and sharply define the slope of his jaw. Her gaze slid to Guy and the indignant anger displayed on his sensitive features. The son was no match for the father. He lacked the ruthless quality, the hard experience that glittered in the gray eyes.

"Take it back," Guy demanded like an offended child. "You take back what you said about her, or . . ." The rest of his threat was contained in his clenched fists.

"She isn't worth fighting over, Guy," was Holt's answer and he started to turn away.

Guy grabbed at his arm and forced him back. "I said take it back!"

His answer was a cold-eyed stare. A chill raced through Diana's bones that had nothing to do with the weather. Holt's silent refusal had backed Guy into a corner and he had tasted just enough manhood to feel obligated to fight his way out, to force his father to regard him as a man to be reckoned with and not ignored.

Holt dodged the right hook Guy swung at him and it glanced off his shoulder. He backed away, but Diana knew he wasn't retreating due to cowardice.

"I am not going to fight you, Guy."

"Take back what you said!" Guy was deaf to all but his need to avenge the insult to Diana, blind to the fact that she stood on the sidelines.

When Holt failed to respond in the way demanded, Guy charged him like a young fighting bull. In the grip of a strange paralysis, Diana was unable to move or call out. Holt defended himself easily, always backing away, always retreating. The blows that landed seemed to inflict little damage. It soon became apparent, even to Diana's inexperienced eye, that it was not the first brawl Holt had been in. She could hear Guy grunting from exertion and frustration. A lucky swing slipped through Holt's defenses, solidly striking his jaw and sending him spinning to the ground.

"Get up!" Panting, Guy taunted him. "Get up and fight!"

Propped up on an elbow, Holt shook his head as if to clear it of ringing bells. He moved his jaw experimentally and looked at Guy. "I said I wasn't going to fight," he repeated calmly and slowly pushed to his feet.

Instantly Guy was attacking, the taste of success making his assault more fierce than before. Twice Holt was unable to block Guy's punches, his head snapping back under the connecting forces of them. Diana's widened eyes saw Holt swing, the blow more instinctive than deliberate, and Guy went down.

The control of her legs returned to Diana's power and she ran the last few steps into the camp, all her attention on the prone figure on the ground.

"Guy!" She felt a flood of guilt for not having tried to stop the fight before he was hurt.

Holt staggered into her path, blocking her from Guy. Blood trickled from the corner of his mouth, coming from a cut inside. He had taken more punishment from Guy's desperate swings than Diana had realized. His eyes had darkened to the color of ominous thunderclouds.

"Stay away from my son." There was a rasping quality to his hard voice. "Haven't you done enough? You've finally got what you always wanted—an open break between me and Guy. Keep away from him."

Her dark head moved in silent denial, but she didn't attempt to come any closer. Holt turned and knelt beside the inert figure, rolling Guy onto his back. The fire cast burnished gold lights on his rumpled brown hair as he bent over his unmoving son.

The walls of her stomach constricted sharply when she saw the bloodied and swelling face, so young and vulnerable in its unconscious state. And all because he had defended her honor. Diana felt sickened, as unworthy as Holt had claimed she was.

"He's hurt."

"I'll take care of him," Holt snapped.

She couldn't simply do nothing, not when it was her fault that Guy was lying there. "I . . . I'll get some water." She walked to the nearest canteen.

As Diana started back with it, the sound of shuffling footsteps heralded Rube's return. He entered the camp carrying an armload of wood. At the sight of Holt bending over Guy, he stopped, bowlegged, and stared.

"What happened? I heard a bunch of commotion goin' on, but I never figure— Is he hurt?" Rube dropped the armload on the dwindling wood pile and hurried over.

Holt took the canteen from Diana's hand, dousing his handkerchief with the water. "He fell." His look dared Diana to dispute his explanation.

"He fell, you say," Rube repeated and peered over Holt's shoulder. "Ain't never seen nobody hurt like that from no fall. Looks to me like somebody hit him. Yep, knocked him plumb out."

"Rube, did anybody ever tell you that you talk too much?" Holt muttered savagely. "I said he fell. Now leave it at that."

"All right, all right, he fell," he agreed with affronted dignity. "Nobody tells me nothin'. Always keepin' secrets. Ole Rube, he don't need to know. But I ain't blind. I can see." He received another silencing look from Holt. "But if you say he fell, he fell. Who am I to be callin' you a liar?" He moved off, still grumbling to himself.

There was a groan and Guy's head moved slightly as he fought to regain consciousness. His eyes opened but it took several seconds before they lost their glazed look. When they focused on Holt, the light of battle leaped back into his expression. Guy started to rise, but Holt pushed him back.

"Take it easy. You had a bad fall." He stressed the last word to impress it on Guy's mind and glanced pointedly to Diana and Rube.

It was the sight of Diana that prompted Guy to contain his anger. "I'm all right," he insisted impatiently and took the handkerchief from Holt, wincing as he pressed it to his split lip.

Holt straightened, moving away, knowing Guy would reject any expression of concern. Carefully, Guy sat up; he was still a bit groggy. Diana felt a surge of maternal desire to comfort him, but she controlled it. She didn't want him misinterpreting her concern, nor did she want him to learn she had witnessed his defeat.

She didn't move to his side, but asked, "Are you sure you're okay?"

His gaze, sullen and bitter, strayed to Holt and

returned to stare at the handkerchief he held. "Yeah, I'm okay."

His look reminded Diana of Holt's accusation that she had ripped their tenuous relationship. They had battled over her, a rift that would not soon be bridged. She hadn't meant it to happen. Years ago, she might have wished it, but she had been a child then with the malevolent dislikes of a child.

"It's going to be a long day tomorrow," Holt announced to everyone in general. "It's time we all turned in." But it was issued to end the conversation between Diana and Guy. All three knew it.

"Diana," Guy's voice was suddenly earnest.

She shook her head. She didn't want a conversation, not when he was so emotionally charged. Diana didn't know what he was about to suggest, but she didn't want to hear it.

"You should rest."

Without giving him a chance to protest, she walked to her bedroll, aware that the length of Holt's separated hers from Guy's. From her bedroll, she watched Guy and Rube follow suit, with Holt being the last.

The stars were brilliant overhead. She stared at them for a long time, listening to the silence. Her gaze strayed to the still form of Holt. He wasn't sleeping, although his eyes were closed. She still disliked him, but the night's event had tempered even that. Diana shut her eyes.

A hand touched her shoulders. Diana awakened slowly to see Holt bending above her. At the look of alarm that sprang into her eyes, his mouth quirked briefly. The half-light of dawn revealed a discolored mark along his jaw.

"Fix breakfast," he ordered. "We're going to break camp in an hour."

Groaning, Diana pushed the blanket aside and rose. Both Guy and Rube were already up and moving about, graining the horses and gathering the saddles. There was little time for idle conversation under Holt's schedule. Breakfast was cooked and eaten with equal haste, the dishes cleaned and packed away. They were on the horses and riding toward a coral sky a few minutes short of an hour. The air was still cool, vaporous clouds forming from their breath.

At mid-morning, Holt reined in his horse and let his gaze follow the direction the tracks were leading. "There's a waterhole in that canyon, isn't there, Rube?" he asked.

Rube paused and looked around. "Now that you mention it, I think there is. Yep, there is. That must be where them wild horses water. It's the only place for miles around that I know of. What're we gonna do? D'ya think they're in there now?"

"I don't know. It's possible. We'll make a wide circle and approach from the upwind side this time, so they won't catch our scent."

An hour later, Diana had her first glimpse of the white stallion. They had approached the waterhole from the north, pausing at the canyon rim. Milk-white, as symmetrically proportioned as any of the Major's blooded Arabians, the stallion stood apart from the grazing mares. A proud sentinel, noble and free.

"He's magnificent," Diana murmured.

"He's fantastic," Guy said with equal awe.

"He's a thief," Holt reminded them. "Those are the Major's mares down there."

His remark heightened the tension that had been present all morning. Diana tried to ignore it. With difficulty, Diana tore her gaze from the stallion to glance at the mares. The familiar white-legged chestnut Nashira was there, along with the prize-winning Cassie. The third mare was a buckskin of good but indiscriminate breeding.

"Find someplace to tie the pack horse," Holt issued the order to Rube. "We'll make our way down that slope. The trees will hide us for a while. Once we're in the canyon, we'll scatter the mares and keep them separate from the stallion. We should be able to manage them easily if he's out of the way."

Dismounting, Rube passed the reins of his horse to Diana while he led the pack horse to a nearby tree with a patch of grass beneath it. Momentarily distracted by Rube's movements, Diana wasn't conscious of her horse's chest expanding. Too late she remembered that the Arabian gelding she rode was the son of the chestnut mare below. Her horse had caught the familiar scent, and with a whickering neigh, he called to her. Holt's reflex was lightning-quick, reaching out to clamp a hand on the horse's nose.

The damage was done. The stallion's head came up, turning in their direction to test the air. His head tossed, as if in irritation that he was unable to catch any scent. He looked at them outlined on the rim. Diana held her breath, knowing if he ran, they would lose the mares, yet at the same time hoping he would flee.

With a mighty snort that seemed to echo through the canyon, the stallion wheeled and raced toward the mares, bunching them together. Cassie, the mare newest to his domination, resisted his attempt to drive her from the grass. He nipped her savagely into obedience.

In a whirl of motion, he sent them racing for the canyon mouth. The stallion brought up the rear, preventing any of the three mares from turning back. Diana stared at the right front and rear legs, moving forward in perfect unison, in opposition to his left side, a fluid, effortless gait, totally natural.

"He is pacing," she whispered, as if she had needed the proof of her own eyes to believe it.

Diana turned in her saddle as Holt released her horse's nose. He lifted his hat and raked a hand through his hair in irritation before setting his hat back firmly on his head.

"Are we going to follow them?" she asked.

He seemed to consider the courses of action open to them before answering. "No. The stallion is already spooked. We can't hope to get close to him until he settles down. They will come back here. I agree with Rube. As far as I know, it is miles to the nearest water."

"But they might not come back until tomorrow," Diana pointed out.

"Whenever he brings them back, we'll be waiting for him."

"How can you be so sure?" Guy challenged, his rebellion now spreading to other areas.

"Horses are creatures of habit. They don't wander from their range. They simply run in circles. The white stallion will be back." Holt reined his horse away from the canyon rim. "We'll make camp in that arroyo and wait. We'll be out of sight, and as long as the wind stays from the south, he can't catch our scent. Rube"—he turned to the man on the ground—"you stay here and watch, but don't let yourself be seen. One of us will spell you in a couple of hours."

"All right, but leave me a canteen. It's gonna get hot up here in the open when that sun gets up another notch. My tongue'll be hangin' out if you don't leave me somethin' to drink. Say, you want me to go down there and fill our canteens?"

"No," refused Holt. "I don't want any human smell around that waterhole. We should have enough to last through tomorrow."

"What if he hasn't shown up by then?" Guy questioned.

"That's a decision that can wait until tomorrow. Bring the pack horse." Holt led out.

Giving her canteen to Rube, Diana followed, leading his horse. Guy was behind her with the pack horse. It was a winding, twisting trail down to the arroyo, farther away than it had appeared. The air seemed dead inside, hardly a breeze stirring to ease the baking directness of the sun.

The horses were picketed in a patch of shade. As soon as they had established an orderliness to the camp, the three of them sought the sliver of shade along the wall of the arroyo. Holt stretched out on the sloping ground, using a saddle for a pillow and tipping his hat over his face. Sitting, Diana hugged her arms around her knees.

"That stallion was something else, wasn't he?" Guy was next to her, on his side, an elbow propping him up. "He was a wild spirit."

"Yes, he seemed—" Diana began.

Holt cut her off. "Don't romanticize him. The stallion is a rogue. He's turned his back on his own kind." He didn't move from his reclining position, his hat tipped forward, arms folded across his flat stomach. "When an animal does that, he's trouble."

"What are you suggesting?" Guy demanded, and electrical undercurrents crackled in the air. "That we shoot him? Destroy him?"

"No," Holt answered with measured deliberation. "I'm suggesting we get our mares back and hope it ends there."

"Will it?" Diana questioned.

"I don't know." He changed the subject. "It's been a long time since breakfast. Why don't you start lunch?"

"Why don't you leave Diana alone? Let her rest." Guy seemed compelled to argue with everything Holt said. "If you're hungry, you fix it."

With commendable control, Holt answered evenly: "It was her idea to come along as camp cook."

"I am hungry, too," Diana lied in an attempt to stop an all-out battle.

"Well, let him—" Guy was still prepared to argue.

"I prefer to eat my own cooking," she insisted and rose.

"I'll help," he offered.

Firmly but politely, Diana refused him, insisting she could manage on her own. The weight of his devotion was growing heavier with each minute. It was a relief to escape it, even with so minor a distraction as fixing lunch.

They ate the hash she cooked in silence. When they'd finished, Diana gathered the plates together.

Holt rose to walk over and help himself to the coffee in the pot.

"You'd better keep the pot warmed for Rube," he told her and glanced at his watch. "Go up and relieve him, Guy."

"You go. I'm going to stay here with Diana."

The flat statement hung in the air like a sword. Holt turned slowly to Guy, and Diana held her breath, seeing the gleaming steel color of his gaze, honed into a sharp, cutting edge.

"You aren't here as a companion to Diana," Holt said with deadly calm. "You are here to work. I have fired men for not doing their job. Is that what you want, Guy?"

Her mind screamed: *No! Don't give him an ultimatum like that!* She forced out a laugh. "Why are you taking Guy so seriously? He didn't mean what he said. It was mostly just some wishful thinking out loud, wasn't it, Guy?"

The area around one side of his mouth and chin was all swollen and discolored. Guy turned the other way so Diana couldn't see that side of his face. His look was sullen as he nodded a reluctant agreement.

"That's all it was," he mumbled. "I'll go up and relieve Rube now."

"Did you have much water left in the canteen you gave Rube?" Holt asked Diana.

"It was a third full, I think," she answered.

"You'd better take another with you," he told Guy.

The extra canteens were beside Diana. She picked out the fullest one and turned to hand it to Guy. He didn't immediately take it from her, a troubled and frowning look on his face as he searched her expression.

"Why do you keep siding with him?" His voice was low and taut, a wealth of bewildered hurt in its stiffness.

"Don't be ridiculous, Guy. I'm not siding with Holt," she denied softly so Holt couldn't overhear.

"Yes, you are. A minute ago—"

"A minute ago you would have been fired. Is that what you wanted?" Diana reasoned.

A grim look entered his expression, hardening his features in a way that was reminiscent of Holt. "No," he sighed and took the canteen from her. "No, that isn't what I wanted." Guy turned away, mumbling, "I'll see you later."

Chapter VIII

Diana watched Guy scramble up the steepest section of the arroyo wall and disappear toward the place where they had left Rube earlier. As she turned back to the dishes, she caught Holt studying her, his expression assessing and cool. He held her gaze for a scant second before calmly turning away.

Her tips tightened. "Thanks, Diana," she issued sarcastically, mocking him. "I appreciated that."

Holt slashed her an icy glance. "Am I supposed to be grateful that you intervened?"

"If I hadn't, Guy would have been leaving," she retorted. "Why did you threaten him with dismissal? It was practically an ultimatum. How did you think he would react? It was self-defeating."

"Self-defeating?" An eyebrow quirked, aloof and arrogant. "If Guy no longer worked on the ranch, he wouldn't live here, either. How long would you be interested in him if he wasn't around?"

Her mouth opened in stunned anger. "You pushed him deliberately?" Diana accused. "That was stupid."

"Perhaps I should take lessons from you in how to handle my son," Holt suggested sardonically. "Maybe I could twist him around my finger then, hmm?"

"Maybe you could!"

"How long are you going to keep Guy dangling on the hook before you cut the line, Diana?"

"I am not dangling Guy on any hook," she denied.

Holt ignored her denial. "When you cut it, he's going to fall. What am I supposed to do? Wait to pick up the pieces when you get tired of playing with your new toy and break it? I'll do everything I can to stop you first."

"What can I do about it?" Diana argued. "It wasn't my idea for Guy to fall in love with me."

"Fall in love with you? You are the goddess Diana. He worships you. He doesn't just love you. And you encouraged him to fall in love with you when you seduced him."

"That's not true. I didn't."

"Guy certainly didn't seduce you. He wouldn't have dared to touch you unless he was invited. You could have stopped him at any moment with just a word. Guy would never have forced himself on you. Why didn't you say that one word?"

"I knew he wanted me, but I never guessed he was in love with me. If I had—" Diana pivoted away in frustration, a lump blocking the words in her throat.

"Why did you make love to him?" he demanded.

"I felt sorry for him."

The admission was barely out of her mouth when a steel vise clamped on her shoulder and twisted her around. Diana stared into a pair of wintry eyes, Holt's features hardened with anger.

"You felt sorry for him?! Why?"

All her nerves screamed at the contact with him. The chemistry between them produced its predictably volatile result. Her dislike of him was as potent as it had ever been in her youth. Hot blue flames blazed in her eyes.

"I'd feel sorry for anyone who had you for a father!" The words carried all the venom she possessed.

Both of her shoulders were seized, his fingers biting savagely into her flesh. He half-lifted her off her feet, pulling her toward him. Her hands gripped his bulging biceps, arms bracing to hold herself away. His face was close to hers, lean and hard, primitive in its ruthlessness, virile in its masculinity.

"You vindictive little bitch." His voice was low and ominous, like rumbling thunder. "Guy thinks you are a goddess and you're made of clay—dirty, clinging clay that any man's hands can mold."

Her heartbeat quickened in alarm. With a kicking twist, Diana wrenched out of his hold, the sleeve of her blouse tearing. She clutched at the material, her eyes wide and accusing when they turned on Holt.

"Do you think Guy will believe that I was the one who had a fall this time?" she challenged.

Holt took a threatening step toward her and Diana pivoted blindly. She had goaded him deliberately, and now she regretted it. She had outgrown her habit of using Guy to get back at Holt, but after all that had happened, he would never believe her.

Diana started to run, as much from herself as from him. A half a dozen steps were all she managed before Holt caught up with her. She tried to twist away. Her legs became tangled up in his. Losing her balance, Diana tumbled to the ground, dragging Holt with her.

For an instant, she was pinned by his weight, but she twisted and wiggled, pushing and kicking from beneath him. He still had a hold on her, pulling her back when she tried to crawl away. Her fingers curled into the gravelly earth as Diana tried to claw precious inches, unable to manage a centimeter. Holt's superior strength was turning her onto her back. Her fingers closed around the gravel in her hand. As he succeeded, Diana flung the sandy grains in his face, momentarily blinding him.

Before Diana could slip free of his iron grasp, Holt recovered. His groping hands found her wrists, spreading her arms above her head while his length covered the rest of her body, weighting her down. Vaguely, Diana was aware of Holt blinking and shaking his head to rid his eyes of the last dust particles, but she was not sorry for the discomfort she had caused him.

Still she tried to strain free, arching her body in an attempt to throw off his weight. Her panting breaths ended in tiny whimpers of futility. Holt held her down until she had no more energy to fight. Her heart was hammering from the effort of her struggles. The muscles in her arms quivered and relaxed, no longer straining to free her wrists from their trap.

At last, Diana looked into the impassive face of her captor. Exhausted and still breathing heavily, she ran the tip of her tongue over her upper lip to moisten its dryness. Holt's alert gaze caught the movement, its attention shifting to her mouth. His pupils darkened to a charcoal-gray, smoldering and intense.

A tiny moan of protest sounded in her throat. Diana was capable of no other movement, not even the slight turning of her head to avoid his descending mouth. It closed over hers, warm and demanding, persuasive pressure moving over the sensitive curve of her lips.

All her senses came to life. The bed of hard gravel was rough beneath her, chunks of rock poking into her flesh. Her arms scraped the ground as Holt drew her wrists down even with her shoulders. Diana tasted the salty beads of perspiration that trickled down from his upper lip to mingle into the kiss. Their combined body heat seemed to fuse them together, sweat heightening the male smell of him, musky and stimulating. The staccato beat of her heart seemed to match the erratic sound of his.

The sensual possession of her lips shivered through her, exciting and arousing, despite Diana's attempts to block out the pleasure it held. Marriage had opened her eyes to the passionate core of her nature, a passion that had not been ignited by Guy's fervent but awkward attempts. And it had been so long since Diana had known the touch of a man wise in the art of arousing a woman. Not until this moment, when the masterful skill was being practiced by a man who had always been her enemy. But if this was defeat, Diana knew she was going to glory in it as her lips softened in an initial response.

That one, small movement was the striking of a match head, igniting a blaze that consumed them both. His tongue probing in the intimate recesses of her mouth sent waves of rapture cascading through her limbs. Aware of his fingers dispensing with the buttons of her blouse, Diana fumbled at those of his shirt. Her body seemed weightless as he lifted to free her of the restricting material of both her blouse and her bra.

The touch of his hand on her breasts was so firm and sure that it seemed they had always been his to caress. The nipples became hard and erect in his palms, sensitive pebbles his mouth had to taste. A curling sensation went all the way down to her toes as Holt rolled his tongue around them.

His hands were never still for an instant, roaming at will about her body, molding the clay of her flesh to his desire. In a mindless whirl of sensual ecstasy, Diana was aware of the remaining clothes being stripped from her. She was dazzled by the knowledge that soon there would be nothing between them. Her hands slid over his back, feeling the uneven marks on his flesh and the hard muscles rippling like living steel.

At the moment of total possession, her hips lifted to meet his thrust, her nails digging into his flesh, like the flexing claws of a cat in a state of satisfaction. She was drowning in a sea of desire. Never had she felt so alive. Nothing existed but the all-encompassing pleasure he gave her and the fervor with which Diana returned it. But it was not a progression without end. It came with a heady rise to delirious heights and a spinning fall to earth.

Diana lay on the ground, her eyes closed, aware of the burning rays of the sun beating down on her naked flesh. She listened to the breathing of the man beside her. For a few serene moments, she felt nothing but the bliss of satisfaction. Gradually, the lengthening silence brought other thoughts.

Turning her head, she looked at him, her eyes wary and vulnerable, screened by thick, curling lashes. She stared at the rugged profile, the closed gray eyes, and his rumpled hair. A pulse throbbed in her neck at the vitality and strength etched in the powerful features. Diana saw him not as an enemy or an adversary, but as a man. And as a man, Holt had no equal. She wanted to reach out and touch him, tell him of the soul-destroying fire of his embrace.

As if feeling her gaze and reading her thoughts, Holt sat up with effortless motion, an action that took him out of her reach and seemed to reject any confidence. Her dark lashes lowered to conceal the flash of hurt.

"At least Guy wasn't totally misguided. You're good."

Within the demeaning statement was a reluctant compliment. But to Diana, it was a backhanded slap that made her feel cheap and promiscuous. Something that had been beautiful now seemed tarnished. She gathered her pride and sat up, reaching for her clothes scattered about the ground.

"This doesn't change anything," Diana told him, refusing to glance in his direction. But she knew everything had changed.

"I never thought for a minute that it would," Holt answered dryly.

Her hands were shaking as she pulled on her jeans, and there was a poignant tightness to her throat. Diana wanted to ask him why he had made love to her and if he really hadn't felt that specialness that had devastated her. But she suddenly lost her natural candor.

There was the sound of clothing being pulled on behind her as she fastened the clasp of her bra. Slipping her arms into the sleeves of her blouse, Diana turned around. Holt was tucking his shirt into his Levi's.

"What now, Holt?" The question fell somewhere between a challenge and a demand.

"I don't know what you mean." His cool gaze raked her briefly, dismissing in its indifference.

"How are you going to make this to your advantage? That's what you've been doing ever since you came here." Diana buttoned her blouse, aware that his steps had brought him closer, but she refused to give ground.

"You have it turned around. You are the one who is always using people."

Holt stopped two feet in front of her. Diana's heart skipped a beat as she met the silvery fire in his look. The flames had been banked, but they hadn't gone out, not for either of them. The embers glowed, ready to be fanned into life.

"Why?" She caught back a tiny, sobbing breath. "Why did it have to be you?"

Holt looked away with seeming impatience and irritation. "I might ask the same question." When he turned back to her, there was something musing and cynical in his expression. "Diana the huntress. Are you going after new game? Do you think it will be amusing if you can capture us both? A double trophy? Father and son?"

Inwardly, Diana reeled from the cruel sting of his words. Any attempt to issue a disclaimer was thwarted by a miniature avalanche of gravel cascading down the slope. Simultaneously, they both turned to the sound, expecting Rube and seeing Guy.

A shaft of cold fear plunged into her heart upon seeing the tortured rage in his young face. Hot tears were on his cheeks and hatred in his eyes when he confronted them on the arroyo floor, legs slightly apart in a challenging stance.

"I saw you!" he told them in a voice that trembled with his violence. "Through the binoculars, I saw you!"

An involuntary cry of anguish escaped Diana's lips, her gaze flying to Holt, now standing to one side of her. Years of control kept his expression calm and impassive; his gray eyes revealed nothing of what was going on inside him.

"Guy—" he began in a level tone.

But Guy was already moving. The saddles and gear were only a step from him, and he moved toward them. For a moment his intention wasn't clear. Then he drew a rifle from its scabbard and pointed it at Holt, aiming it from his hip.

"I saw you rape her!" he accused in a sobbing cry. "I'm going to kill you!" Guy cocked the rifle. "Move away from her."

Gasping, Diana looked at Holt. An intense pain, pure agony, flashed across his face. It held no fear of death, only the searing torment that the gun aimed at him was held by his son. The entire force of it seemed to be transmitted to Diana. But the glimpse was fleeting. Again, iron control masked Holt's reaction.

"If you saw"—Holt took a step forward and to one side, away from her—"then you know it wasn't rape."

"You told me all those lies about her because you wanted her for yourself," Guy accused, lifting the rifle to his shoulder. "You'll never touch her again."

"Guy, don't!" Without being aware she had moved, Diana was between the two men. "My God, he's your father!"

"What good are fathers?" he retorted bitterly.

Holt was pushing her aside, rejecting the shield of protection her body offered him. With slow, deliberate strides, he started toward Guy.

"Don't come any closer," Guy warned, the muzzle of the rifle wavering slightly.

Holt stopped when there was barely five feet between them. "At this distance, you can't miss, Guy. So when you pull the trigger, be certain you won't regret it."

Diana ran to Guy, her legs shaking with every step, her heart pounding in terror. She grabbed at his arm. "If you care about me at all, don't do this!" she pleaded.

His finger trembled on the trigger, but he didn't look at her. Her widened gaze darted to Holt. The piercing metallic look in his eyes was impossible to hold, and Diana didn't see how Guy could meet it. In another second, she would have reached for the rifle barrel, but it wasn't necessary, as Guy pointed the muzzle at the ground.

"If you go near her again, the next time I will kill you," Guy warned.

It was over and Diana sank weakly to her knees, trembling. Holt turned and walked several yards away, eliminating the possibility of further confrontation. The polished wood of the rifle butt touched the ground near her. Her shaking fingers lifted a curtain of tangled black hair and tucked it behind her ear.

Guy's hand rubbed across his forehead and roughly wiped the tears from his cheeks in a gesture that said he was waking from a nightmare. Reality had been much worse than a nightmare. Diana closed her eyes, trying to shut out the horrifying memory of it. She felt the tentative touch of Guy's hand on her shoulder.

"Did he hurt you?"

"No." She nearly choked on a bubble of hysterical laughter. "No, he didn't hurt me."

"Where's Rube?" Holt's voice cut into the quiet exchange.

"He's still up there," Guy answered curtly.

"Go relieve him." It was an order.

Guy hesitated before announcing, "Diana is going with me."

Holt's gaze flicked over the pair of them. "Why tell me? She doesn't need my permission."

Guy's mouth tightened as he glanced down at Diana. "Come on." He extended a hand to help her to her feet.

Diana didn't know what to do. Half of her wanted to stay with Holt. The other half knew she had to go with Guy or risk a whole new explosion. Her shattered nerves couldn't withstand another such scene.

Placing her hand in Guy's, Diana rose and walked with him. As he helped her up the steep slope, she forced herself not to look back at the solitary figure of Holt watching them leave.

It was a long, punishing climb on foot to where Rube waited. Her legs were aching and she was out of breath by the time they reached him. The physical pain felt good, overwhelming the mental torment for a while.

"It's about time you came back," Rube grumbled. "I'd just about decided you was gonna leave me up here. I s'pose the food's all dried up by now an' ain't fit to eat. What'd you mean by runnin' off like that, anyways?" he demanded of Guy. "You took off out a here like a bull after a bee stung his privates." His squinting eyes turned to Diana. "An' what happened to you?"

She guessed her face was still white, her eyes not yet losing their anguished look. When his gaze touched the torn sleeve of her blouse, her hand moved to cover it.

"I tore it on a bush," Diana lied.

"Ya gotta be almighty careful out here. Ya can get some bad scratches from some of these bushes." Rube shook his head in warning. "Infection sets in an' then you're in a bad fix."

"I wasn't scratched."

"You're mighty goddamned lucky, then. The way it tore your sleeve, it coulda—"

"Don't you think you'd better get down to camp?" Guy interrupted.

"First you go tearin' off without so much as a 'bye, ya leave, an' then you're hustlin' me to go. But I can take a hint. I know when I'm not wanted. I'll go." Rube moved off, still grumbling under his breath.

In a few minutes, his wizened figure was out of sight and Diana sat down in the shade of the juniper tree near the canyon's rim. She didn't glance at Guy when he joined her. Seconds ticked away in silence, each one louder than the last.

"I hate him," Guy muttered in a savage release of emotion. "If you hadn't been there, I would have killed him."

"Don't talk like that." Diana rose in agitation, hugging her arms about her knotted stomach. "I don't want to hear it."

Then Guy was on his feet. "Why did you let him do it?" There was the pain of bewilderment in his voice.

"It just happened, that's all." She kept her back to him, fighting the twinges of guilt. "I can't explain how or why."

His arms circled around her waist to draw her close. "Oh, God, I love you so much, Diana." His mouth moved against her hair as he spoke. "All I want is to cherish and protect you. You need never to feel insecure as long as I'm around, Diana. I promise." Her hands had closed around his wrists, intending to escape his embrace, but his curious statement caught her by surprise and she hesitated. "I know what it's like to be lonely and to need somebody—anybody—to show that they care. But I care, Diana. I've always cared. You never have to turn to anybody else but me."

His mouth moved lower to nuzzle her neck, but her senses were indifferent to his caress. There was no more hesitation as Diana unwrapped his arms from around her waist and stepped away, rejecting his embrace and his rationalization for her behavior.

"What's wrong?" Guy frowned.

"Everything. Don't you see?" she demanded impatiently. "I can't go from your father's arms straight into yours." She turned away, confused, irritated, and miserable. "I'm going back to camp."

"You can't go back down there with him!" he protested.

"Oh, God." Her laughing sigh was bitter. "After what happened between you and Holt, you don't honestly think he still wants me. He'd probably rather see me dead. You needn't worry, Guy. Nothing is going to happen. Besides, Rube is down there now."

Her descent to the arroyo camp was a slow one. At the crunch of her boots in the gravel bank, Holt turned to face her, a light flashing in his eyes. Her heart leaped at the involuntary movement he made toward her, but he stopped himself, his features hardening as he pivoted away. Diana's heart plummeted to her toes. It was what she had expected, but it didn't make it any easier to accept.

"I thought you was gonna stay up there with Guy." Rube scraped the last bit of hash from his plate. "If I'd o' known you was comin' down, I'd o' walked with you, but you didn't say a word about comin' back."

"It was too hot up there."

"I coulda told ya that, but ya didn't ask. Nobody asks me nothin' . . . nor tells me nothin', neither," he complained. "Not that I care. Don't make no goddamned never mind to me."

If it wasn't for Rube, there wouldn't have been any conversation around the campfire that night, a fact that didn't escape his notice.

"The air around here is so goddamned thick a body could cut it with a knife," he observed. "Ain't no one 'cept me strung ten words together all at once. Course, it never occurred to any of you to let me in on what's goin' on. Nah, there ain't no need in tellin' Rube nothin'. Just keep it 'twixt yourselves." Diana caught the quelling look Holt sent him. "I know, I know," Rube acknowledged it. "Why don't I just shut up? It ain't none of my business."

Chapter IX

By mid-afternoon of the following day, the stallion had still not brought the mares to the canyon's waterhole. The last of their canteens of water was empty. The decision Holt had postponed had to be made now, and Guy reminded him of it.

"We're out of water. What are we going to do?" he challenged. "Our horses haven't had any since this morning."

"We'll wait until five. If the stallion hasn't brought the mares in by then, we'll go to the waterhole."

They waited. Five o'clock came and went with no sign of the white stallion and his mares. Diana sensed Holt's reluctance to enter the canyon, but the overriding concern was their own need for water.

"Saddle up," he said when he saw Rube's signal that there was no movement in the canyon. "We'll take the horses in and let them drink their fill."

On horseback, the climb to the canyon rim seemed shorter. Rube saw Guy leading his saddled horse and smiled widely.

"I figured you was gonna leave me perched up here like some goddamned bird. I was gonna hitch a ride if ya did," he declared. "If I gotta be sittin', I'd rather be astraddle a horse. 'Sides, it's bound to be cooler down there, rather than these skillet-hot rocks up here."

"Get on your horse, Rube," Holt said with thinly disguised impatience.

Muttering to himself, Rube took the reins from Guy and swung his bowed legs into the saddle. With Holt leading the way to the canyon floor, Diana was last, leading the haltered pack horse minus its pace.

The lengthening shadows made the canyon seem much cooler than the higher plateau of the mountain. At the waterhole, Holt and Guy refilled the canteens, adding purifying tablets to the containers as a precaution, while Rube and Diana held the horses. When their drinking water had been gathered, the horses were led forward to drink.

Diana splashed water on her hands and face, the tepid water cool to her skin. "Be nice to take a bath," she murmured to no one in particular.

But Rube was quick to take up a chance at conversation. "When you're chasin' wild horses, ya shouldn't bathe. Ya ain't even s'posed to change clothes. Confuses the smell. I read about one fella that did that, never bathed nor changed clothes. He'd follow a herd 'til they'd get so used to his smell, they wouldn't even run when he came around. He herded 'em right into a pen without them even knowin' they was bein' caught. Nope, ya shouldn't bathe when you're chasin' wild horses."

"I'm sure you are in favor of that, Rube," Holt commented dryly.

"Now what are you insinuatin'? I bathe just as regular as the next fella," was the indignant retort. "Ain't nobody ever accused me o' bein' dirty."

Unkempt, perhaps, Diana thought, glancing at the stubble of beard growth on his weathered face, but not unclean. But she, nor either of the other two, had the desire to tease him as they would have a few days ago.

With a sigh, she straightened and gazed toward the canyon mouth. It was pure chance that prompted her to look in that direction. Her muscles froze as she saw an alabaster statue standing several hundred yards away.

"Look," Diana whispered.

The others turned, similarly freezing in their tracks. The white stallion saw their shapes and lifted his nose to the air, testing it for their scent. He advanced a few feet, floating over the ground in that peculiar rocking gait of his, his long tail streaming behind him, his mane rippling like white silk in a gentle breeze. Suspicious, the stallion stopped again, becoming as motionless as an exquisite living sculpture.

Diana was conscious of nothing but the sight of him, the sense of awe and enchantment. The stallion was as wild and free as the soaring eagle, with equal pride and nobility. Excitement thundered through her veins.

The wind carried the stallion's scent to their horses. This time Diana was prepared when her gelding turned to view the strange horse, her hand closing over his nose to silence him. But the shifting movements of the horses turning to stare curiously at the stallion seemed to be all the confirmation he needed of danger.

His snorting neigh was undoubtedly an order for the mares behind him to retreat. Wheeling on his hind legs, the stallion struck out for the mouth of the canyon. Diana would have stood there watching the beautifully fluid picture, but Holt was already springing into his saddle.

"Come on. We'll never get closer than this," he ordered.

His horse was bounding after the fleeing band before the others were in their saddles. With the burden of the pack horse, Diana was destined to eat their dust as they galloped in pursuit. Their horses were fresh but water-logged, and it slowed them down.

They kept in sight of the band. The buckskin mare raced in the lead with the white stallion crowding the rear of the other mares, not letting them slow their headlong flight. His pacing stride made him appear to glide over the ground, effortlessly and tirelessly.

The shadows lengthened as the sun dipped lower. At times, Diana lost sight of the mares, but always the gleaming white of the stallion guided them like a beacon light. No matter how hard they pushed their horses, they couldn't seem to close the gap between them and the fleeing herd.

The buckskin mare seemed to know every hill and hollow intimately. Swerving sharply, she ducked into the narrow opening of an arroyo and the stallion drove the stolen mares after her. Rube and Holt were the first to enter the opening, followed by Guy. Diana was much farther behind. She heard the squealing cry of horses and shouts from the men. Before she could urge her horse through the opening, Guy and his horse were coming out.

"They're trapped!" he shouted in elation.

Almost instantly, Rube and Holt were riding out of the narrow opening. Holt was dismounting before his horse plunged to a stop. He didn't waste time exclaiming over their triumph.

"Let's get a barricade up," he said to Rube. "Guy, Diana, be ready in case they try to come out."

Working with a speed and ingenuity Diana would have marveled at if she hadn't been so alert to the sounds coming from inside the arroyo, Holt and Rube erected a barricade of brush, stones, and dead limbs.

"It don't look very substantial," Rube panted when they were finished.

"It isn't," Holt acknowledged. "But it looks like it could be. We'll just have to hope the stallion doesn't decide to test it."

"Well, he'll be goddamned reluctant to get cornered in that narrow chute of an opening, so it could be he won't make a try at the barricade."

"I hope so."

"Are you sure there isn't any way for them to get out?" Diana dismounted now that there was no longer any need to guard the opening.

"There must have been once, or that mare wouldn't have led them in there," Rube insisted. "I thought I caught a glimpse of a small landslide that carried away one wall of the arroyo. Could be there was a trail out, but the slide buried it. They're boxed in there just as big as you please. We couldn't o' driven 'em into a better trap.''

"Are we going in there and rope the mares?" Guy was still on his horse, a lariat in his hand.

"It's getting too dark to see," Holt said. The sun was behind the horizon, leaving a crimson afterglow to light the sky. Soon that would be fading to purple. The sheer walls of the arroyo would make it even darker inside its confines. "And our mares are almost as wild-eyed as that stallion. They can't get out of the arroyo, so rather than risk an injury from panic, I think we should let them settle down overnight. In the morning, we can catch our mares and let the stallion and the buckskin go.''

"Do you mean we're going to camp here for the night?" Diana questioned. Then she instantly protested, "But all our food and gear is—''

"We are camping here," Holt stated in an uncompromising tone. "We'll build a fire right in front of the barricade just in case the stallion decides to investigate it. The fire should keep him back. As for the food and bedrolls, I guess we'll have to go hungry and sleep close to the fire to stay warm.''

"I might be able to scare up a jackrabbit or a chukar," Rube suggested. "Don't fancy the idea of goin' without any goddamned thing to eat.''

"If you can see it to shoot it, you are welcome to try," Holt answered.

"Always gotta come up with somethin', don't ya?" Rube grumbled. "Just can't give a fella credit for comin' up with an idea. Nah, ya gotta poke holes in it. If ya can go without eatin', so can I. Here, take my horse.'' He shoved the reins into Holt's hands. "If you're gonna be that way about it, I'll just gather up some firewood and get a fire goin'. Probably ain't gonna get done lessen I do it.''

"I think I'll see if I can't find a jackrabbit before it

gets too dark." Guy picked up on Rube's idea, pulling the rifle out of the saddle scabbard and dismounting.

"The horses will need to be walked to cool off," Holt said as Guy passed Diana the reins to his horse. "They worked up a hot sweat."

Holding the reins of her horse and Guy's, as well as the lead rope of the pack horse, Diana began walking behind the horses Holt led. Slow, monotonous circles they made in front of the arroyo as Guy disappeared into the shadowy dusk and Rube wandered about, loading his arms with wood fuel.

The dominating sounds came from inside the arroyo. The angry squeals of the trapped horses were punctuated by the trampling of hooves around their natural enclosure. Their frenzy seemed to fill the air, clawing at sensitive nerves until Diana wanted to tear down the barricade herself and set them free. Common sense kept her from giving into the impulse and she tried to appear as stoically indifferent to their cries as Holt did.

From somewhere out in the purpling desert came the explosive report of a rifle shot echoing through the night. Diana paused to look in the direction she believed the shot had come from, absently stroking the muzzle of the horse at her shoulder. There was an empty gnawing in her stomach, endurable for the moment, but not for long.

"I wonder if Guy hit anything," she mused aloud.

"We'll know when he gets back to camp," was Holt's clipped response.

Rube's fire was crackling into full flame when Guy returned triumphantly to camp. He carried a scrawny jackrabbit by its long ears, held high for all to see the evidence of his successful hunt.

"Ain't much, but it's better than nothin'," Rube conceded. "Let's get it cleaned and skinned and on a spit. You always was a good shot, Guy. There was a day when I coulda done it, but . . ." He let the rest trail off unfinished.

"I never thought a jackrabbit could look as delicious as a steak. It just shows how hungry I am," Diana remarked with a laugh.

"I know what you mean," he agreed.

The look he darted at Holt was smug and arrogant; he had accomplished something Holt had said couldn't be done. But Holt was stringing a picket line for the horses, ignoring the byplay around the fire, as if he found Guy's game of one-upmanship beneath his notice.

Rube took his knife from its sheath, the blade gleaming in the firelight. Guy handed him the rabbit and walked over to his horse, returning his rifle to the saddle scabbard. The pride of accomplishment had diminished from his expression at Holt's failure to acknowledge it. Gradually the noises from the arroyo had reduced to angry snorts and restless pacings, the initial panic of the captured horses subsiding.

"It's going to be chilly tonight," Guy commented, pausing beside Diana.

"Yes." It wasn't difficult to guess the direction his thought was taking him, and Diana sought to avoid it. "But the fire will keep us warm, and, thanks to you, we'll have food in our stomachs. So it won't be too bad."

His mouth opened to make a response, but Holt's approach stopped him. "I'll take the horses," Holt said, reaching for the reins Diana held.

His presence brought an added chill to the already cool air. Handing him the reins, Diana avoided looking at him directly, aware of the silently bristling Guy beside her. As Holt led the horses to the picket line where the others were tied, Diana turned toward the fire.

"I'd better give Rube a hand with the rabbit," she said.

Guy followed her like a bodyguard, unwilling to let her be more than a few feet from him. The rabbit was skinned and cleaned and Rube was using a sparing amount of water to rinse the blood away. "Puny, ain't it?" Rube slid the carcass onto a stick.

"Beggars can't be choosers," Diana reminded him, taking the spitted rabbit and holding it over the flames, while Rube drove a pair of forked sticks into the ground for the spit to rest on.

The rolling snort of the wild stallion seemed to come from directly behind her. Diana glanced over her shoulder in alarm, staring at the blocked arroyo entrance. There was a rustling of dead brush, and the muffled thud of hooves in sand.

"He's checking out the barricade. Chase him back, Guy," Holt called from the picket line.

Walking toward the arroyo, Guy clapped his hands loudly. "Hiyaa! Get away from there!"

His shouts were followed by a crashing sound. "Look out!" Holt called.

The warning came too late, as a white mound suddenly burst through the barricade. Guy had no chance to get out of the path of the stallion. He attempted to dive to the side and was knocked to the ground by the onrushing horse. Right on its heels came the mares.

At the first glimpse of white, Diana had frozen in shock. As the white stallion swerved toward her, a second obstacle in the way of his escape, his ears were snaked flat against his head, menacing ivory teeth bared, hatred blazing in his dark eyes.

"Diana!"

She heard Holt's shout, but she was powerless to move, mesmerized by the awesome fury charging toward her. The stallion was a bounding leap away when a driving weight hit her side, tumbling her to the ground and knocking the breath from her lungs. Crushed by the same weight that had struck her down, Diana was helplessly pinned.

Her dazed senses were aware of pounding hooves thundering past, but it took a full second longer before she realized the force that held her down was Holt.

Flat on her stomach, tasting what seemed like a mouthful of gritty soil, Diana was conscious of his hard body spread protectively on top of her. By then the horses had stampeded by, but the sensation of danger still thudded in her ears.

"Are you all right?" Holt levered himself off.

Spitting out the grit from her mouth between gulps of air, Diana managed a breathy, "Yes."

Holt didn't wait to see whether her answer was merely brave words or the truth. With a muffled curse, he was pushing to his feet.

"The horses," he said in a muttering explanation.

As she rolled onto her back, Diana thought at first that he was referring to the stallion and mares until she heard the plunging, panicked sounds coming from the picket line. It was their own horses being stampeded into flight by the wild ones. The prospect of being afoot this far from the ranch drove Diana to her feet and sent her running after Holt.

The pack horse was already racing into the night. A second was pulling at its knotted reins until the leather snapped, unable to take the strain. As it whirled to follow the other fleeing horses, Holt stood in its path, waving his arms to turn it back. Diana hurried to the three that were still tied, rearing and plunging in panic, and tried to calm them.

"Whoa, boy, easy now." Diana's firm, soothing voice talked to the dodging horse.

Out of the corner of her eye, Diana saw him grab for the reins as the horse bolted past him, and miss. The remaining horses were beginning to respond to her quieting words, still snorting and tossing their heads, eyes rolling, but no longer tugging at the reins. Holt moved swiftly but smoothly to the nearest horse, untying the reins.

"You aren't going after them in the dark?" Diana protested.

"I might catch them." Holt swung into the saddle. "They'll be halfway back to the ranch by morning."

He didn't immediately set out after their fleeing mounts, but reined the excited and prancing horse to the edge of the camp circle. Diana knew one rider could only hope to catch one horse, but two riders might possibly bring back both. Untying the reins of her gelding, she ducked under the picket line and mounted.

"How's Guy?" Holt called out.

On the other side of the fire, Diana saw Rube bending over Guy, who was sitting up, his head cradled in his hands. She had forgotten all about the stallion knocking him to the side when it broke out of the arroyo.

"He got his bell rung, but he'll be all right," Rube answered, turning to see Holt astride his horse. "Where the hell do you think you're goin'?"

"Two of our horses got loose."

"You ain't goin' after 'em now? You'll break your goddamned neck!"

There was more, but Holt was already turning his horse around and sending it bounding into the night shadows, with Diana right behind him. At the sound of hooves pounding after him, Holt glanced over his shoulder.

Before his grim look could be put into words, Diana shouted determinedly, "I'm coming with you! You need me!" She was secure in the knowledge he couldn't force her back to camp without turning back himself.

Into the night they raced. The sliver of moon cast insufficient light to illuminate the ground. Blindly they galloped, only a sixth sense telling the horses of the footing beneath them. It was a reckless, heart-stopping ride, with Diana clinging to the saddle, never knowing whether the next stride would leap over an obstacle or descend a hollow.

A black silhouette of a racing horse crested a rise ahead of them, head held to the side to keep from tangling its feet in the trailing reins. Their first objective had been sighted. Holt whipped his horse with the reins and Diana did the same. The escaping mount's headlong flight had been reduced to a steady gallop. Within minutes, they overtook it.

From her tomboy years, Diana knew the routine by heart. They approached on either side of the horse, forcing it to run straight rather than swerve away from its captors. Holt was on the side nearest the trailing reins. She saw him lean in the saddle to grab for them.

A split-second later, her horse was falling and Diana was somersaulting over its head into the emptiness of night. A stifled cry of surprise was caught in her throat. She flew through the air for what seemed an eternity before hitting the ground, but it all happened in the blink of an eye.

The jolting impact knocked the wind from her. Diana lay on the ground, the pain in her chest too intense for her to move. She had fallen free of her horse, which was thrashing a few feet away from her. It was rising to its feet shaking like a dog as she took the first painful gasp for air.

The pounding hooves of more than one horse vibrated the ground beneath her. "Diana!" Holt called out to her.

"Over here." It was a weak, breathy answer.

Yet somehow he managed to hear it. Within seconds he was kneeling beside her, a dark shadow looming over her. "Are you all right?"

Diana had already tested the mobility of her limbs and could answer truthfully, "Nothing is broken. I just had the wind knocked out of me, that's all. You caught the horse," she observed shakily.

"Yes," Holt said in a terse response that indicated it was unimportant. "What happened?"

"My horse fell," she said, stating the obvious. She reached out with her hands. "Help me up."

As he pulled her into a sitting position, Diana gasped at the stinging pain in her left elbow. She reached to explore the cause and her fingers came away wet and sticky.

"What's wrong?"

"I hurt my elbow when I fell."

"Let me see." When he reached to turn her elbow toward the faint moonlight, his forearm brushed against the pointed tips of her breasts. Her flesh tingled at the contact. His arm hovered there a fraction of a second longer than necessary, enough to make Diana aware that he was conscious of the intimacy.

"You must have scraped it when you fell. We'll have to clean it when we get back to camp," Holt announced and moved a few inches away from her.

It was dangerous to play with fire. Yet like a moth, Diana was attracted to the flame, knowing her wings would be singed, but not caring. But the flame had turned cold. She suppressed the impulse to arouse its heat.

Tucking her legs beneath her, Diana started to rise. A wave of weakness buckled her knees and she had to clutch at Holt for support.

"I'm shakier than I realized." She tried to laugh away her momentary collapse, make it light so she could ignore the firm strength of the arms that held her. "I'll be all right as soon as I catch my breath." She leaned against him, letting him take her weight.

"We'll go back to camp."

"We still haven't caught the other horse," Diana protested.

"We don't stand much of a chance of finding it in the dark, not now. Besides, one fall is enough. The next time you might break your neck," Holt told her roughly.

Her head was tipped back to better see his face. The brim of his hat shaded his eyes, but she could see the tautness of his lean jaw. A yearning shivered through her.

"Would you care, Holt?" she asked in an aching whisper.

Her question brought a long moment of utter stillness as he gazed down at her. Then his fingers were brushing granules of sand from her cheek and curling into her hair. His head moved downward.

An inch from her lips, he growled, "What do you think?"

There was reluctance in his kiss, as if he resented the fact that he found her physically desirable. It mattered little, as his kiss provided fuel for the smoldering embers of their passion. White-hot flames melted them together. There was a searing, sweeping urgency to their embrace, an insatiable lust that transcended physical bounds.

It was a wild coming-together. Afterwards, Diana lay in his arms, awash from the primitive delights that had swept her high on a tidal wave of pure passion. Holt's breathing was slowly returning to normal, but she could hear the uneven thud of his heart beneath her head. It excited her to know she had driven him as insanely mad with desire as she had been.

And it had been against his will, too. Diana wasn't a fool. She knew that, because of Guy, Holt wished her to the ends of the earth, but the potent attraction between them had been more than either of them could deny.

Almost of its own volition, her hand glided slowly and smoothly across the flat muscles of his stomach to the hardened wall of his hair-roughened chest, a caress there hadn't been time for before. She moved her head slightly in the cradle of his arm to watch the play of her fingers across his tanned flesh. Absently, Diana's lips touched his collarbone. She inhaled the warm, male scent of him. It was like a drug, and she was becoming addicted to it.

At the light touch of her lips to his skin, the hand at her waist tightened its grip, relaxing after a second to lightly caress her hipbone. His free arm crossed over to gently massage her shoulder, not interfering with her hand as it explored his chest.

It was all the invitation Diana needed. Turning more fully into his arms, her mouth began to languourously taste the salty flavor of his skin. His hands fastened on her waist and shoulder to pull her up and above him, the sensitive tips of her breasts brushing the cloud of dark hairs on his chest.

Gray eyes, dark like burnt silver, scanned her features. Their look held experience, most of it hard. Diana wanted to beg him not to speak and destroy the wonder of their lovemaking as his callous words had done the last time. His jaw was clenched in a forbidding line.

When he spoke, the words came out in a grudging mutter. "I want you again, Diana."

"Holt." She said his name in an aching sigh that echoed his wants.

Drawing her up more, his mouth sought the valley between her breasts, lazily and sensuously investigating its every shadow before slowly following the swelling curve of a breast to its darkly pink bud. Her fingers curled into his shoulders as Holt let his tongue leisurely explore it. With equally unhurried interest, he repeated the same attention to her other breast.

Easing her down, he made his way to the hollow of her throat and found the pleasure point along her neck that sent shivers of delight down her spine. He nibbled her ear lobe and with tasting kisses searched out each feature of her face, leaving her lips 'til last. Then he teased them until they trembled with the need to know the fullness of his kiss.

When he kissed her, a steady flame burned them, hotter and stronger than the fiery but brief combustion that marked their previous union. This time everything was in slow motion, as if they wanted to savor each precious second of the gratification of their desires. Words would have only spoiled the silent worshipping of their bodies.

Chapter X

The stars were crystal-bright in the night sky. The silence during their lovemaking had carried into its aftermath. It seemed all wrong now. Diana's troubled eyes watched Holt's dark shape moving around the horses. When he approached leading the horses, she made a project of tucking her blouse into her jeans.

"Your horse is lame," Holt stated flatly. "You'll have to ride Guy's."

His shuttered expression made Diana shiver. "Is it serious?" She walked to her horse, scratching its forehead.

"It doesn't seem to be; looks like a pulled muscle in his left foreleg. There's very little swelling and he's willing to put weight on it, although he does favor it." With the explanation made, Holt handed her the reins of the third horse. "Here. We'll have to take it slow on the way back, so we'd better get started."

There was no reference to the reason why they had lingered in the night. Holt seemed to be pretending that they had never made love. Diana wasn't able to allude to it, either.

Mounting the third horse, Diana reined it behind the gamely limping horse Holt led. As Holt had said, its injury necessitated a slow pace. That allowed Diana too much time to think. Which wasn't good. Her thoughts kept focusing on the lean figure riding in the lead, a man as raw and untamed as the land they rode through.

Diana didn't know how many long minutes had dragged by when a horse whinnied from the darkness to their left. Holt's horse whickered an answer. They both reined in at the sound of trotting hooves approaching.

"It's the pack horse," murmured Diana when its shape became distinguishable.

"It must have gotten lonesome and come back for some company of his own kind," Holt surmised. "Catch his rope."

It shied briefly when Diana reached for the rope dangling from its halter, but didn't attempt to elude her a second time as it nuzzled the neck of her horse. With both missing horses in tow, they started out again for the camp, a distant glow of light in the night's darkness.

The light grew steadily brighter. Several hundred yards away, Diana could make out the two figures by the fire: one wizened and bent, sitting close to the fire; and the second tall and supple, standing and staring out into the night, impatience and tension in his posture. How could she have forgotten Guy?

Her gaze slid to Holt's wide shoulders. He rode easily in the saddle. There was no squaring of the shoulders, no indication at all that he was mentally bracing himself for a meeting with his son. How long had they been gone? Diana wondered. Long enough, she was sure, to make Guy suspicious. She felt trapped by the tangled web of her emotions.

As they neared the camp, the sound of their horses brought Guy striding out to meet them, his expression a glowering mask of challenge. He grabbed at the bridle of Holt's horse to stop his short of the picket line.

"Where have you been?" he demanded.

"Catching our horses." Holt dismounted with an unconcern Diana envied.

"What took you so long?" Guy wasn't satisfied with

the answer as his narrowed gaze studied Holt's bland features.

"Yeah." Rube echoed his curiosity, following Guy at a slower pace. "I practically had to hogtie him to keep him from goin' out lookin' for ya. If ya hadn't come back just now, I probably would have."

"Diana's horse fell," Holt said, as if that was the reason for the delay. At the stricken look of concern that flashed onto Guy's face, Holt's mouth quirked in a taunting line. "She wasn't hurt," he added before Guy could take the first step toward Diana, "only her horse. Do you want to take a look at that left foreleg, Rube, and see what you think?"

Handing the reins of the injured horse to Rube, Holt stepped back to take the pack horse's lead from Diana. Guy was already at her side, reaching up to help her dismount. There was no way she could avoid his assistance.

"Are you all right?" he asked.

"I'm fine." Diana heard the brittle quality in her voice. The very last thing she wanted to talk about was herself and what had happened out there. "But what about you? How are you?"

It was the wrong moment to hand the reins and lead rope to Holt. Diana caught the expression of contempt etched in his features and whitened under it.

"I'm okay, just a headache and a bruised shoulder." Guy flexed his right arm and winced. "You look chilled. Better come over by the fire and warm up."

Agreeing that she was cold, Diana allowed him to lead her to the campfire. Neither Holt nor Rube followed until the horses were unsaddled and bedded down for the night. Until then she had to listen to Guy relate the apprehensions he had felt when he learned she had gone after the horses with Holt. She also had to conceal the truth—that his alarm had been justified. The instant Holt and Rube joined them, he fell silent.

"Come here, Diana," Holt ordered. She stiffened, aware of the accusing look Guy shot her, all his doubts and fears returning in a flash.

"Why?" she questioned warily.

"I want to look at your arm," Holt reminded her dryly and held up the compact first-aid kit.

"Your arm?" Guy repeated. "What's wrong with your arm? I thought you weren't hurt."

"I scraped my elbow." Diana had forgotten all about it, so minor had it been. "It's hardly serious."

"But it should be cleaned and disinfected," Holt insisted.

She couldn't disabuse his common sense. She hesitated as he sat down in front of the fire, then walked the few steps to kneel beside him, offering her left elbow for his inspection. The impersonal touch of his fingers pushed aside the torn material of her blouse sleeve. Diana stared into the fire rather than at the dark head bent near her elbow.

Holt turned away to open the kit. "Slip your arm out of the sleeve."

It was a logical request, Diana knew, since the torn fragments of her blouse would merely hamper his attempt to clean the abrasion. Guy made a muffled sound of protest, but Diana was already unbuttoning her blouse and pulling her left arm free of the sleeve. As a concession to Guy's modesty, she pulled the loose side of her blouse across her front, as if Holt did not know her body more intimately than Guy did.

Holt took no notice of her action. With an efficiency of time and technique, he cleaned and applied disinfectant to the abrasion. Finished, Holt returned the first-aid kit to the saddlebag. Diana was left with the sensation that she had just been treated by a stranger.

"Thanks." Some of his coolness was reflected in her voice.

As Diana was slipping her arm back into the sleeve, Rube remarked, "If you ask me, you was lucky to get by with just a scrape. You could get yourself bad hurt chasin' horses out there in the dark. I didn't give you a goddamned chance in hell of findin' 'em after that stallion scattered 'em. You coulda knocked me over with a feather when I seed you leadin' both of 'em in."

"We were lucky, I guess," Holt conceded.

"Lucky?" Rube snorted. "We all was lucky. Lucky that all our horses didn't take off for parts unknown. I thought we was gonna have a goddamned stampede on our hands when that stallion came chargin' through here."

"There was absolutely no warning," Guy recalled. "The stallion caught us all unprepared. I can't get over his cunning. He just came up to the barricade and knocked it down without any hesitation. Then he attacked us. When he came charging at me, I thought he was going to kill me. He even tried to scatter our horses so we couldn't chase him."

"Don't be attributing intelligence to something that was purely instinct," Holt said. "The stallion knew he had entered the arroyo, and the entrance was the only way out. He charged you because, like the barricade, you were in his way. Our horses merely panicked in the confusion. There was no attack."

"There is somethin' in what you say," Rube admitted. "But it ain't necessarily true that a wild stallion won't attack, 'cause he will. You talk about hell on four feet. You saw what he did to the Major's stud."

"As powerful as that white stallion is, why hasn't he challenged one of the mustang stallions for his herd? Why raid our ranch? It doesn't make sense when there are wild mares in these hills," Guy said.

"Well, now, there just might be an answer to that." Rube crouched near the fire, rocking back on his heels. "When I was mustanging as a boy, some of the old-timers told me that some of the finest, well-built wild stallions they ever saw ran without mares. They reckoned as how these rogue stallions figured they was too good for ordinary mares. Could be that's how this white stallion figured it, too, until he got him an eyeful of the Major's blooded mares. An' there ain't no wild stallion that won't do a bit of stealin' of domestic stock if'n he gets the chance."

"That's quite a theory," Holt said with mocking skepticism.

"I never said it was a fact," Rube defended. "But that's what they told me. Could be just a tall tale, for all I know. I just passed it on for whatever it was worth. I never claimed it was gospel."

"True or false, the fact remains we're going after the mares at daybreak. There's been enough talk and excitement for one night." Holt said. "It's time we tried to get some sleep."

No one argued with his suggestion, least of all Diana. The saddles were positioned around the fire as headrests. Diana lay down as close to the radiating warmth as possible, draping the stiff and coarse saddle blanket over her shoulders. She exchanged good nights with Guy and Rube, but offered none to Holt when he remained silent.

Closing her eyes, Diana tried to sleep, but she couldn't keep out the thoughts that were crowding in. Soon Rube was snoring, and the slow, steady breathing of Guy indicated that he, too, was asleep. For a long time, she lay there, the ground hard beneath her, the night chill creeping over her skin. Her eyes were tightly closed, but sleep wouldn't come.

There was a movement, the sound of someone quietly rising. Her lashes lifted a fraction. Through their narrow slits, Diana's eyes saw Holt add a few more limbs to the fire, then stand motionless before the flames. The flickering light threw his craggy features into sharp relief, a look of deep concentration toughening the lines.

Very quietly, Diana sat up. She hardly made a sound, yet his head jerked toward her. Undeterred, she joined him.

"Can't you sleep, either?" she asked softly so as not to disturb the others.

"I was adding more fuel to the fire." This didn't answer her question.

Drawing the sweat-stiffened saddle blanket more tightly around her shoulders, Diana tried to ignore the decided chill in the atmosphere. "I haven't thanked you for saving my life," she said. And, at his blank look, she explained: "I mean when you pushed me out of the way of the stallion. I forgot to thank you for that."

"Did you?" The insulting sweep of his gaze over her body seemed to say her thanks had been given by deed, not word. She was unable to control the shudder of hurt that went through her. "Cold?" Holt inquired with decided indifference.

"Of course." It was an abrupt response, underlined by rigid pride that asked not a thing from him, not even sympathy or concern.

"You could always go lie down beside Guy. I'm sure he'd be delighted at the chance to keep you warm."

Tears stung her eyes, anger and hurt mixing together. "How can you suggest that after I let you make love to me, I go sleep with your son? What kind of a woman do you think I am?" she questioned in taut demand.

"You've turned my son against me. Do you really want me to answer that question, Diana?"

"Then why . . . out there, we . . . you . . ."

Holt knew the confusion she was trying to put into words, and he turned to face her. "Do you think I don't wish now that when your horse fell, I would have put my hand around that pretty neck of yours"—as he spoke, his hand carried out the action he described, the cool touch of it on her neck paralyzing Diana—"and put my thumb under your chin. One little snap and I could have broken it and blamed it on the fall. With you dead, I might have a chance of getting my son back."

Instead, he had made love to her, and Diana could see how bitterly he regretted it. Looking into those hard, gray eyes, she felt fear. He was so completely controlled and in command of his emotions.

"Why don't you do it now?" She had to challenge him.

The pressure of his thumb on her chin increased

slightly, but Diana didn't flinch or let her gaze waver from his. Something flickered in his eyes. Cynical amusement? Reluctant admiration? It was too fleeting to recognize. The pressure eased a second before his hand came away from her throat.

"You'd thumb your nose at the devil himself if he told you that you couldn't have what you wanted." Holt sighed tiredly, "Go to sleep, Diana."

He turned away and walked back to his own makeshift bed, leaving her with little choice but to do the same. Curled in a tight ball, Diana stared into the flames. Holt made her sound very self-possessed. Funny, she didn't feel that way.

An hour after sunrise, Rube was smothering the campfire coals with sand. The horses were all saddled. Since Diana's horse still showed signs of favoring his left foreleg, the only horse that remained for her to ride was the pack horse. It was not a horse she would have chosen, but the only other alternatives were to walk or ride double with one of the others. Diana opted for the relative discomfort of the pack horse.

"What are we going to do?" Guy asked after climbing into the saddle. "Are we going back to the waterhole?"

"No. We have the stallion spooked, so we might as well keep him running," Holt stated. "We'll trail him from here."

"Aren't we going back to our camp?" Guy protested.

"We aren't. Rube is," Holt corrected and turned to the older man. "You take Diana's horse and pack what you think it can carry, without putting too much strain on him. We'll meet you—"

"For God's sake, Holt!" Guy interrupted angrily. "We haven't eaten since yesterday noon. We can't go chasing after those horses with no food in our stomachs. We have to go back to camp and eat."

Hesitating before making a response, Holt's gaze swept over the three of them. Diana agreed with Guy. She was already beginning to feel slightly light-headed from hunger, but she didn't say so.

"All right," he agreed. "You three go back to camp, eat, and divide everything the horse can't carry among you. Here's the binoculars." Holt gave the case to Rube. "I'm going to trail the stallion. Find a high vantage point and look for me. More than likely, his range is going to pivot around that waterhole, so I'll be somewhere in your vicinity."

With that, the party split up, three of them riding toward the canyon several miles away, and Holt searching the ground for the distinctive tracks of the wild stallion and his mares. The lame horse kept the pace slow for the trio of riders.

"Why don't you two ride ahead?" Rube suggested after they had gone about a mile. "You can have breakfast cooked by the time I get there."

"Good idea, Rube," Guy agreed with alacrity and dug his heels into his horse's flanks to send it cantering forward.

Diana's pack horse lumbered after him, his rough gait not helping the queasy emptiness of her stomach. They cantered half the distance and trotted the rest of the way, an equally jarring experience for Diana. But it kept conversation to the minimum. Slowing as they entered the arroyo where they had camped, they both saw the destruction at the same time and reined in their horses.

"My God! What happened?" Guy stared around him in stunned disbelief.

"Maybe it was coyotes," Diana suggested as he dismounted.

"I don't think so." He shook his head. "Look at this."

Diana swung down from her saddle to look at the tracks he indicated. They were made by horses, un-shod, which meant wild. She stared.

"That wild stallion did this," Guy declared.

"Why?" she asked. Then she insisted, "It's impossible."

"Is it?" he countered.

Diana shook her head in confusion. "Let's see what we can salvage."

The destruction was not as serious as it had first looked. The bedrolls had been kicked and scattered about. They needed to be shaken free of sand and neatly rolled up. The supplies, too, looked as if a whirlwind had struck them. Outside of a few dents, the cooking utensils were undamaged.

However, their food supply had not been so fortunate. Diana was on her knees trying to save what she could of the flour dumped out of its sack when Rube and Holt rode in. She wasn't surprised to see Holt, since he had been tracking the stallion.

"The stallion was here," Guy announced. "He practically destroyed every bit of our food supply." His attitude very plainly challenged Holt to explain that away if he could.

"How bad is it?" Holt directed the question to Diana.

"We were getting low on everything, anyway, so there isn't much left now. Enough for two meals, maybe," she answered.

Holt shifted in his saddle, looking around him as if he expected to see the white stallion looking down at them and laughing.

"Are you gonna fix breakfast?" Rube wanted to know. "I had my mouth all set for some flapjacks. I s'pose that goddamned stallion went and ruined that. Do you reckon he did it a' purpose?"

"Man smell," Holt said. "He brought the mares straight over here from the arroyo for water. Probably caught the scent of our things and connected it with the same smell that had trapped him."

"Last night he tried to drive away our horses," Guy argued. "Now he's practically destroyed our food supplies. Are you trying to tell me the stallion didn't know what he was doing?"

"Our horses panicked last night," Holt reminded him. "They would have if it had been a herd of cattle stampeding out of that arroyo. The stallion didn't single out our food. It just happened to be the most susceptible. It wasn't cunning, Guy. It was instinct."

" 'Pears to me that Holt is right," Rube agreed, and Guy pivoted away in disgust. "I've seen a wild horse trample to pieces the hide of a mountain lion. It didn't matter to the horse that it was only the hide and not a flesh-and-blood cat. Looks like that white stallion did the same goddamned thing here." Rube dismounted, shaking his head, and glanced at Holt with faint indignation. "Would you look at that? Here Guy was so all-fired hungry, and he ain't even got a fire started. Seems to me like I'm the only one around here that knows how to start a fire. It never seems to get done less'n I do it."

"Why don't you start the fire and just shut up, Rube?" Guy muttered.

"Don't you go growlin' at me, you little pup," Rube bristled. "It's one thing for your pa, here, to be a-tellin' me to shut up. He's—"

"Yeah, I know," Guy broke in bitterly. "He's the head honcho around here."

"That will be enough, Guy." Holt's voice sliced firmly through the air.

Diana glanced apprehensively from one to the other. It was the first time the shredded relationship between father and son had surfaced when someone other than herself was present. She held her breath, waiting to see if this exposure would lead to a full-scale explosion.

Guy turned away, mumbling, "I'll help you with the fire, Rube."

"You just hold on there a minute," Rube said. "There ain't no need in startin' a fire 'til Diana tells us whether we're gonna have some food. I ain't gonna do it just for practice."

"I think I have enough for a stack of flapjacks apiece," she responded to the indirect question.

Holt swung down from his saddle. "Guy, let Rube start the fire while you and I pack up this gear."

"See? What'd I tell you? I'm the only one around here that can build a goddamned fire," Rube grumbled to no one in particular as he walked toward the blackened circle of ashes from their previous fires.

As hungry as Diana was, the food tasted like chalk in her mouth, but she forced it down, anyway, knowing she would need it before the day was over. She glanced around the circle at the others quietly eating. With all their gear left at this camp last night, neither Holt nor Guy had shaved this morning. Since they had returned, neither had taken the time. The shadows of a dark beard growth accented the bluntly chiseled features of Holt's face, making him look tough and forbidding. Guy's fair coloring made his short stubble less noticeable. As for Rube, he hadn't shaved since they left the ranch. He scratched the salted dark growth almost constantly.

They were a disreputable-looking group, haggard and covered with trail dust. It made Diana conscious of what her own appearance must be—hair unbrushed, no makeup, as dusty as the others. The sleeve of her blouse was torn at the elbow. The only other blouse she had was the one Holt had ripped. With a sigh, Diana knew there was little that could be done about it even if she felt like it, not when Holt was so anxious to get on the trail.

The last of their gear was packed away when the meal was finished. Although the Arabian gelding Diana had been riding did not seem as lame, the packload he carried was decidedly light, the rest of the gear divided equally among them. And Diana was still astride the packhorse.

Rube had already left the arroyo camp to pick up the stallion's trail when Holt handed her the lead rope to the gelding. "When we catch up with the stallion, keep up with us as best you can," he ordered. "Don't get lost because I don't want to come looking for you."

"I don't want you to come looking for me," she retorted, aware of the double meaning in her reply.

"Why does Diana have to lead the gelding?" Guy argued, seemingly ready to pick a fight over anything. "Let Rube have him."

Holt's mouth thinned. "In the first place, Diana's horse is slower than ours, so a lame horse isn't going to slow her down that much. Secondly, it could turn out to be a wild ride after those horses. And I don't want to see her break her neck."

"I wouldn't think that would upset you," Diana taunted. "In fact, I would have thought you'd be glad to be rid of me."

It was a cool gray look he leveled at her. "I don't like the idea of carrying your body home to the Major."

"I see." She sat rigidly in the saddle. "It isn't me getting killed that would bother you. It's facing the Major."

"You got it," he snapped and stepped into his saddle.

"Dammit, Holt!" Guy swore, but Holt had already started his horse in Rube's direction.

"Leave it alone, Guy." Now that Holt had moved away, all her stiff-necked pride left in a wave of tiredness.

"But—"

"I don't mind bringing up the rear. After the fall I took last night, the last thing I want to do is go on another hellbent-for-leather chase across these mountains." It had nothing to do with it, but it was an excellent excuse.

One that Guy accepted. "I wasn't thinking," he apologized.

"It's all right." Tugging on the lead rope, Diana clicked to the gelding to follow as they started after Holt and Rube.

The pace was slow and Diana had no difficulty keeping up as they trailed the band of horses. Shortly before ten o'clock, they spotted the small herd grazing

on a slope dotted with junipers. The same as the first
time, the stallion was to one side standing guard, alert
yet relaxed.

"There he is," Guy whispered, an excited, throbbing sound that matched the rapt look on his face.

"If that stallion stays true to his pattern," Rube
began quietly, leaning in his saddle toward Holt,
"when you jump him, he's gonna run to the left an'
circle back to the canyon. We can run the herd in
relays. Sooner or later, the stallion will abandon the
mares an' take off by hisself, hopin' to lead us away.
That's when we can get back our mares."

"All right." Holt nodded agreement with the proposal. "I'll start them running here. You and Guy
station yourselves three or four miles apart along the
route you think the stallion will take. You stay here,
Diana. If Rube is right, the stallion will be coming back
this way." Then his gaze was on the other two.
"Whoever is running the herd when the stallion breaks
away is to stick with the stallion. Keep him running
while the others catch the mares."

The packhorse Diana was riding wanted to follow
the other horses as they moved out with their riders,
but she held it back. Rube and Guy split off to the left
while Holt started for the herd.

From her vantage point, she watched Holt work his
way slowly along a dry gully, letting the soft sand
muffle the sound of his horse's hooves. There was
almost no breeze. As he neared the slope, she saw the
stallion come to full alertness, small ears pricked in
Holt's direction.

When Holt came into the stallion's view, the white
horse did not snort in alarm and send the mares flying.
Instead, he whistled a shrill challenge, his long ivory-
colored tail standing straight out. In a prancing pace,
the stallion came boldly toward his adversary.

"My God," Diana murmured, her pulse leaping in
fear. "He's going to attack him."

Holt had to be aware of the stallion's unusual
reaction, but he kept riding his horse forward, not

slackening its cantering stride. A hundred feet separated them when the stallion whirled, retreat becoming wiser than valor. Screaming and snapping at the mares, they leaped away as one, bunching together. Again the buckskin mare took the lead while the pacing stallion drove them from the rear.

The horses raced away from Holt as if he was standing still. His horse galloped, but Holt did not urge it into a flat-out run, but kept the wild band in view. They disappeared over the slope. Standing in the stirrups, Diana strained for a glimpse of them, waiting for them to come into view on the left where Rube had said the stallion would direct them. Within minutes, she saw them, the mares racing, the white stallion pacing effortlessly behind them.

Soon they were lost to her sight, only dust clouds marking their course. Diana waited, feeling her heart pounding with excitement and wishing she was part of the chase. An interminable amount of time passed, so much that Diana was beginning to wonder what had gone wrong.

Then, off to her right, she saw them, cresting a knoll and coming toward her. The buckskin mare was still in the lead, but running heavily now. Obviously tiring, the other two mares were being brutally driven onward by the stallion, baring his teeth and nipping savagely at the slightest sign of lagging. Rube came galloping steadily behind them, closer now than Holt had been.

The mares thundered past within fifty feet, lathered and blowing. The stallion's pacing stride still seemed effortless as he relentlessly pushed his harem. His coat was wet and caked with dust, no longer a gleaming white. Large nostrils were distended to drink in the air in enormous gulps. He would not be run into the ground for a long time.

Approaching the slope where they had first been routed, they had to cross the gully Holt had used. It didn't look more than four feet wide. The buckskin mare slowed, gathered herself, and leaped mightily

across it. The two blooded mares followed. The bank
crumbled under one, sending it tumbling to the bottom. It was the young prize mare, Cassie. She struggled to get to her feet. The stallion hesitated on the
other side, then glanced at the pursuing rider. With an
angry shake of his head, he left the downed mare and
streaked after the remaining two members of his herd.

"I'll get the mare!" Diana shouted to Rube. "You
go on!"

A wave of his hand indicated he had heard her. He
didn't attempt to jump his horse across the gully, but
swerved into the dry wash, his horse plunging up the
opposite bank.

When Diana reached the gully with the injured
gelding in tow, the mare had just staggered to her feet,
shaken but apparently unharmed. After a tired and
half-hearted attempt to elude Diana, the mare stood
quietly while Diana looped a rope around her neck.

She was leading both horses back to her vantage
point when she heard a shout. Glancing over her
shoulder, she saw Holt and Guy cantering toward her.
Holt motioned toward the fleeing band, calling something that she couldn't understand. Diana turned in the
saddle, standing in the stirrups.

As Rube had predicted, the white stallion had left
the mares. Breaking his pattern, he had swerved off to
the right with Rube giving chase. The wild buckskin
mare was continuing the route, but the older Arabian
mare, Nashira, was already slowing down.

Immediately Diana understood Holt's signal and
followed at a trot as he and Guy struck out for the
mare. They caught her as easily as Diana had roped the
other mare. When Diana reined in beside them, Holt
had dismounted and was looping the rope around the
mare's nose, making a crude halter. He did the same
with the rope around the other mare's neck.

"Let's catch up to Rube," he said.

The white stallion was headed into rough country,
still pursued. Rube was blind to those that followed

him as he continued after the horse. Diana's arm ached from tugging on the rope and pulling the horses on, but she wouldn't quit.

Climbing a steep hill, she topped out on a plateau. Guy and Holt were not far ahead of her. Beyond them, she could see Rube and the white shape of the stallion. Rube finally looked behind him and stopped, waiting for them to catch up to him. When Holt and Guy reached him, there was an earnest conference. Diana frowned, not understanding why, until she joined them.

"The stallion's trapped," Guy told her. "There isn't any way off this plateau except the way we came."

She could see him pacing restlessly back and forth beyond them and turned to Holt. "What are you going to do?"

"Let him go," he said. "We've driven him off his range. Maybe he won't come back."

"We could catch him," Rube insisted. "He's tired, I'm tellin' you. Guy and me can rope him and you catch his heels. It'll be easy as pie. We'll never get another chance like this one."

"What would you want with a wild stallion, Rube?" Holt asked grimly. "He isn't any good to us. You'd have to kill him before you could break him. We have what we came for. Now let's get the mares back to the ranch."

"I'm tellin' ya—"

"Look!" Guy pointed toward the stallion. "That's suicide!"

The stallion disappeared over the edge of the plateau amidst a rattle of loose rock. They all rushed to the point where he had disappeared, reining their horses in short of the rim. Halfway down the almost perpendicular slope of shale-like rock was the white stallion, sitting on his tail and sliding. An avalanche of small rock wiped away what little balance the horse had. He fell, rolling the rest of the way to the bottom.

"If he comes outta that without a broken leg," Rube muttered, "I'll be goddamned if—"

The stallion lay at the bottom, motionless. "He's dead," Guy choked, and Diana swallowed at the tightness in her own throat.

Then his head moved, lifting up. A second later, his thrashing legs were kicking him up on his feet. With a vigorous shake that sent dust flying, the stallion stood. He took a few steps and swung into his rolling gait. His stride was slow and vaguely leaden, but the stallion was unharmed.

Diana let out the stunned breath she had been holding.

"Did you see that?!!" Guy exclaimed. "My God! How did he do it?!!"

"I didn't see a scratch on that white hide of his'n!" Rube declared.

"I thought he'd break his neck for sure," Guy added.

"It's a pity he didn't," Holt said dryly, not at all impressed by the miracle he had just witnessed with them.

"You can't mean that," protested Diana.

"I do. I have a feeling that stallion will be back." The way Holt was looking at the pacing white stallion reminded Diana of a hunter watching his prey escape him. There was a certain unconcern, a knowledge that he and the mustang would meet again. But that impression was ridiculous. Diana mentally shook it away. Holt had no interest in the stallion. He'd come only for the mares.

"Why did he do it?" Guy was still dazed by what he had seen.

"The stallion was trapped and he knew it," Rube answered.

"But to go over the edge like that?" Guy shook his head.

"Mustangs have been known to do goddamned near anything to keep from bein' caught. They'll jump off cliffs or dive into swollen rivers. Some of 'em just flat prefer death to a cowboy's rope."

Holt turned his horse away from the rim and started

back the way they had come. The others followed with
Rube still rambling on with his narrative.

"When I was mustangin', I heard stories about wild
horses that refused to eat or drink after they was
caught. All the hay and water was right there before
'em and they died. A fella told me once about a time
he'd roped this wild stallion. He and a couple other
fellas were takin' the mustang back to their place.
They had to cross a little stream. The fella claimed
there wasn't more'n six inches of water in it. Well, he
said that wild stallion buried his nose in that water and
they couldn't get his head up. He drowned, drowned in
six inches of water. An' another fella told me about a
wild horse that got caught in a bog. H——"

Diana wasn't listening to his tales. She was remembering that instant when the white stallion had gotten
up after Guy had declared he was dead. Holt had said
the stallion would come back. Would he?

Chapter XI

The western sky was streaked with fuschia when the ranch buildings came into sight. The horses picked up their pace, hurrying toward the promise of oats and water and rest. Tired and hungry, too, Diana doubted if she had the strength to stay in the saddle another hour.

A welcoming committee of ranch hands greeted their return, questions flying. All of which Diana ignored, leaving it to the others to answer them. She smiled a weary thanks at the man who took her horse.

"The Major says he knows you'll want to clean up first, but afterward you are all to go to the main house, Holt," Floyd Hunt said. "And he said not to worry about eating. He'll have all the food you want on the table."

"Thanks." Holt nodded. His eyes looked years older than his body when he glanced at Diana. "Tell the Major we'll be up in less than a half-hour."

"Yes."

On saddle-weary legs, she walked to the main house. The Major was in the living room. He looked up and smiled when the screen door slammed shut behind her.

"How was the horse hunt?" He added ice cubes to a glass.

Diana took a deep breath, then answered simply, "Successful."

"How about a drink?" he offered.

"A shot of whiskey on the rocks," she ordered without hesitation.

Taking a crystal decanter from a tray, he splashed a measure of the amber liquor over the cubes in the glass. "You look awful," he said, walking over to hand her the glass.

"Thanks." A wry smile curved her mouth.

"When the boys told me you were coming, I had Sophie fill your bathtub with hot bubbly water. It's waiting for you."

"No wonder people accuse me of being spoiled." Diana laughed briefly and kissed his cheek.

She sipped at the glass and started for her room, unbuttoning her grimy blouse as she went.

"Who says you are spoiled?" The Major followed.

Holding the glass in one hand, she struggled out of her blouse, tossing it on the floor of her room. Without stopping, she continued on to the private bath, steaming and scented from the water-filled tub.

"Holt, for one," she answered. Setting the glass on the marble sink top, she began shedding the rest of her clothes.

"Do you want your robe?" her father called from the bedroom.

"Yes." Diana stepped into the mound of bubbles atop the water.

"So Holt thinks I have spoiled you," the Major commented as he carried her robe in and hung it on a door hook. "Were the two of you at loggerheads all the while you were gone?"

Up to her neck in bubbles, Diana closed her eyes, trying to shut out all the memories of what had been between her and Holt. "Do you mind? I'd rather not talk about him."

"You were gone longer than I expected." He changed the subject.

"Yes," Diana sighed as the hot water soothed her aching muscles.

"Are the mares all right?"

"Cassie has a couple of nasty-looking bites on her rump. They are both a little thin, but otherwise, they're in good shape," she told him.

"I thought I noticed a horse limping."

"That was mine. Holt thinks he pulled a muscle. Nothing serious, though."

"How?" he asked. "And how did you hurt your elbow?"

"I had a fall. My horse lost its footing and went down. I did a glorious somersault over his head." Diana smiled at the frown of concern that appeared on her father's face. "It isn't the first time I've taken a tumble, Major."

"No, I guess it isn't," he agreed.

"How was everything at the ranch while we were gone?"

"Fine. No problems at all."

"And the stallion, Fath?"

"He's recovering and doing very well so far. It's too soon to tell how much use he'll regain of his foreleg. He could be crippled, but we won't know for some time. That's enough talking." He smiled. "You relax in that tub for a while. When you're through, come to the dining room. Sophie is fixing a mountain of sandwiches."

As he turned to leave, Diana remembered, "I forgot to tell you. Holt said he'd be up in half an hour."

There was an acknowledging nod at the message. Then he left. Diana relaxed in the scented water, closing her mind to all thought and taking in only the sensual pleasure of the bath.

Afterward, Diana wrapped a towel around her freshly washed hair, securing it turban-fashion atop her head. Pausing in front of the mirror, she brushed mascara on the luxurious thickness of her dark and curling lashes and applied coral-tinted gloss to her lips.

She tied the sash of her robe and walked barefoot to the dining room.

The Major greeted her with a smiling and assessing look. "Much better."

"I feel better, too." But her reply was lost to the echoing thud of footsteps on the porch.

An instant later Holt walked in, followed by Guy and Rube. The gray eyes touched on her first before directing their attention to her father, and Diana felt the immediate tensing of her nerves. They had all taken the time to shower and change, and to shave the beard growth from their faces.

Holt looked fresh and vital, showing no evidence of having spent the better part of the last four days in the saddle. But Diana noticed the bruise on his jaw had turned a bluish color. The Major would have been blind not to see it.

He gestured to it and laughed. "What does the other fella look like, Holt?" At that instant, Guy turned and the Major saw his split lip and bruised cheek. His gaze returned to Holt, sharp and silently questioning.

"We sure did have us a trouble-prone time, Major," Rube inserted. "Guy, here, falls down. Holt runs into somethin'. Diana gets her blouse torn on a bush. That white stallion tries to run our horses off, then wrecks our camp an' destroys our food. I ain't et since noon."

"Is this all true?" The Major frowned when Rube recounted the mustang's deeds.

"Embellished slightly," Holt said.

"What—" Then he stopped. "The explanations can wait. Sophie has the food on the table. Come eat."

When Diana reached the table, Guy was there, holding out her chair. His look glowed with ardency and her own gaze fell under it. As he pushed her chair to the table, he bent low.

"You look beautiful," Guy murmured near her ear, "like a queen."

"Thank you." Diana carefully avoided glancing in Holt's direction as Guy took the seat beside her.

At first no one spoke, too intent on filling their

empty stomachs. The Major waited patiently until he could no longer contain his curiosity.

"Tell me about the stallion."

"He's about fifteen hands, solid white, good conformation, and is running with a wild buckskin mare. He paces," Holt added, almost as an afterthought.

"He what?" Diana understood the incredulous look on her father's face. They had all experienced the same stunned surprise when they had seen it with their own eyes.

"The stallion's a goddamned sidewheeler," Rube inserted in affirmation. "We chased him for more'n four hours today, an' he never once broke stride. You shoulda seen him, Major, rollin' from side to side like a goddamned rockin' chair. It was somethin' to behold."

"You are serious about this, aren't you?" the Major said.

"Perfectly serious." Holt helped himself to more potato salad.

"It's the Pacing White Stallion come to life again—that's what it is," Rube declared. "You've heard stories about him, haven't you, Major?"

"The Pacing White Stallion? Yes, yes, of course I have." He sat back in his chair, seeming to consider the information.

"Did he really exist?" Guy asked skeptically.

"Yes, he existed," the Major answered, then qualified it. "But I have always been of the opinion that there was more than one white stallion that was known to pace. The chronicles of the West are filled with stories about the Pacing White Stallion. He was referred to by various titles: the Pacing White Mustang, the White Steed of the Plains, and so on. You must understand that white horses were never a rarity in the Old West."

"But a horse that paced?" Guy shook his head, hanging on to his disbelief.

"The majority of the horses in North America came from Spanish stock. The Spaniards had a strain of natural pacers, said to pace as fast as other horses could gallop. The extinct Narragansett pacers of the East Coast are believed to have been descendants of a Spanish stallion. As a matter of fact, this pacing breed from Spain was better preserved in South America than here. I read somewhere that these South American horses were usually light-colored—gray, palomino, or white—with black skins," the Major offered in substantiation and paused. "So it's your theory, Holt, that this white stallion is a throwback to that Spanish blood."

"It isn't mine, it's Rube's," Holt said. "But after what you've said, it seems reasonable."

"A fascinating theory. I wish I had seen him," the Major declared.

"Doubt if you'll get a chance now. We chased him clear into Utah." Rube's words were muffled by a mouthful of sandwich.

"We came close to the line. I don't know if we crossed it." Holt wouldn't let Rube exaggerate the length of the chase.

"But you think the stallion will come back," Diana reminded Holt of his comment out on the mesa.

Holt seemed reluctant to answer, but finally admitted a cool, "Yes, I think he will." He glanced at the Major. "It might be best if we keep all the mares close to the ranch yard for the next week or so."

"Do whatever you feel is necessary," he said.

"With Shêtan dead and Fath injured, we'll be needing a new stud." Holt shifted the subject. "I'll start making phone calls tomorrow to see what I can find. Depending on what's available, I'll either lease a stallion or buy."

Diana stared, aware that Holt had neither asked nor consulted the Major about his plan. He had simply informed her father of what he was going to do. The discussion became centered on the merits of various bloodlines. Diana didn't take part, Holt's announcement nagging at her.

Covertly, she studied her father. Age and illness had taken their toll. The Major was no longer the strong, indomitable man of her youth. His dark hair was steadily graying, his tan fading into a pallor, jowls sagging his once firm jawline. Tiny tremors shook his hands.

Somehow, she had thought he would recover. Now Diana realized he would never again be the man he once was. There were glimpses of his former self, but they were shadows without substance. The Major had turned over his command to an outsider and had become merely a figurehead. He seemed suddenly a pathetic man, and her heart cried out at the change. He was old and weak and sick. She was overwhelmed by an urge to hide him from the eyes of others.

Diana interrupted the conversation. "It's getting late, Major." And she immediately felt like a mother reminding a child of his bedtime.

"What?" He looked at her blankly for an instant. "Oh, yes, so it is."

The meal was finished. There was no more reason for the others to linger. Holt took the hint and pushed his chair away from the table, rising to his feet.

"Excuse us, Major. I think we'll call it a night, unless there is something else you want to go over with me."

Diana bristled at the patronizing words, pretending the Major was still in charge when Holt knew he wasn't. Who did he think he was fooling?

"No, I don't think so," her father responded, his tiredness showing. "Floyd can fill you in."

As Diana rose to hurry the others on their way, Guy was on his feet beside her, his low voice eager and questioning: "Diana—"

She didn't know what he was going to ask, but she cut him short. "I'm tired, Guy." She moved to her father's chair, her fingers curling around the wooden posts of the chair back, her attitude protective and possessive. "Good night." She directed it to all three of the men and received the same response as they left, Rube hastily wrapping two sandwiches in a napkin to take with him.

When they were alone, Diana said, "I don't know about you, but I'm going to dry my hair and go to bed," as a means of prompting the Major into getting the rest he so badly needed.

"I am tired, too," he agreed. "These last few days must have been quite an adventure for you."

"Yes, they were." Diana hid the fact that they had been anymore than that. "Good night."

"Good night," he echoed.

The Major was at the breakfast table the next morning when Diana entered. He looked rested after his night's sleep, and it eased some of her concern.

"Good morning, Major," she greeted him cheerfully. "Good morning, Sophie," she added when the housekeeper appeared. "Just toast and juice this morning, please."

"Yes, Miss." The housekeeper retreated to the kitchen.

"It's a beautiful morning, isn't it?" Diana poured herself a cup of coffee from the urn.

"It certainly is." The Major eyed her indulgently. "But something tells me you have more on your mind than the weather."

"You guessed right." She was glad she didn't have to find a way to lead into her subject. "Last night I did some thinking and decided I should take over some of the ranch responsibilities while you are recovering."

"Holt is pretty well in charge of everything," he reminded her.

Don't I know it, Diana thought, but said, "I know you've had to depend on him a great deal. Under the circumstances, there wasn't anyone else you could delegate authority to, but I'm home now. There isn't any work on the ranch that I don't know firsthand, through the sweat of my own brow, you might say." She laughed, trying to keep it all light. "There isn't any reason I shouldn't take over the responsibilities. Holt has done a good job, but you have said yourself that no one takes care of somebody else's property as well as he would his own.''

"That's true," he conceded.

"Besides being capable and experienced, I want to get involved. It's only natural since I am your daughter," she reasoned, "and this is my home, too."

"I can hardly argue, can I?" The Major looked vaguely pleased.

"I hoped you couldn't." She couldn't keep a triumphant smile from curving her lips.

"I'll discuss it with Holt at lunch."

A confused fire sparkled her blue eyes. "Why do you need to discuss it with him?"

"You don't remove a valuable man from his command without a private talk first, unless you want a mutiny on your hands. It requires tact," he explained with more than a trace of indulgence. Sophie returned with Diana's toast and juice and immediately disappeared into the kitchen. "We'll talk to Holt at noon," the Major said. "After you've finished your breakfast, find him and ask him to come to the house early if he can."

"All right," she agreed readily.

There was a spring to her stride when she later walked down the incline to the ranch buildings. Horses and riders were gathered near the stable. Guy she recognized, but Diana could find no sign of Holt. Separating himself from the other riders, Guy rode to meet her.

"Hi." He stopped in front of her, a beaming smile lighting his face. "Would you let Sophie know that Holt won't be here for lunch?"

"Why? Where is he?" A flash of irritation issued the questions in a rapid-fire burst.

"He left early this morning to go look at some stallions—said he wouldn't be back until late tonight." There was a faintly bitter twist to his mouth. "Good riddance, I say."

Her lips thinned into a tight line. "He certainly isn't wasting any time trying to acquire a new stallion."

"We have three mares coming in season and no stud to service them." Guy wasn't defending, merely explaining.

"Yes, you're right." But it didn't lessen her sensation of frustration.

"Holt left orders to bring the mares and colts to the inner paddock. That's where we're going now," he said. "Why don't you ride along with us?"

"No." It was an absent refusal, her attention already wandering from Guy.

"All you ever say anymore is no." He read the rejection in her look. "Why don't you just tell me to get lost? That's what you used to do."

Diana turned back to him, her hand lifting to protest, but Guy was already reining his horse around to rejoin the other riders, his features set in angrily hurt lines. Diana didn't call him back.

When she went to bed that night, Holt still hadn't returned, and the message still had to be delivered. After breakfast the next morning, she again ventured into the ranch yard in search of him.

Diana stopped one of the men. "Where is Holt?"

"In the stables treating one of the mares."

"Thanks." She was already walking away. In the stable, she found Holt and one of the hands in the stall with Cassie, treating the bites inflicted by the white stallion. Diana stepped inside the spacious stall. "I'll hold her. You can go, Tom," she told the man at the mare's head.

Before the man relinquished his hold on the halter, he glanced at Holt for confirmation of the order, then obeyed it. That didn't set well with Diana. Before she had married and left, no one had questioned an order from the Major's daughter. It was another indication of the subtle changes that had occurred in her absence.

With a firm grip on the halter, she talked soothingly

to the mare, letting Holt finish his task before explaining why she was there. He stepped away from the mare's hip and capped the bottle of antiseptic.

"Did you find a stallion?" Diana asked first.

"Maybe." At last, he glanced at her, appraising gray eyes sweeping over her. "But that isn't what brought you here. What do you want?" Blunt and to the point.

She felt her senses stirring to the virile force of his presence, a purely physical reaction that she couldn't control. Holt appeared totally indifferent to her.

"The Major wants to talk to you. You are to come up to the house early for lunch." Her voice shook slightly as she relayed the message.

"I can't. I won't be here at noon." Holt walked out of the stall into the wide stable corridor. "Tell him I'll be there this evening."

Diana followed him, stiff-legged with anger. "The Major says 'Come' and you say 'Wait.' There was a time you would have jumped at his bidding!"

"I have never jumped," Holt corrected. "I did what he asked me, and I still do. If he was aware I had made a previous appointment, he would be the first to postpone our meeting. And if it was vital that he see me, he would say, 'Come now.' "

Any response Diana might have made was checked when she stepped outside and saw a pickup driving into the yard, bearing a government insignia on its door. Irritation forgotten, Diana hesitated, glancing at Holt.

"What do you suppose he wants?" She nibbled at the corner of her lip.

"We'll find out shortly."

The pickup stopped in front of the main house. Together, Diana and Holt walked toward it. A short, squat man in his mid-forties climbed out, dressed in typical work clothes of Levi's and plaid shirt, a straw Stetson on his head. He started for the house, then saw them approaching and stopped.

"Good morning."

"Good morning." Diana returned his greeting with her most disarming smile. "Is there something we can do for you?"

"It might be the other way around." His voice was gruff, but his expression was pleasant. "My name is Keith Jackson. I'm with the Bureau of Land Management, here to see Mr. Somers."

"I am Diana Somers, his daughter." As she responded, the man politely removed his hat, revealing a shiny and balding head. "My father isn't very well. Perhaps I could help you."

The man glanced hesitantly at Holt as if he was reluctant to speak to a woman. Holt extended a hand in greeting. "I'm Holt Mallory, the Major's ranch manager."

"It isn't exactly necessary that I speak to the Major himself," the man admitted, addressing himself to Holt. "I'm sure you can provide me with the information I'm seeking."

"I'll try," Holt said with a pleasant, congenial air. "What is it you want to know?"

"We've heard reports at the Bureau that you've been having trouble with some mustangs," he said.

"Where did you hear that?" There was a faintly amused and scoffing note in his question.

"You know how these stories get around." The man laughed. "Somebody tells somebody else, and they tell somebody else. Sooner or later it filters through to us."

"What did you hear?" Diana asked, silently holding her breath.

"That some wild stallion stole a couple of your mares."

"We did have two mares that were missing," Holt admitted. "We had to go out looking for them, but when we found them, there wasn't any wild stallion with them."

Diana's lips twitched in amusement at the half-lie, half-truth. The white stallion hadn't been with the mares when they had recovered them.

"Oh, I see," the man hesitated. "We also heard rumors about a stallion fight. Was there anything to that?"

"Yes, unfortunately, there was." Holt nodded. "We don't know how it happened, since there weren't any witnesses. Maybe somebody didn't secure the latch properly on one of the stud pens. One of our stallions is dead and the other was injured," he said, implying it was a result of a fight between the two.

"I'm sorry to hear that," the man offered sympathetically.

"It was a loss," Holt agreed. "The stallion that was killed was a proven stud. He isn't going to be easy to replace."

"I can imagine. I've heard the Major raises some high-priced horses. Well," he sighed, "it looks like I've driven all the way out here for nothing. You don't seem to be having any problems with the mustangs."

"There's plenty of water and forage this year," Holt said as if that explained it.

"Yes, for a change." The man slipped his hat back on his head, preparing to leave. "If you have any problems with the wild horses, will you contact us?"

"Not willingly." Holt smiled dryly. "Personally, I think the present law protecting the wild mustangs stinks."

The look Diana gave him was a mixture of anger and alarm, but the man didn't seem upset by the remark. He chuckled and shook his head.

"It is an opinion shared by a majority of ranchers," the man declared. "We'll see you. Have a good day."

"Same to you," returned Holt.

"It was a pleasure meeting you, Miss Somers."

"Yes. Good-bye, Mr. Jackson." When the man had started his pickup and was reversing out of the yard, Diana turned to Holt, demanding, "Why on earth did you have to say a thing like that?"

"If I had been too cooperative, he might have gotten suspicious. As it is, I probably sounded no different than a hundred other ranchers he's talked to."

"I always believed you were cunning, but I never realized that you were such an excellent liar," Diana retorted. "I'll have to remember that."

The pleasantness had left his face, leaving cool mockery in its place. He simply smiled and walked away.

"Tell the Major I'll see him at seven-thirty tonight," he offered over his shoulder.

Chapter XII

Promptly at seven-thirty, Holt arrived at the main house. At the sound of his footsteps on the porch, Diana left the study and walked into the living room just as he entered.

"The Major is in his study." Diana turned to lead him back the way she had just come.

The Major rose from behind his large walnut desk when they entered. "Holt," he greeted him, reaching across the expansive desk to shake hands. "I've missed seeing you at lunch these last couple of days."

"I've been busy."

"I know you have." He nodded. "Diana, why don't you bring us some coffee?"

She returned in a matter of minutes carrying a china service on a tray. The Major and Holt were engrossed in a discussion about a stallion Holt had seen. Setting it down on the desk, she began pouring. As Holt reached for his cup, he noticed the three cups on the tray. His gray gaze sliced to her, aware that Diana was including herself in this meeting.

As he sat back in his chair, Diana took her cup and sat in the wingbacked twin to his. She sipped at her coffee, letting the Major bring up the reason for the meeting in his own time. In the meantime, she made no attempt to take part in their discussion about the stallion and its breeding.

At last, Holt concluded with, "There are two more

stallions I want to see before I make my final decision."

"I wasn't aware yours was the final decision," Diana inserted with cool dryness.

"The statement wasn't meant to be taken literally," Holt replied.

"Holt has an excellent eye for horses." The Major seemed to defend him. "As a matter of fact, Holt is the one who selected Fath."

Diana stared at the black mirror surface of her coffee, containing a surge of resentment. "I wasn't aware of that."

"We still haven't seen enough of his colts to be certain my choice was the right one," Holt said.

"Enough to give promise," the Major insisted. "But this is taking us off the track. I didn't ask you to come here to discuss stallions, Holt."

"I didn't think so." Holt drained his cup and set it back on the tray. "What did you want to talk to me about, Major?" His gaze glanced off Diana, aware that she was involved.

"Diana has expressed an interest in overseeing the operation of the ranch," the Major stated.

"Which means I'm out of a job," Holt countered, almost indolently relaxed and unconcerned.

"It doesn't mean that at all," the Major assured him, trying to smooth over the rough spot. "What Diana has in mind is assuming my role while I'm recovering. Your position would remain the same. You would only be answerable to a different party."

An eyebrow arched in a dismissing gesture. "I'm afraid that wouldn't work."

"Why?" Diana spoke up, challenging. "Would it bother you to take orders from a woman?"

"I don't object to taking orders from a woman," Holt corrected, turning his flint-hard gaze to her, "only to taking them from you." The glove of challenge was hurled back in her face.

"I know you and Diana have had your differences in

the past, but—'' Her father attempted to lessen the tension suddenly sparking between them.

"I'm sorry, Major." But there was no apology in Holt's clipped voice. "If I don't work for you, I don't work here at all. Things either stay the way they are, or you indulge this whim of your daughter's and I leave."

Diana went cold, guessing what her father's words would be before he said them. "Of course, I don't want you to leave. Nor was it Diana's wish, either."

But the taunting glitter of Holt's gray eyes seemed to dispute that claim. All Diana had wanted was to assume her rightful place as the Major's daughter.

"Major"—her voice was shaking—"do you mind if I speak to Holt alone?"

Initially, her request was met with silence. Then her father rose from his chair. "Yes, perhaps it's best if the two of you iron this out alone."

After the Major had left the room, Holt rose from his chair and walked to the fireplace, resting a hand on the mantelpiece. Diana's heart seemed to be pounding louder than the clock on the mantel.

"All right, Diana, what is it you have to say to me?" Holt challenged. "What do you have in mind? A little blackmail? I suppose you are going to threaten to tell the Major that I attacked you unless I agree to stay."

His sarcasm took her breath away. "Are you going to deny that you did?" she demanded finally.

"And a very unwilling victim you were, too," he mocked.

Diana pushed out of her chair, tremors quaking through her body. "It isn't fair!" she declared stridently. "I'm his daughter, his own flesh and blood, his only child! I should be in charge, not you!"

Holt faced her, impassive and unyielding. "That is for the Major to say."

"Why did you have to make him choose?" she cried, feeling her emotions being ripped apart. "You knew he would choose you, didn't you?" Diana accused, tears filling her eyes. "He always has picked you over me! Always!" Her hands doubled into fists.

"Diana, don't be ridiculous." He took a step toward her.

"It isn't fair!" His broad chest offered an easy target for her blurred vision. She struck at it with her clenched fists, her breath breaking into angry sobs. Holt caught at her wrists, giving her a hard shake that snapped her head back.

"The Major made a business choice," he insisted. "There was nothing personal in it."

The rough shaking had stopped her sobbing breaths. Now hysterical and mocking laughter bubbled in her throat. "Wasn't there?" Diana returned. "He's never needed me. Why should he? He had you." The tears began rolling down her cheeks, stream after stream.

"You don't know what you are saying," Holt muttered.

Diana could no longer see the blurred outline of his angular, male features. She was drawn inside the circle of his arms, her head forced to rest against his shoulder. She felt the point of his chin against her forehead, his hand uncertainly stroking the black silk of her hair.

"It's true, Holt," she mumbled against his shirt. "It's been true ever since you came here."

"No, Diana, it isn't," he said firmly.

Lifting her head in order to see his face, Diana found herself staring at his mouth, so well defined, strong, and male. Her mouth was open to speak, but no words came out. His hand stopped its stroking to cup the back of her head. Inch by slow inch, his mouth moved closer until his warm breath was playing over her nose and cheek and teasing her lips. Diana's heart fluttered in anticipation. She was keenly aware of the male contours of his body against her curved shape. His gaze roamed over her face, coming to a rest on her parted lips.

His mouth made feather-light contact with hers. "I swore I wouldn't get near—" Holt cut off the end of the sentence he muttered against her lips and gave in to a compulsion stronger than his resistance.

Diana trembled at the initial hard and expert pressure of his kiss. As the first response tingled through her, she felt him stiffen a warning instantly before he abruptly broke it off. When he didn't, her eyes opened onto his profile and the intense concentration etched there.

As if sensing her gaze, his low voice ordered: "Listen." Her head moved in dazed protest. "Something is bothering the horses," he explained in the same low, almost whispering, tone.

Over the hammering of her heart, Diana finally heard the disturbed sounds, curious whickers and alarmed snorts and restless movement. Yet there was no indication of panic.

"The stallion?" Diana made the suggestion a question.

A grimness settled into Holt's face. "Yes." He released her. "The stallion."

His long strides carried him to the study door. Diana followed him at a running walk. There was no sign of the Major as they passed through the living room and out the screen door. Once outside, the direction of the sounds became discernible. They were coming from the large paddock where the mares and colts had been penned.

A half-moon gleamed silvery-white in the night sky to light their path. Holt vaulted the first fence they came to, not waiting for Diana as she climbed over it. She heard someone behind her and glanced over her shoulder to see Rube hurrying toward her.

"It's that goddamned white stallion, ain't it?" Rube hauled himself over the fence after her. "I heard the mares stirrin' an' knew right away what was excitin' 'em." He talked as he walked, a steady stream of chatter that Diana ignored.

Holt reached the paddock fence, ahead of them, climbing the rail to get an overall view of the pasture area. Diana joined him, hooking a knee over the top rail for balance, and Rube did the same.

"There he is!" Diana pointed to the far end of the paddock.

On the other side of the distant fence, the moonlight glistened on the white coat of the stallion. He was pacing back and forth along the fence, seeming to float over the ground. Animated, his muscled neck arched, head tossing, his tail held high and streaming out behind him like a white banner, the stallion issued low, whickering calls to the mares, cajoling, coaxing, and persuading. They were slowly succumbing to his equine charm, the uncertainty of alarm leaving their responses.

Diana was mesmerized by the sight, unaware of the other ranch hands who had joined them, drawn by the disturbance. Deaf to their whispered exclamations, she didn't hear the word from Holt that galvanized them all into action. Nothing pierced the entrancing scene until the shouts and whistles from the men scattered the shadowy shapes of the mares grouped near the far fence line. The white stallion froze into an alert statue of animated expectancy, eyeing his two-legged enemies. Tossing his head, the stallion pivoted with the grace of a dancer and sped into the night.

"So that was the wild stallion." The Major was standing at the fence, slightly winded, excitement and grimness quarreling with each other in his expression. "I wish I'd gotten a better look at him."

"Magnificent, isn't he?" Diana murmured.

"Like no mustang I've ever seen," he admitted.

With the stallion gone, the men began to filter back, talking among themselves. Holt's familiar shape separated from the others to come to the fence where Diana and the Major waited. The moonlight bronzed his lean features, making silver chips of his eyes.

"He'll be back," he predicted flatly. "We'll have to keep a man on watch, take four-hour shifts."

"I agree," the Major said, although he hadn't been consulted.

"Maybe we'll be lucky and he'll give up after a few unsuccessful attempts to steal our mares." Holt stared at the dark mountains where the stallion had fled.

"No doubt he will." The Major glanced at them. "The two of you, did you—"

"You don't need to worry about losing Holt," Diana interrupted. "We've come to an understanding. He'll continue running things and I'll stay out of his way. I will keep on working with the horses, halter-breaking the new foals, and I thought I'd help you with the bookwork, but that's all."

Diana was already regretting the emotional scene with Holt at the house. It had exposed her weaknesses. Even though they enjoyed a mutual and powerful sexual attraction, there was too much bad blood between them, Guy, the Major, and the bitter rivalry. In a sense, Holt was still her enemy. She gave him this victory.

"Then it's all straightened out," the Major said.

This time it was Holt who replied: "Yes, it is." His gaze locked briefly with Diana's, measuring and steady. Then it was sliding to her father. "Excuse me, Major. I need to arrange the watches with the men."

"Go right ahead. Have a good trip tomorrow." When Holt moved off in the direction of the men, the Major turned to Diana. "Shall we go back to the house?"

"Yes." She stepped down from the fence rail. "Where is Holt going?"

"He's flying to California to look at a stallion there. I am relieved you and Holt came to an understanding," her father said as they started back.

"Yes."

"I have always wished the two of you could get along. Holt would have made a good husband for you. He's hard-working, loyal . . . but," the Major sighed, "it wasn't to be. It's a good thing I didn't try any parental matchmaking."

Diana nearly stopped dead at his comment. "Is that why you hired him? As a prospective husband for me?" She could have added: *Is that why you groomed him and trained him to take over the ranch?*

"Good heavens, no!" He laughed at her suggestion. "I hired him because he had the qualifications to fill the position I had open at the time. It was . . . three or four years later before I began to think of him in conjunction with you. By then you had already made a habit of rubbing each other the wrong way. I hoped the friction between you might spark something more. When it didn't, that was that."

"And you never said anything."

"No. The last thing I wanted for you was a loveless marriage," he said.

"Love can sometimes be an ugly thing."

"You are thinking of Rand and what happened between the two of you," the Major guessed. "It wasn't love he felt for you, or he wouldn't have spread those stories about you. Love is a warm and wonderful thing."

Diana's heart nearly stopped beating. "You heard those stories?"

"Yes, I heard them," he admitted.

"I—"

"It isn't necessary for you to explain," interrupted the Major. "Just forget them."

And Diana could tell by his tone of voice that he didn't want to hear an explanation. He wanted the subject dropped and forgotten by both of them. Slipping her fingertips into the front pockets of her jeans, she let the conversation drift into less turbulent channels. Somehow it didn't ease her conscience to learn the Major had heard the stories and chose to ignore them.

The stallion paid a second visit to the mares the following night. The accompanying noise awakened Diana and she had trouble getting back to sleep. It was late when she rose that morning. The Major had already breakfasted and was taking his morning rest.

At loose ends, Diana strolled out of the house

toward the stables. The sun was already warm on her skin. By afternoon, it would be hot. A haze covered the mountains, a cloud shadow racing across the slopes.

"Diana!"

She turned at the sound of her name, recognizing Guy's voice. She hadn't seen him at all these past two days, not since he had hurled those embittered words at her and ridden away to bring the mares up.

A breath-stealing pain swept through her at the long, effortless strides that were carrying Guy to her. Did he know how strongly his mannerisms sometimes reminded her of Holt? Diana mentally shook away the thought and noticed the flowers in his hand.

As he stopped in front of her, his gaze, uncertain and intent, searched her face. "A peace offering."

She took the bouquet from his hand. "Wildflowers. They're lovely, Guy."

His tension seemed to melt at her response. "I did it deliberately—chose wildflowers, I mean," he explained with a self-conscious laugh. "I thought about buying flowers in town, but these are you. You are a wildflower, Diana—delicate, untamed, and vulnerable to man's intrusion. The other day I was trying to make you grow where I wanted you to grow. You can't do that with a wildflower. I'm sorry. Will you forgive me?"

Why did he have to be so thoughtful and considerate? She was so tired of hurting people and letting them down. It would have been better if he had stayed angry with her . . . better for him. Diana couldn't let Guy continue to idealize her.

"I was rude when I refused you so abruptly. The only excuse I have is that I had other things on my mind," Diana said.

"We all have times when we don't want to be with people." His look was adoring.

Diana stared at the yellow flowers, drawing in a grim breath. "You shouldn't be so understanding, Guy. It isn't natural."

"The only thing that comes natural to me is loving you." His voice changed its pitch becoming vibrant and husky. "It seems that I've loved you all my life, Diana."

"Don't say that." Her hands tightened around the flowers, crushing the stems.

"All right, I won't say it anymore." But they both knew it wouldn't change the fact. "I was coming up to the house to see you. I have to drive into Ely to pick up a part. I thought maybe you'd like to ride along. It'd give you a chance to get away from the ranch and maybe do some shopping."

The idea was appealing. Instead of refusing his invitation, as she knew she should do, Diana accepted it. "Are you leaving now?"

"In about an hour. I have a couple of things to do first, and"—he glanced down at his work clothes, dusty, with horsehairs clinging to the denim fabric—"I want to clean up."

"That's fine," she agreed.

The hour's delay gave Diana a chance to change and leave word with Sophie as to where she was going. Dressed in a gypsy skirt and a white peasant blouse with a gathered neckline, Diana went in search of Guy. He wasn't in the ranch yard. Since he hadn't mentioned which vehicle they'd be taking, she walked to the fourplex.

Pausing at the screen door of the largest unit, Diana knocked once, calling, "Guy?"

A fan whirred loudly inside, circulating the warm air. Without hesitating, Diana walked inside. Her head was tipped at an angle, listening for sounds of movement. It had been several years since she had been inside these living quarters. The living room, dining room, and kitchen were all one room, with two small bedrooms branching off of it, as well as a bath. Everything was neat and orderly, almost impersonal. Then Diana noticed a pair of trophies sitting on a shelf. Curious, she walked over. They were marksmanship trophies with Guy's name inscribed on the gold plate.

A wooden rifle rack was on the wall above them, empty.

A bedroom door opened and Diana turned. Holt stared at her, halted in the act of closing the door. Diana, too, was motionless, her breath lodged in her throat, her heart skipping beats all over the place.

There was no doubt he had just stepped from the shower. His wet hair glistened darkly. His chest was bare, a sheen of moisture on the muscled flesh. Dark trousers emphasized the slimness of his hips and the width of his shoulders. Primitive and dangerous, there was a funny curling in the pit of her stomach.

His eyes made a slow, insolent sweep of her, twin tongues of silver lightning licking over the straining swell of her breasts against the white fabric and the draping folds of her skirt at the hips. Her senses reeled under the sensual impact of his look.

"Are you here to welcome me home?" His voice was taunting, derisive, and cynical.

"I . . . I didn't know you were back." Damn! Why was she stammering like some silly teen-ager? He unnerved her, yes, but did she have to show it so plainly?

"I got back about twenty minutes ago." He closed the bedroom door, continuing to face her, his feet slightly apart in a stance that suggested command.

"I was at the house. I didn't hear you."

The fan was on the kitchen counter behind Holt. *My God,* Diana thought, *I can smell him, the soap, the shaving cologne, the musky animal scent of him.* A suffusing heat enveloped her, heady like potent wine.

Holt glanced pointedly around the room. "Are you making an inspection tour of the premises?"

"I am riding into town with Guy. I was supposed to meet him in an hour."

Suddenly the temperature in the room seemed to drop below the freezing point. His features became encased in a bronze mask that was aloof and forbidding. The silent messages that had been disturbing her were broken off.

"What are you doing here?" Holt asked in a cold, flat voice.

Confused, Diana thought the reason for her presence was obvious, but she explained, anyway. "I didn't see Guy out in the yard. He had said something about cleaning up, so I came here."

"He isn't here."

"Obviously—"

"I mean," Holt interrupted her laughingly defensive reply, his manner grim and snapping, "he doesn't live here anymore!"

Diana was too startled by his announcement to respond immediately. "Where . . .? Why . . .?" She stammered out of her stunned silence.

"Do you really think he'd live under the same roof with me, considering how much he hates my guts?" he hurled with the lashing force of a whip.

Diana recoiled under the sting. "I didn't think. When—" She couldn't get the rest of the question out.

"He slept in the barn the night we got back. The next day he cleaned out that old trailer and moved his things into it. I'm surprised he didn't tell you." Holt was sarcastic. "With the seclusion and privacy of the trailer, he could have entertained you for a couple of hours in the evening."

"I have barely seen Guy since we came back, and spoken to him even less!" she flared.

"You always were easily bored with him," he said with disgust.

"Do you think I don't know how I treated him in the past? Do you think I'm not sorry now?" Her protest came in a passionate rush for understanding.

"Are you trying to make up for it? Is that what you're saying?" Holt challenged. Then he immediately backed off, muttering, "What the hell does it matter? You've taken him out of my reach, Diana. There isn't anything I can do to stop you. He's yours . . . to play with or destroy." He turned away.

"I don't want him." She stopped, staring at the faint, crisscrossing scars on his back. Her forefingers remembered the ridges they had felt when they had caressed his flesh. Her memory was jogged to that long-ago summer when she had first seen them, and Diana repeated the question she had asked then: "Those scars on your back—how did you get them?"

She watched the constricting of his muscles as Holt stiffened at her question. With rigid strides, he walked to the kitchen counter and removed a glass from the cupboard.

"Go find Guy." He deliberately ignored her question.

Holding the glass under the faucet, he turned on the cold-water tap. Drawn by an irrepressible urge, Diana followed him. A step behind him, she stopped, her attention riveted on the pale golden marks on his otherwise tanned skin.

"Did . . . someone whip you?" she murmured. Her hand reached out to trace the fading white lines. "Why?"

At the touch of her fingers, the glass crashed to the sink as Holt pivoted, grabbing her hand in a vise-like grip, crushing together the slender bones of her fingers. A deadly fury blazed in his eyes.

Her head was tipped back, the waving curtain of raven-black hair swinging free of her neck. In an effort to ease the pain of his bone-crushing hold, Diana swayed closer to him. She could feel his solidly muscled thighs through the folds of her skirt. The physical contact suddenly drove out all her fear. Her eyes, the darkly brilliant blue of a sapphire, smoldered with the ache she felt, the longing to know again his possession.

Her wants were unmistakable. She felt Holt catch at his breath and saw his gaze narrow on her lips, moist and enticing. The pressure of his grip eased slightly as his other hand moved to her shoulder. The instinctive knowledge throbbed through her that in another second she would be crushed in his arms.

Chapter XIII

"Diana?" Outside, Guy's questioning voice called her name.

As swiftly as the moment of desire had come, it fled. Part of her wanted to press her body closer to Holt's, make him aware how well her curved shape molded itself to the male contours of his and make him forget that Guy was outside looking for her. If she had felt the smallest chance of success, Diana would have abandoned her pride and self-respect, become as wanton and bold as any creature in love. But Holt was already rejecting her initial, hesitant advance, forcefully and angrily pushing her away from him while winter eyes froze her with contempt.

Not a word was said. Her gaze finally fell under the force of his. Diana turned and walked calmly to the screen door and pushed it open. A smile automatically curved her mouth as Guy turned at the sound.

"I've been looking for you," Diana said in a surprisingly steady voice.

Guy glanced at the closing screen door. Did he know Holt was back? Diana wondered. No sound of movement came from inside. His hand reached to take her arm and lead her toward the ranch pickup parked close by.

"I don't live there anymore," Guy said. "I moved out."

186

"You didn't say anything to me." Diana feigned ignorance, masking it in a statement of half-truth.

"I'm sleeping in that old trailer over by the gas tanks." He opened the door for her and gave her a hand into the cab. "It isn't much." He looked at her and Diana realized he had never mastered the art of hiding or controlling his feelings. "It needs a woman's touch, Diana."

She could have cried at the ardent appeal, but she was much more adept at controlling her reactions. "Not mine," she said brightly. "I've had my fill of the 'happy homemaker' role for a while. Someone else will have to fix it into a cozy love nest for you." Diana smiled, trying to ease the sting she knew her joking words had caused.

"Funny." His mouth twisted in a pained smile. "I don't feel like looking for anybody else."

Diana dropped her mask to plead. "I don't want you to love me, Guy. I don't want to hurt you."

His gaze fell from hers as he closed her door. "There isn't any way you can change it," Guy murmured and walked around to the driver's side.

For the first few miles from the ranch, neither spoke. Guy was the first to break the silence with a tentative comment about the horses. Diana responded and the tension began easing. One remark led to another. Soon they were talking with all the naturalness and long-shared friendship that had been present the first few days after Diana had returned, before everything had gotten so complicated.

As the truck approached a shaded picnic area and rest stop along the highway, Guy slowed down and glanced at Diana, his blue eyes sparkling. "What do you say we stop here for a breather? There's a cooler in back with a couple of cans of beer and pop."

"You just happen to have it along, huh?" she teased.

"It's part of my emergency kit in case I have a flat tire and my mouth gets dry and dusty as the desert while I'm fixing it." He had slowed almost to a full stop. "Well? What's it going to be? Are you thirsty? I'm in no rush to get to town unless you are."

His manner and mood suggested nothing more serious on his mind than playing a little hooky, and Diana found herself agreeing. "Let's stop."

Guy swung the pickup across the lane and onto the graveled cul-de-sac, parking under the gnarled trees. Switching off the motor, he hopped out of the cab.

"What'll you have, Miss?"

Diana answered with his same mock seriousness. "A cold can of pop." He made her feel incredibly young, still in the carefree days of her teens.

"What flavor?"

"What have you got?"

A wicked light danced in his eyes, laughing and teasing and suggestive. "Since you asked—"

Diana held up a hand, laughing, to stop him. "Surprise me."

Sighing with mock regret, Guy walked to the open bed of the pickup. There was the clink of aluminum cans and the swish of poptops being removed. Then he was back, sliding behind the wheel and passing her a cold can of cola. Diana leaned her head against the back of the seat and relaxed.

"Mmm, it's good," she murmured.

"There's nothing like a cold drink on a hot day." His own was a beer, the aroma of the malty beverage drifting through the cab.

Her gaze wandered absently out the window, noting the full litter barrels. Odd bits of paper and a few cans were scattered on the ground near the picnic tables. She and Guy weren't the only ones who had stopped here to enjoy the shade and the silence.

"A lot of people use this place, don't they? Some less considerate of the next person than others." Diana drew Guy's attention to the litter.

"It gets plenty of use," he agreed. "It's a popular place for beer parties and . . . it's kind of a lovers' lane."

Lulled by their recent camaraderie, Diana missed

any significance in the remark and teased, "Is that the voice of experience speaking? How many times have you used it to party with a girl?"

Guy took a swallow of beer and swished the rest around in its can. "If you tell me how many times you've been here, I'll tell you," he challenged.

"That's easy. I have never been here before. The boys I dated in high school never quite got up enough nerve to go out and park with the Major's daughter."

When he lifted his head, that look she dreaded to see was back in his eyes. "I'm glad you haven't been here with anyone else, Diana, because neither have I." He set his beer on the dash of the truck and turned in the seat to face her. Suddenly the large cab felt very confining.

"Then it's a first for both of us," Diana said brightly, ignoring what he was implying. "We've had a little beer party here together. At least you've had the beer." She gestured toward his can. "You'd better drink up before it gets warm."

"Diana, don't ignore me. Don't treat me like—"

"I'm not ignoring you, Guy." She gave up the pretense. "I just don't wa——"

"Don't talk." He slid closer, his arm circling her shoulders. Diana had a choice either to submit to his embrace or cringe against the door. She chose the first, carefully wedging an arm between them, trying to keep him at a distance. "You're so beautiful, Diana. I know I've told you that before, but it's true."

"Guy, don't!" She tried to be patient with him, firm without being harsh.

"I mean it. I'm not just saying it," he insisted. "Your hair is like satin." He reached out, curling a lock around his finger and stroking its smoothness with his thumb. "Black as midnight and shiny like the stars."

With a slight turning movement of her head, the strand of hair slipped from his fingers, falling back with the others. Undeterred, Guy touched his hand to her face, tracing the sweeping curl of her lashes.

"And your eyes, they are so blue I could drown in them," Guy murmured.

Diana tried to stop his exploring fingers, reaching up and circling his wrist with her hand. She firmly pushed his hand away from her face.

"And I love your mouth. God, I love your mouth."

Distracted by her efforts to remove his hand, Diana hadn't noticed his descending head. The warmth of his breath, smelling of beer, fanned her skin in warning. She made the mistake of turning toward him and found her lips claimed by his kiss. She started to twist away.

"Don't say no to me again," he begged.

His plea went straight to her heart, freezing her with its utter vulnerability. She let him kiss her, remaining stiff and unresponsive to his ardent pressure. But feeling sorry for him now was not the answer. Hadn't she learned that from her last mistake?

Diana twisted away from his kiss, but Guy didn't seem to care; he transferred his attention to her neck. His moist, nibbling attempt to arouse her only sickened Diana with a sense of guilt. A choked sob came from her throat, and Guy thought it was a moan of desire.

"I love you, Diana." His hand was pushing the elastic neckline of her blouse off her shoulder. "I love everything about you." His mouth never left her skin, his lips moving against it as he spoke.

"Guy—"

But he seemed unwilling to let her speak until he was through. "I love your beauty, your skin, your bones." She was straining, trying to push him away, fighting him as gently and determinedly as she could. In his inexperience, Guy seemed only to believe she was trying to find a more comfortable position or aid him in his lovemaking. His hand slid inside the expandable neckline, cupping the underside of her breast and holding it like a priceless art object.

"And I love your breasts." His voice was raw with desire. "They are so round and full, with dark rose centers more beautiful than any pictures I've ever seen. I want to—''

"No!" Her hands lifted his face, trying to keep him from the object of his desire. Her breaths were coming in little sobs.

Guy seemed destined to misunderstand. He let her move him away, but when he raised his head it was to seek her lips. Diana eluded his mouth, letting it find instead her cheek. When he tasted the salty moisture on her skin, he drew away, frowning at the tears on her cheeks.

"Diana, what's wrong? Why are you crying?" His voice, breathless with passion, was confused and concerned. Diana looked back at him, knowing she was crying for him, as well as for herself.

She looked away, angrily wiping the tears from her face. "I want you to stop it." Diana avoided his gaze, not wanting to see his reaction. Feeling sorry for him was not a reason to keep giving in to his desires. Neither was guilt for past wrongs. Diana adjusted the neckline of her blouse and opened her purse to find her lip gloss.

"I'm sorry." Guy was on his own side, his hands gripping the steering wheel, his head lowered. "I love you so much," he groaned. "I just got carried away."

With the lip gloss in her hand, Diana flipped down the visor to reveal its rectangular mirror. "You might take a few minutes to find out if the girl is willing."

Was that her reflection in the mirror? So cool and composed, and, yes, beautiful? Her blue eyes were as bright as polished gemstones. The traces of smudged mascara seemed only to darken the outline of her thick lashes. Her hand was steady. Nothing revealed how shaken and sickened she was by the trap she had sprung on herself.

"Every time I get near you, I remember the way I felt that first time. Even when I'm not with you, I remember. God, you were so beautiful, Diana, with your body . . . your skin all shiny from the water. You were mine to touch and kiss, every inch of you. When I made love to you, it was as if we became one person. After I came in you, lying beside you, knowing a baby might start growing, I—"

"No baby, Guy. I wasn't that foolish." She felt suffocated and sickened. "Give me your beer can. I'll throw it away."

Guy obeyed her request automatically, only half-aware of what she had asked. When she opened the door and stepped down from the truck, it penetrated. Guy followed.

"You said before it was good, that you didn't regret it. You weren't lying to me, were you, Diana? You weren't sorry we made love?"

"No." Not then. The bitterness of regret had come later. She set the cans in the overflowing trash barrel and turned to walk back to the pickup. Guy blocked her way, his gaze searching her face.

"Then why don't you want me to make love to you now? I know you said you didn't want to get seriously involved with anyone yet, but I can't believe that's why. It's something else, isn't it?"

"Guy—"

"It's because Holt raped you, isn't it? He's the one who's made you freeze up inside. I should have killed him!"

"No! Will you stop looking at me like a saint incapable of doing anything wrong! It wasn't rape!"

An incredulous frown spread across his face. "Did you want him to? You've always hated him as much as I have. I can't believe you actually wanted him to—"

"I didn't—not at first." She searched desperately for a way to explain something she wasn't sure of herself. "How can I make you understand? Sex and love don't necessarily go hand in hand, not even for a woman." Diana looked away, shamed by how readily she fell into the arms of a man who despised her. "Believe me, it doesn't make me feel very proud to admit it."

"You regret it?"

"Yes, I regret it." Her answer was accompanied by a short, bitter laugh.

Guy refused to believe the worst of her. "It still doesn't change the fact that Holt forced himself on you when you weren't willing. I saw you fight with him, trying to make him stop. Nothing you can say makes what he did any less brutal. Look what it's done to you. He should pay for it."

Her heart cried out: *My God, don't you think he is?* Didn't Guy realize his hatred for his father was the most vicious form of punishment that could be rendered? Her throat ached. Diana doubted that mere words could penetrate the wall of hatred. Hadn't she shown Guy how to lay the bricks?

"Try to forget it, Guy." Her voice sounded as tired as she felt. "Don't you think it's time we started for town?"

His agreement was grudgingly given. Diana sat close to the door. As they drove onto the highway, the wind blew through the open window, tangling her hair into rumpled black curls. For several miles, there was only the whine of the tires and the roar of the motor. This time it was Diana who spoke first.

"Have you ever asked Holt how he got those scars on his back?" There was a pause, but Guy never took his eyes from the road.

"Yes, I've asked him."

"And?"

"He never gave me an answer."

Very little else was said until they reached the outskirts of town. Guy slowed the truck to a stop at one of the main intersections and glanced at Diana.

"Where would you like me to drop you off?"

"Anywhere downtown is all right. I'm just going to do some window-shopping. How long will you be?"

"About an hour." The traffic light changed to green and Guy shifted gears, stepping on the accelerator.

"Where shall I meet you?"

Guy stole a glance at his watch, secured around his wrist by a wide leather band. "That'll make it about noon. We could have lunch before we head back to the ranch if you want.''

"I'll meet you at the hotel around noon then,'' Diana agreed.

"You aren't still mad at me, are you?'' His question was hesitant, asking reassurance that his behavior had been forgiven.

Diana gave it to him. "I was never mad at you, Guy.'' How could she be when none of what happened was his fault? It was her fault, she had gotten herself into this emotional tangle.

Guy let her out on a street corner of the downtown shopping area. Diana wandered in and out of a few stores, but she was only going through the motions. She was just looking because it was what she had said she was going to do.

Twenty minutes early, Diana walked into the hotel. A handful of players were at the slot machines inside the entrance. There was the grinding sound of arm levers being pulled, the whirl of spinning reels, and occasionally the ringing of jackpot bells and the clunking of coins falling into a metal tray.

The sights and sounds were too familiar to Diana to be noticed. She walked past the row of slot machines and up the short flight of steps. The blackjack and craps tables were virtually empty of players. One of the dealers smiled and nodded to her as Diana walked by on her way to the hotel coffee shop.

The noon-hour crowd was already beginning to fill the restaurant. Diana glanced around for an empty booth to wait for Guy. A waving hand caught her eye.

"Come sit with us, Diana.'' Peggy Thornton motioned her to their booth.

"I'd love to, but I'm supposed to be meeting Guy here for lunch.'' Diana walked toward their booth. "I didn't expect to run into you here. Where are the kids?''

"Sit down and have an iced tea with us while you're waiting for Guy,'' Peggy urged. "We left the kids with my mom." She glanced at her husband, sitting beside her. "Alan decided I needed a rest from them. So he brought me into town to do a little shopping and take me out to lunch. Isn't he a doll?"

It was obvious the outing was a rare treat for Peggy. It was such a small thing and so easily arranged that Diana became irritated at Alan for not doing it more often. Peggy was sitting beside him, almost radiant in her happiness.

"Sit down, Diana." Alan Thornton added his invitation to his wife's. "What will you have? Coffee, maybe, instead of tea?"

"Iced tea is fine."

As Alan called their waitress over, Diana started to slide into the empty booth seat opposite the couple. Only it wasn't empty. Holt was already seated there, a full cup of steaming coffee in front of him. Somehow she hadn't seen him; she had just assumed that Peggy and Alan were alone.

"I didn't know you were here." The statement bordered on an accusation as Diana hesitated at the edge of the seat.

"Do you want to change your mind about the tea?" Holt baited.

"Of course she doesn't!" Peggy laughed. "What a silly thing to say. Sit down, Diana. Don't mind him. I've been meaning to call and talk to you, but Amy has been sick and I've had my hands full."

Reluctantly, Diana slid onto the seat beside Holt. All her muscles were tensed, her nerves stretched thin, her senses tuned to his nearness. She knew she was sitting rigidly, but she seemed unable to relax, to be natural.

"How is Amy? I hope she's better." The words came out stilted and insincere, but Peggy didn't seem to notice.

"Yes, she's better, but I think Sara is coming down with the bug now. And she is so much more demanding when she's ill that I dread to think of having her sick in bed with both little ones to take care of, too. Ah, motherhood," Peggy sighed. "It's good to have a few hours away from it."

"She says that," Alan inserted, "but it's all talk. Since we left the kids at her mother's this morning, Peg has called twice to see how they are. If she would tell the truth, she'd rather be with them right now."

"I would not. I enjoy having you all to myself without one of the kids tugging at me, wanting this or that." She hugged his arm.

"Alan! Why, you old son of a gun!" A male voice exclaimed in delighted greeting. "I haven't seen you since— Hell! I can't remember when it was!"

An older man came up to the booth, clamping a hand on Alan's shoulder and vigorously shaking hands with him. Diana had a vague recollection of the man, a former rancher in the area who had sold out and retired. A turquoise nugget decorated his string tie, and an equally elaborate silver belt buckle was studded with turquoise. Alan introduced the man as Ed Bennett.

"You're the Major's daughter." His broad grin was turned to Diana. "My, you sure have grown. The last time I saw you, you weren't knee-high. Miss"—he motioned to the waitress—"bring me some coffee." The jovial man took it for granted that it was all right to join them. When he sat down beside Diana, she was forced to slide closer to Holt to make room for him. "How is your father? I heard he wasn't well. Heart trouble?"

"Yes. He's much better now."

Her pulse was running away with itself. The imprint of Holt's muscled thigh was being branded into hers. Her shoulder was pressed against his arm, until he lifted it to rest it on the back of the seat. Instead of providing more space, the action seemed to nestle Diana against him. He smelled clean and fresh with that slightly musky male scent that disturbed her so.

The rancher returned his attention to Alan and Peggy, making Diana feel even more isolated in the corner with Holt. "Why are you in town?" Her voice was low, edged with a thin anger. She turned slightly to look at him, her gaze lifting no higher than his smoothly shaven jaw.

"The stallion I bought will be arriving this afternoon. I'm waiting to pick him up." His reply, too, was low, letting the other three at the booth continue their conversation. Holt sipped at his coffee, apparently indifferent to her forced closeness.

"Why here?" Diana heard the faintly haughty note in her voice, as if she was attempting to put him in his place. It was purely defensive. "Why not—"

"I'm having the stallion flown in," he interrupted. "The pilot is to call me from the airport when they arrive."

He set the cup down and, figuratively, set Diana down at the same time. Moisture had collected on the outside of her iced-tea glass. It cooled her fingers when she wrapped them around the glass, but it didn't cool the heat rushing through her veins.

Diana could hear the others talking, but their words didn't seem to penetrate. Good Lord, what were they saying? She tried to concentrate. It was no use. She was much too conscious of the even rise and fall of Holt's chest against her arm. The warmth of his body heat was drugging her mind, but she had to keep cool.

Her breathing was shallow. She was afraid to move. Through the upward sweep of her lashes, Diana glanced at his face, so male and craggy, full of aloof, virile charm. Masked gray eyes were studying the shadowy cleft between her breasts, exposed by the scooped neckline only because he was looking down. Holt must have felt the faint tremor that went through her because his gaze lifted to her lips. There was a dizzying sensation of possession, his animal magnetism making her weak.

"Diana, there's Guy." Peggy's voice broke through the haze, her message snapping the spell. "Guy!" Diana turned as Peggy waved to Guy, searching the room. "Over here!"

"Hi, Peg, Alan." Guy walked to the booth. "I was looking for . . . Diana." The pause came when he saw her and lengthened at the sight of Holt.

"Pull up a chair and sit down at the end," Alan invited.

"Thanks, but I think this booth has more people than it can handle now. Diana and I will find a table." The look in Guy's face was that of a man coming to the rescue. The worst of it was that Diana wasn't certain she wanted to be rescued. Where Holt was concerned, she seemed to be without pride.

"Lots of luck, Guy." Alan laughed. "The place is packed. There isn't a free table to be had. Besides, there's plenty of room here. Steal a chair from somewhere and join us."

"Well, I . . ." Guy tried to think of an excuse.

Their waitress was at the next booth and Alan turned in his seat. "We have another one joining us. Will you find him a chair? We'll be ready to order when you do."

The decision was taken out of Guy's hands. Diana felt a twinge of guilt for not greeting him, especially when Guy became sullen and uncommunicative, answering in monosyllables during the meal, sulking like a child. With his gaze rarely leaving the two of them for long, Diana took care to ignore Holt while literally rubbing elbows with him.

The waitress came back to refill their coffee cups and carry away the luncheon plates. Holt covered the top of his cup with his hand.

"No more for me," he said. His gaze slid over Diana to the man seated on the outside end of the booth. "Would you mind letting me out? I want to check at the desk to see if there have been any calls for me."

The retired rancher stood up and Diana slid out so Holt could leave. She had become so accustomed to the lean, hard strength of his body against hers that it felt strange sitting in the booth without Holt beside her.

"It doesn't look like Holt's coming back," Peggy observed after several minutes had passed.

"Probably not," Alan agreed. "I saw him paying his check at the register before he left the restaurant."

"What was he doing here, anyway?" Guy demanded with near belligerence.

Diana explained about the new stallion that had been purchased. "Holt probably had a message that the plane had arrived."

"I guess." But there was still irritation in Guy's tone. He glanced at his watch. "It's time we were going back to the ranch."

"Not yet!" Peggy protested. "Diana and I have barely had a chance to talk. Can't you stay a little while longer?"

"We'd like to, but I have to get back to work." Guy tried to make his refusal polite and firm.

"Diana doesn't have to go back. Do you, Diana?" Peggy turned to her. "Alan and I can take you home. We go right by your ranch, so it isn't out of our way. We can have a long talk. And I have some shopping to do. You can come along with me. It's been ages since I've been shopping with a girl friend. Alan has some errands to do. So, please, say yes."

There wasn't any other answer Diana wanted to give. The prospect of a long ride with Guy in his present mood was definitely not appealing. And she, too, wanted to spend a few hours with her friend.

"Of course I'll stay. It sounds like fun." She turned to Guy, ignoring his resentful look. "Tell the Major that I'm staying in town with Peggy and Alan."

There was a fleeting second when Diana thought he was going to insist she accompany him. Then Guy was nodding curtly and turning to leave.

Chapter XIV

The retired rancher, Ed Bennett, had spotted another old acquaintance and had gone over to talk to him. Alan had decided it was time to start running his errands. When Peggy suggested a visit to the hotel's powder room, Diana agreed.

She stood in front of the mirror, brushing out the snarls the wind had made in her hair. Peggy was retouching her lipstick, a necessary bit of color in her pale face. She caught the reflection of Diana's gaze in the mirror.

"Guy sure seemed jealous of you and Holt."

The brush in Diana's hand stopped in mid-stroke, then continued with new vigor. "What are you talking about?"

"Come on, Diana. He has always had a crush on you. You are woman enough to know that. What started out as a bad case of puppy love seems to have grown into the real thing—green-eyed jealousy and all."

"Guy thinks he's in love with me." There was no point in denying that. "But you are wrong about there being anything between Holt and me. We never have been able to stand each other."

"Funny, I had the impression—" Peggy stopped in mid-sentence and shrugged. "Alan always tells me that I have a very vivid imagination."

200

"You must."

Peggy put the tube of lipstick back in her purse and turned away from the mirror. "Ready?"

Diana paused to fluff the sides of her hair with her fingertips, then nodded. The powder room was on the second floor of the hotel. As they came down the steps, Diana saw Holt standing behind one of the players at the blackjack table near the foot of the stairs. Her heart did a little somersault. He hadn't left, after all.

As if aware of her approach, Holt turned, metal-gray eyes pinning hers. The floor seemed to roll beneath her feet, but it was only the trembling of her knees. He stepped forward to intercept them.

"Holt," Peggy said with some surprise, "we thought you'd left."

Diana picked up on the comment. "Hasn't the plane arrived?"

"Not yet. Where's Guy?"

"He's gone back to the ranch. I'm riding home with Peggy and Alan."

"Yes. We're off to do some shopping. It will be a first for Diana, since I'm going to be dragging her through all the children's departments. She'll be an expert on rompers and playsuits after she follows me around."

"Since you are staying in town for a while, you might as well ride back to the ranch with me. It will save Alan a stop." The glint in his eye challenged her to refuse.

"We don't mind," Peggy insisted.

"Besides," Diana added, "you don't know when you'll be leaving."

"According to the flight plan the pilot filed, the plane won't be arriving for a couple of hours. You can give me a hand with the stallion."

Why was he suddenly seeking her company? Diana couldn't help being skeptical. She wanted his, but she doubted that the reverse was true. So why was he asking her? Not because of the new stallion.

Curiosity, if nothing else, made her say, "We are supposed to meet Alan here at the hotel when we're through shopping. If you haven't left to pick up the stallion, I'll ride back with you." Diana made certain that she didn't sound eager for his company.

"All right."

"See you later, maybe," Peggy said and turned to walk away.

Diana started to follow her, but Holt caught her hand. She stopped, feeling something hard and metallic being pressed into her palm. A light glittered in his eyes, challenging and cold, as he released her hand. Her fingers curled around the object. Heat burned her cheeks as Diana's sense of touch recognized it as a key, a room key. She would have hurled it at his face, but Peggy turned around.

"Aren't you coming, Diana?"

She held his gaze for another full second, outraged anger choking her. "Yes." Finally she turned, slipping the key into her purse before Peggy noticed it. "Yes, I'm coming."

The key seemed to add twenty pounds to the weight of her purse. Diana felt it growing heavier and heavier with each passing minute that brought them closer to the time when they were due to return to the hotel.

As Peggy had warned, their shopping tour was limited to the children's departments. Diana, who had previously had no interest and no reason to be interested in children's clothes, found herself surrounded by miniature garments.

"Sara is so hard on clothes. By the time Amy gets them, they are almost in rags. Brian, of course, gets hand-me-downs from both girls. And I never realized how many of their baby clothes had ruffles and lace and all pastel colors—which upsets Alan to no end when he sees Brian dressed in them." Peggy flipped through the clothes hanging on tiny hangers. She held out a tiny denim overall outfit. "Isn't that cute?"

"It's darling," Diana agreed.

Peggy looked at the tag and rolled her eyes. "The

price is a crime. You just can't pay that much for clothes they'll outgrow in a few months. I am simply going to have to learn how to sew."

"When would you have time?" From what Diana had seen, Peggy had her hands full twenty-four hours a day.

"At night when they're all asleep." Peggy seemed to consider the idea. "I think I'll talk to Alan about buying a good secondhand machine. It would be practical since I take all my patching to my mother's and do it on her machine.

Peggy looked through the rest of the little outfits and ultimately purchased some inexpensive little T-shirts and shorts. As they left the children's department, they passed the ladies' clothes. A jersey dress patterned in green and gold caught Diana's eye.

"Look, Peggy. With your coloring, that dress would be perfect on you." Diana instinctively knew she was right. The material would soften the bony thinness of Peggy's figure, and the colors would bring out the rich auburn shade of her hair.

"It is beautiful, isn't it?"

"Try it on," Diana urged.

"No." Her laugh was just faintly self-conscious. "The children are the ones who need clothes, not me. I have a closet full of skirts and dresses from when I was teaching school."

Which was almost ten years ago. "They're out of style by now." The flush that crept into Peggy's cheeks made Diana wish she had bitten off her tongue.

"They'll come back in style. In a couple of years I'll be the best-dressed woman around."

"Every woman needs a new dress now and then. It's good for her ego."

"Maybe, but I'll pass on this one."

Diana suddenly became determined that her friend, who had so little, should have this dress. "It was made for you, Peggy. If it's the money that's bothering you, I'll buy it as an advance Christmas present."

"I know your heart is in the right place, but I can't

let you do it. Alan would guess and his pride would be hurt. Besides, where would I ever wear a dress like that? With the kids, we hardly ever go out. And that dress is too bold for Sunday church. Thanks just the same, Diana."

Damn Alan and his pride, Diana thought as she left the store with Peggy. Damn him for asking Peggy to scratch out a living with him on that two-bit ranch. They couldn't afford the first child, and damn him for getting her pregnant with two more. Her hand closed over the flap of her purse, aware of the key that burned inside. Damn all men!

"Alan is probably waiting for us at the hotel." Peggy was oblivious to the anger that had whitened Diana's face. "Shall we head back?"

Alan mustn't be kept waiting, Diana added bitterly in her mind. "Yes, we might as well," she agreed with almost deadly calm.

At the crosswalk opposite the hotel, a smile lighted Peggy's face. "See? I told you he would be waiting for me."

Alan Thornton was standing at the hotel entrance. The frown that had been on his face cleared when he saw them across the street with the light.

"Is your shopping all done?" He took the packages from Peggy's arms and crammed them in his own.

"All done. Have you been waiting long?"

"Not long." He turned to Diana. "I saw Holt in the hotel about twenty minutes ago. He said you were riding home with him."

"Yes. I'd better go see if he's ready to leave."

"I'm glad you stayed, Diana. It was fun. Come over to the ranch sometime soon and visit me, okay?"

"Soon, Peggy," she promised.

With a wave to the departing couple, Diana entered the hotel. A search of the casino and restaurant found no sign of Holt. She hadn't expected it would. She knew where he would be waiting for her.

Anger seethed inside her like a bubbling volcano before an eruption. Opening her purse, her fingers closed around the room key. Furtively, she stole a glance at the number before hiding the key in her closed fist.

Climbing the stairs to the second floor, Diana walked past the ladies' powder room, entering the corridor of hotel rooms. The hallway was blessedly empty. No one was about to see her glancing at the numbers on the doors.

When she found the right room, she knocked once and waited. No sound came from inside. Diana hesitated only a second before inserting the key into the lock and turning it. She opened the door and saw Holt standing at a window, staring out the panes through a veil of smoke curling from the cigarette in his hand. She swept into the room with contained fury, her skirt whirling about her legs.

At the click of the closing door, Holt gave her a sidelong look without turning from the window. "Somehow, I didn't think you'd show up."

"Didn't you?" she fumed. "What did you think I would do?"

"You'd better keep your voice down unless you want someone complaining to the management." He walked to an ashtray and calmly crushed out his cigarette.

"What do you suppose the management is thinking now?" Diana hissed. "Do you think they aren't speculating about why you rented a hotel room?"

"They know why." Holt smiled without humor. "As a matter of fact, I rented three rooms: one for the pilot, one for the co-pilot, and one for the handler who's accompanying the stallion. They will be staying over for the night and flying back to California in the morning."

"And whose is this?"

"Does it matter? I'm making temporary use of it until the switchboard relays the message that the plane has arrived. It's better than standing around downstairs waiting for the call."

Wary, still not completely believing what he said,

anger sparkling in her eyes, Diana questioned, "How much longer before the plane arrives?"

"A couple of hours."

"That's what you said the last time."

"So I did." He was regarding her lazily through his masked expression, a coiled alertness in his indolent stance. "Weather delayed their takeoff."

"And you expect me to wait here for two hours?" she demanded.

"It's less boring then being downstairs."

"You're bored, is that it?" Diana was so angry she was trembling. "Am I supposed to entertain you? What do you want me to do? Strip off my clothes and hop into bed like some whore? Here's your key!" She hurled it at him. "You know what you can do with it. I'm leaving."

It bounced off his chest and clattered to the floor. "Alan and Peggy have already gone."

"So what? There's more than one way of getting back to the ranch." She hesitated, knowing where he was vulnerable and using it. "Such as calling Guy and having him come and get me." A blazing fire leaped into his eyes before they narrowed dangerously. "He'll be glad to rescue me from your clutches." Diana added more fuel with malicious satisfaction and pivoted to leave.

She had taken one step when Holt seized a handful of hair at the back of her head. "Like hell!" He yanked her back, twisting her into his arms all in one motion.

The vicious tugging at her tender scalp drew a gasping cry from Diana, which Holt ignored. She lifted a hand to the back of her head to try to ease the pain and found herself locked in the steel trap of his arms.

With her head forced back by the continued pulling of her hair, Holt stared into her eyes for a long minute. Her breath was stolen by fear and something else. She couldn't speak, not in protest or pain.

"Damn you," he muttered.

His mouth came down hard on her lips, grinding them against her teeth. Diana heard the whimpering

cries muffled in her throat. The ever-tightening circle
of his arms flattened her breasts against his chest, the
buttons of his shirt digging into the soft flesh. Black-
ness swam at the edges of her mind.

The pressure of his mouth changed subtlely, cruelty
becoming demand. Diana answered it, the treachery of
her senses releasing the floodgates and letting the
passion flow forth. His hands rubbed her sore scalp,
fingers tangling in the black silk of her hair. Her arms
were around his neck, lifting herself on tiptoes to more
easily reach his mouth. A steel band circled her waist,
lifting Diana the rest of the way off her feet. Carrying
her thus, Holt walked the few steps to the bed,
following her down to the mattress.

The volcano of anger that had been simmering near
an eruption became an explosion of desire. His touch,
his kiss, the feel of his body burning against hers
aroused her, as always, to the primitive animal needs
of the flesh. The spouting fires grew hotter and hotter
at the wayward caress of his hands and the nuzzling of
his mouth along the pulse point of her neck. He was
driving her to the edge, knotting her stomach into a
tight ball of need, a pulsing ache twisting her body.
Her frustrated writhing had worked the length of her
skirt around her waist. Her hips were moving in
instinctive and automatic reaction to the teasing massage of his hand.

"Do you want me to stop, Diana?" His voice
throbbed huskily against the curve of her neck. "Do
you?"

A soft moan of protest came from her throat,
knowing what her answer was and hating him for
making her say it. Why didn't he take her and be done
with it, satisfy the needs that were assaulting them
both?

Holt levered himself away from her. "Do you?" he
demanded again.

She closed her eyes against the blazing sheen of his.
"No," was her barely audible reply.

But she didn't receive the assuagement of his hard

kiss. Instead, Holt pushed himself off the bed. "Take off your clothes." At her choked cry of protest, Holt began unbuttoning his shirt with savage impatience. "I don't want to be explaining ripped clothes when we leave the hotel, and the way I feel right now—" His mouth snapped shut on the rest of the sentence as he turned away.

With shaking hands, Diana pulled the blouse over her head and unfastened the waistband of her skirt. She stepped out of it as she rose from the bed, trembling with shame and a desire that she couldn't control. Removing her sandals and nylons, she balanced alternately on one foot, aware of the sounds of Holt undressing behind her. As her nylons fell soundlessly on the pile of her other clothes, there was silence. Diana turned, lifting the sides of her hair and holding it away from her face.

His gaze swept slowly over her long legs, slim hips, and full breasts, stopping finally at her face. For the first time in her life, Diana was conscious of her nakedness, as well as his. One coarse or demeaning word from him and she would have fled rather than face the humiliation of surrendering. Conflict warred in the expression on his hard, lean features. His hand lifted, his fingers barely touching the jutting curve of her cheekbone.

"Why do you have to be so damned beautiful?"

Diana knew. In that flashing second, Diana knew. Holt wanted her more than he despised her. He couldn't control what he felt any more than she could. He, too, was caught in the dangerous whirlpool of passion and it was dragging them both down. With the desperation of two lovers reaching for each other in death, they came together and let the whirlpool take them where it wished.

Afterward, weak and exhausted, Diana lay in the crook of his arm. She closed her eyes, afraid to speak in case words diminished the wonder of what she had experienced. Holt gently wiped the tears from her cheeks and drew the bedcovers over them both. With the comfort of his arm around her, Diana let herself drift away, floating on a cloud that avoided reality.

Once something disturbed her and Diana stirred restlessly. A soothingly low voice near her ear quieted her. "Ssh, baby. Sleep." And Diana obeyed the gentle command.

Sometime later a coolness began to chill her skin. She rolled over to snuggle closer to the fiery heat of Holt's body. When she didn't immediately encounter his solid form, her hand groped beneath the covers. The fact registered through the haze of her half-sleep that he wasn't there.

An instant later her eyes opened, her mind surfacing to full consciousness. The room was empty. His clothes were gone. A long, rectangular patch of yellow sunlight streamed through the window. It was late, nearly sundown.

Diana sat up in the bed. With a groan, she buried her face in her hands. Why did she have to wake up alone? It would have made it all so much more bearable if she had awakened in Holt's arms. Diana bit her lip to hold back a sob.

With a burst of movement, she threw back the covers and slid out of the bed. She walked to the bathroom and stopped at the sight of her sleepy and love-drugged face in the mirror, and the lost look in her eyes. Pivoting sharply away, Diana turned on the shower. She wrapped a towel around her hair to protect it from the wetness of the spray and stepped into the tub-shower, drawing the curtain shut. The needle-like jets of water pummeled her skin, driving out the numbness. She stood beneath the spray, her head back, her eyes closed, her hands raised, her palms open in silent worship to the reviving water.

The rushing deluge flooding over her deafened Diana to any other sound. When the shower curtain was jerked open, she cried out in startled alarm. Holt stood there, impassive in his regard. Her breath came back slowly. She stepped closer to the tiled wall, letting the shower spray come between them as if it shielded her somehow.

"Where have you been?" Her question accused and quivered with hurt.

"The plane arrived." He continued to hold the shower curtain aside, watching her, his gaze not lowering from her face, shiny and beaded with water. "I had to get the stallion loaded in the van and bring the crew back here."

"The crew." Diana remembered that this hotel room belonged to one of them. "I'll make the bed up as soon as I am out of the shower. I suppose they're waiting downstairs."

"The pilot and co-pilot are bunking together, so there's no hurry to vacate the room." Holt let go of the curtain and turned to the side. It remained partially open and Diana could see him undressing.

"What are you doing?" She sounded breathless.

Her eyes rounded into large, blue saucers as Holt stepped into the shower. He seemed taller, his shoulders, wider, dwarfing her. His shoulders and back shielded her from the brunt of the spray. She stared into his eyes, darkening into charcoal. His lean, muscled form seemed larger than life, all bronze sinew rippling under the cascading water.

A reborn heat was firing her veins, but Diana didn't move as Holt took a bar of soap from the shelf and lathered his hands. Her lashes fluttered down at the sensual touch of his soap-slicked hands on her neck. There was a crazy, wild singing in her ears as he lathered every inch of her with slow, massaging caresses. Fingers, palms, breasts, legs, navel, all tingled with the erotic cleansing of his hands. Diana was clinging to the hard flesh of his shoulders when her passion-weakened limbs would no longer support her. His mouth closed over hers in a long, drugging kiss.

Water ran over their faces and their entwining bodies. Its warm temperature was nothing compared to the fiery heat that fused them together. The water

turned cool before they did. For long minutes Holt
held her in his arms, waiting for the tremors to end in
his own body, as well as hers.

Then he was lifting her out of the shower and
wrapping a towel around her. The towel around her
head was sodden, her hair damp when Diana shook it
free. She saw the swing of velvet-black hair in the
mirror and glanced at her reflection. She looked so
very different from how she ever had before. Without
vanity, Diana admitted to a radiant beauty that
frightened her a little.

Holt's reflection joined hers, hard, lean, and very
male. He stood behind her. Diana watched his dark
head lower to the curve of her neck and heard a
quickly indrawn breath before realizing she had made
the sound. His hands slid down her arms, crossing
them in front of her as he explored the pulsing vein in
her neck. Turning her around, Holt lifted her in his
arms and carried her into the bedroom, dim now in the
purpling dusk of night.

Side by side, they lay in the bed, their lips meeting in
an occasional kiss, but mostly they simply enjoyed the
freedom of touching one another. Her hand was on his
shoulder, sliding across to his spine. Diana felt the
faint ridges on his hard flesh.

"How did you get them?" She shifted her head on
the pillow to see his face.

"Get what?" He rubbed a knuckle in the little
hollow behind her ear.

"Those scars."

"I don't remember." And Holt leaned over to kiss
her lips, but Diana didn't want to be sidetracked just
yet.

"That's the same thing you said a long time ago
when I asked you." She moved an inch out of reach of
his mouth.

"Are you surprised my story hasn't changed after all
this time?" There was a lazy curve to his mouth, and
his hand cupped the back of her head so she couldn't
elude him again.

"Somebody used a whip on you. Why?"

His answer was a hard, silencing kiss. Diana surrendered to it, responded to it, but the instant he released her, she fought back through her befuddled senses to the topic.

"Tell me what happened, Holt."

A muscle along his jaw rippled in impatience. "This isn't the time to be recalling ugly memories."

Her fingers traced the faint marks on his back. "It must have been very painful. Was it?"

As he had that morning, Holt was dragging her hand from his back. He pinned it to the mattress, looming above her, a cold anger flashing across his face. It dissipated just as quickly as his gaze roamed over her features.

"I've never met a woman like you." It was a grudging compliment, issued almost in growling irritation. "You mess up a man's head until he can't think straight."

"I do?" Diana felt an exhilarating sense of power at his admission.

"You knew you were tearing my guts out today when you kept rubbing up against me in that booth," he accused. "You were all but sitting in my lap."

"Not deliberately." She touched a hand to his cheek, stroking the smooth hollow of his jaw. "I couldn't help it. The booth was meant for two. It was either your lap or that man's."

"I even convinced myself that I didn't give you the room key so that this would happen."

"Then why did you want me here?" Diana frowned.

"It doesn't matter. This is really why I wanted you all to myself. It's why you came, too, isn't it?"

"Yes," she admitted without hesitation. Anger had merely been an excuse. She had wanted Holt to make love to her.

"Then we both have what we wanted."

His head moved down, his mouth kissing the exposed hollow of her throat. His weight shifted on the mattress and his hand was curving on the underside of a breast, lifting the nipple to his lips. It grew into a hard, sensitive bud under the manipulation of his tongue. Her skin quivered as he made a matching rosebud of the other. Content with his success, Holt let his attention wander to the swelling curves of her breast and down to her rib cage. The muscles of her stomach constricted spasmodically as he explored the recesses of her belly button. When his downward descent continued, Diana stiffened.

"Holt, no." Her protest came in an apprehensive whisper.

He laughed at her softly, without malice, his breath warm against her ultra-sensitive skin. "Do you mean you still have some inhibitions left, or do you want me to say 'grace' first?"

A crazy, wild tingling was taking over her limbs. "Holt, please, Rand never . . . he considered it . . ." Diana never got the rest of the words out as a searing, breath-stealing fire swept through her.

Chapter XV

Purring like a kitten, Diana snuggled closer to his side. She tried not to examine too closely the wildly sweet emotions she was feeling. She just wanted to feel them and not look ahead to see where they might lead. Her fingers lightly stroked his shoulder and arm. Even relaxed, his flesh was hard and muscled. It was crazy the way she couldn't seem to have enough of touching him.

"Do you have any family?" Diana wondered aloud, her voice a soft whisper. "I can't remember you ever leaving the ranch. Were you raised in Arizona?" She let her nose be tickled by the hairs on his chest, inhaling the scent of him. At his silence, her thoughts wandered further. "Your wife . . . Guy's mother—I know you split up when he was small, but you must have loved her once. Didn't you?"

"That's typical. A man takes a woman to bed and she thinks she's entitled to know his life history."

For all his amused and mocking tone, there was a closed look about him when Diana tipped her head back to see his face. She laughed softly in her throat.

"You'd like to tell me to shut up, wouldn't you, the way you always do with Rube? It won't work, not with me." Her hand slid up to the tanned column of his neck where a fingertip began tracing a lazy circle near his ear. "You'll have to find some other way."

214

"Like this?" His fingers closed around her throat, exerting pressure and lifting her face to his. With hard demand, Holt covered her lips, kissing her into silence before his mouth blazed a fiery trail to the curve of her neck.

"God!" Diana felt the taut breath he released against her sensitive skin, his mouth nibbling here and there. "I'm beginning to memorize the smell of you. I could find you in the dark."

"It is dark."

Diana arched closer to him, shooting fires racing through her veins. She had believed her passion was burned out, but his touch, his kiss, his nearness was rekindling it again.

At her growing arousal, Holt accused, "You are an insatiable bitch."

But Diana felt the hardening bone against her skin. A feline smile curved her lips. "What does that make you?"

With a quick twist, Holt rolled her onto her back, pinning her shoulders against the mattress. Then he was lowering his body onto hers, his mouth finding hers in a fiercely consuming kiss. The fire raged out of control.

For a second time, Diana fell into an exhausted sleep in his arms. She felt at home there, more comfortable than in her own bed, the most natural place in the world to be. Even in sleep, there was a trace of a smile on her lips.

A hand gently shook her shoulder. "Wake up, Diana." With a negative movement of her head, she cuddled closer to the hard pillow she had made of his chest. "Come on. Wake up." Holt's voice became firm. "It's almost midnight."

Moaning a protest, Diana forced her eyes open. Holt took his arm from around her and tossed back the covers. She sat up, covering her eyes when he switched on the light. The mattress shifted as he climbed out of bed and walked to the bathroom, where he had left his clothes.

"Get dressed," he ordered.

Diana obeyed. She was fastening her sandals when he walked from the bathroom. Except for the darkening shadow of a beard, he looked vital and fresh, tobacco-brown hair gleaming in the artificial light.

"I'll bring the truck and van around and wait for you in front of the hotel."

Before leaving, he tossed the room key on the dresser to save leaving it at the night desk. The door closed as Diana took the hair brush from her purse. The image of her love-softened face in the mirror held her spellbound. Anyone looking at her would know she had been made love to very thoroughly and had enjoyed it. There wasn't a trace of haughtiness or arrogant pride. Diana knew, at this moment, she was very, very vulnerable.

The thought of Holt waiting for her lifted the brush to her hair. A touch of lip gloss and Diana was ready. There were voices in the hallway outside the door, and the first crush of reality began to press on her. She waited until she heard the closing of doors before she ventured out. She almost ran to the staircase.

As she descended the steps, Diana felt like she was running a gauntlet of eyes. On the surface, no one seemed to pay undue attention to her, no more than any halfway attractive woman would receive at that hour of the night. Yet, Diana was weighted by the knowledge that she might be recognized by local people. Would they wonder where she had been? Would they guess she had been in one of the hotel rooms with her lover? Would the gossip about her divorce feed their imaginations? Would the rumor get back to the Major?

Diana almost burst out of the door, away from the suffocating atmosphere of the hotel into the fresh air and silence of the night. The truck was idling in the street on the other side of the cars parked in front of the hotel. Diana ran to the passenger's door and climbed in, her heart pounding. Holt shifted the truck into gear and started out slowly. Diana could hear the shifting of hooves in the horse van drawn behind the truck.

"I hope the Major isn't worried about me." It was an attempt by Diana to communicate the twinges of guilt she was experiencing at her immoral behavior.

"He knows you are a big girl now. He won't be waiting for you to come home."

The indifferent response wasn't what she had hoped to hear. "I suppose not."

When they reached the open highway, the truck picked up speed, staying within the limits because of the van it pulled and the precious cargo of a blooded Arabian stud it contained. Diana rested her head against the seat back, letting the cool wind blow through the open window over her face. She closed her eyes.

Holt seemed so distant, and she wondered why. Was he thinking about the Major, too, and wondering what his reaction would be if he learned? She turned her head to look at him, his bold, aquiline profile outlined by the moonlight.

"Would it bother you if the Major knew?"

There was a second's hesitation before he answered, simply, "No," his attention not leaving the road.

She wished she could say the same, but old habits die hard. "Don't you think he'd be upset if he found out?"

"It's unlikely he would find out unless you intend to make a full confession and tell him how we spent the afternoon and evening making mad, passionate love." There was a cynical, taunting quality to his voice that sliced at an open wound. "If he did, what would you expect him to do? Play the outraged parent? I was married at the point of a gun once. It won't happen twice."

"He could dismiss you."

It was an ineffectual thrust. "We are two consenting adults. Your father is a man. Given the same set of circumstances, the Major wouldn't have behaved any differently than we did."

"No, he wouldn't fire you." She could hear the acidity in her tone, but couldn't prevent it. "He needs you. He depends on you. And you were just doing what any normal, red-blooded American male would have done in your place."

God, Diana wished she hadn't brought up the subject. Why hadn't she left it alone? She turned her face to the window, staring at the looming, dark mountains flanking the highway. The tires whined in the silence. Diana closed her eyes again, not sleeping, but losing herself in the droning hum.

Miles later the rhythm altered as the truck slowed down. Diana opened her eyes to glance out Holt's side, expecting to see the light from the ranch yard. He caught her look and nodded to the right.

"Would you like to stop here for a while?"

Diana looked in the direction he had indicated and recognized the rest stop where she and Guy had been this morning. Her gaze jerked back to Holt, wary and alarmed.

"Why?"

"You found it an idyllic spot before. I thought you still might be in the mood."

"You saw us." She wanted to leap at him and claw his eyes out.

"I left shortly after you and Guy did this morning. When I saw the ranch truck parked there, naturally I slowed down. It was entirely possible that you were having a mechanical problem." Holt started out speaking in a cool, flat tone, but she could hear the anger mounting. "That was before I had a glimpse of what was going on inside the cab. You are a consummate little actress, Diana. If I hadn't seen you with Guy this morning, I might have believed that—" He didn't finish it, his mouth thinning into a hard line.

"Was that your motive for this . . . the hotel room . . . everything?" Raw pain screamed through her nerves. "Some perverted kind of logic that said, 'if she's with me, she isn't with Guy'? Plus it was cheaper than some visit to a chicken ranch.''

Cold and ruthless, steel-gray eyes flashed to her. ''Maybe that's the solution—just make love to you until you're too exhausted to look for sex with any other man—most of all, Guy.''

Diana turned away holding back tears. She felt sick and sickened. Holt had all but called her a tramp, as he had done before. Right now, Diana felt like one. The miles to the ranch couldn't fly by fast enough. She felt the truck accelerate and guessed Holt shared her wish to get home quickly.

The silence between them was unnerving. It seemed forever before Diana saw the lights at the ranch winking through the grove of trees. Holt pulled the truck up to the stud pens, stepping out of the cab before the motor had completely died. Diana's leaden feet were much slower. By the time she walked to the rear of the van, he already had the ramp down and was leading the stallion out of the trailer stall.

Diana's gaze swept absently over the latest addition to their breeding program. The new stallion was a dapple-gray with black points, iron-gray shading to silver, fine-boned and finely muscled. A small muzzle, small pointed ears, an arched neck, and spirited carriage showed all the characteristics of a well-bred Arabian. The stallion pranced at the end of the lead, blowing out rolling snorts and testing the strange smells of his new surroundings. His concave head turned toward the distant paddock where the broodmares were held. He caught the scent of his future harem and sent out a strident, whickering call to them.

''Quiet, fella.'' Holt patted the sleek neck. ''You'll meet them soon enough.''

An eruption of sound came from the paddock, shouts and a rifle shot, followed immediately by frightened neighs and the thundering of hooves. Diana raced to the stud corral, climbing to the top rail, mindless of her billowing skirt. Far off in the distance, she saw a ghost-white shape floating over the desert sage, moving ever closer to the shadowy recesses of the mountains. Their return had coincided with the night visit of the mustang stallion.

The commotion made the new stallion fractious. Holt had his hands full trying to hold him and calm him. "Open the stable door and the one to his stall," he snapped the order to Diana.

Practicality demanded that she obey. Stepping down from her fence perch, she hurried to the stable, pushed open the door, and went on to the large stall that had been Shêtan's. Moving out of the way as Holt followed, she didn't linger in the stable. Outside Diana walked swiftly toward the main house. Her path through the shadowed yard took her by the larger stable-barn. Gravel crunched to one side of her, and Diana jumped in alarm.

"Sorry we waked ya." Rube stepped from the darkness. The barrel of the rifle in his hand gleamed in the yard light. "It was that goddamned white stallion again."

"I guessed that." She let him think she had been asleep at the house.

He noticed her downward glance at the rifle he held. "It's a-gettin' to be that the sound of a rifle shot is the only thing he respects."

"You didn't shoot *at* him?"

"Hell, no! Do I look like some kinda goddamned fool?!! I ain't gonna risk hittin' one of the Major's mares. He'd have my skin if I did that. 'Sides, Holt never gave no orders about killin' the horse, only scarin' him off."

"I'm sorry, Rube. I should have known you wouldn't be irresponsible. Good night."

"Good night." He was grumbling to himself as she walked away.

A light was on in her father's room, the door standing open. "Is that you, Diana?" he called as she entered the hallway.

"Yes, Major." She paused at the door, her heart in

her throat, wondering what she would say if he asked her where she had been.

"I suppose all that racket was because of that wild stallion?" Pajama-clad, he looked half-asleep and exceedingly tired.

"Yes, it was."

The Major sighed in resignation and reached to switch off the lamp on his nightstand. "I should have known. Good night."

Morning brought only questions about the new stallion from the Major and a rather absent comment: "It must have been late when you returned. No trouble with the stallion, I hope."

Diana had her answer ready. "No. Some weather system delayed the plane's takeoff from California."

Since he didn't ask, she didn't have to find an answer for how she and Holt had amused themselves in the interim. She almost gagged on a piece of toast. "Amuse." God, that was the right word. Holt had amused himself with her while extracting a savage revenge.

The excuse of a genuine headache kept her from accompanying the Major to the stud pens to see the new stallion and allowed her to skip lunch, thus avoiding Holt for one day. She spent most of the afternoon lying on her bed. Diana felt like one big ache—physical, as well as emotional, and sincerely hoped that Holt was as sore as she was. Two sleeping pills taken after the evening meal ensured her of a night of sound sleep. Nothing disturbed her.

"How do you feel this morning?" The Major's question greeted her as she arrived at the breakfast table.

"Much better." Her head felt slightly woolly. Diana blamed it on the aftereffects of the sleeping drug.

"Rest is a marvelous cure, especially when there are

no disturbances in the night." He passed her the pitcher of orange juice.

"Yes." She didn't catch the significance of his remark.

"We didn't have a visit from that wild stallion."

Diana lifted her head. "Oh. Maybe he's finally given up."

"I hope so."

After breakfast, Diana resumed her ritual of a morning ride. She rode far out in the desert, away from all signs of civilization. She raced a jackrabbit until he outmaneuvered her nimble gelding and escaped. She paused to watch a flock of desert bluebirds skim across the top of the sage. But, inevitably, she had to return to the ranch.

There seemed to be virtually no one about the ranch yard. All the vehicles except one were gone. Since it was still too early for lunch, Diana wandered to the stud pens, wanting to see the new stallion in the daylight.

When she saw Guy in the pen working the gray stallion on a lounge line, Diana hesitated, then continued forward. His back was to her as she climbed the fence to sit on the top rail. He turned slowly with the circling horse and finally saw her. She spoke before he could.

"Beautiful, isn't he?" The stallion was even more impressive in the daylight.

"Dynamite." He halted the horse and walked forward to unsnap the line. "That's enough for today, fella." The stallion tossed his head and trotted away, moving lightly on his feet. Guy coiled the lead as he walked to the fence. He joined her on the top rail and watched the stallion. "You weren't at lunch yesterday."

"I had a headache. Sophie brought me some soup."

"I've never known you to have headaches. In fact, I can't remember you ever being sick."

"That's true. But this last year, with Rand and me breaking up and the divorce, I've had a lot of headaches. Nerves, the doctor said. But they rarely last very long." God, she was turning into an excellent liar.

"Did you enjoy yourself with Peggy the other afternoon?"

"We had a marvelous time."

"You said they were going to bring you home."

It was finally out. It was almost a relief. "I know."

"But you didn't come home with them."

"No. I rode back with Holt."

"And it was late, too. I know because I was up until midnight, and you still weren't back then."

"The plane that flew the stallion in was delayed by bad weather."

"What did you do all that time?"

The proprietorial demand in his voice irritated her. There was an icy sparkle in her blue eyes when she turned to look at him. "You know that you don't have any right to cross-examine me this way."

He couldn't hold her level stare. "Jeez, Diana, I—"

A pain-pitched squeal screamed through the air. Diana's gaze jumped to the enclosure where the mares were penned. They were milling together in agitation, colts whinnying in unknown fear. Amidst the mostly dark bodies and the dust stirred by their hooves, Diana caught a flash of white.

"My God, the stallion is inside the fence," she said, drawing in an incredulous breath.

"How did he know there was no one guarding the mares during the daytime?" For an instant, they were both paralyzed by disbelief. Then Guy vaulted from the fence. "I'm going to run the gray inside. You go get a rifle and meet me at the paddock."

Diana raced for the main house, the one place where she knew for sure where the rifles were kept. Her mad dash didn't stop as she slammed into the house straight to the gun cabinet, stretching to reach the key on top.

"What's the matter, Diana?" The Major stood in the study doorway.

"The white stallion is in with the mares." Unlocking

the door, she grabbed a rifle and a box of cartridges, pausing only to make certain they were the right caliber.

"Now?!!"

"Yes." Diana pushed her way past him and raced out the door.

Her lungs were on fire by the time she ran across the large ranch yard and behind the long stable to the paddock. The muscles in her legs quivered as she forced them to climb her over the fence. On the other side, she paused to catch her breath and looked for Guy. He was halfway across the paddock, walking toward the horses at the far end. She could hear a cracking pop sound and realized he had grabbed a whip from the stable.

Diana started after him at a stumbling run. She could see the white stallion clearly now. He had cut two mares out of the herd—Nashira and Cassie, the two mares he had stolen before. He drove them to a break in the fence where two rails were down. But the white stallion wasn't content to reclaim his former property. Once the two mares were outside the enclosure, he returned to the herd, never flicking an ear at the man who hurriedly approached.

A bay mare with a colt at her side was singled out by the stallion. Frantically, the mare tried to elude him and return to the safety of the herd, but snapping teeth and slashing hooves turned back every attempt. Finally, the mare and colt leaped over the low rails and joined the other two obediently waiting for the stallion.

As the stallion went back for a fourth, Diana twisted a foot and fell to her knees. Guy was still fifty yards away. She had neither the strength nor the breath to call to him. And they were running out of time.

Resting the rifle on her thighs, she flipped open the box of cartridges and began shoving shells into the chamber. She glanced up once. This time the stallion had selected a gray mare, also with a colt. The mare had started to lie down in an effort to resist the stallion's attempts, but a savage nip on her flank brought the mare to her feet.

Diana's trembling fingers had only managed four bullets. She cocked the rifle, hoping it was enough. She fired into the air, the explosion deafening to her ears. The mare and colt were racing for the broken fence with the stallion pacing at their heels. She fired again and again and again. Then the hammer clicked. After lowering the rifle, Diana brushed the hair out of her eyes.

The four mares, two colts, and the white stallion were fleeing for the mountains. Two of the mares already knew his directions. The two with foals were learning. And the stallion, white as snow with a gait as smooth as glass, was a hard taskmaster.

"My God, did you see that?" Guy dropped to his knees beside her, shaking his head in wonder as he stared after the fast disappearing horses. "He took four this time, just as neat as you please, right from under our noses."

"Four mares and two colts," Diana corrected him breathlessly. There were footsteps behind her in the tall grass. She turned as the Major strode toward them. He looked winded, yet strangely exhilarated.

"Wasn't anyone around? Didn't anyone see the stallion before he got in with the mares? Wasn't anyone watching?"

"No." Guy scrambled to his feet. "Who ever thought the stallion would be so bold as to make his raid in the daytime? It was fantastic."

"Yes, I know. I saw it."

"Should we go after them now? Try to catch up with them before they reach the mountains?"

"No." The Major shook his head. "At the rate they're traveling, they'll be in the mountains by the time you get a horse saddled and leave the yard. But get that fence fixed before any of the mares stray through it."

"Right away." Guy handed the coiled whip to Diana

and started for the fence break at a jog.

Her breathing had returned to normal and Diana pushed to her feet, the rifle hooked under her arm, the muzzle pointed at the ground. She glanced at her father, not liking the pallor in his face.

"You shouldn't have come."

"It's probably the closest look I'll ever get at that white stallion." He was staring sightlessly at the mountains, as if he was seeing it all again. In that look, there was conflict. Admiration for a magnificent piece of horseflesh was overshadowed by the threat the horse represented.

"Let's go back to the house, Major." Diana wasn't certain he had heard her, but finally he turned to start back.

"There was a lot of superstition in the Old West about white horses. Some of it even extends into the present day." He seemed to be speaking his thoughts aloud, aware of his audience of one, yet blind to it. "It was believed white horses were weak and lacked endurance. During Crook's campaign against the Sioux in '76, a troup of his cavalry was mounted on white horses, but they stood up no better than the other horses. The Indian's didn't want a white horse because it was too easily seen at night. Probably the same reason why mountain men—and later, the cowboys and other western men—avoided riding white horses. Yet, despite all this prejudice, a white horse is still a symbol of pride and power and supremacy. How many great men and conquerors rode white horses? The list is probably endless. A strange contradiction," he murmured to himself. "A strange contradiction."

Chapter XVI

Seated at the lunch table, Diana studied Holt through her lashes. He had looked at her only once, when he'd entered the house and acknowledged her presence with a curt nod. His expression was grim, angrily grim. He reminded Diana of a jungle cat that had been riled and was pretending to ignore the object of his anger while his tail lashed the air with mounting rage. A shiver danced over her skin and she let her gaze slide to his hands, the hands that had such intimate knowledge of her body.

Waves of heat washed through her, the heat of desire. She stared at her plate, fighting back the flood of longing, and tried to concentrate on the words he was saying instead of the ache in the pit of her stomach.

". . . take an extra string of horses and enough supplies for a week, just in case. We'll leave tomorrow at first light."

The Major nodded agreement with the plans and asked, "Who are you taking with you?"

"Rube, Guy, myself, and probably Don."

This time Diana didn't invite herself along. Guy gave her an expectant look. He seemed extremely tense, deeply troubled, and angered by something. It was a razor-sharp glance he darted at Holt, but he didn't say a word.

Diana spent the afternoon doing the ranch paperwork. By dinner's end, she was ready to escape the confines of the house, but she wandered no farther than the wood porch. Using an upright post as a backrest, Diana sat on the porch railing, her legs stretched out on the flat board. She watched a lingering sunset painting the distant mountain slopes with yellow and orange.

From the lengthening shadows of the shade trees, she saw Guy approaching the house. Instead of walking onto the porch, he came to the rail where Diana sat. He looked up at her, his expression confused and tense.

"Will you walk with me? There's something I have to talk to you about."

It was on the tip of her tongue to beg off by saying she was tired, but the urgency in his tone made her decide to go along. He wasn't suggesting a romantic stroll, hand in hand into the sunset. Something was seriously bothering him, and it wasn't her.

"All right."

She swung her legs off the rail to hop to the ground. Guy's hands closed around her waist to help her down. Then he shoved them in his pockets and started walking back through the trees, his stride long and revealing an inner agitation. When they were away from the house, Diana put a hand on his arm to stop the running walk.

"What is it?"

Guy stared at her, searching her face with an intensity that brought a frown. "Has the Major said what he plans to do about the white stallion?"

"No." Her frown deepened.

"He hasn't talked to Holt about it?"

"All they have discussed is getting the mares back. Why?"

"Because I think . . ." He raked a hand through his sandy hair. "I think Holt is going to kill him."

"What? Did he say that?"

"No." His hand doubled into a fist, clutching the air

as if trying to grasp some invisible line and hold on. "It's just a feeling I have. But I know I'm right."

"No." Diana didn't want to believe it.

"You know what he thinks about the stallion," Guy argued. "He considers it a pest, a nuisance. He'd have no more compunction about killing it than a fly. Don't you see? Holt probably wouldn't say anything about it to the Major, because I don't think the Major wants to have the stallion destroyed."

"I think you are being overly dramatic." She moved away to escape the mist of panic Guy was trying to envelop her in. He caught at her arms and turned her back to face him.

"What if I'm right? What if, when Holt rides out of here tomorrow morning, it's with every intention of coming back with the stallion dead?"

"Then you'll have to stop him—*if* that's what he intends to do."

"Me? How? Who's going to listen to me? Holt? Rube? Don? They all think I'm still a snot-nosed kid. Besides, he can convince them of anything. Rube and Don will do whatever he tells them. I couldn't stop them. He's the boss. But you, you're the Major's daughter, you could."

"Holt would never listen to me," Diana argued.

"But if you were along, he might think twice. And the other two would listen to you, because you would be speaking for the Major. He may not hold the reins, but he still owns the bridle. You've got to come with us."

"No." She turned her head away. Guy didn't know what he was asking. "You talk to the Major."

"It wouldn't do any good. Holt and the Major are as close as . . ." Guy impatiently searched for a comparison.

". . . a father and son." Diana's voice was flat.

"Yes, as a father and son should be," he agreed. "It's up to you, Diana. Do you want the stallion dead?"

"No!"

"Then do something." He cupped her cheek in his hand and forced her to look at him. "Have you ever seen a more beautiful animal in your life than that stallion? Wild and proud and free. Picture him with a bullet hole in his head and his brains spilled all over the ground. That's what's going to happen, Diana!"

"No!" She shut her eyes, but it only made the mental image clearer.

"You've got to come along."

"Holt won't want me to go with you."

"So what? He couldn't stop you the last time, and he sure as hell won't be able to stop you now. You've got to come along."

Diana hesitated. There was just enough logic in the conclusions Guy had drawn to make it the truth. Didn't she know how ruthless Holt could be? Hadn't he indicated before that he felt the stallion should be destroyed? Hadn't she seen the look of a hunter in his eye?

"I'll come," she agreed at last.

"I knew I could count on you." Relief swept over Guy's face. "I knew you'd be on my side in this. I'm going to enjoy seeing Holt's face when I tell him." He laughed with triumph. "They're getting everything packed and ready to go for in the morning. I'll go down now to let them know you're coming so there'll be provisions for you."

"All right." She was less enthusiastic about her decision, but once committed, Diana wouldn't back down. "I'd better get my things ready."

The birth of a new day came silently. There was little talk among the departing group of riders. What was exchanged was said in hushed tones. The Major had not been surprised by Diana's decision. He had said he expected it. Rube and Don had welcomed her into the hunt. Holt had not offered her any greeting at all.

They crossed the valley to the mountains at a

shuffling trot. Don was in charge of the fresh string of horses and Rube led the two packhorses. Guy rode beside Diana while Holt took the lead. Their destination was the waterhole in the mountain canyon. Holt occasionally checked the stallion's trail to verify that their general directions were the same.

An hour into the mountains, Diana noticed a pair of circling dark objects in the sky. "Look." She pointed.

"Yes, I see them. Those scavenging ravens are having a feast on something," Guy commented with grim acceptance of nature's laws.

The farther they rode, the closer they came to the area where the scavenging birds were gathering and landing. The dead animal was going to be very close to the route they were taking. A gully cut down a mountain slope by the runoffs of rain yawned ahead of them. They had crossed it before, the first time they had gone after the stallion. Its sides were steep, but negotiable by a horse and rider.

Holt reined his horse in at the edge, paused, then sent his horse down the slope. His descent was followed by a chorus of caws and flapping wings as the large black birds took flight in alarm. As Diana and Guy reached the gully, Holt was dismounting. At the bottom was the body of one of the colts. Holt crouched on one knee beside the inert form. A gagging lump was in Diana's throat as Rube and Don rode up.

"Its neck is broken." Holt straightened, his mouth hard and thin.

"Prob'ly took a tumble comin' down this gully. Poor thing was prob'ly all tuckered out after comin' all this way. It's a shame. It's a goddamned shame," Rube grumbled.

"Get a shovel out of one of those packs so we can bury him." Holt's horse was nervous, tugging at the reins, disliking the smell of blood and death.

When the colt was buried, they pushed on, a solemn group. At the waterhole, there were fresh tracks, lots of them. The stallion had brought the mares here and left. Diana stared at the churned-up earth.

"He was trainin' them new mares." Rube spoke behind her, reading the curious expression on her face and guessing what she was thinking. "A wild stallion always has to teach a new mare to take his orders. Sometimes he spends hours bunchin' 'em together or sendin' 'em runnin'. He'll even keep 'em from water 'til he says it's okay. He probably had a time with that mare that lost her colt."

"Yes, I suppose so." Diana shielded her eyes from the afternoon sun and looked back to the waterhole where the others had taken the horses to drink. "Where do you think they are now?"

"Ain't nowhere near here, I'm a-bettin'. We'd better be gettin' back with the others an' see what Holt has up his sleeve, don't ya think?"

Together they returned to the waterhole, Diana walking to her horse and Rube moving toward Holt. He was uncinching his saddle. He flicked a glance at Rube and continued his task.

"We're saddling the fresh horses. Don, Guy, and I are going to ride out and see if we can locate the herd. You can set up our base camp here."

Diana turned at his announcement. "Here?" she questioned his decision. "But if our camp is here, the horses won't come in for water."

"The stallion won't. If the mares get thirsty enough, they might." He swung the saddle off his horse to the ground and draped the damp pad over the horn. He never once looked at her, only through her at the others. "We'll be back in three hours."

Twenty minutes later the three men had changed to fresh horses and were riding out of the canyon. Rube and Diana set to work establishing their camp. Rube chose a site a discreet distance from the water to enable the smaller wild animals to come and drink without feeling too threatened by humans.

When the men returned in three hours, the camp was all set up. The horses were staked out to graze. A fire was burning, started by a grumbling Rube, who claimed it was the only reason he was along. Diana had their meal all prepared and ready to cook. The coffee had already boiled.

"Did ya see him?" Rube waited to take the reins of the horses as the men dismounted.

"We didn't even get a glimpse of him," Guy answered as Holt walked to the fire and poured himself a cup of coffee without so much as a glance at Diana, who stood right beside it.

"Didn't ya trail him?"

"We lost the tracks in some rough ground, made a couple of sweeps in the area, but couldn't pick it up again." Don walked to the fire. He was a small wiry man with balding hair and had a perpetual smile weathered into his face and a complexion that blushed easily. "Damn, that coffee smells good. Where are the cups?"

Together Rube and Guy unsaddled the horses, rubbed them down, and staked them out with the others. Diana started cooking the meal, Holt's silence pressing on her like a deadening gloom. Don wasn't extremely talkative, either, influenced by Holt's lack of conversation and a natural reticence about making casual conversation with the Major's daughter.

They were all seated around the fire, cross-legged, plates balanced in their laps, eating. "It ain't a-gonna be easy gettin' close to that goddamned stallion this time," Rube said, chewing his food as he talked. "I'll bet he'll spook at his own goddamned shadow. Chances are he's gonna see us long before we see him, an' he'll send them mares a-flyin' when he does. We got ourselves a job cut out for us this time. What we need is an airplane."

"What we need is a heliocopter in this terrain, but we might have to do some explaining if we rented one." Holt scraped the last bit of food from his plate and set it down. Rolling to his feet, he walked to the fire and refilled his cup. Without a word, he left the camp circle and wandered into the dusky shadows.

"What's with him, anyway?" Rube mumbled, but no one answered.

When the others were finished, Diana cleaned up the dishes and packed them away. The coffeepot was practically empty. She swished the grounds.

"I'm going to get some water for coffee in the morning," she told the others.

"I'll get it for you," Guy offered, springing to his feet.

"No, thanks. I have to make a trip out there, anyway."

She walked the short distance to the waterhole. Scrubby cottonwoods rose on the near bank of the water. Through the shadows cast by their limbs, Diana saw the moonlight glinting on the smooth surface of the water. It was a beacon to show her the way.

Kneeling on the sandy edge, she let a little water flow into the coffeepot, swished it around, and poured it on the ground. Then she dipped the pot deeper into the water to fill it. A red light glowed a few feet away, the burning tip of a cigarette. It was Holt. He had seen her come and hadn't spoken.

"The silent treatment isn't going to work," Diana said irritably. "If you think by shunning me, my feelings are going to get hurt and I'll go back to the ranch, you're wrong."

"Why did you come?" His voice came to her from the night's stillness, low and impersonal. "Couldn't you stand the thought of being separated from Guy for a week?"

She rose, rigid and angry that he could accuse her of wanting anyone else. "That had nothing to do with it."

"Didn't it?" He moved from the concealing shadows, looming in front of her, the brim of his hat shading his face.

"No, it didn't."

"Your sudden decision didn't have anything to do with that furtive little stroll you and Guy took last night, out in the trees where no one could see you."

"For your information, all we did was talk, and I don't give a damn whether you believe me or not!" Liar, a little voice inside taunted.

"Talk?" Holt mocked her. "You spent a very long time talking."

"We had a very fascinating subject to discuss—namely, you." She saw his head draw back in surprise and knew she had scored a point. "Guy believes that you plan to kill the stallion. He intends to stop you."

"And you?"

"I don't want to see him killed. I'm sure the Major doesn't, either." She could feel the air crackling with his anger.

"We have two horses dead, the stallion, and now the colt—both of them because of that wild mustang. If a coyote got in a chicken coop, you'd shoot him. If a mountain lion started attacking the cattle, you'd track him down and kill him. If a sheepdog began killing sheep, you'd have him put away." He spoke in an ominously low voice. "What does it take to make the two of you see that this horse is just another animal that's gone bad?!!"

"You are going to shoot him."

"No. We are here to get the mares."

"Holt—"

"Diana?" Guy was calling for her.

"Go on. Lover boy wants you." Holt stepped away.

Diana hesitated, but she didn't want Guy finding her with Holt and have to fend off all his jealous questions. She picked up the coffeepot and started back for camp.

"I was beginning to wonder what had happened to you." Guy met her halfway.

"I'm a big girl." She laughed away his concern. "I can take care of myself. And if I can't, I have a healthy scream."

Fifteen minutes went by before Holt came back to the fire, approaching the camp from a different direction. Diana knew he hadn't wanted Guy suspecting that they had met or talked when she had gone to the waterhole.

An hour later they were all stretched out in their bedrolls. When Diana fell asleep, she dreamed about the hours she had spent with Holt in the hotel room. It was a warm, wonderful dream where everything was perfect, minus the bitter ending.

A hand touched her shoulder and a familiar voice told her to wake up. She opened her eyes and looked into Holt's face. Suddenly it all seemed part of her dream. She smiled at him, all loving and soft.

"Wake up," he told her again, his jaw hardening.

"Good morning." It was almost a purr.

Her arms curved around his neck and she stretched like a cat. Diana saw the frown on his face, but she knew how to make it go away. Lifting her head, she pressed her lips against his mouth, moving, tasting and persuasive. His momentary resistance gave way to hard demand. His kiss drove her backward against the hard ground, a hand cupping her breast. Her lips parted to experience to full ecstasy of his possessive kiss.

Suddenly, there was nothing as Holt abruptly levered away from her, cursing silently beneath his breath. The gray eyes were cold and angry when he looked at her startled and confused face.

"Fix the coffee while I wake up the others."

The dream vanished as Diana realized where she was. Her gaze swept the half-circle of sleeping figures. Shaking in reaction, she sat up and reached for her boots.

The breakfast was thrown together in a hurry, not one of her better efforts, but no one seemed to notice; or at least they were too polite to comment about it. Don was saddling the horses while Diana finished cleaning up. She noticed he had saddled neither of her horses.

Holt handed her his empty cup and Diana challenged: "Why isn't my horse being saddled?" When he didn't immediately answer and gave her one of his shuttered looks instead, her temper flared. "If you think I'm going to hang around this camp like some squaw while you go out looking for the mares, you had better think again."

"You—"

"I don't take orders from you." She never gave him a chance to answer. "Don, saddle my horse!" Diana called to the hand. "I'm going with the rest of you." And she turned back, challenging Holt to override her command.

"It's your neck." With an invisible shrug, Holt turned away.

All day they searched for the stallion and the mares, coming back to the camp at noon to change horses and eat. Twice they caught a glimpse of the band, miles away and running. At nightfall they returned to the camp, hot, tired, and hungry.

The second day proved as unsuccessful as the first. The third day wasn't any better. As the horses entered the canyon at a tired shuffling trot, Diana felt there was an acre of Nevada soil clogging her pores. When they dismounted at the camp, she handed her reins to Guy.

"Would you mind taking care of my horse? I'm going to try to wash some of this grit away before I fix our supper."

"That's the best thing I've heard all day." Guy took her reins, a weary smile on his mouth. "Save some water for me."

Pausing to pick up a pot that would serve both as a basin to hold the water and a means to heat it, Diana started for the waterhole. As she was leaving, she saw Rube approaching the camp circle.

"When you get the fire going, Rube, why don't you reheat the coffee left over from this noon?" Diana tossed the suggestion over her shoulder, not slowing her strides.

She could hear him talking to himself as she moved away. "Get the fire goin', Rube. Put the coffee on, Rube. You'd think I was a goddamned—" His mumbles faded into the wind.

In the shade of the cottonwoods, Diana flipped the hat off her head to hang down her back suspended by the string around her throat. Bending at the water's edge, she dipped the pot into the pool. The water felt cool and refreshing against her hand. It intensified the sticky, grimy dust which coated her skin.

Taking the handkerchief from her pocket, Diana moistened it in the water and began wiping the rivulets of sweat from her neck and throat. Wetting it again, she began wiping her cheeks and forehead, a preliminary rinsing in anticipation of heated water and soap back at camp. Footsteps approached through the trees. Diana didn't bother to look around.

"Wouldn't you love to just dive into the middle of that pool, Guy? What I wouldn't give for a nice cool bath!" she sighed longingly.

"And to make love afterward—is that what you have in mind?"

Holt's taunting voice brought Diana to her feet. The icy control in his face sent her heart thumping against her ribs. He was standing very close, an arm's reach away, and his manner was threatening. The water was at her feet. Diana couldn't back away.

"Why are you twisting an innocent comment into something suggestive? That wasn't what I said or meant." Her defense was in attacking.

"Wasn't it?" he countered through clenched teeth. "You are forgetting that I know you." He took a step forward and Diana tried to slip past him, but he caught her easily. Contact with him ended her resistance. His hand cupped the back of her head, forcing her to look at his face. "It's been a long time, hasn't it?"

Her body trembled. It didn't matter what Holt was referring to. Her flesh knew how much it had missed the caress of his hands and the fire of his kisses. Diana gazed at his powerfully male features, her senses clamoring in response to his hard and punishing embrace.

As if sensing her response, Holt began covering her cheeks, eyes, and mouth with rough kisses. "You wanted to dive into the pool, splash and swim naked in the water"—growling the accusations against her skin—"later, to crawl up on the bank and make love. That's what you and Guy did that other time."

Diana twisted her head away, hating him for bringing up that misadventure with Guy. "Yes." Her voice was raw and rasping with pain. "So you could watch. You get some vicarious thrill out of watching us, don't you?" The hand gripping her arm tightened so fiercely she thought the bone would snap. She didn't find out what his method of retaliation might be as Guy's voice shattered the moment.

"Hey, Diana, what's keeping you? Did the waterhole run dry or—" He emerged from the trees and froze. His face went first, white with shock, then livid with rage. "Let her go!"

Alarm pulsed through her, aware the scene was teetering on the edge of violence. She strained against Holt's hold. He glanced down at her, a cold smile in his eyes.

"Sure. But she needs cooling off."

As he released her, Holt gave her a push. She stumbled backward into the water. A gasping cry ripped from her throat as Diana lost her footing on the slippery rocks and sat down with a resounding splash. Stunned and outraged, she couldn't will herself to move.

"I warned you to stay away from her. If you've hurt—"

"Save it." Holt's voice sliced off Guy's threat. "I think your lady fair needs rescuing."

Torn between wanting to go to Diana's aid and confronting his father, Guy did neither as Holt strided past him into the trees. With his second option eliminated, Guy waded into the water.

"Are you all right?" He took the hand she extended to him and pulled her upright.

Her Levi's were sopping wet. Water filled her boots. Her blouse was splattered where it wasn't completely soaked. Her rump tingled from the hard landing, but she was otherwise unhurt.

"I'm okay."

"I ought to—" Guy cast a murderous look over his shoulder.

"Forget it." Diana shouldered the blame. "It was my fault. I made him angry." Just by breathing.

"What happened? What did you say?" He kept a hand at her elbow as they waded through the shallow water to dry ground.

"Does it matter?" She shrugged away his question. "After these last three days, we're all tired and irritable. Holt's temper was on a short fuse. It didn't take much of a spark to light it. Just leave it at that."

"I suppose," he gave in grudgingly. "But if he—"

"Do me a favor, Guy?" Diana sat down to pull off her boots and empty out the water squishing inside them. "Go back to camp and get me some dry clothes. And don't pick a fight with Holt," she added with heavy impatience. "It isn't worth it."

"One of these days, I'll kill him." He breathed in deeply, then nodded a reluctant agreement and walked away to carry out her request. Cold shivers raced over Diana's skin.

Chapter XVII

The morning of the fourth day they came upon the band and the chase was on. As they had the previous time, they pursued the horses in relays, each rider taking a leg, including Diana. This time the stallion refused to leave the mares, relentlessly driving them on, sporadically stampeding them in an effort to escape the pursuit.

The sun had angled past the midday point into the afternoon and Diana marveled at the endurance the band displayed under the stallion's leadership, especially that of the white stallion. He seemed to cover four times as much ground as the mares, darting back and forth to keep any mare from lagging.

More than half a mile behind the herd, Diana watched the stallion suddenly accelerate to slice his way through the small band and force the buckskin mare in the lead to swerve in the direction he wanted her to go. Satisfied, the stallion fell back to the rear and continued pushing them on. She realized his domination was total.

It was exemplified further when the young colt could no longer maintain the pace and fell behind. Its mother tried desperately to stay with it, but the stallion unmercifully forced the mare on with raking hooves and snapping teeth.

When Diana overtook the foal, it was still trying to

stagger after the herd. Its weak, puny whinnies for its mother were plaintive, lost sounds. Frightened and too exhausted to flee, it stood trembling as Diana approached.

A mile ahead, she knew another rider was waiting to take over pursuit of the herd. She couldn't leave the colt behind. Reining in her horse, she dismounted and walked slowly toward it, leading her horse and talking softly to the colt. It jerked its head away at the first touch of her hand, then submitted to the contact.

She tried to lift the colt onto her saddle, but it was almost a dead weight in her arms. Diana couldn't lift it high enough to drape it over the saddle. Setting the colt on the ground, she tried to think of another solution.

The cantering hooves of several horses came from behind her. With her hands on her hips, Diana turned as Holt rode toward her, leading two fresh mounts. He checked the horses to a stop, a frown gathering on his forehead.

"What's wrong?" He hadn't seen the colt until after he had asked the question. "Is he hurt?"

"Exhausted."

Guessing her problem, Holt swung out of his saddle. "I'll hand him up to you." Diana mounted and waited while Holt picked up the foal and draped him across the saddle in front of her. "Take him back to camp. He's probably hungry, as well as tired. If you have any dried milk, mix some up for him. If not, feed him some sweetened water. Who's ahead of you?"

The colt struggled briefly, then quieted under Diana's hand. "Don, I think. He should be waiting about a mile up."

"We'll keep pushing the stallion until sundown." Holt remounted. "Take care of the colt. I'd like to take one of them back alive to the Major." He rode off and Diana started back to camp at a walk.

It was dark when the four men rode into the camp. The evening meal was simmering on the edge of the fire. Diana sat close to the warmth. The chestnut colt was curled up beside her like a puppy dog, its dainty head resting on her lap, sound asleep.

"How's the colt?" Holt walked over to examine it, squatting on his heels beside her.

"Doesn't seem to be any worse for the experience." Diana tried to match his impersonal but conversational tone.

"I think he's decided he doesn't need his mother now that he has you," Guy observed.

"It's amazing how everything seems to eat out of your hand." Holt's caustic murmur was barely audible, but Diana heard it.

"He's lucky he didn't break one of those spindly legs, considering the rough ground we went over today," Don said, reaching for a plate Diana had stacked in readiness by the fire. "Is it all right if we eat?"

"Help yourself," Diana insisted. "I've already had mine."

"That little fella is lucky to be alive." Rube joined them around the fire. "I had an old mustanger tell me one time that some stallions will kill the colts rather than have 'em hold back the whole herd. It ain't a common practice, mind ya. But it's been known to happen. An' I wouldn't be surprised at anything from this stallion."

"Tomorrow should do it," Don said. "If we push that band as hard tomorrow as we did today, we'll get those mares."

"They could be miles away by morning." Diana watched as the men dished up their plates.

"Ain't likely. Maybe the stallion isn't, but them mares are goddamned tired—too tired to eat, probably, or get much rest. They won't be more'n a couple of miles from where we left 'em," Rube predicted.

He was right. Approximately two miles from the point where they had abandoned the chase the night before, they found the stallion and mares. Showing no sign of weariness, the white stallion had the mares bunched and at a run within seconds after sighting the riders.

It seemed to start out as a repetition of the previous day. Then Diana began to notice that each relay rider was following closer and closer to the herd. Instead of the distance varying from a mile to a half-mile, it became a half-mile to a quarter-mile. The mares were tiring badly. Only the tyranny of their master kept them going. And the stallion still refused to leave them. It was as if he knew the riders were after the mares he had stolen.

The sun was a white-hot ball directly overhead and Diana was on her third relay lap, driving the herd down a long mountain valley. They were approaching an area where a smaller valley intersected with the main one. The buckskin mare had always tried to veer into it, leading the band where the terrain was rougher and pursuit more difficult. Rube was stationed there to keep the herd heading straight down the main valley and take Diana's place in the chase.

Diana eased her horse into a slow canter as the buckskin mare angled for the mouth of the smaller valley. Almost immediately, Rube appeared in the center of the opening to race down the center of the main valley. The lead mare swerved away violently, the other mares following, finding the reserve strength to break into a hard gallop. Rube urged his horse into a canter to intercept the path of pursuit and relieve Diana.

Her horse willingly responded to the checking pressure of the bit and slowed into a hard trot, tossing his head, foam flicking from his lathered neck. As Diana watched Rube angle toward the band, she saw the white stallion become aware of his second pursuer. With a shake of his white mane, he switched directions. A whistling scream rent the air in challenge. Her eyes widened as the stallion charged at his enemy, his neck snaked low, his ears flat against his head.

"Rube!" Diana screamed in warning.

But Rube had already seen the sudden attack and was pulling back on the reins. His horse sensed the danger from the stallion and reacted with fear, plunging and fighting the hands on the reins. Diana could see Rube waving his arm and shouting, trying to scare off the stallion. She spurred her horse toward him.

Like a white fury, the stallion charged at the horse and rider. Rube tried to avoid it, manhandling his mount into a pivot. His horse panicked and reared. Rube clung to its neck like a monkey, but the horse overbalanced and fell backward onto his rider.

The white stallion wasn't satisfied to have his pursuer downed. With his ears back and his mouth open, he came again. Rube's horse scrambled to his feet and out of the way. Rube tried to do the same, but the white stallion was on him, iron hooves pounding him to the ground.

Diana's tired horse was stretched out in a run, skimming over the sage and grass, whipped by the reins on his flanks. The stallion whirled to face his new threat. For a terror-ridden moment, Diana thought he would attack her. But his blazing eyes turned to the fleeing band of mares, beginning to scatter without his commanding presence. In a flash, his long pacing stride was sending him after the mares, his harem.

As she neared the man on the ground, Diana pulled back hard on the reins. Her horse slid to a stop, momentarily stumbling to its knees before righting itself. In her haste, Diana jumped and fell out of the saddle, unconscious of the sobs that were coming from her throat. She saw Rube move as she ran to him, her legs trembling from the shock of what she'd seen. He was lying on his side, moaning, when she reached him.

"Rube?" Diana carefully rolled him onto his back.

"Don't move me," he groaned, choked, and began coughing up blood.

"Oh, my God!" She was completely unaware of the tears in her eyes as she scrambled to her feet and ran to his horse. Grabbing the rifle from his scabbard, Diana fired it in the air three times in rapid succession. Then she raced back to his side, dropping the rifle on the ground.

"Goddamned stallion," Rube coughed.

"Lie still. Please, Rube, lie still. The others are coming."

He seemed to lapse into unconsciousness. Not knowing what else to do, Diana ran to her own horse for the canteen. Wetting her handkerchief, she began wiping his face and the blood from his mouth. His shirt was torn and there were marks all over his chest where the stallion's hooves had struck him.

It seemed forever before she heard the galloping sound of approaching horses. All three—Holt, Don, and Guy—arrived within seconds of each other. Diana rose, knees quivering, to meet them.

"What happened?" Holt snapped out the question as he brushed past her to kneel beside Rube.

Diana wasn't certain that he listened when she told him. She was surprised at how steady her voice sounded, considering how she felt inside. Although tears still welled in her eyes, she had stopped crying. She was partially aware that Holt was trying to determine the extent of Rube's injuries, checking his pulse and other vital signs. He was alive. Diana saw Holt rock back on his heels, his hands doubling into fists as he stared at the man.

"Goddamn you, Rube," he muttered beneath his breath, but the cursing seemed to be for his own helplessness and the frustration it brought.

With eyes still closed, Rube's mouth twisted in a painful smile. "Screwed myself up, didn't I, Holt?" He started coughing again, spitting up more blood.

"You'll make it. Just hold on." It was an order, impatient and angry. Both emotions were in his expression as he straightened, hard gray eyes regarding Don and Guy in turn. "Take Rube's horse and ride for the ranch. Get some help out here. And you, Guy, go back to camp and bring back some blankets. You go with him, Diana."

"No!" She had the horrible feeling he was sending her away so she wouldn't be around when— Diana refused to finish that thought. Don was in the saddle and spurring his horse toward the ranch.

"Let 'er stay, Holt." Rube's hoarse voice unexpectedly argued in her behalf. His right hand made a weak, reaching movement toward her, and Diana bent to her knees beside him, taking his hand and holding it, because she sensed it was what he wanted. Opening his eyes seemed to be an effort. They were glazed with pain when he looked at her. "Your eyes are as blue as heaven. I was always gonna tell ya that from the time ya was a little tyke. Yessir, like heaven." He started coughing again. She fumbled for her handkerchief and wiped the trickle of blood from his chin. The tears were building up again. "There might not be no angels waitin' for me where I'm a-goin', so I'd better have one sittin' with me on this side of the Beyond."

"Go on, Guy," Holt ordered. "Ride!"

Diana glanced up as Guy reined away from them. Holt was stripping the saddles from the three remaining horses. He left them on the ground and carried the saddle blankets over to keep Rube warm.

"You're wastin' your time, Holt." A spasm of pain contorted the wizened features, leathery and gray beneath his tan.

"Ssh!" Diana touched her fingers to his lips. They came away sticky and warm with blood. "Don't talk, Rube. You've got to save your strength."

"Don't ya be a-tellin' me to shut up. Everybody's always a-tellin' me to shut up." He was indignant and hurt. "When a man's dyin', he's got a right to talk. An' people oughta listen instead of always ignorin' him."

"We'll listen, Rube. We'll listen," Diana promised, a tear sliding down her cheek. "But you aren't dying."

Again there was that twisted smile, but Rube didn't correct her last statement. He closed his eyes and seemed to rest for a while, as if the last outburst had taken a great toll on his strength. Holt was crouching on the opposite side of him, sitting on one heel, his expression unbearably grim. Diana knew her chin was quivering, but she couldn't control it.

"It's just as well I never married." Rube began talking again. "No goddamned daughter of mine would ever have been as perty as you. I used to pretend you was my little girl. Ain't that a laugh?" He tried to laugh, and he started choking again on his own blood, but he managed to add, "Imagine me thinkin' I was the Major."

Diana closed her eyes, squeezing them tight, and felt the tears running down her cheeks. She had never guessed, never suspected, that Rube had thought of her in that light. Why did a person always find out these things when it was too late?

"You're a good man, Rube." Her voice was small and taut. "Loyal and dependable. The Major always said so."

"Hell, you're a goddamned liar." He smiled and looked pleased despite the pain that twisted his face.

"Why don't you rest for a while, Rube? We can talk some more later," Holt suggested.

"Yeah, we'll talk more later," he agreed and seemed to sigh, as if he was very, very tired. His gnarled fingers continued to curl around Diana's hand, and she made no attempt to disengage them. When he hadn't moved for several minutes, Holt lifted an eyelid.

"He isn't dead?" She clutched at Rube's hand, staring at Holt.

"No. He's unconscious."

Diana swallowed at the lump in her throat. "He's bleeding internally, isn't he?"

"Yes." Holt pushed to his feet.

"Isn't there something we can do?"

"No." Holt turned away, lowering his head to rub the back of his neck.

Diana maintained her vigil at Rube's side, holding his hand, hardly changing her position. Her back and shoulders ached and her legs were numb. When Guy returned with the bedrolls from camp, they stripped the saddle pads away and covered him with the blankets from the bedrolls.

Rube stirred and coughed. "It's cold. Ain't nobody . . . gonna start a . . . goddamned fire?" His voice seemed to gurgle when he talked.

"Guy will do it this time," Diana told him, but he had seemed to drift away. She didn't know if he had heard her.

A fire wasn't needed for warmth, but Guy built one, anyway, to have something to do, more than anything else.

Two hours later, Rube died, quietly, without struggling. Diana slipped her hand from the loosened grip of his fingers, her eyes dry as Holt pulled the blanket over Rube's face.

Stiff and silent, she walked to the fire. She felt cold and sick. Someone put a blanket around her shoulders. She didn't know who and she didn't care.

Almost a full hour later, the whir of a helicopter broke the unearthly silence. Diana flew back with Rube's body and no one questioned why.

Chapter XVIII

A sack of clothes to be given to the Salvation Army sat outside the door of the small apartment. Diana put the last of the canned goods from the cupboard into another sack and carried it outside, as well. She walked back into the two-and-a-half-room unit. She checked the bathroom again to be sure she hadn't overlooked anything.

In the bedroom, she paused to stare at the brown suit laid neatly on the bed, and a white shirt, the only one Rube had owned. A stringed tie with a liberty-head dollar was on top of the suit, and a pair of boots sat on the floor by the bed, the polish not hiding the scratches of use. Everything there was destined for the funeral home.

The closet and chest of drawers were empty. Diana noticed the small drawer in the night table and walked over to open it. The only thing in it was a dog-eared Bible. Diana frowned. She had never known Rube was a religious man. She couldn't remember him ever going to church. She opened it and found a name scrawled on the inside cover—Anna May Carter Spencer. His mother?

Sighing, Diana turned to carry it to the kitchen table, where the rest of his meager personal possessions were collected in a basket. Something slipped from the pages of the Bible and fluttered to the floor. It was an old photograph, a picture of her when she was eight or nine. Diana's jaw tightened briefly as she replaced the picture in the Bible. She set it on the table instead of in the basket.

Diana tried to remember what she'd thought of Rube when she was growing up, but no impression lingered. She guessed she had taken his existence for granted, never concerning herself with what his dreams might be. If anything, she had probably regarded him as a silly old coot, in an indifferent sort of way. Everyone had dreams.

There were footsteps and the screen door to the far unit of the fourplex opened and closed. Diana glanced around the small, empty room and picked up the basket containing Rube's belongings. She carried it outside and walked to the last unit.

Her knock on the screen door brought Holt's response of: "Come in." He was drying his hands on a towel as she entered. He turned, irritation flitting across his face when he saw her. The gray eyes seemed to look very old and very tired. "What is it?" He hung the towel on a hook.

Diana was too numbed to be upset by his unwelcoming tone. "I have been cleaning out Rube's place. There are a few personal items here that I didn't know what to do with." She set the basket on the table. "There isn't much: his razor, a pocketknife, his watch, a radio, and a couple of other things—nothing that's worth very much, but I thought . . ."—she shoved her hands in the pockets of her jeans as Holt walked to the table—" . . . maybe there's something here that some of the boys might like to have. I thought you would know and could see that they got it."

"Yes, I'll take care of it."

She continued to stare at the contents of the basket. "There's a sack of canned goods, too. The flour was wormy. Stuff like that I had to throw out. There's some beer in the refrigerator and some butter and eggs. I left it there for the time being. It isn't much, is it?" Her voice cracked on the last sentence.

"You should have let somebody else do this." Holt sounded grim, angry with her.

"I wanted to do it." Diana lifted her gaze to him. "You see, I never knew . . . Rube was just . . ." A shudder quaked through her. She saw the half-movement Holt made toward her, as if to offer comfort. The bone-chilling numbness became too much and she turned to him. "Hold me. Please, hold me."

There was a second's hesitation before he gathered her into his arms and rocked her gently. His body heat slowly began to thaw her benumbed state. She began to feel again, with her heart and her mind and her senses. There was pain and guilt and grief . . . grief for a man she had never really known. She wound her arms around Holt's waist, drawing on his strength. Tears began to gather in her eyes, the first tears she had shed since the accident yesterday.

Now the shock of Rube's death had worn off and Diana began trembling in reaction as the tears fell. Her face was buried in Holt's shirt, the dampness on her cheeks moistening the material. The steady beat of his heart was comforting, as was the hand stroking her hair. Aching, Diana pressed closer to the solidness of his support and felt the brush of his mouth against the top of her head.

Spreading her fingers over his shoulder blades, Diana lifted her head to rub her brow against his jaw and chin, like a cat wanting to be stroked and reassured. She felt the warm pressure of his mouth against her temple in response. His caresses of solace continued; he kissed her eyes and the tears from her cheeks. His hands were moving over her body, seeking and massaging away the hurt until there didn't seem to be an inch of her that hadn't felt the touch of his hands. His embrace was gentle and healing. Diana shuddered against him in relief.

"It isn't right," she said of Rube's death, her voice breathless as Holt's mouth nuzzled the black hair near her ear.

"Nothing is right." His response was muffled by the silken thickness of her hair. "What I'm feeling right now is wrong, but what the hell does it matter?"

With a sweeping mastery, his mouth closed over her lips and parted them. Diana became engulfed in the flame of his passion. It ignited her fiery core and she responded with all the abandonment of previous times.

Lifting her off her feet, Holt carried her into a side room and set her down beside an unmade bed. There, he undressed her and laid her on the bed. The sheets were warm with the smell of him. The mattress groaned as it took his weight. In the next second, Diana was glorying in the feel of his naked torso against hers, the white-hot flame of their desire fusing them together in an explosion of wondrous sensations. The force of it lifted them higher than they had ever gone before. It took a long time to come down.

Even then, neither of them wanted to bring it to a total end. Her head rested in the crook of his arm. Diana was smoking the cigarette Holt had lit for her. The ashtray they shared was on his stomach. Suddenly she found it easier to speak of Rube.

"It all happened so fast. I saw the stallion charge and his horse rear over with him. It didn't seem like I was that far away. If I had reached him sooner, before the stallion trampled him, he might not be dead now."

"If you had reached him sooner, both of you might be dead. You can't think like that, Diana. There was no way of predicting what happened. The only thing that might have saved him would have been getting him immediate medical attention. It was too far away."

"I've known Rube all my life. Yet, in all these years, I never once guessed that he thought of me in any special way. I just took him for granted, the same way I did with Guy. They were just conveniently around when I . . ." The sentence trailed off as Diana sensed the sudden stillness that had come over Holt. She stared at the smoke curling from the cigarette and the ashes building on its tip. They had been so close. Now Holt had withdrawn. "I wish I hadn't mentioned Guy," she murmured.

"It doesn't matter." He crushed out his cigarette and handed her the ashtray.

"It does matter! You keep accusing me of being sexually involved with him, that we're having an ongoing affair. It isn't true."

"It doesn't matter," Holt repeated in a hard, flat tone.

Tears stung her eyes as she snubbed out her cigarette. "Please." The muscles in her throat had constricted, making her voice husky and taut. "I don't want to argue with you about Guy, not this time." Not the way they had done every time before in the aftermath of their lovemaking.

There was a pause as he inhaled deeply and released the breath in a long sigh that bordered on regret. "Neither do I, Diana." Holt turned on the mattress, caught her chin in his hand and kissed her, but he didn't let it deepen into passion. He slipped his arm from beneath her and sat up on the edge of the bed.

Love sprang from the eternal well of her heart. Rising, Diana moved to where he sat, her hands gliding over his shoulders to circle his chest. She pressed close to him and kissed the fading white scars lining his back with crisscross marks. It was a release of deep emotion rather than a desire to have him make love to her again. Gently, Holt unwound her arms from around him and partially turned to set her away, ending the embrace without rejecting it.

"It's almost noon," he said.

Nodding, she made no attempt to reach for him as he rose. Diana remained in bed, watching him dress, feeling she had the right to such an intimacy. Her gaze kept being drawn back to the scars, her blue eyes clouding over with question. Holt turned and intercepted the look. He hesitated, then reached for his shirt, hiding the old marks from her sight.

"My father beat me when I was a child." Holt

buttoned his shirt, seemingly indifferent to the words he had just spoken. "He was a rodeo clown. My mother showed me pictures of him. He followed the circuit, so he wasn't home much. I used to wish that he'd never come home. Every time he did, I got a beating for something, and once he started hitting me, he couldn't stop. My mother would be crying and begging him to quit, but I was usually unconscious by the time he stopped."

"Oh, my God, Holt, no!" she choked out the protest.

"I was eleven when a bull crushed him against a fence and broke his leg. He came home for a week after he got out of the hospital. He had a rawhide quirt and he used that on me instead of his hands."

"But surely there was someone—your teacher, a neighbor . . ."

"That was before adults ever admitted there was such a thing as child abuse. What a parent did to a child was his business, enforced by the excuse that the kid probably deserved it." His mouth quirked cynically.

"But surely there was something that could be done about it, wasn't there?" Her mind recoiled from the idea that he had been hopelessly trapped in the situation, with no way out.

Holt didn't answer immediately, taking an abnormal amount of time tucking his shirttail inside his pants. "A few months after he whipped me, my mother told me he was coming home for the weekend. When she went to buy groceries, I ran away. I swore he was never going to beat me again. Two days later the police found me and brought me back. My mother was home alone. She said he was out looking for me and he'd promised never to hit me again. But when he came home and I saw the look in his eye, I knew it had all been a lie. He started yelling at me for upsetting my mother and worrying her out of her mind. When I saw the quirt in his hand, I ran for my mother's bedroom. Because she was alone so much, he had insisted she keep a loaded shotgun in her closet. I remember him saying once that if you were going to shoot something at close range, a shotgun was better than a handgun. I don't know if it was in my mind to scare him with it, or kill him. I cocked it and pointed it at the door. When he came through, I pulled both triggers.''

Diana felt sick. She knew she had gone white. Holt's face was impassive, registering no emotion. He buckled his belt and reached for his boots.

"There were never any charges filed, because of the circumstances and the fact that I was a juvenile. But they put me in a home for a few months, then released me to my mother. We moved away then . . . to Arizona.''

"I . . . I'm sorry." It seemed such an empty thing to say.

"If I had the moment to live over again, I'd do the same thing." Holt walked out of the bedroom.

It was several minutes before Diana recovered enough to rise from the bed and dress. There didn't seem to be anything left to say when she joined him in the main room.

"I have to check on one of the horses. I'll see you at lunch." He held the screen door open.

"Yes." Polite phrases that avoided the stark truth they both knew. Son hating father . . . in the past and in the present.

A brisk ride in the warm, morning sunlight had not eased her conscience. Rube's funeral was tomorrow, but the depression and guilt Diana felt had nothing to do with his death. She walked her horse slowly to the stables, skirting the main buildings in an effort to avoid others. She watched the horse's head bobbing from side to side as it walked.

"Diana! Hey! Come on over!" A voice broke through the mist of her mind. "Why didn't you tell me you were going for a ride? I would have come along."

At the sound of her name, Diana had automatically stopped her horse. On her left were the gasoline barrels, mounted above the ground on steel supports. Beyond them was the old trailer that Guy had partially restored as living quarters. He was sitting in a dilapidated lawn chair, half the webbing broken. The chair was in the shade cast by the trailer.

"Come on over and talk to me!" He motioned toward her. There was something unnatural both in his voice and his actions.

The temptation was to ride on, as if she hadn't heard him, but it was hardly possible now that she had stopped and looked in his direction. With a sigh, she turned her horse into the narrow gap between the supports for the gasoline barrel and a machine shed.

"It sure is hot this morning, isn't it?" Guy didn't move from his slouched position in the chair when she reached his trailer.

"It isn't too bad."

"Get down. Get down." He waved her off the horse. "Sit with me and talk." He rose from the chair, swaying unsteadily for a minute. "You can sit here. I'll get another chair from inside."

As Diana dismounted, Guy walked very erectly into the trailer and came out with a second lawn chair in equally bad condition as the one he had offered her. He set his beside the one she was to occupy.

"How about a cold beer?" There was a faint slurring of his speech.

"No, thank you."

"I think I'll have one. Be right back." He smiled and went inside the trailer once more.

Stacked around the chair were a half-dozen empty beer cans, the aroma fresh in the air. Diana realized that Guy had been drinking, and it wasn't even noon. She sat carefully in the lawn chair, and the thin webbing held.

"Sure you don't want a beer?" Guy came back out with one in his hand.

"No, I don't."

He sat down in the chair beside her, slouching into

his former position. He took a swig from the can, then stared at it, something sad flickering across his sensitive face.

"It's Rube's beer," he said. "The boys gave it to me when they divided up his stuff. Floyd took his watch and Don wanted his wristwatch. I was going to take his radio, but the damned thing didn't work." Guy laughed at that and looked at Diana. "Are you sure you don't want to have a beer on old Rube?"

"I doubt if there's any left," Diana murmured dryly.

"There's still a couple of cans," he assured her.

"I'll pass."

"You know"—he leaned his head back to stare at the sky—"we ought to have a wake for Rube. He'd like that. A rip-roaring, beer-busting wake. Shoot some craps, maybe. He loved dice. How he used to talk to them! He was a lousy poker player, though. You could bluff him out of any pot. He loved to gamble, but he was afraid to risk a dollar. Did I ever tell you he taught me how to gamble?"

"No, you didn't."

"He was a lousy teacher." Guy sighed and drank some more beer. "He didn't have any family, did he?"

"None that he ever talked about. The Major thought he had a sister somewhere, but Floyd thought she had died a few years ago. They're trying to find out."

"I don't imagine there'll be very many people at the funeral tomorrow—just us from the ranch. Rube didn't have hardly any other friends except us. Maybe a couple of hands from other ranches who worked here at one time or another." His fingers tightened around the can. There was a popping sound as the force dented the aluminum. "Did I tell you Holt took his saddle! The bastard!"

Diana whitened at the violence in his voice. "Don't say that?"

"Why not?" Guy was faintly belligerent. "It's the truth. That's what he is and what he's always been. You know it, Diana. You feel the same as I do about him. Besides"—he didn't give her time to refute the last statement—"if it hadn't been for him, Rube would be alive."

"That isn't true. You can't blame Holt. It was an accident. I was there. If anyone's to blame, it's me for not reaching him sooner."

"No, it isn't your fault. There wasn't anything you could do. No, it was Holt," Guy repeated. "And he's blaming that wild stallion."

"It was the wild stallion that trampled him, not Holt," she reminded him sharply.

"But Holt was the one that got us out there. It was all his damned plan. He should pay for what he's done. First you, then Rube. I hate the bastard."

"That's the beer talking, Guy. I refuse to believe you are actually saying any of this." Diana trembled, partly in anger and partly in horror.

"How can you defend him after what he did to you?" He sat up in the chair, glaring at her.

"What do I have to do or say to get it through your head that I wanted him to make love to me?!!!" she cried out in frustrated anger.

"I don't believe you. You're just saying that. You wouldn't want him, not when you hate him as much as I do. You've always hated him."

"I don't hate him anymore. I . . ." Diana had second thoughts about saying more than that.

"That bastard—"

"Don't say it," she warned. It wasn't any use trying to reason with Guy, not in his present condition. "If you're going to keep talking like this, I'm leaving."

"No." With an alacrity that belied any dulling of his reflexes from alcohol, Guy was on his feet, catching her arm before Diana could take a step toward her horse. "Please, don't leave. Stay with me for a little while." His blue eyes were contrite and beseeching. "I'm sorry for swearing like that in front of you. It just slipped out."

He seemed such a little boy, despite his man-hard

grip on her arm. It made it difficult for Diana to stay angry with him, the same as it had years ago when he'd looked at her with those calf eyes.

"It wasn't your swearing that upset me, Guy. It's your attitude toward Holt. Don't you see that he's tried to make a home for you, seen that you had an education? He's never mistreated you, has he?"

But her protests only brought an angry frown to his face. "He's made of stone. You have more emotion in your little finger than he has in his entire body. He doesn't care about me."

"Maybe it's all locked up inside him and he doesn't know how to let it out. He cares about you. That's why he warned me to stay away from you, because he didn't want you to be hurt by me."

"He warned you?" His face clouded over darkly. "That's why you keep pushing me away. You're afraid of him, afraid of what he might do to you." Ignoring her head shaking in denial, he crushed her into his arms and buried his face in the waving thickness of her raven hair. "I won't let him hurt you, Diana. Don't you know that?"

Diana closed her eyes, realizing that Guy fancied himself as her dragon-slayer. "I am not afraid of Holt." She strained for breathing space. "I don't need to be protected from him. I don't want to be protected."

"All this time you've been telling me it was because you didn't want to get serious, you didn't want to get involved." Guy hadn't listened to a word she'd said. "And it was him threatening you. That's why you didn't ask me to ride with you this morning."

"No. I wanted to be alone and think. I didn't want anyone with me," Diana insisted.

"When he raped you out there, I should have—"

"It wasn't rape. How many times do I have to tell you that?" Diana argued in frustration. "If I wasn't willing, don't you think I would have scratched his eyes out? And I'm the Major's daughter. You know yourself how close Holt and the Major are. Do you think Holt would have forced himself on me and risked losing the Major's respect, as well as his job? Don't be stupid, Guy. Open your eyes and face the truth.''

"You're afraid of him." His hand was moving along her spine in what was meant to be an arousing caress. He began kissing her hair, seeking her face, but Diana twisted her head far to the side. "We'll run away, far away from here, you and I, where Holt's threats can't frighten you.''

"I don't want to run away. This is my home." Hadn't anything penetrated that alcohol haze?

"All right, we'll stay here. Anywhere you want to be—that's where I want to be. I'll do anything you want," he vowed huskily. "I'll saddle a horse and we'll go riding together. When it gets too hot, we'll stop at the pond and go swimming like we did before.''

"No." Her strangled cry fell on deaf ears.

"I love you so much, Diana. I just want to be with you. Hold you in my arms. Kiss you. Let's go to the pond," Guy moaned. "I promise you it will be as beautiful as it was before.''

"No!" Summoning all her strength, Diana twisted out of his arms, stepping backward to glare at him, frustration igniting her temper. "I'm sorry I ever went there with you.''

"You don't mean that." He was frozen with shock and disbelief. "You said you weren't sorry.''

"Not then, but I am now. Oh, God, don't you see?" Her fingers raked her hair as she searched impatiently for a way to make him understand. "We were friends. I made the mistake of letting you become too intimate and it's spoiled the relationship between us. Now, every time you're near me, that's all you want to do. And I don't want you to make love to me again.''

His mouth was contorted with pain. "But you said you cared about me.''

"I do care about you, but I don't love you." Diana wasn't sure anything she was saying was getting through to him. "Guy, I don't want to hurt you.''

"You're trying to protect me, aren't you? You're afraid of Holt and afraid I might do something to stop him. That's it, isn't it? You're trying to protect me."

It was hopeless. "You're drunk, Guy. When you sober up, maybe some of the things I've said will sink in. There isn't any point trying to make you understand when you won't listen and keep twisting things around, trying to find motives that don't exist." She walked to her horse and stepped into the saddle.

"I'm not drunk," was his indignant denial. "I've had a few beers, but—"

Diana tapped a heel against the horse's ribs and it broke into an eager trot toward the stables.

Chapter XIX

Diana flipped through the pages of a magazine, but the contents didn't hold her interest. She was restless, on edge, her thoughts constantly turning back to the argument with Guy this morning. And there was Holt, and the funeral tomorrow, so many things pressing on her mind. She tossed the magazine aside in a rush of unconcealed agitation.

"Why don't you drive into town this afternoon, Diana?" the Major suggested gently. "You need to get away from the house for a while, I think. All these preparations for Rube's funeral are beginning to prey on your mind."

"It isn't that," she said and rose from the sofa to walk to the window. "Besides, if I went to town, I'd stop at the funeral home."

"I still think you need a change of atmosphere for a few hours. I haven't seen you smile at all in these last couple of days. Go see Peggy. That woman's smile has always been contagious."

"Yes," she breathed in. "Maybe you're right. I'll go see Peggy. I won't stay long, though." Diana started for the door. "But don't forget to get some rest this afternoon."

"I can take care of myself," the Major insisted. "You just run along."

Taking the station wagon, Diana drove to the

263

neighboring ranch. The yard was empty of vehicles, but the sounds coming from the house assured her that Peggy was home. She knocked once on the screen door and walked in.

"Peggy?"

"Yes," came the answer from another part of the house a few seconds before Peggy came to the kitchen, bouncing a fussing baby in her arms. Her auburn hair was in rollers, her white blouse stained with the baby's spit. "Hi, Diana." Her smile of greeting looked harried. "I was just putting the girls to bed for their afternoon nap. Come in and sit down. How about some iced tea? I know I'd love a glass."

There were dark circles under the woman's eyes. Diana thought Peggy should be the one taking the nap. The woman looked positively exhausted.

"You sit down and I'll get the tea."

"I'm not going to argue." Peggy laughed tiredly. "There's a pitcher of tea in the refrigerator and glasses in the left cupboard by the sink." She sat down at the kitchen table while Diana prepared the cold drinks. The teething ring slipped from the baby's fingers and he started to cry until Peggy retrieved it for him. "I was so sorry to hear about Rube. I called yesterday morning and talked to the Major. What a terrible accident."

"Yes, it was." Diana carried the two glasses to the table and took a chair.

"Alan said he saw you at the funeral home last night. Have you finished making all the arrangements for the services?"

"Yes. There probably won't be many people attending, so we're just having a small service at the funeral home, and a graveside service, of course."

"I suppose the boys at the ranch will be the pallbearers."

"Yes." Diana nodded and glanced up as she caught a flash of red out of the corner of her eye. The oldest girl was hesitating in the archway leading from the kitchen to the rest of the house. Her mouth was drooping in a half-pout and there was still a trace of tears on her cheeks.

"Mommy, I want a drink," she demanded.

"No, you are not getting a drink!" Peggy flared at the sight of the girl. "You march right back into your room and get into bed! I mean it!"

"I don't want to take a nap, Mommy." She began to cry, fresh tears spilling from her lashes.

"Sara Kay Thornton, you get into that bedroom before I get the paddle and give you something to cry about," Peggy threatened.

"No, Mommy, no!" Instead of obeying, the little girl began dancing in frightened agitation, crying harder.

Peggy shifted the baby in her arms and rose from the chair. The baby lost his teething ring and he started crying. As Peggy picked up the round paddle lying on the counter, the little girl started screaming not to be spanked. For a few minutes it was sheer bedlam as Peggy chased the girl back to her room, applying a few swats along the way.

"Stop crying!" Peggy's voice carried into the kitchen. "And don't you get out of that bed again until I tell you!" She returned trying to soothe the fussing baby, who wouldn't be quieted until the teething ring was back in his mouth. Peggy grimaced tiredly as she sat in her chair. "That's another rebellion put down. I hope I don't have to live through a week like this again, what with Sara just getting over the flu and Brian cutting teeth and Amy certain that she isn't getting her share of attention."

"You look exhausted."

"I am." She smiled. "But I'm getting very good at catnaps. Mom is coming out tomorrow to sit with the kids so Alan and I can go to the funeral."

Diana sniffed at the acrid odor in the air. "Is something burning?"

A horrified look spread over Peggy's face. "Oh, my God! The cake! I forgot all about it!" She set the baby on the floor and rushed to the stove, pulling open the oven door. "It's ruined," she moaned and reached for a potholder. "Damn this oven!" She lifted out a rectangular cake tin. "Just look at that! One side is burned and the other is still doughy. The back of the oven is hotter than the rest. To get anything evenly baked, you have to keep turning the pan." Peggy poked at the contents of the pan. "I forgot all about it, and now I'll have to throw the whole thing out." The baby crawled over to her feet, whimpering.

Diana shook her head. "How can you stand it? I mean, how can you put up with all this?" She found Peggy's situation intolerable. "I don't mean just the kids crying, but the stove that doesn't bake, the refrigerator that doesn't keep things cold, and a husband who doesn't lift a finger to help, who keeps you barefoot and pregnant, instead. You can't even afford a new dress." It all burst out before Diana could stop to consider what she was saying.

Peggy stared at her for a stunned minute, then let her temper fly. "How dare you imply that I don't have anything worthwhile in my life! You have a very beautiful brass bed to sleep in, but it's empty when you crawl between the covers. When I go to bed, Alan is there to hold and love me and share his dreams with me. You may be able to dine on steak every night while we eat hamburger. Sitting at my table are my husband and three beautiful children. Who is at yours? This house isn't much, not as fine as the Major's, but it's filled with love. I'm the one who is rich, and you're the one who's poor, Diana. If you can't see that, then I feel sorry for you!"

"Peggy, I—"

The anger in his mother's voice started the baby crying in earnest. Peggy reached down and picked him up. "I think you'd better leave, Diana." Her gaze was proud.

Diana didn't know how to undo the damage her thoughtlessness had done. Rising from the chair, she walked slowly to the door and turned. The baby had his fingers in Peggy's mouth. Diana watched Peggy hold them away as she kissed him on the forehead and hugged him close. There was a lump in Diana's throat as she walked out the door, closing it quietly.

It was a long, slow drive home. She parked the wagon in front of the house and fixed a smile on her face that the Major expected to see before walking up to the porch. As she opened the screen door, the telephone rang.

"Somers Ranch," she answered.

"Diana? It's me, Peggy. I forgot to mention something else that I treasure—your friendship. Can you forgive me for flying off the handle like that?"

"After the things I said, I don't see how you can forgive me," Diana declared in amazement, her voice choking up.

"We've both been under a strain these last few days. Let's forgive and forget, okay?"

It was hard to get it past the lump in her throat, but Diana finally managed a tremulous, "Okay."

"Good. I'll see you tomorrow."

"Yes, tomorrow."

The funeral service was simple and the mourners few. It was windy at the cemetery, dust-devils whipping across the road. Diana stood beside the Major, a black armband circling the sleeve of his dark suitcoat. Both Guy and Holt were among the pallbearers, standing apart from each other. With bloodshot eyes and a pallor to his skin, Guy looked as if his drinking binge had continued yesterday after Diana had left him. Holt seemed removed from the proceedings, indifferent to the droning voice of the minister and the wind that ruffled his sun-brown hair.

When the interment service was over, the small gathering of mourners milled together for a few minutes. Alan and Peggy Thornton came over to offer their formal condolences to the Major, the closest thing Rube had to a family.

"Peggy, about yesterday," Diana began hesitantly.

"It's forgotten, remember?" She gave her a quick

hug, a gesture completely unaffected and natural. "We'll see you at the ranch."

Others were waiting to speak to the Major, and the Thorntons moved on. Everyone had been invited to the ranch for coffee and refreshments after the funeral. Those who lived close by had accepted. The rest chose not to make the long journey.

The group had begun to disband, returning to their cars. The minister and his wife had accepted the Major's invitation to ride to the ranch in the station wagon with himself and Diana. The narrow path leading to the parked vehicles forced Diana to walk behind them to the car.

They were almost there when a hand lightly grasped her elbow, not impeding her progress. Her startled gaze found Holt at her side. Diana hadn't seen him for the last several minutes and had been under the impression he had already left the cemetery. He met her look briefly, his thoughts hidden behind a wall of gray stone, and continued at her side to the car.

The warmth of his touch spread through her. Diana wanted to turn into his arms and let the hard feel of his body drive out all the talk of dust and ashes, death and graves. At the car, Holt let his hand fall from her arm and Diana felt a life-support system had been removed. She trembled.

"Are you all right?" The question was low, not reaching the ears of the others near them.

She lifted her head. Her black hair was pulled severely back into a coil at the nape of her neck. The simple black suit she wore made her complexion seem paler than normal, intensifying the blue of her eyes.

"I'm fine." In her mind, Diana added: *As long as you are with me*.

Looking at his lean, tanned features heightened her desire to be crushed in his arms and feel the searing pressure of his mouth on her lips. Her eyes must have revealed her consuming hunger, because she heard his quickly indrawn breath and saw the sudden darkening of his light-colored eyes. Unconsciously, she swayed toward him and Holt pivoted abruptly to face the Major.

"I'd like a few words with you, Major, later on today, when it's convenient."

"Whenever you wish, Holt."

With a brief nod to the minister and his wife, Holt moved away, not casting a glance in Diana's direction. A chill of apprehension shivered through her. Why did he want to speak to the Major? And why did the knowledge that he did make her so uneasy? Her gaze slid to the eastern mountains and she had to suppress a shudder of fear.

At the ranch everyone linked her quietness and preoccupation to Rube's death. No one seemed to notice how seldom her gaze strayed from Holt. Despite this feeling of foreboding, it didn't override her sense of obligation as hostess. When she saw the minister and his wife standing alone, Diana walked over to speak to them, suggesting they help themselves to more refreshments, but they declined.

"This is a fine turnout," the minister commented.

Diana glanced around the room, knowing if it had been the Major's funeral, the people would be spilling into the yard. "There aren't many."

"No, but those who are here sincerely cared about Mr. Spencer and have gathered for that reason, not out of a sense of social obligation."

Mr. Spencer. It sounded odd. He had always been Rube. His last name had probably been forgotten by half the people here, Diana thought, but didn't say so.

"We will miss him," she admitted instead.

"I understand Mr. Spencer had worked for your father a goodly number of years."

"He's been here ever since I can remember. I've known him all my life." Unaware she hadn't used the past tense, only aware that she had never known him at all.

"It was such an unfortunate accident," the minister's wife murmured, "to be dragged and trampled by your own horse."

Was that the explanation that had been given? Diana hadn't known. No one outside the ranch had questioned her about it. The involvement of the white stallion had been concealed. How easily she could have let it slip.

"It was unfortunate."

"I understood you were there when it happened?" the woman questioned, her gentle smile ringed with sympathy.

Diana nodded. "Yes."

"Was he able to speak before he died? I do hope he was able to make his peace with God." The only remark made by the minister's wife was almost a fervent prayer.

"Rube was in a great deal of pain. He knew he was dying, and . . . yes, he did speak of heaven." She didn't think Rube would object if she stretched the truth to ease the woman's mind.

"I am so glad."

"Excuse me, would you?" Diana requested, needing to retreat from this conversation. "I should check to see if Sophie needs any help in the kitchen."

Again the couple extended their sympathies before she left them. Carrying out her statement, Diana walked to the kitchen, certain that the competent Sophie wouldn't require her help. The housekeeper was scraping and stacking the plates that had been used.

"Is everything all right, Sophie? Do you need anything?" A glance around the kitchen seemed to indicate everything was under control.

"Everything is fine, Miss," was the bland response to what had been perfunctory questions. When Diana would have left, the woman turned hesitantly from the dishes. "This is a fine thing you and the Major are doing." At Diana's puzzled look, the housekeeper went on to explain, somewhat nervously: "I mean the funeral, the marker for his grave, and having all these people out here.''

"Thank you, Sophie.'' She couldn't think of anything else to say.

"Rube was always . . . very fond of you, Miss.'' The woman seemed uncertain, as if afraid she was speaking out of turn. "Holt told me you were a great comfort to Rube when he died.''

"I . . . thank you.'' Diana couldn't remember Sophie ever speaking at this length unless the subject dealt with household matters. She supposed Rube's death had touched them all in one way or another.

The housekeeper turned back to the dishes, her sparse frame beginning to bend with the accumulation of years, the braided coronet atop her head revealing the thinness of her graying hair. "I wasn't sure that you'd ever taken any notice of Rube. You were always so wrapped up with the Major as a child, and he was so wrapped up with you. There never seemed to be room for anyone else in your lives. I know Rube can see what you're doing for him, and I know it will make him happy.''

And Diana realized Sophie was speaking for herself, revealing how she had felt all these years. She let her hand rest lightly on the woman's shoulder for just a second.

"Thank you, Sophie.'' And she knew it was the first time she had touched the woman with any measure of affection.

Leaving the kitchen in silence, Diana returned to the main room. Automatically, her gaze searched for Holt. She saw him as he approached the Major, say something to him which received an agreeing nod, and walk with him toward the privacy of the study. The audience Holt had requested was going to take place now, Diana realized.

She moved quickly across the room in the direction of the study, nodding to those who spoke to her, but not allowing any of them to sidetrack her into a conversation. She opened the door within seconds after Holt had closed it. Impatience flashed in the look he gave her when she entered.

"How are you feeling, Major?" Diana walked to her father's side. "You aren't getting too tired, are you?"

"No, I'm fine." He sat down in the leather-covered chair behind the desk. "Holt merely wanted to speak to me in private for a few minutes."

"I see. You don't mind if I sit in, do you?" She was firmly ensconced in one of the side chairs when she issued the challenge.

Holt's voice was dry, his irritation contained. "I doubt if my objections would make any difference." He didn't take a chair, but stood in front of the desk, indicating by this action that whatever he had to say wouldn't take long. "I'm going after the mares in the morning . . ."—adding after a pregnant pause—". . . and the stallion."

"No!" Diana had the premonition all along that this was what the discussion would be about.

"I'm afraid I must agree with Diana," the Major said soberly. "I think it's time we turned the matter of the wild stallion over to the Bureau."

"Their hands are tied. The law prohibits the killing of any wild horse. If the Bureau tries to catch that white stallion, someone else could end up dead or maimed."

"Leave the stallion alone. Let him keep the four mares," Diana argued.

"If I thought four mares would appease him, I might agree with you, but it wouldn't." Although he was responding to her argument, he addressed it to the Major. "The stallion will be back for more. Why shouldn't he? They are virtually free for the taking. He doesn't have to fight any other stallion for ownership of the mares. Any fear the stallion might have had for man seems to be vanishing. He isn't simply a nuisance anymore. He has become a menace." Holt stated his case in a flat, unemotional tone. "The stallion has to be destroyed."

"No!"

"There is logic in what you say, Holt, but—"

"I am not asking your permission, Major," he interrupted. "I would have preferred to ride out in the morning without telling you of my intentions because I don't want you to be involved. I am taking full responsibility. Whatever repercussions come from what I do will be solely mine."

"You aren't going alone?" There was concern in the Major's acceptance of Holt's decision.

"No. Don has asked to go with me"—he hesitated—"and I imagine Guy will come along."

"He doesn't know yet?" Diana held her breath.

"Not yet."

"He'll do everything to stop you."

"He'll try."

"Don't do it, Holt."

But he was already ignoring her again. "I probably won't see you until we get back, Major."

"Take care."

"I will."

Turning on his heel, Holt walked to the door. Diana stared after him, searching for any argument to change his mind, but finding none. The door closed and she turned to appeal to the Major, the only one Holt might listen to.

"You've got to stop him."

"How?" His look was tired and indulgent. "I can't stop Holt. He is a man. I can't keep him from doing what he feels has to be done."

"But he works for you. If you—"

"Are you suggesting that I threaten him with dismissal, Diana? It wouldn't work. He'd call my bluff, because that's all it would be. And if I did carry it out and fire him, Holt would go after the stallion, anyway. You heard him. He wasn't asking for my permission because he knew I wouldn't give it."

She knew all that, but she refused to accept it. "You can't let him do it!"

The Major tipped his head to the side in a curious

thoughtful pose. "Are you concerned for the stallion or Holt?"

"Holt is a human being. The stallion is just a horse, an animal. Of course I'm concerned for Holt." Diana rose in agitation.

"And that is your only reason?" he probed.

"There has to be a way to stop him. You love him, too," she protested, too concerned to care what she was admitting. "You've treated him as your son almost from the day he came here. Holt has been everything to you that I could never be. How can you let him do this when you care about him as much as I do?"

"It is true. In many ways, I have treated Holt like a son. But I don't like what you are implying." His brow was furrowed. "My affection for him has never taken precedence over my love for you, my own daughter. Given the choice when you were born, I would never have traded you for ten sons like Holt."

"Then stop him. Stop him for me!"

"I would do anything humanly possible for you." There was sorrow in his aging features. "I would give you the moon if I could, Diana. But what you want isn't within my control. I can't stop Holt, not even for you."

"There has to be a way." She clung desperately to the hope.

"I know of nothing that could sway a man like Holt from his course once he's set it." He shook his head sadly.

"I have to try if you won't." Diana started for the door, then hesitated. "If I can't persuade him to change his mind . . . I'm going with him tomorrow."

Stern denial flashed across her father's expression until he realized that, like Holt, Diana wasn't asking for his permission. The look faded.

"I can't stop you, either," he admitted.

"Thank you." Tears misted her eyes, but Diana quickly blinked them away. "I wouldn't have liked to disobey an order from you, Major."

"Wait." He halted her when she would have left. "Why don't you give me a few minutes to rejoin our guests and you can slip out the back way, without being waylaid by a lot of people wondering what happened to their hosts." Her father smiled indulgently. "I presume you are going to speak to Holt now, aren't you?"

"Yes, I am." Fighting the premonition that it was all a waste of time.

Rising from his chair, he walked around the desk to the door where she stood. "Give me five minutes." In a spontaneous and unexpected display of affection, he bent and kissed her cheek. "Good luck, my dear."

Chapter XX

Five minutes later, Diana was slipping out the side door and working her way through the trees to the fourplex. A knock on Holt's door received no answer. She walked in, calling his name, but the rooms were empty.

She hesitated. Where else could Holt be? Perhaps at the stables, beginning the preparations for the morning's journey, she decided. She hurried out of the unit toward the stable, the spikey heels of her shoes forcing her to slow her pace over the rougher, graveled ground.

Sliding open the stable door, Diana paused to let her eyes become adjusted to the relative gloom of the barn. A horse whickered in its stall, the aroma of horses and hay strong in the warm air. There was no movement around the stalls, so she turned to the tack room.

At that moment, Holt's voice called, "I'm in here, Don."

His back was to the door when she entered. He hadn't changed clothes, although his suitcoat and tie were tossed over a bench. He was bent over the packsaddles.

"We've got a weak cinch here that will have to be replaced. Hand me a new one."

When there was no sound to indicate his command

was being heeded, Holt glanced over his shoulder. A muscle tightened in his jaw as he straightened and turned to face Diana. The white dress shirt was unbuttoned at the throat, accenting his rugged good looks. She felt the fluttering in her stomach, his raw animal magnetism working its magic on her.

"You know why I'm here," she said.

"I can guess." His voice was as dry as the desert wind.

His level gaze swung away from her as he walked to the wall where various sizes and lengths of cinches hung. Holt selected one and carried it back to the packsaddle. Diana realized he would continue to ignore her as long as she let him. She walked to where he worked, replacing the old cinch with the new.

"Holt, look at me," Diana ordered with impatience.

His eyes made a raking sweep of her before returning to his task. "You aren't exactly dressed for the stables, are you? Don't wander too close to the stalls or you'll end up with manure all over your shoes."

"You didn't change clothes, either," she pointed out and immediately became irritated with herself for letting his comment sidetrack her from the issue.

"I came to check the equipment we'll be needing in the morning."

He didn't look up. Perspiration was beginning to make his shirt cling to his skin, the white material molding to the rippling muscles in his shoulders and back. His physical attraction was beginning to sway her attention again. She closed her eyes in an effort to shut it out.

"Don't go, Holt."

"It's no use, Diana. You're wasting your breath." His answer was clipped, discouraging any more discussion.

"What do you think you are going to accomplish?" she argued.

"Two things. I'm going to get the mares back and get rid of the stallion, eliminate a potentially dangerous problem."

"Is it as simple as that?"

"Yes."

"Are you sure?" Diana challenged. "Or have you appointed yourself to avenge Rube's death? Do you think by killing the stallion you are going to compensate for Rube's death in some way?"

"Dammit to hell, Diana!" The packsaddle and cinch were discarded in a burst of lightning temper as he rose to confront her, scorching her with his anger. "Isn't Rube's death proof enough that the stallion has to be destroyed?!"

"No, it isn't! Because you're just using it as an excuse. You've been obsessed with this stallion from the beginning. You have wanted the stallion dead since you knew of its existence. First it was because he killed our stallion, then the foal that died of a broken neck. Now Rube's death makes you feel justified in going after the horse so you can hide your obsession behind a cloak of vengeance. Don't do it, Holt. Don't go after him."

"If anyone around here is obsessed with that horse, it's you and Guy. You've listened to all those legends Rube and the Major told you about the other white stallion and you've become convinced he has been reincarnated. He is a wild horse, a rogue. Nothing more."

"No, I'm not obsessed by him," Diana denied his accusation, suddenly becoming calmer. "I know what it's like to be obsessed by something. For years I was insanely jealous of you—without cause, as it turns out."

"Jealous?"

"Yes, jealous." She nodded. "From the first moment I saw you with the Major, I hated you. I never fully understood why until just recently. But when I saw you, I knew instinctively that you were all the things the Major would have wanted in a son. I hated you for it."

"But you are his daughter, his only child. He adores you." His frowning gaze searched her expression.

"Don't you see? That was the problem. I was his daughter, a girl." Even now, there was a faint bitterness in the laugh she gave. "The Major never said he wished he'd had a son instead of me. But this . . ."—her hand made a sweeping gesture to envelop everything around them—". . . is a very macho environment. Isn't it taken for granted that a man would rather have a son? So somewhere along the line, I got the idea that the Major wished I had been a boy. I tried to be what I thought he wanted—riding and roping, more at home in boots and jeans than in skirts. When you came, you changed it all. First it was not exercising the stallions, then not going along on the roundup, because I was a girl. Suddenly the Major wanted me to be a lady. He didn't want me the way I had been, and I thought it was all because of you, because you had become the son I had tried so hard to be. I hated you. I wanted to get rid of you. I even used Guy to try to make your life so miserable here that you would leave."

Holt turned to the side, savagely raking his fingers through his hair. She could hear the cursing ejaculations beneath his breath. Diana wanted to touch him, but she knew any attempt would be knocked aside. He was angry and she didn't blame him.

"After a couple of years, I finally realized there wasn't anything I could do to make you leave," she continued. "So I started out to become whatever the Major wanted. I felt I had to be the best at everything so he'd love me. When he had the first attack, I wanted to take care of him. But he said no, he had you and he didn't want me tied to the ranch. He wanted me to marry. My God, I'm afraid I even married Rand because I thought he was the kind of son-in-law the Major wanted. Do you know what the Major told me a few weeks ago?" Diana paused as Holt's smoldering, dark gaze swung to her. "That he used to wish I would marry you. If I had known that back then, I probably would have married you to please him, no matter how much I resented and despised you."

God, she wished Holt would say something, release all that contained fury, instead of standing there, all raw masculinity and coiled power. She was baring her soul to him. Didn't he realize what a weapon she was handing him? He could destroy her. Or maybe was that what he was waiting for?

"You see, Holt, I know what it's like to be obsessed. There was no rhyme or reason to it. I created it all in my mind." Diana was practically begging him to understand. "I am not obsessed with the white stallion, but you are. I don't think it's just because of the horses we've lost, or even Rube's death. In some way, I think you've blamed the stallion for that first time you made love to me—a case of 'if we hadn't been chasing him, it wouldn't have happened,' and Guy wouldn't have seen us and started hating you to the point of wanting to kill you. It isn't true, Holt. That chemistry between us was always there. If anything, the stallion merely served as a catalyst."

His nostrils flared as he took a deep breath, the muscles standing out along his jaw. The hard silver sheen of his eyes was angry and forbidding. Hadn't anything she'd said penetrated that stony exterior?

"I am not obsessed with the stallion. He simply has to be destroyed," Holt stated.

"Don't go after him." Diana couldn't explain this terrible feeling she had inside. "I'll do anything you say, if only you'll promise to leave the stallion alone. Do you want me to leave the ranch and never come back? Go somewhere far away where Guy could never find me? Tell me what you want me to do and I'll do it. Only, don't go after the stallion, Holt."

"Stop being so damned dramatic! It's a job, something that has to be done. That's all!" he snapped.

"Maybe I am." Her shoulders lifted in a shrug of confusion. "I—" Diana couldn't get any words past the sudden constriction in her throat.

It was no use appealing to him. He wouldn't listen. The Major hadn't been able to dissuade him. Why had she thought she could? All the fight seemed to drain out of her, leaving her oddly weak. He stood so close, his strength so indomitable. It was easy to glide across the small space and wrap her arms around him, resting her head against the solid wall of his chest.

"Don't go," she heard herself murmur.

At the initial contact, his muscles tensed, rigid in resistance to her unconscious advance. "Diana, for God's sake—" Holt began angrily, but the minute his hands touched her to push her away, they tightened to hold her.

Diana felt the brush of his mouth against her temple and lifted her head, hungrily seeking his kiss. The erratic hammering of her pulse was the only sound she could hear. His mouth devoured hers. His fingers began tugging at the pins holding the sleek coil of her hair in place. When it was free, Holt ran his fingers through the black confusion tumbling about her shoulders.

"I wanted to do that at the cemetery," he muttered against her throat.

Diana's senses were spinning beneath the passion of his touch. That familiar craving to be closer to him still took hold of her. She was aware of his wide-legged stance and her hips arching against him, wanting to feel the throbbing pressure of every muscle and sinew in his length.

It would have ended between them as it always did if it hadn't been for a voice calling, "Hey, Holt, are you in here?" Don's voice. A second later there was only silence as Holt lifted his head, his arms staying protectively around Diana, shielding her face from the man standing in the doorway, flushing twenty shades of crimson. "God, I'm sorry. I didn't mean to . . . excuse me." The embarrassed apologies were tumbling out in mumbled words.

Holt's sharp voice cut through them. "Catch the horses we'll be riding and bring them up to the stables."

"Yessir," was the relieved response before Don scurried away.

Only then did Holt set Diana away from him. He took a step away and bent to pick up the cinch to the packsaddle. Diana watched him, part of her remaining under the influence of the warm, wonderful confusion of his embrace.

"I . . . can't change your mind about going tomorrow?"

There was something self-mocking in his sideways glance. "I'm tempted to let you try, but, no." He shook his head decisively. "You can't change my mind."

"Then I'm going with you," Diana stated.

"I think I knew that, too." Holt offered no argument.

Diana waited, wanting him to say more, but he continued his task of replacing the old cinch. Quietly she turned and walked from the tack room, retracing her path to the main house.

Diana shifted in the saddle, uneasily aware of Guy's eyes boring holes into her back. She glanced at Don, directly ahead of her as they wound single file into the mountain wilds. Face it, she told herself, we are all a bit nervy. The freshness of Rube's death had made them all unnaturally silent. They all missed Rube's incessant chatter which had previously filled many a silence. Last night, watching Don build the campfire, there had been a painful knot in Diana's throat.

They had located the wild band an hour ago. Holt was setting up the relay posts now. The wearing-down process would begin soon, the same tactic that had cost Rube his life, but the only one guaranteed to succeed. The first order of business was to recover the mares. Then the stallion would be taken care of.

In the lead, Holt reined in his horse and signaled to Guy that he wanted him to take up a position here. Guy stopped and they continued on without him. One by one, they took their positions until Holt was left to initiate the chase.

For three days they trailed the small band, always

keeping at a distance, respecting the savage defense the stallion could launch if a rider's nearness posed a threat.

On the fourth day, and after almost six full days in the saddle, Diana's aching muscles numbed her entire body. A leg was hooked around the saddlehorn, an elbow resting on her knee, a hand supporting her head. Her horse stood in the shade of a gnarled pinion tree, stomping his leg at a persistent fly. Bone-tired, Diana dreaded to hear the sound of horses. When it came, it would mean it was her turn to take over the chase. She didn't want to move. She didn't think she could move.

A sharp crack split the air and her head jerked up. A cold chill of fear raced down her spine at the immediate repetition of the sound. A rifle shot. A signal. Diana unhooked her leg from around the horn, unaware of any stiffness or pain, and slipped the toe of her boot into the stirrup. She waited for the third shot, a signal of distress.

There was a long pause, then two shots fired in rapid succession. Her knees started shaking as relief washed through her. Two shots meant the stallion had separated from the mares. Diana reined in her horse in the general direction of the sound and started off.

Diana was the last to arrive on the scene. The weary mares were already roped and haltered. They were in sorry condition, their ribs showing, bodies dehydrated. Guy and Don were using the water from their canteens to temporarily slake the horses' thirst. She stopped her horse beside Holt. There was weariness in his lined features, and a certain ruthlessness of purpose, too, as he gazed off into the distance, no doubt in the direction the stallion had taken.

"We have the mares," Diana spoke quietly, appealing to him again to change his mind. "Let's go back now."

His gaze swung slowly to her, hooded and gray. With a faint, negative shake of his head, he said, "No," his mouth quirking dryly at her persistence.

"The mares can't go another mile," he said. "They need a day of rest, food, and water before they can be moved anywhere."

"And the stallion?" Diana looked in the direction Holt had been gazing. There was no sign of him.

"He's tired. He has to be." The last biting statement cast doubt on the first.

"Holt, let him go," Diana repeated tightly.

"She's right, Holt." Guy's look glittered defiantly over the lean figure in the saddle. "You've got the mares back. Isn't that enough?"

"No, it isn't," he retorted with a snapping, thin edge to his patience. "Don"—he turned to the other rider on the ground with the mares—"since I'd be wasting my time ordering either of these two to stay with the mares, you're stuck with them. Water them again in about half an hour. Rest them for another hour or so. The waterhole is about three miles from here. By then you should be able to move them there and stake them out in the grass. We're going to find the stallion."

Without waiting for arguments or protests or agreement, Holt reined his horse away and urged it into a canter. Swearing, Guy scrambled into his saddle as Diana rode after Holt. The terrain was rough. It was difficult for either of them to overtake Holt with the head start he had on them.

Three miles later Holt stopped on the crest of a low ridge. When Diana and Guy joined him, they saw the white stallion about a mile away, standing in the shade of some rocks, his dusty-white coat plainly visible against the darker background. He was resting, a perfect target. It was with relief that Diana realized the stallion was out of range.

"You're really going to kill him, aren't you?" Guy accused suddenly, "You said so all along, but I kept—" His voice cracked on a note of despairing anger.

There was no indication that Holt had heard a word he'd said. "I want you to flush the stallion out of those rocks, Guy. If you can, head him down that wash. It's the obvious avenue of escape, so he'll probably choose it on his own. Diana, do you see where that wash opens into the valley?" He pointed. "I want you to wait in that stand of trees. Make certain the stallion is well past you before you show yourself. Keep your distance. He should break for the smaller valley past that hill. Let him. That's where I'll be waiting."

There was no need to state why he would be there. From that hill, Holt had a clear field of fire in either direction the stallion chose to take, down the main valley or into the smaller one. Diana tried not to think what would happen after that.

"I'm not going," Guy said. "I'm not going to ride out there and help you murder that stallion. You aren't going to make me a party to this. Diana isn't going to help you, either. And without us, you can't do it."

"Diana?" Holt's steel gaze became riveted on her. She shook her head in mute protest. "It has to be done. The Major knew it. So do you."

"Don't pay any attention to him, Diana," Guy ordered. "He can't make you do it. And he hasn't got a chance on his own."

Confused and torn, Diana looked from one to the other, father and son. Her love for Holt and a fear for his safety pulled her one way, while Guy's arguments to spare the stallion and her own premonition that it would be dangerous to pursue him yanked her the opposite way. She saw Holt gather his reins.

"Make up your mind, Diana," he said quietly.

"She isn't going to help you," Guy declared with faint triumph, a smile curving his mouth.

But Diana knew he was wrong. With a whipping lash of the reins, she set her mount down the ridge, deafening her ears to Guy's angry cry. She didn't look back and slowed her horse to a trot once they reached the flat, rocky ground. Diana could no longer see the white stallion, only the jutting rocks he had been using for shade from the sun. She set her course for them and refused to think what she had committed herself to or what the outcome would be.

When the stallion came into view, he was still standing in the shade, poised and staring in her direction. Diana didn't ride any closer, aware of Holt's unnecessary admonition to keep at a safe distance. Her horse pranced slightly under the tight rein. The stallion tossed its head, as if daring her to come closer. After several seconds, he left the shade and broke into a rolling pace, choosing, as Holt had predicted, the dry bed of a wash. Diana followed at a trot, increasing her mount's gait to a canter as the distance widened.

Chapter XXI

The stallion was not as tired as Diana had hoped. He had held his initial burst of speed for more than a mile, forcing her to push her mount in order to keep pressure on the stallion. Without Guy or someone to relieve her in this heat, the pace was beginning to tell on her horse. There was still a long way to go before they reached the hill.

Leaving the wash, she glanced toward the stand of trees. For some reason Diana had expected to see Guy there. Possibly she had thought her decision might have influenced his. There was no one in the trees. She was on her own. Shutting her mind to the bone-weary ache of her muscles, Diana urged her horse into a canter before the stallion left them behind on the flat valley ground.

The hill grew larger and larger. She tried to concentrate on the stallion and not look for the flash of sunlight reflecting off a rifle barrel. The stallion moved steadily closer to the hill. So far, he hadn't committed himself to either the small valley or the larger one, but the stallion was within range of the rifle. Her stomach began churning with nausea, waiting for the explosion that would strike down the wild stallion. She closed her eyes, not wanting to see the mustang topple to the ground.

Suddenly her horse swerved sideway, half-rearing.

Diana lost her grip on the saddle, slipping to the side. She grabbed for the saddlehorn, half-aware of the jackrabbit leaping into the sage in panic. She couldn't regain her balance as her horse took a frightened leap forward, unseating her completely. Diana felt herself falling and the ground rushing up to meet her. Her arms reached out to break her fall. There was the hard impact as she rolled, then nothing. Everything went black.

When she came to, she was lying on her stomach. Diana was conscious of a hot wind blowing on her arm. Something snorted and there was moisture on her skin. Her lashes fluttered. There was a blur of white in front of her eyes.

Shock seared her into full consciousness as Diana realized the stallion was standing near her, investigating the pursuer that had fallen. Instinct warned her not to move, but it was sheer terror that kept her motionless.

Through the veil of her lashes, she saw the white stallion toss his head and paw the ground only a few short yards from where she lay. It was as if he was challenging his enemy to rise and fight him.

Nostrils flared and reddened, the stallion's head was extended toward her, the thick white forelock falling forward to half-cover his dark eyes. His white coat was lathered and dirty, yet neither factor detracted from the fact that he was a powerful brute. Viewed from the ground, as Diana saw him, he was terrifying. She had seen what those ivory teeth and iron hooves could do. A cold sweat covered her skin, blood curdling in her veins.

Almost simultaneously, there was the sound of a rifle shot and dust was kicked into the air to the right and beyond the stallion. It came from the direction of the hill where Holt was to be. The stallion's head came up, yet he didn't flee. A second shot struck the ground nearer to the stallion. Spinning on his hindquarters, the mustang started to bound away as a third shot laid a red crease along the root of his tail. Diana heard his squeal of pain and rage before he leaped into full stride.

The paralysis left and shock waves of relief shuddered through her body. Her first breaths came in frightened gasps, strength returning slowly to her paralyzed muscles. She pushed to her knees, shoving the hair away from her face and waiting for the tremors to subside.

A galloping horse approached. Turning, Diana saw Holt vaulting from the saddle, rifle in his hand, as his mount slid to a stop. She stumbled to her feet. Before she could take a step to meet him, he was there, drawing her into his arms, the hard metal of the gun behind her back.

"Are you all right?" His husky demand was the most beautiful sound Diana had ever heard.

She clung to him, the solidness of his male length absorbing the tremblings of her body. His fingers roughly pushed the hair away from her face, then cupped the side of her face, lifting it up for his inspection.

"I'm fine," Diana insisted shakily.

His gaze burned over her face, a brilliant silver fire that dazzled her eyes. "Don't ever do that to me again!" Holt snapped. "I had visions of—" He didn't finish that. He didn't have to because Diana had had her own visions of ending up like Rube or trampled to death like the Arabian stallion. "For God's sake, what happened?"

"A jackrabbit spooked my horse and I . . . I fell off. I must have blacked out for a couple of seconds. When I came to, the stallion was standing there." Diana closed her eyes, not wanting to remember the fear that had consumed her.

His mouth covered hers, fierce and gentle, both at the same time. It was all so crazy. Diana felt crushed, yet cradled, safe from harm, yet assaulted. To all sensations, she responded with equal fervor. The knowledge seared through her that a few minutes ago she could have been killed and never again have felt his embrace. She wanted to cherish the feeling and have it forever burned into her flesh, too. They remained locked in each other's arms for timeless seconds, each more precious than the last, his mouth trailing fire over every inch of her face and neck.

"It's a miracle that stallion didn't hurt you," Holt murmured at last, pressing her head to his chest, his jaw and cheek rubbing her hair.

"I don't think he knew whether I was alive or not." Diana strained closer to the comforting wall of his chest, eyes closed.

"Thank God, you had sense enough not to move," he muttered.

"Sense?" Her laugh was shaky with reaction. "I was petrified!" She felt him smile against her hair.

"Are you sure you weren't hurt when you fell?" He held her away, his expression serious. "You didn't hit your head?"

"I don't think so." Diana touched her head, feeling no soreness or bump.

"You're not riding after that stallion again." It was neither an order nor a comment, but a flat statement, issued in a deadly grim voice. "You're not taking any more risks of being harmed."

"And you? Are you still going after him?"

"Yes."

"Who's going to help you?"

"There's still Don," Holt reminded her, both aware of Guy's mutiny. "Let's get you back to camp."

"Where is my horse?" Diana glanced around, most of her view blocked by his wide shoulders.

"He must have bolted for home after—" The drumbeat of horses' hooves interrupted his answer. They both turned as Guy came riding into view, leading Diana's horse. Holt's arm remained around her shoulders, although they both shifted to allow more space between them.

Guy reined in. "I heard the shots. I didn't know whether something was wrong or if you had . . ." He didn't finish that. "I found your horse on the way, Diana. What happened?"

"He spooked at a rabbit and I fell."

"That precious stallion that you are so eager to save almost made her victim number two!" Holt snapped.

"Holt scared him away," Diana added quickly when Guy paled at the announcement.

"Were you hurt?"

"It's a little late to be concerned about that now, isn't it? When you weren't around to help," Holt challenged.

"Not a scratch," she assured Guy. "Just a few bruises from the fall."

"Did it ever occur to you, Holt, that if you hadn't gone after that stallion in the first place, there wouldn't have been a chance of her getting hurt?" Guy angrily countered the challenge with one of his own.

"It occurred to me." His hand gripped Diana's elbow and propelled her toward the horse Guy held. The firmness of his control was transmitted through his touch. After giving her a leg up into the saddle, Holt took the reins from Guy, handed them to her, and walked to his own horse.

"I suppose you're going after the stallion now," Guy snapped.

Before answering, Holt mounted and rode over to the two of them, his eyes a wintry gray. "No, tomorrow. We're going back to camp now." He moved his horse out and they followed.

"Goddamn it, Holt! You don't have to kill him!" Guy rode up level with him, twisting in the saddle to confront Holt.

"We've been over this, Guy."

"You don't have to kill him," he repeated. "You can catch him. And if he can't be tamed, then you can turn him loose, transport him miles away from here."

"That doesn't solve the problem. It only puts it on someone else's doorstep." Holt nudged his horse into a canter, bringing an abrupt end to the discussion.

Guy fell back to ride beside Diana. "Damn him!" He glowered at the ramrod-straight figure, riding so easily in the saddle.

"He's convinced he's doing the right thing. You can't change his mind, Guy."

"And you?" Fiery blue eyes were turned on her. "Are you convinced he's right? You've gone over to his side, haven't you?"

"Does there have to be sides?" Diana tried to dodge the question.

"You know damned well what I mean. Why did you help him? Why did you go after that stallion when he told you to? His hands were tied. He couldn't do anything without us. Why didn't you stay with me?" His barrage of angry accusations fell on her.

Diana tried to avoid a direct answer. "Does it matter?"

"Yes, it matters! And while you're at it, you might try to explain why the two of you were so cozy before you saw me riding up. You were clinging to him like a leech!"

"I had just had the wits scared out of me not five minutes before," she defended angrily. "Did you expect me to just shrug it off?"

"And that's all it was?" He was derisively skeptical. "If you were so scared, why didn't you run to me for comfort when I came? You know how much I care for you, how much I love you. But you just stayed glued to his side. Why?"

"You have no right to question me," Diana warned.

Guy reached over and grabbed her reins, forcing her horse to stop. "I want to know what's going on," he demanded. "Here lately you've been leaping to his defense every time I mention his name, and you never give me a straight answer. I love you, and that gives me a right to know where you stand."

"Let go of my horse," she ordered and cast a glance at Holt, but so far he wasn't aware they had fallen behind.

"Not until I find out. Are you with him, or with me?"

A surge of temper made Diana retort, "With him!" Guy's possessive attitude had become more than she could take on top of all that had happened. "I love him!"

He recoiled as if she had slapped him, his complexion paling beneath his tan. "You're lying!"

Diana immediately regretted her outburst. She knew how he felt. Why hadn't she broken it to him more gently, with some of the compassion that had originally gotten her into this predicament with Guy? The anger faded from her face, intense sorrow darkening the blue of her eyes.

"I'm sorry, Guy. I truly never meant to hurt you."

"You're lying!" He denied her statement again, not heeding her abject apology. "You can't be in love with him! My God, he's my father! You can't—" He seemed to choke on his own rage, tears welling in his eyes.

"Do you think I don't know that? Do you think I wouldn't change it if I could?" Diana heard her own voice trembling. "Falling in love with Holt wasn't something I planned. It was the last thing I wanted."

"I don't believe you." He shook his head, gritting his teeth as waves of pain flashed across his face. "It can't be true. You have always hated him. Not even the Major . . ." Guy stared at her. "The Major," he repeated. "That's it, isn't it? You're saying this because it's what the Major wants. He's always treated Holt like a son. Now he wants you to make it legal, is that it?"

"No," she denied. "What the Major wants has nothing to do with the way I feel. Not this time."

"You're lying!" The truth was too painful, and Guy rejected it.

"For your sake, I wish I were."

He glared at her for another minute, then let go of her horse and yanked his away. Digging his spurs into its sides, he sent it racing across the valley, angling away from the direction Holt was taking. Holt reined in to wait for Diana.

"Where is Guy going?" he asked when she caught up with him.

"I . . ." Diana hesitated, not certain how much she wanted to tell him. "I think he wanted to be by himself for a while." She felt his penetrating look, but Holt didn't question her about Guy's reasons for wanting solitude.

Back at camp, dusk was purpling into night and Guy still hadn't rejoined them. Holt sat by the fire, seemingly unconcerned by his son's absence, yet Diana saw his gaze seeking the source of every sound coming from the night's shadows. Don straightened and stared into the darkness.

"Maybe we should go look for him," he suggested. "He could be hurt."

"We wouldn't stand much of a chance trying to find him in the dark." Holt didn't move from his supposedly relaxed position. "He has his rifle. If he's in trouble, he can signal us. He probably wandered farther from camp after that stallion than he realized. He's probably camped somewhere for the night. He's old enough to take care of himself. If there's no sign of him by morning, we'll look for him."

"S'pose you're right," Don agreed and sighed. "Distances can be pretty deceiving out here. He probably didn't give himself enough time to get back to camp before the sun went down."

"Either way, there isn't anything we can do about it tonight. We might as well get some sleep."

"Right." Don walked to his bedroll.

Like Holt, Diana was sitting on her bedroll, but she made no move to lie down beneath the blanket. She couldn't sleep. And she wasn't going to make any pretense of trying. Instead, Diana rose and added more wood to the fire, standing close to the flames. The radiating heat seemed incapable of warming the chill of apprehension shivering through her.

"Cold?" Holt was beside her, draping her blanket around her shoulders.

"Scared," Diana whispered.

His hands remained on her shoulders, rubbing them gently. Across the fire, Don was rolled in the blanket, his back turned discreetly toward them. Diana relaxed under Holt's soothing caress, swaying back against his chest. Unaccountably, she shivered and his hands tightened on her flesh.

"Let's sit down." The pressure of his grip both helped and forced her to the ground beside the fire. Using a saddle as a backrest, Holt gathered her blanket-bundled figure into his arms to rest against his shoulder in the crook of one arm, a comfortable and familiar position. "It was a frightening experience this afternoon."

Diana tipped her head slightly on his arm to look up at him. "Were you scared?"

There was a disturbing darkness to his eyes as the muscle in his jaw constricted tautly, then relaxed. "You know I was," was his low and simple answer.

Diana didn't pursue that leading statement to its logical conclusion. She couldn't; not yet. She quieted the leaping of her heart and looked away from the compelling male features into the darkening sky.

"Where do you suppose he is?"

Holt didn't have to ask who. "He's out there somewhere. He's all right. Sulking, no doubt."

"Sulking?" Diana thought that a peculiar word choice.

"Yes, sulking." His hand smoothed the hair on top of her head. "Whenever you didn't do what Guy wanted, he used to sulk for hours—in his room, or the hayloft, somewhere private. Whenever he got over his anger, he'd come out. And he was angry today because you helped me try to get the stallion."

"Yes, partly," she admitted and levered onto an

elbow to look at him squarely, her blue eyes rounded and troubled. "Holt, I was with Guy only one time. I know you think there were others, but there was only that once."

"No, don't, Diana." A frown of irritation darkened his face. "Leave that in the past, where it belongs."

"No, I'd rather try to make you understand than have you imagining." She rushed on before he could stop her. "When I came back here, there were all those ugly stories about my divorce. I thought I had escaped all that, but I hadn't. And it felt like everyone was looking at me as if . . . Then there was Guy, always being so kind and considerate, adoring and gentle in his sensitive way. I remembered the way I had treated him, used him to get at you. It wasn't exactly a pleasant memory. But here he was telling me that I was the most beautiful woman he'd ever known. I needed that. I was starving for it. I tried to pay for what I took from him. Afterward, when he told me he loved me and started talking about getting married, I . . . realized I had made things worse and I didn't love him, but he kept insisting I would. He just wouldn't believe me today, either."

"Is that what you argued about?"

Diana didn't immediately answer, shifting to lie back in the crook of his arm. His fingers plucked at the folds of the blanket.

"I . . . told him I was in love with you."

Everything seemed to become very still. "Are you?"

"Yes." Her voice was remarkably steady.

"And Guy didn't believe you?"

"No. He accused me of lying, of pretending to care for you to please the Major. But that isn't true, Holt. For the first time in my life, I don't care what the Major wants or what would make him happy. I just know I love you." Diana hesitated. "I know you only want me sexually and I—"

His fingers twisted cruelly into her hair, forcing her around. "I want you sexually and every other damned way," Holt muttered, his gray eyes racing over her startled face. "God knows I've tried to hate you. I even tried to pretend the lust I felt was a way to get revenge for all you'd done. But it isn't simply lust or sex. I *love* you, Diana."

She gave a little cry of breathless joy before his mouth crushed hers into silence. Their cup of life overflowed with the fullness of their love for each other. Wondrous contentment flooded through Diana when the kiss ended and his hand remained to gently and adoringly trace her features.

"I want us to be married, Diana," he told her huskily. "When we get back, we'll get the Major's blessing and have a quiet little ceremony."

"Yes." She kissed the work-roughened skin of his hand.

"There will be talk, you know that," Holt warned her. "Some damned nosy busybody is going to say I married you to get my hands on the Major's ranch. They'll say I married you for your money."

"It's true, isn't it?" she teased, then sighed languidly. "I don't care what they say. I don't care what anybody says." And she immediately knew that wasn't true. Diana shivered. "What are we going to do about Guy?"

A grimness settled over his features. "There isn't much we can do. Whatever happens is going to be up to him."

"Holt, don't go after the stallion tomorrow. We have the mares. Let the stallion go."

"You know I can't." She heard the impatience in his voice. "If it isn't tomorrow, it will be next week."

"You don't have to destroy him," she argued. "For Guy's sake, couldn't you . . . catch him, take him to some other part of the country, and turn him loose to run free?"

"It wouldn't solve—"

"I know it wouldn't solve the problem," Diana interrupted. "But don't you see? It would be a gesture. Guy would have to realize that you spared the stallion's life because it was what he wanted. It wouldn't make up for . . . everything, but it would mean something. It isn't too much to ask, is it?''

''No.'' Holt took a deep breath and let it out slowly, his voice grim. ''No, it isn't too much to ask.''

''You'll do it?''

''Yes, I'll do it.'' He nodded.

''Thank you.'' Diana pressed a kiss into the palm of his hand, her fingers curling tightly around his.

''I just hope to hell Guy thanks me for it,'' he muttered.

''He will.'' But she wasn't nearly as confident as she sounded. Any gratitude Guy might experience would never compensate for the damage their love would do to him. They both knew it.

Holt's arms tightened around her. For the time being, Diana let herself dwell only on the fact that he returned her love. Morning and its problems would come soon enough. But at least they could face them together. She let her head rest on the pillow of his shoulder and closed her eyes.

The campfire began to flicker and die. There was only the glowing red embers in the night when a sound, a muffled footstep, awakened her. She started to open her eyes as even that dim light was blocked by something tall and dark. The arm around her waist tightened in warning, although the steady rhythm of Holt's breathing hadn't altered a fraction. He, too, had heard the sound and was cautioning her not to move.

Guy was standing there, staring at them. The air seemed to crackle with tension. Anger, hatred, jealousy—all seethed in the invisible undercurrents. He seemed to tower above them for an eternity. Diana wondered if he could hear the frightened drumming of her heart.

''You're back.'' Holt's low voice seemed to vibrate through the charged air.

''Yes.'' It was a savage hiss.

''Diana's asleep.''

"So I see." The sarcasm in Guy's voice made Diana wince.

"You'd better get some sleep yourself," Holt suggested, so very calm. "We're going to catch the stallion in the morning. That isn't very far off." He put just the slightest emphasis on the word "catch."

For a long minute, there was no response. Then Guy moved away to his empty bedroll. A shooting star flamed across the sky. In the grasses, a horse stomped and blew a soft, rolling snort. Diana lay for a long time, listening to all the comfortable night sounds, dreading morning, because she knew it hadn't ended.

Chapter XXII

"You found your way back in the dark, I see," Don commented as Guy joined them for coffee. "You must have cat eyes."

Guy grunted a noncommittal answer and filled his tin mug from the speckled pot. A sullen grimness seemed permanently etched into his features. Studiously he avoided looking at either Diana or Holt, showing them with his brooding silence that nothing had been forgiven.

The sun had crested over the eastern horizon, a yellow ball that was brilliant but not yet blinding. Diana flipped the hotcake on the griddle, wondering if anyone besides Don had the appetite to eat this breakfast she was cooking.

One of the mares staked in the thick grass of the canyon floor whinnied softly. "Have you grained the horses this morning?" Holt addressed the question to Don.

"Not the mares. I grained the horses we would be riding before you saddled them."

Holt slipped the razor into its case and wiped the excess lather from his shaven face. He glanced toward the picket line where their riding horses were tied.

"Leave your rifle with Diana," he told Don. "Since she's staying behind to take care of the mares, she might need it."

"Will do," Don agreed and started to rise.

"You can get it after you eat." Diana handed him a plate with a stack of steaming hotcakes in the center. She started pouring more batter on the griddle. "How many cakes do you want, Guy?"

The upward sweep of her gaze was caught by the icy and angry blue of his eyes. With a violent flick of his wrist, he dumped the remainder of his coffee into the fire, the sizzling hiss matching his temper.

"You can take your cakes and shove—"

"Guy! That's enough!" The low command from Holt spun Guy around.

"And as for you, you—" Guy couldn't seem to find words vile enough to describe Holt.

Another mare whinnied. The sound was followed by the milling of hooves and a second, throatier neigh. "My God!" Diana hear Don exclaim and turned to see the white stallion floating down the rear slope of the canyon toward the meadow where the mares were tethered.

"He's come to get the mares back!" he declared. Before the last word was out, the stallion had reached the first mare and tried to drive it back the way he'd come. The rope held her, stretched taut with the horse's attempts to obey the steed that had become her master. "With those teeth, he could bite the rope in two with a single snap of his jaws."

"He isn't a trick horse, so he doesn't know that." Holt started for the picket line where the saddled horses waited. The geldings were resting, aware of the intruding stallion in the canyon, their own impotence forgotten.

"Hey, Guy, give me your rifle." Don motioned toward the Winchester next to Guy's bedroll. "I've got a clear shot from right here."

Diana's glance ran swiftly to Holt, who hesitated, then on to Guy. Don's statement had broken his enthrallment with the sight of the stallion. His hardened, yet very expressive features seemed to be waiting for Holt's reaction.

"No shooting, Don. We're going to catch the stallion."

"What?!!" Stunned, Don turned away from the mountain meadow to stare at Holt. He was at the picket line, untying his prancing horse. Holt's concession amounted to an about-face as far as Don was concerned, but it didn't soften Guy's expression, his blue eyes still icy with bitter anger. "But you said—" Don started to protest, his legs slowly moving him toward his saddled horse.

"We may not have intended to use the mares for decoys"—Holt swung into his saddle—"but that's what they've become. We'll have a better chance to rope that white stud."

An angry squeal reverberated across the walls of the canyon. Diana turned to see the white stallion lashing out with his hind feet at the staked mare. The vicious kick missed by inches as the mare sidestepped and struggled wildly to be free. The rope that held her became tangled in her hind feet and the mare went down.

The snapping, biting attack from the stallion could not bring the mare to her feet, not with the binding rope around her legs. Screaming in anger, the stallion switched to another mare and sent her galloping to the end of her rope.

The wild commotion had excited all the horses. Holt's mount was almost cantering in place, straining at the bit, neck arched unnaturally high. At the edge of the camp circle, he waited for Don, who was having difficulty mounting his horse. Holt untied the lariat on his saddle and began shaking out the loop.

"Are you coming?" He shot the question at Guy.

After a stony silence came the cold and condemning reply. "You don't need me. Not you."

"You're my son. I've always needed you." The instant that was said, Holt glanced over his shoulder to see what was keeping Don. He didn't make any further attempt to persuade Guy to help them.

Diana wanted to scream at Guy to go with Holt. It

could be essential to have three riders to rope the white mustang. But the time when Guy would listen to any of her arguments was over. That left only one alternative.

"I'll go with you." She started toward the picket line.

"God, no!!" It was an explosive refusal that halted her immediately. "Stay here," Holt added in a less violent tone, "where I know you're safe!"

The argument she had been inclined to offer died on her lips. It had been years since she had done any roping. Diana realized her ineptitude could prove to be more of a hindrance than a help. She turned away from the picket line in mute acceptance of Holt's decision.

Finally in the saddle, Don joined Holt, his fractious horse plunging with nervous excitement. He, too, shook out his lariat, all business now. Any indecision or doubt he expressed at Holt's announcement had vanished. His entire concentration was on the task at hand.

"How do you want to handle it?" he asked Holt.

"The stallion's going to determine that. Chances are he is going to charge one of us when we approach. If it's me, you throw the first loop. We'll try to stretch him between us. Don't miss," Holt warned. "Ready?" Don nodded, pulling his hat down low on his forehead and shifting the saddle to be sure his cinch was tight and the saddle wouldn't slip. "Let's keep some distance between us so the stallion has to make a choice."

With pressure relaxed on the reins, the horses bounded forward together. There was chaos in the desert meadow. The stallion's rage at the mare's inability to obey his commands made Diana tremble. She cast a despairing look at Guy, standing a few feet away, like an observer, showing no emotion.

The space widened between the two riders as they approached the grassy area. They kept to the open, not wanting to become entangled at a critical moment with any of the ropes tethering the mares. The white stallion saw them coming, tossing and shaking his long mane in a flash of temper. Diana held her breath, knowing that any second the wild horse would cease to threaten. He would rush out to meet his enemy.

His shrill whistle of challenge shivered over her nerve endings. Seeming to catapult himself forward, the stallion charged. Diana's heart rocketed in fear, the image of Rube's horse going down with him flashing in her mind's eye. Lightning-swift, the horse bore down on Don.

Out of the corner of her eye, Diana saw Holt's loop snake through the air. His aim was true and the rope circled the white neck. He made a quick dally around the saddle horn and braced himself for the moment when fifteen hundred pounds of charging dynamite hit the end of the rope. Don was waiting for that second, too, his loop lazily circling the air above his head, seemingly oblivious to the danger of the onrushing stallion.

That moment never came. The instant the stallion felt the first tightening of the rope around his neck, he seemed to change directions in mid-stride. Whirling, the white fury charged at Holt, neck stretched flat, mighty jaws open. A cry of alarm tore from Diana's throat, drowning out Holt's shout to Don.

Spurring his horse, Don started to chase the stallion, tossing his loop. As it started to settle on the white head, the stallion swerved the fraction necessary to duck it. While Don swiftly gathered in the empty rope, Holt was trying to reel in the slack of his and keep his horse out of the path of the stallion.

Diana wanted to shut her eyes. It was becoming a nightmare. Her fingernails had dug into her palms until they were bleeding. Tears began stinging her eyes and she blinked them away, fighting through the blur to see what was going on.

The stallion was twisting and turning, relentlessly pursuing Holt. A striking hoof hit Holt's gelding in the shoulder. His mount staggered under the blow, recovered, and eluded the next charge of the stallion. But

Holt's success in keeping out of reach of the stallion's jaw and hooves was the source of Don's failure. He couldn't find a clear opening to cast his loop. If Holt and his horse weren't in the way, then the stallion was switching directions to follow them and Don's rope was catching air.

The stallion's jaws ripped a chunk of flesh from the flank of Holt's mount and the neigh of pain made Diana's blood run cold. Don tried to maneuver himself into a better position, swinging around the horse and rider. A mare plunged frantically out of his way to the right.

"Look out!" Diana screamed the warning, but it was too late.

Don had unknowingly ridden too close. His horse's feet became entangled in the rope holding one of the mares. It went down heavily, trapping Don beneath. The horse tried to struggle to its feet while Don strained to pull his leg free.

Holt was on his own. There would be no help from Don. Diana saw him unwind the rope dally from around his saddlehorn and throw the rope free. He stopped trying to elude the stallion and attempted to outrace him, break off the encounter. Before his horse could achieve full stride, the stallion was crashing into him and he went to the ground. Holt dived free of the saddle, rolled, and came up crouched on his feet. The stallion ignored the downed horse, just as he had done with Rube, and charged for the man on the ground.

"Help him!" Diana cried to Guy, tears streaming down her cheeks. Her blurring gaze slid to the rifle near his feet. "The stallion is going to kill Holt! You've got to stop him!"

Holt darted out of the way of the stallion's first charge. There wasn't a flicker of emotion on Guy's face as he slowly bent and picked up the rifle. He simply held it in his hand and watched. Holt dodged the rearing, pounding hooves trying to beat him into the ground.

"For God's sake, help him, Guy!"

Guy cocked the rifle, but he didn't raise it to his shoulder. An iron-hard club of a hoof struck Holt to the ground. More pile-driving blows hit the ground as he escaped them by inches. Diana's horror-widened eyes saw Holt clutching the upper part of his left arm as he tried to weave out of the stallion's way.

"Guy, you've got to shoot!" She was pleading, begging.

Diana could see what he was thinking. If Holt were dead, she would turn to him, in his opinion, no longer bound by the Major's wishes.

"You can't let him die!" she whispered. Her head moved from side to side in helpless denial. "Guy, he's your father. You can't just let him die."

For what seemed an eternity, Guy stared at her. God, couldn't he see he was killing her, too? Diana cried silently. With a muffled sob, she turned away. Holt had somehow lost his footing and was stumbling to his knees, unable to check his fall because of his injured arm. Diana saw him trying to crawl out of the way of the tearing stallion with only one good arm to aid him.

"Holt!" It was a scream from her heart, filled with all the agony of love. She started to run to him.

With her first step, there was an explosion behind her. The white stallion staggered drunkenly onto all four feet, but, with jaws open, he went for Holt. A second shot and the mustang crumbled into a white heap on the ground.

Diana ran, her chest bursting with pain and fear. The wall of tears was so thick that she could hardly see where she was going. She had a vague image of Holt pushing to his knees, and relief soared on an eagle's wing.

"Give me a hand!" a voice called out to her. "I can't reach the rope to cut it!"

A blurry sideways glance recognized Don, still trapped by his fallen horse. She hesitated, then rushed over and took the knife from his hand. As Diana sawed the blade through the rope twisted around the gelding's rear legs, she was distantly aware of Don muttering in frustration.

"The damned horse not only fell on my leg. He fell on my rifle, too. There wasn't anything I could to to help Holt."

"Are you hurt?" It was her voice, but Diana wasn't aware of asking the question.

"Nothing's broken."

Diana stepped back the instant the rope was cut through and unconsciously jammed the knife blade in the sandy ground. She was already running toward Holt when thrashing legs kicked the horse to its feet. Don was following at a considerably slower pace, dragging his right leg.

Holt was resting on his knees, his right hand tightly gripping the upper part of his left arm. His head was tipped back, his face white with pain when she reached him.

"You're alive! Thank God, you're alive!" Her throbbing whisper was a prayer as her shaking fingers ran over his cheek and jaw in reassurance. "Your arm—"

He attempted a smile, warmth in the look he gave her. "My shoulder's broken, but that's all." Holt started to move and winced. "Help me up." Brushing the tears from her cheeks, Diana looped his right arm around her neck, taking as much of his weight as she could to help him to his feet. She flashed a concerned glance at his face and saw him staring at the white horse only a few feet away. "The stallion's dead."

"Yes." For the first time Diana let herself glance at the equine shape. The milk-white coat was dusty and splattered with crimson. In death, the white stallion did not look like the mythical horse of classic form and beauty. His neck was too thick and heavily muscled, his barrel too long, his chest too narrow. He was a horse, possessing no qualities to set him apart from any other mustang except for his size and the fact that he paced, but never would again.

"Guy killed him," Diana murmured. The first shot

had hit the stallion in the chest and the second in the head, bringing instant death. Tears filled her eyes as she realized the full importance of what Guy had done. She looked up at Holt. "He saved your life, Holt. He killed the stallion to save you."

Holt looked toward the camp. Diana turned and saw Guy standing where he had been, the rifle lowered. Although she couldn't see his face, Diana knew he was watching them. Slowly, Guy turned away and walked to the picket line. He shoved the rifle in the scabbard and mounted. With one last glance in their direction, Guy paused, then kicked his horse into a canter and rode out of the canyon.

"He's leaving. He won't be coming back."

At his flat statement, Diana lifted her gaze to Holt's face. His features were chiseled in stone, revealing no more than his voice had, but there was a liquid silver sheen to his eyes.

"Maybe he'll come back . . . someday." She stared at the trailing cloud of dust.